Who Sent Clement?
By Keith A Pearson

For more information about the author and to receive updates on his new releases, visit...

www.keithapearson.co.uk

"It is when we are most lost that we sometimes find our true friends."

— Brothers Grimm

NOVEMBER 1988

Edward Baxter's journey home usually took around fifty minutes.

Not on that evening, though.

Fourteen miles from home and the traffic on the motorway had barely crept above walking pace in almost an hour. He found himself behind a stationary white van, its brake lights steadfastly glowing red. The rain continued to fall heavily as the windscreen wipers on his Austin Maestro rhythmically whumped back and forth.

He let out a sigh and stared down at the copy of *James and the Giant Peach* on the passenger seat; a present for his seven-year-old daughter. He couldn't wait to see her face when he handed it to her, and that thought raised a smile.

The brake lights on the van disengaged and it slowly moved forward. He slid the gear stick into first and followed.

Wary it might be yet another false dawn, he tentatively moved through the gears until the Maestro hit thirty. His right foot twitched nervously, ready to dab the brakes again if the white van stopped for the umpteenth time.

The procession continued to move cautiously forward.

Apart from the van ahead of him, there was little else to see beyond the rain-dappled windows. A curtain of black sky hung over the hard shoulder to his left, and the equally black tyres of a lorry filled the window to his right.

The speedometer displayed his speed at forty. He let himself relax a little. Hopefully the worst of the delays were behind him.

His hope was short lived.

The brake lights on the van lit up, and the expanse of empty tarmac in his windscreen quickly shrunk to barely thirty yards. He pressed his foot down on the brake pedal.

"Not again," he groaned.

For ten minutes, his right foot switched between the accelerator and the brake pedal. With no opportunity to move beyond first gear, his left hand remained redundant.

Mild agitation moved towards sheer frustration. He just wanted to get home.

The Maestro crawled forward for a long minute until the van stopped again. He cursed under his breath and gazed off to his left, hoping for a change in the vista. He spotted the edge of a blue sign with three diagonal stripes — three hundred yards to the next motorway exit. It wasn't the exit he usually took but it had to be better than another six miles of congestion.

He checked his left mirror and swung the car onto the hard shoulder. He knew it was only supposed to be used in emergencies but he doubted a three hundred yard dash to the exit would land him in trouble.

Seconds later, the Maestro sped down the exit ramp, away from the motorway and away from the queue of stationary traffic.

He was free at last.

At least he thought he was.

The rush hour traffic was almost as slow as that on the motorway. Thankfully, he knew a short cut. He navigated two roundabouts before a tortuous crawl along a two-mile stretch of dual carriageway. He took a left turn onto a quiet lane which meandered across the countryside. It would take him to within a mile of his home. Very few people knew of the shortcut and for that he was grateful.

Keen to make up for lost time, he pushed the Maestro up to forty. The headlights provided a tunnel of light in the darkness, illuminating the hedgerows which bordered the ribbon of greasy tarmac.

A sharp left-hand bend crept up on him.

He dabbed the brake pedal and the book on the passenger seat slid forward, disappearing into the darkness of the footwell. It pulled his attention for barely a second, but sufficient time for the car to enter the bend.

As he returned his eyes to the road, his heart dropped to his stomach. He buried the brake pedal into the floor and the front wheels locked. The Maestro slid across the rain-slicked tarmac, the steering wheel of no use to him.

If he'd hit the brakes a split second earlier, the point of impact would have been different. The finest of margins.

But he didn't.

The Maestro launched from a low berm on the outer edge of the lane. All four tyres lost contact with the road and the residue momentum propelled the car towards a five-bar gate. That gate had only been replaced two weeks before, its wooden predecessor finally losing the battle with rot.

The replacement was unforgiving.

Metal struck metal as the steel gate and the body of the Maestro become entwined. A steel cross section snapped away, and the jagged end pierced the car's windscreen.

Silence.

He could feel the wetness, the warmth. He could see the length of steel tubing embedded in his chest, just below his collar bone. If it had been on the left, rather than the right, he knew he'd already be dead.

As he could barely catch a breath, it was scant consolation.

He knew his time was short but he wasn't scared of what awaited him. He was scared of what awaited his wife, and his young daughter.

Husband. Daddy. Neither home tonight. Neither home ever again.

His breath was almost spent and his life expectancy could only be measured in seconds.

He smelt earth, and petrol. A flicker of yellow light reflected in the rear view mirror. Fire, he thought.

His eyelids flickered and his chest stopped moving.

The final seconds.

As he prepared to leave, he felt a presence. Help maybe? Too late he thought.

A voice whispered, although he couldn't be sure if it was just his imagination; a cruel trick played by an air-starved brain.

"We will watch over her."

It was the last sound he heard.

The final question his mind would ever pose — *who are you?*

He died without an answer.

The Maestro and its occupant were reduced to skeletons by the ensuing fire.

Ashes to ashes, dust to dust.

BETH BAXTER'S BEDROOM

PRESENT DAY...

1

I used to love bedtime.

I'd lie in my childhood bed with my dad sitting beside me, and we'd pluck the prose from the pages of my favourite books. For half-an-hour every evening we'd enter our own little fantasy world — it was our time, our world.

After my dad kissed me goodnight and turned out the light, I would snuggle beneath my duvet to dream of handsome princes, unicorns, and cats in hats.

Two years later, my dad walked out of that bedroom for the final time. The man who filled my sky left an empty horizon. I had to read my own stories to fill the void he left behind.

I grew into a solitary adolescent, content in my own company. With every passing year, memories of my dad, like my childhood dreams, slowly ebbed away.

My love of books remained.

At some point I passed seamlessly from teenager to young woman. But while my peers hankered for handsome young men on the beaches of Ayia Napa and Ibiza, I hankered for Orwell, Woolf, and the Brontës.

My love of books became an obsession.

Somehow, life then bowled past at a frightening pace. One moment I'm dressed in robes and a mortar board, standing on the steps of Durham University for our graduation photos, and the next, I'm a thirty-six-year-old woman, living with Karl — a planning officer from Croydon.

Whatever future I envisaged as a young woman, it probably wasn't this.

"For fuck's sake, Beth, just let it go, will you?"

I sit up in bed and cross my arms.

"No, I won't," I snap. "I'm sick and tired of finding your dirty laundry scattered around the house."

My thirty-year-old fiancé rolls his eyes like a sulky teenager.

"Whatever," he grumbles. "I'm tired."

He rolls onto his side and pulls the duvet tight around him. The snores soon follow.

And this is my life.

It's been one month since Karl transitioned from boyfriend number five to fiancé. We've been together just over four years, and despite the fact I've agreed to marry him, I'm not sure if I'm totally in love with him. I'm not even sure I know what love should feel like.

When I was young, my expectations were drawn from the cream-coloured pages of tatty paperbacks. I hoped for Jane Eyre and Edward Rochester, Elizabeth Bennett and Fitzwilliam Darcy, even Heathcliff and Catherine.

If life has taught me anything, it's that the real world is a pale imitation of fiction.

I do *like* Karl though, a lot. He possesses a boyish charm and a carefree attitude that balances my pragmatic outlook on life. There's a lot to like, but he doesn't set my heart racing. He doesn't make me want to swoon, if indeed swooning is still a thing. I'm fairly sure no man has ever made me swoon and that is a major disappointment.

But in spite of Karl's propensity to leave skidmarked underpants on the bathroom floor, he remains the best of a bad bunch.

Boyfriend number one was Kevin — the man-boy who stole my virginity. I say stole, it was more of a smash and grab. The event took place in his bedroom on New Year's Eve, 1999.

As the clock ticked down towards the new millennium, Kevin grunted away. I recall lying there and thinking how utterly underwhelming the whole experience was, and how much it bloody hurt. My physical pain was brief, as was Kevin's stamina. He dumped me three weeks later and the emotional pain lasted a lot longer than eighty-six seconds.

Boyfriend number two was Danny and we dated for over a year. I met him during my second year at university and we connected immediately through our mutual love of literature. We would spend most weekends lying in bed, reading, smoking French cigarettes, eating takeaways, and occasionally making love.

I actually thought he might be 'the one', right up until the moment I entered his dorm room unannounced, and found him performing fellatio on his tutor, Philip. While I was shocked, obviously, it did explain why Danny always seemed more enthusiastic about Byron and chicken madras than having sex with me.

After a fairly barren period, I started dating Stuart when I was twenty-two. My first proper, grown up relationship. After eleven months of dating, we moved in together and I spent the next five years wondering why. Stuart single-handedly destroyed any remaining preconceptions I had about men, and not in a good way.

He didn't have a romantic bone in his body, and our love life was duller than celery soup. He was also obsessive about personal hygiene, to the point where he'd decline any sexual advance unless I'd showered within ten minutes of said advance. I once suggested he might like to go down on me — a big mistake. Instead of hungrily assaulting my nether regions, Stuart looked at me in horror before listing the various strains of common bacteria my mimsy might host.

Andy was boyfriend number four. What I learnt from Andy is that men who are passionate sometimes have a tendency to share that passion around; quite liberally in his case. He was an incredibly adventurous lover and knew exactly which buttons to press. His problem was one of multi-tasking; he was pressing so many buttons in so many places, it eventually caught up with him. He was as addictive as crack, and just as debilitating. It's a shame he screwed with my head as much as he screwed other women. I really liked Andy.

So here I am with boyfriend number five; my future husband, my fiancé. He's not perfect but, I suppose, neither am I.

I'm a little too short and a little too fond of cake. My shoulder-length chestnut hair is more an annoyance than an attribute, and some say my light blue eyes are cold.

But to quote Gloria Gaynor, I am what I am.

I nestle down under the duvet and slowly drift off to sleep.

Eight hours later, I awake to an empty bed. Karl is always up first. He usually wakes up with boundless energy and irksome enthusiasm. I prefer to wake up gently and slowly ease myself into the day. I'm green tea and Radio 3, whereas Karl is double-espresso and Kiss FM.

I wearily plod to the bathroom and take a shower.

I return to the bedroom and throw on a pair of aged jeans and a shapeless black jumper; function before fashion. My hair is then scraped into a ponytail before I invest two minutes applying makeup.

A quick glance in the mirror. Presentable.

I head downstairs where Karl is eating breakfast at the table in our reclaimed kitchen. I say *our*, but the kitchen, and indeed the entire house, is actually mine — unfortunately, so is the accompanying mortgage.

Together with boyfriend number three, Stuart, I purchased 14 Elmore Road almost ten years ago. It's a twee, two-up, two-down Victorian terraced house and I love it. When I split with Stuart, I used a chunk of my father's inheritance money to buy his share. That money was scant consolation for losing a father but without it, there is no way I would have been able to extract Stuart from my life and keep my beloved home.

"The kettle has just boiled," Karl mumbles as he chews on a slice of cremated toast.

"Thanks. Is the radio loud enough?"

He shrugs and returns his attention to a magazine.

I turn the radio down and make myself a cup of green tea.

"What's the magazine about?" I ask.

"Motorbikes. I'm thinking of getting one," he replies. "Here. Look at this."

He holds up the magazine to show me a picture of a lurid green death machine.

"Very nice."

I could not be less interested. Still, it's good to see Karl reading something other than a newspaper, although I suspect he might just be looking at the pictures.

"Lovely, ain't she?" he says wistfully. "Does 0 to 60 in 2.6 seconds."

Karl continues to fawn over the picture while I tuck into a bowl of wholegrain granola.

I indulge him. "How much does one of those things cost?"

"North of twenty grand."

I almost choke. "Unless we win the lottery, you'll have to make do with pictures for the foreseeable."

He looks up at me with doe eyes, deep and brown.

"Man can dream can't he?"

I flash him a smile and he returns his attention to the pictures.

Karl *is* an unquestionable dreamer.

He dropped out of college at seventeen to start an events company. That lasted eight months. Undeterred, Karl moved on to his next big idea. By the time he'd reached his early twenties, he'd started, and subsequently folded, a dozen different ventures. His entrepreneurial spirit withered with every failure and he eventually settled for a career with the local council.

Somehow, he found himself starting as a glorified tea boy in the planning department. Credit to him though; he worked his way through the system and became a planning officer two years ago. But even against the backdrop of planning applications and building regulations, Karl kept dreaming.

I like that about him. Everyone needs a dream, don't they?

"Anyway, gotta shoot, babe," he says as he gets up from the table.

He strides over and plants a kiss on my forehead.

"Might be late tonight," he says. "Four o'clock meeting with a developer which will probably overrun."

"Overrun into the pub by any chance?"

"You know me so well, babe," he replies with a wink. "That's why you'll make the perfect Mrs Patterson."

I pad over to the sink and rinse my bowl. Karl nestles up behind me and wraps his arms around my waist.

"So when are we going to set a date then?" he purrs.

"I'm still thinking about it. I like the idea of a summer wedding though, so maybe July next year."

"Not sure I can wait ten months."

From the moment he proposed, Karl has been a little too enthusiastic about our wedding timetable. If he had his way, we'd be heading down the aisle next weekend. I, on the other hand, prefer to take my time and plan the big day with military precision. A psychiatrist might suggest a deeper rooted reason for my procrastination.

I turn around and put my hands on his shoulders.

"Good things come to those who wait, Karl."

He scrunches his face in a way I find hard to resist. Much like a puppy, Karl is too cute to be annoyed with for any length of time.

"You're the boss," he says. "But don't you go getting cold feet on me."

I run my fingers through his unkempt, butterscotch-coloured hair.

"I won't. Promise."

He responds with a lingering kiss.

"I need to get going. Seeya tonight."

He grabs his magazine and darts out of the kitchen. Seconds later, I hear the front door open and close.

I've never been blessed with children, but I imagine it must occasionally be a relief when they leave for school and the house is quiet. Despite my lack of offspring, Karl's departure summons a similar feeling.

I wipe crumbs from the table and put Karl's plate in the sink. As lovely as his backside might be, I think I'd trade it for a change in his untidy ways.

I finish my tea and slip my coat on, taking a moment to check the contents of my handbag before I head out the front door.

The sky is a cloudless blue and the air crisp. Autumn is by far my favourite season, followed by winter, spring, and then summer. I'd rather be too cold and able to warm up than too warm and unable to do anything about it. There's nothing nice about being hot, bothered, and claggy. No, summer definitely isn't for me.

I walk the twenty yards along Elmore Road to where my car is parked. I unlock the doors with the remote control and stand for a moment to appreciate my new car; a custard-yellow Fiat 500. I say new, but it's actually nine years old. I've owned it for just over a month and the way it came into my possession still makes me smile.

My previous car, a battered old Fiesta, had spectacularly failed its MOT — I think the precise term used by the mechanic was 'death trap'. I spent the subsequent days searching in vain for a replacement within my shoestring budget. On the third day, I left the house to find the Fiat outside, adorned with a giant red bow. Karl, who had supposedly left for work ten minutes prior, was standing proudly next to it with the passenger door open, and he invited me to sit inside.

Still confused, on Karl's suggestion I opened the glove box, where I discovered the ownership documents, in my name. If that wasn't surprise enough, I also found a small box containing an engagement ring. As I turned to Karl, he was already down on one knee and the question was subsequently popped. Of course I said yes. How could I not?

It later transpired that a week prior to his proposal, Karl had actually won ten thousand pounds on a lottery scratch card. I did ask him if the proposal would still have materialised without his windfall. He claimed it would, although I suspect my ring might have sparkled with cubic zirconia, rather than diamonds. And I dread to think what sort of shitty car I'd now be driving around in.

With that thought in mind, I clamber into the Fiat and give the dashboard an appreciative pat.

I set off for work in surprisingly good spirits for a Monday morning, and ten minutes later I pull into a parking bay behind a shop — my shop, to be precise.

I left university in 2003 with a degree in English and little idea what to do with it. I considered, and quickly dismissed, careers in teaching, journalism, and advertising; the three main paths usually taken by English graduates. I sought my mother's advice and she imparted a pearl of wisdom my father had offered her — if you do a job you love, you'll never work again.

By early 2004, I had decided what I was going to do with my future. I wanted to create a legacy from my father's wisdom, and money, so I decided to launch Baxter's Books. The venture sucked half of my father's inheritance money from my bank account.

I remember the day the shop opened as if it were yesterday. Such excitement, such enthusiasm. Unfortunately, both were tainted by naivety.

Back then, the shelves were stocked with thousands of new books and the smell of fresh print was divine. For a few years, my dream of owning a book shop was every bit as wonderful as I had hoped.

Then, Internet shopping became a thing.

If that wasn't bad enough, some genius then decided we no longer needed physical books, and a raft of digital e-readers hit the market.

By 2011, the till was starting to gather cobwebs and I was forced to let all but one member of staff go. Ten months later, she was also made redundant and I was forced to run the shop solo. It was impossible to compete with online stores so I had to make a radical change to my business model. I had to clear my dwindling stock of new books and replace them with second-hand stock.

The smell in the shop changed from divine to desperate.

Six years on and I'm just about able to pay myself a half-decent wage. Some days I still love it. Most days it definitely feels like work.

2

Baxter's Books sits in a row of six shops, located in a back street on the edge of the town centre. Three of the shops stand empty, and have done for some time. Besides my shop, there's also a newsagent and a tanning salon. The three of us, clinging on.

On the plus side, the rent is cheap.

I get out of the car and fumble around in my bag for the shop keys. Despite checking they were there only ten minutes ago, I panic after barely a second of searching. I don't know why I panic. If I have forgotten the shop keys, what difference will it make if I have to return home to fetch them, and subsequently open twenty minutes late? It's not as though there will be a queue of customers waiting impatiently at the front door.

I locate the keys and breathe a pointless sigh of relief. I undo the lock on the sturdy rear door and tug it open.

The rear half of the building is divided into two rooms: a staffroom for when I actually had staff, and a large stockroom for when I actually had stock worth storing. A door leads from the staffroom into the main shop.

I hang my coat and bag in the staffroom, put the kettle on, and head into the shop to unlock the front door. There's no queue.

Before I took possession of the shop, it was formerly a high end boutique so I didn't need to spend too much on fixtures and fittings. There was already a custom-made counter, and the stripped wooden floorboards were stained and polished. I had all the walls painted in terracotta red and my mother's second husband, Stanley, fitted shelving across three of the walls. There used to be four tables in the centre of the space, back when I had piles of lovely new books worthy of display. Those tables now sit idle in the stockroom.

With the door unlocked and the 'open' sign displayed, I duck below the counter and turn on a CD player which pipes music through speakers embedded in the ceiling. The system was installed by the previous tenants but I guess they left in a hurry and forgot to take it with them. Their loss was my gain. Back in the shop's heyday, we mainly played contemporary jazz to provide a more sophisticated ambience. I'm above such pretensions these days and throw an Adele CD into the slot.

I head back into the staffroom, make a cup of tea, and return to the shop. I take up position behind the counter and gaze across the empty shop — just me, Adele, and thousands of dog-eared books.

It's nearly eleven o'clock before the first customer enters; a man close to pension age, conservatively dressed in a fawn sweater and brown slacks. He flits from shelf to shelf, plucking books in a seemingly random manner. He inspects each book for a few seconds before returning it to the shelf.

He repeats this process for almost an hour, retaining just two paperbacks. I'm not sure why, but marathon browsers have become my bête noire, and my annoyance slowly simmers.

"Excuse me, sir," I call across the shop. "Were you looking for something in particular?"

The man turns to face me. "No. I think I'm done here, thank you," he replies.

He wanders across to the counter and hands over the two paperbacks.

"That'll be one pound fifty, please," I say, as I drop the books into a paper bag.

He rummages through the pockets of his jacket and pulls out a small leather pouch. He inspects the contents and looks up at me.

"Would you take a pound?"

"You want to haggle over two seventy five pence paperbacks?" I reply incredulously.

"Every little helps," he squeaks.

Give me strength.

"Look, sir. Would you wander into a branch of Waterstones and ask for a third off the latest John Grisham novel?"

"I'm not really keen on Grisham," he replies.

"You're missing my point," I sigh. "But, tell you what. Why don't we call it a pound-fifty and I'll throw in a free mystery novel? What do you say?"

He perks up. "Oh, okay. That would be most agreeable. Thank you."

He plucks the correct change from his pouch and places it on the counter. I swipe the coins in one hand and scan the barcodes with the other. I drop the coins into the till and slam it shut.

"Let me get your free mystery book."

I reach below the counter, pull out a copy of *Fifty Shades of Grey*, and hand it to him.

"Enjoy."

He eyes the book with some level of disdain.

"What is this?" he asks.

"Erotic fiction. It's very popular."

The man is about to complain but I step from behind the counter and usher him towards the door.

"Have a nice afternoon, sir. Do call in again."

I nudge him out of the door, and as he wanders away, I allow myself a satisfied smile. I've managed to rid myself of a tight-fisted customer and another copy of *Fifty Shades of Grey* — only ninety six more copies to go.

The busiest part of the day is usually around lunchtime. Today is not a good one though, and I only sell a few dozen paperbacks. By three o'clock the shop is empty so I take the opportunity to check the day's takings on the till — a shade over twenty pounds.

In view of the rent, rates, and utility bills, which have to be paid before I am, my hourly rate of pay sits way below the legal minimum wage. Selling used paperbacks is not a sustainable business model.

Almost on cue, the door swings open. A balding, middle-aged man in a grey cardigan and black jeans barges in, carrying a large cardboard box.

"Afternoon, Beth," Eric pants, clearly struggling with the box. "Got some stock for you."

I glance at the box and inwardly groan. This is what my business has descended to — buying boxes of second-hand books from charity shops for a tenner each.

Eric volunteers for a muscular dystrophy charity and delivers their cast-offs once a week. They usually only want glossy, hardback books on their shelves so everything else gets boxed and sent my way. I have no idea what's in the box, nor can I cherry-pick the contents. It's a lottery, but the only sustainable way of securing regular stock for the shop.

However, it does occasionally pay dividends if I stumble across a first edition or a collectible book. Without those occasional finds, the business would have folded by now. The downside is that I end up with multiple copies of the most popular books, hence the vast pile of *Fifty Shades of Grey* I'm struggling to offload.

"Thanks, Eric. Just drop it down here please," I reply, pointing at a space on the floor by the counter.

Eric staggers over and gratefully drops the box to the floor. I pull a tenner from the till and hand it over to him.

"Cheers, Beth. Got time for a cuppa?" he asks, while staring at my tits.

"Sorry, Eric. As much as I'd love to, I've got a lot of stock to sort. Another time?"

He beams a lecherous smile. "Of course. Another time."

Eric leaves, but his pungent aftershave decides to hang around a while longer.

As I contemplate whether to dig into the box of literary dirge, or make another cup of tea, the front door opens again.

A woman walks in. I'd guess she's possibly in her mid-twenties, but her face has a hard edge, courtesy of some aggressive contouring.

As she strides over to the counter, I'm slightly taken aback by her attire. I don't like to generalise, but she doesn't look the bookish type: short red skirt, three-inch heels, leather jacket, and far too much nine-karat.

"Can I help?" I ask.

She looks me up and down. "You own this place?"

"I do."

"I'm looking for a book," she declares.

Thank Christ she isn't looking for a job.

"Okay. Was there a particular book you're looking for?"

She pulls a scrap of paper from her pocket and studies it for a second or two.

"It's called, *Lies in Plain Sight.*"

"Can't say I've heard of it. Let me check on the computer."

I step back behind the counter and conduct a search with our rudimentary stock software. No results.

"Sorry. It doesn't look like we have it in stock, but I might be able to order it in for you."

"Yeah, alright. Do that."

I search my supplier's website and find two books with similar titles.

"Do you know the name of the author?" I ask.

"K Patterson."

"K Patterson?" I parrot.

"That's what I said. Want me to spell it?"

"No, no. I know how to spell it," I splutter. "You threw me for a moment. Coincidentally, it's also my fiancé's first initial and surname."

"Fascinating."

Sarcastic cow.

"Give me a moment and I'll check."

Neither author is called Patterson.

"Sorry. I can't find any book with that title and author."

"Maybe I got the author's name wrong," she says. "What are the other authors called?"

I list the names of the two authors: Shorter, and Davies.

"Order the one by Davies then," she says.

"Okay. I'll need the ten pounds payment up front."

She pulls a purse from the inside of her jacket and extracts a ten pound note, which she slaps on the counter. I ring the sale through the till and give her a receipt.

"If I can take a name and phone number, I'll call you when it comes in," I say.

"Can't give you a number as I'm changing my phone at the moment. I'll call in next week."

"Can I at least take your name then?"

"Dakota."

I'd have bet my bottom dollar her name was something trashy like Britney or Destiny.

"That's an unusual name. Did you know the Dakota people are part of the native Sioux tribe, in North America?"

"Ugh?"

"Forget it. I'll see you next week."

"Yeah, you will," she replies with a smirk.

She turns on her three-inch heels and sashays out of the shop.

By the time the door closes, I've made my mind up about Dakota — I don't like her, not one bit.

The rest of the afternoon delivers just four more customers to my door; two of whom spend a few pounds each. By closing time, the till reports sales to the tune of £27.25. Not my finest day.

I consider sorting through Eric's box, but a lack of motivation puts paid to that idea. Besides, it will give me something constructive to do tomorrow.

I lock up and make my way home with thoughts of the tight-fisted pensioner and Dakota still summoning irritation. I do wonder if I've reached that time of life where I'm just inherently cranky and less tolerant. Nearly thirteen years of dealing with the public is enough to test anyone's patience.

Deep down I know that's not really the reason for my annoyance. On the whole, most of my customers are lovely, and the occasional troublesome customer comes with the territory. No, deep down I'd rather not be selling books — I'd rather be writing them.

Sadly, I can't.

When my thirtieth birthday arrived, I decided I was going to be a novelist. With mind-boggling naivety, I sat down with my laptop and waited for the prose to flow.

I'm still waiting, and last week I started novel number eighteen.

That might suggest there are seventeen prior novels. There aren't. There are seventeen novels I've started and abandoned, ranging in length from a dozen pages to a handful of chapters. Even when I have managed to put down a few thousand words, I inevitably run out of inspiration and the story rambles listlessly towards a dead end.

Such is my frustration, I have given my collection of failed novels a name — the short and the shit. And every time I start, and give up, it breaks my heart just a little more.

I'm told it could be writer's block but I don't think so. A block suggests there is something there to be blocked. I suffer from writer's void, in that I have a head full of nothing.

Karl thinks it could be because I'm such a ravenous reader, and my mind is so crowded with other people's stories I can't find my own. Maybe he's right, or maybe I just don't have that creative spark or vivid imagination required to pen a novel.

What I do know is that I've taken on a whole new appreciation of books I once labelled as trash. No matter how much I might have once sniffed at their writing, those authors put their words down and told their story. They found a willing publisher, and readers prepared to pay for their work. My scorn is now envy.

I did originally wonder if my sheltered life was to blame for my lack of inspiration. I've never really done anything of note or been on any epic adventure. I know I'm being disingenuous though; there are plenty of published authors who've led lives more uninspiring than mine, but still created masterful works.

Stephen King walked straight out of university into fatherhood, and worked a series of low paid jobs while writing *Carrie*.

John Steinbeck was married and running an ultimately unsuccessful manufacturing business when he wrote the first of his sixteen novels.

Joanne Rowling was a single mother, living on state benefits, when she penned the first Harry Potter novel.

Extraordinary stories crafted from ordinary lives.

I guess you've either got it or you haven't. I'm struggling to accept that perhaps I don't have it.

So, for the foreseeable future I will continue to run my book shop, taunted by the thousands of bound reminders that I can't do what I really want to do.

3

I step through the front door to an empty house. I was so focused on dissecting my day I completely forgot Karl said he would be late home from work. I decide to take advantage of the calm and head up to the bathroom.

I light half-a-dozen scented candles and drop a lavender bath bomb into the tub.

Ten minutes later, I ease myself in and close my eyes. If there's a better feeling than sinking into a hot bath, I've yet to experience it.

Ever the optimist, and fuelled by nothing more than blind determination, I turn my attention to ideas for my eighteenth novel. Ideas drift into my mind before being quickly dismissed, each one more preposterous than the last.

A divorcee's harrowing legal battle for custody of her cat? *Tears For Mr Mittens.*

Awful.

A desperate child trying to escape the shackles of his middle-class upbringing, and his battle with kale addiction? *The Hell of Highgate.*

Stupid.

A woman who embarks on a brief, but steamy affair within a small, suburban accountancy practice. *Thirty Nights with Nigel: Sexy Excel.*

Dumb.

What the hell is wrong with me? I am an intelligent woman with a first class honours degree in English. Why is my head full of this mush?

Not even the soothing scent of lavender can temper my annoyance.

I get out of the bath, slip into my pyjamas, and head down to the kitchen. I rethink my dinner plans and knock up a cheese omelette which I pick at while watching TV in the cosy confines of my lounge.

A movie trailer during the ad break grabs my attention — *Fifty Shades Darker,* based upon the book by E. L. James; the follow-up to my literary nemesis, *Fifty Shades of Grey.* The release of a new movie might actually be a good thing, and help to reduce the mountain of Ms James's books in the shop. I make a mental note to put a display in the window tomorrow. There must be somebody left in the country who hasn't read it.

I finish my omelette and settle down on the sofa to watch the soaps. Maybe an hour of mindless escapism will reboot my imagination.

Halfway through Coronation Street, I hear the front door open. It's then slammed shut before heavy feet stomp up the stairs. Clearly Karl is home. I pause the TV and listen. He's in our bedroom, directly above the lounge, and I can hear drawers being opened and closed with increasing force. I'd guess he's probably lost something but I can do without his childish tantrums this evening. He can find whatever it is without my assistance.

I return to Coronation Street.

Five minutes later he storms in, looking harassed.

"I left an envelope on the chest of drawers. You seen it?" he snaps.

"And a good evening to you too."

"Not now, Beth. I need to find that envelope."

"Alright, calm down," I plead. "What does it look like?"

"Like a fucking envelope," he blasts back. "What do you think it looks like?"

Karl rarely gets angry but he's currently approaching an apoplectic breakdown. Whatever he's lost, clearly it's important and I don't wish to stoke his fire.

"Try the top drawer in the kitchen, next to the fridge."

He darts out of the lounge without thanking me.

The Case of the Missing Envelope by Beth Baxter — Desperate.

Karl returns to the lounge a few minutes later.

"Sorry, babe. I didn't mean to snap. It's been a stressful day."

"It's okay. Did you find it?"

"Yeah. Where you said it was."

He leans over and kisses me on the forehead.

"Thanks."

"So why has your day been so stressful?" I ask. "Did your meeting not go well?"

He flops down on the sofa and stares blankly at the TV.

"Actually, I'd rather not talk about it, if you don't mind?" he replies.

"Okay. Whatever."

"Tell me about your day."

"Dull. Although I did have an odd enquiry at lunchtime."

"Really?" he says, paying more attention to the TV than me.

"This young woman came into the shop looking for a specific book — *Lies in Plain Sight.*"

"Right," he says, as he scowls at something on the screen.

"Funny thing was, she thought the author was called K Patterson."

"Yeah, funny. Have you eaten?"

"I have. Do you want an omelette?"

"Please."

I think I might be wasting my time trying to engage my fiancé in conversation. I try one last time before I head off to make his dinner.

"This girl was so thick she didn't even know her name was the same as the Sioux tribe."

"Eh? Right. Tribe."

"Karl. Are you actually listening to me?"

He's still staring at the TV as he answers. "Yeah, yeah. Woman wanted a book and her name was Sue."

I lean across and slap his shoulder. "Karl, at least pretend you're listening to me."

"Sorry."

"I didn't say her name was Sue. I said her name was the same as the Sioux tribe."

"You've lost me."

"Her name was Dakota, like the Sioux tribe," I groan. "Oh, just forget it."

I get up to head for the kitchen but Karl grabs my wrist.

"What did she look like, this Dakota woman?" he asks, his attention now firmly fixed in my direction.

"Mid-twenties, I guess. A few inches taller than me, dark hair, trashy dress sense. Why?"

"Um...doesn't matter. Forget it."

"Karl?"

"Sorry. I...I thought it might be one of the girls from the office playing a prank."

"She didn't strike me as a typical council employee, unless you've recruited a former lap dancer recently?"

"No," he laughs nervously. "Just an odd coincidence I suppose. Forget it."

He stares off into the distance, not focused on either me or the TV.

"Are you okay? Karl?"

"Yeah, I'm fine. Work stuff," he replies in a low voice.

He seems unsettled. I'm about to ask why when he springs up from the sofa.

"Forget the omelette, babe. I have to drop some paperwork off to an architect. I was going to do it on the way home but it slipped my mind."

"But Karl, it's nearly eight o'clock," I protest.

"It's a set of plans. They need them for a meeting first thing tomorrow. Won't be long."

He darts out of the lounge before I can argue.

And this is the man I have agreed to marry. For all the boyish charm and his romantic gestures, Karl can also be flighty and erratic. I suppose they're traits from opposite sides of the same coin. Better than the alternative, though. I tried dull and dependable with Stuart and nearly died of boredom.

You can't have your cake and eat it, Beth.

I disagree with myself and head into the kitchen, intent on having my wicked way with Mr Kipling.

I consume two slices of lemon drizzle and a hundred pages of an Ian Rankin novel before Karl eventually returns.

"Two hours to drop off some plans? Really?" I chide.

"I'm sorry, babe," he pouts. "I got a call while I was out. Toby had some work issues he wanted to discuss out of the office, so we met for a couple of pints."

"You could have called."

"I know. I just lost track of time."

I do my best to look cross but it's unconvincing.

"I might get an early night. I'm shattered," he adds.

He shuffles over and kisses me on the cheek. He does look tired, and his chocolate-brown eyes are circled with dark rings.

"Okay, honey. Night."

It's not unusual for Karl to be in bed before me. I'm not sure if it's a scientifically proven fact or an old wives' tale, but apparently the time of day you were born determines if you're a morning person or a night person. I was born at ten at night while Karl entered the world just as the sun was putting its socks on. I'm happy to sit up past midnight while Karl is usually dead to the world by then. It's a contributory factor to the dwindling frequency of any bedroom-related antics.

I return to my book and read for another hour.

I finally head upstairs at eleven thirty. Karl is snoring away, louder than ever. I climb under the duvet and try to block out the noise.

Every time I get close to drifting off, Karl mumbles something unintelligible or throws out an errant limb. This goes on for almost an hour before I give up.

I grab my pillows and traipse across the landing to the spare bedroom. The mattress on the guest bed might be lumpy but at least the room is quiet. This is not the first time I've resorted to sleeping in here. Every time Karl has a major planning project nearing a deadline, his sleep becomes increasingly disturbed. I've long since given up trying to wake him as it only serves to put us both in a bad mood the next day.

I fall asleep within a few minutes.

Six hours later, I wake up; disorientated, and with a crick in my neck courtesy of the lumpy mattress. I head straight to the bathroom and take a shower before returning to our bedroom. The duvet and fitted sheet are in a twisted ball in the centre of the bed. Karl must have been thrashing around in his sleep like a fish on a hook. God forbid he'd have the decency to make the bed.

I get dressed and waste five minutes untangling the twisted linen before I make the bed. I stomp down to the kitchen with every intention of venting my annoyance at Karl.

He's not there.

There's a scribbled note on the table, next to a mug containing coffee dregs, and a bowl encrusted with remnants of cereal. I snatch the note up and read it.

Had to be in the office early. Sorry about the mess. Love you xxx

That man infuriates me sometimes. I screw the note up and throw it in the bin.

Breakfast is eaten through gritted teeth.

I don my jacket and check the contents of my handbag before leaving the house, irritation still niggling.

When I pulled into our road last night, I had to park the car almost sixty yards from our front door. As much as I love my house, the road in which it's situated is a nightmare for parking. There are seventy terraced houses along our road and every home possesses at least one car. That equates to over one hundred cars requiring a parking space along a narrow Victorian road. It's a constant bone of contention among the residents.

I stomp along the pavement, car keys in hand. I activate the remote central locking and the indicator lights flash a greeting. I climb in, drop my handbag onto the passenger seat, and turn the ignition key. A deep breath to calm my irritation and I pull away from the kerb.

Barely fifty yards later, I realise something isn't right.

There's an odd rumbling noise coming from below the car and the steering is all over the place. I pull over to the kerb.

Some of the more militant residents try to protect their parking spaces by placing traffic cones in the road. I wonder if I've inadvertently run over one. I get out of the car to check.

I'm about to kneel down and inspect the underside of my car when I spot the problem — both tyres are flat.

I dart around to the other side and, to my horror, find two equally flat tyres. All four tyres are as flat as a witch's tit.

This must be the work of kids. The little shits.

I stand on the pavement, unsure of what to do, other than to cuss several times. I consider calling Karl but I know I'll regret it later. I pride myself on being a strong, independent woman and I don't need a man to solve my problems. All well and good, but sometimes I hate my own bloody-mindedness.

I traipse back to the house and return five minutes later with a foot pump.

I kneel down and unscrew the dust cap from the first wheel. As I affix the pump valve, I spot the problem; a problem the foot pump won't solve. I bend down and inspect a four-inch-long slit in the tyre wall. Some bastard has slashed the tyre with a knife.

I scramble to my feet and check the other tyres — all three have also been slashed.

I cuss again, with a slightly more coarse selection of swearwords. What type of low-life arsehole would do such a thing?

I'm now late for work and in need of four new tyres. It's time to swallow my feminist principles.

I call Karl.

It rings a dozen times before he picks up.

"It's not a good time, babe. I'm just going into a meeting," he blurts.

"Screw your meeting. Some bastard has slashed the tyres on my car."

"What? You sure you haven't just got a puncture?"

"No, Karl. I might not be mechanically minded but even I can spot a four-inch slash in a tyre."

The line goes quiet.

"Karl?"

"Yeah, alright," he snaps. "Just get a taxi to work. I'll sort it out later."

"Why would somebody do that to my car?"

"Beth, just go to work will you. I've gotta go."

He hangs up.

If it were not for the fact I'm in full view of my neighbours, I'm pretty sure I'd be stamping my feet and screaming by now. If I wasn't livid before, I certainly am now. Bloody kids. Bloody fiancé. Bloody, bloody, everything.

I take a moment to regain my composure and ring a cab firm. They don't have a car available for at least half-an-hour.

More cussing ensues.

I throw the foot pump in the boot, lock the car, and stomp towards town.

Woe betide anyone who gets in my way.

4

It takes me twenty five minutes to walk to the shop and I open the front door at quarter past nine. Opening late only adds to my irritation.

I don't know why I'm so concerned about opening on time. It's just a symbolic gesture; something to remind myself that I do still have a business to run, albeit a struggling one. If I let myself become complacent with opening and closing times, it'll become a habit, and start to manifest in other ways. I'll stop caring about how the stock is displayed or if it's properly categorised. I'll stop changing the displays in the window. I'll stop hoovering the floor or dusting the shelves. Bad habits are the hardest to break so for the sake of my own pride, I try to keep the shop functioning like a proper shop.

I make myself a cup of camomile tea in the hope it will ease my rising blood pressure.

I dig around under the counter and unearth a classical music CD. Beethoven's *Moonlight Sonata* feels appropriate; soothing, yet mildly sombre. I slip the CD in and hit the play button. The sound of a piano echoes around the shop as I sip my tea and try to calm down.

I can't.

I hate feeling helpless and I need to do something. I call the local police station to report the damage to my tyres.

I've never had cause to report a crime before and I'm not sure what to expect. Maybe a swarm of crime scene investigators will descend upon my road and put a white tent around the car. Perhaps forensic experts in paper overalls will dust for prints and swab for DNA samples. Maybe a seasoned detective inspector will corral his best investigators and demand the culprit is found before their shift ends.

A six-minute call suggests none of those things will happen.

An uninterested desk jockey gives me a crime reference number and tells me that an officer will be in touch within the next few days. Far from putting my mind at rest and easing my irritation, the call leaves me incensed.

Vandalism in any guise has to be the most pointless of crimes. What possible motive can there be? I can understand why people steal things. I can understand how emotions can push a person towards violence. But vandals? As far as I'm concerned, they should all be burned at the stake. Yes, that's what should happen.

I picture the scumbag who slashed my tyres, tied to a stake and screaming for forgiveness. It's a horrid thing to think but it does make me feel slightly better.

An hour later I've calmed down a little. I'm about to head into the stockroom in search of some old promotional posters for my *Fifty Shades of Grey* window display, when the door opens.

It's Eric again, with yet another box of cast-off books.

"Morning, Eric," I sigh. "I wasn't expecting you again this week."

"Morning, Beth," he chirps. "We had a visit from the fire safety officer yesterday and got a slap on the wrist for having too much stock out back. We spent all evening yesterday sorting through it, and I've got another two boxes of books in the car."

This is all I need.

"Look, I'm really sorry, Eric, but I've had a few problems with my car this morning. I can't really afford to shell out another thirty pounds."

"Oh, don't worry about it. Pay us when you've got the money. We have to get this stuff out of the shop."

"Right. Thanks."

Eric stacks the box on top of the one from yesterday, still sitting by the counter, and returns to his car.

Once all three boxes are deposited, Eric departs. Mercifully, he didn't ask for tea this time.

I stare at the boxes and decide to leave them be. I need to get the window display sorted before I restock the shelves.

It takes me a while to locate the stash of promotional posters, buried in a box at the back of the stockroom. When the shop used to stock new books, we'd receive promotional material from the publisher with every order of a new release. The posters are a painful reminder of better times. Indeed, *Fifty Shades* was one of the final promotions I ran before I decided to give up on selling new books. I distinctly recall scraping every last penny I had to acquire thirty copies, in the hope it would sell like proverbial hot cakes. I sold them all but the profits were a drop in the ocean. Too little, too late.

Little did I know that one day I'd have enough of the damn things to create my own library of mummy smut.

I pull the posters from the box and carry them out to the shop.

My merchandising skills aren't great, but I manage to create something resembling a half-decent display. Finally, I stick two of the posters in the window together with a printed sign, knocked-up on the computer — *This Week Only: Fifty Shades for Fifty Pence.*

As I take a step back to admire the display, my mobile rings.
"Hello."
"Is that Miss Baxter?" a male voice enquires.
"Yes it is."
"Ah, good. I'm PC Kane. I understand you've got a problem with some damage to your car?"
"That's correct. My tyres have been slashed."
"Sorry to hear that. Have you got a few minutes to talk?"

I confirm I have, and my initial disappointment with the police eases a little as PC Kane lends a sympathetic ear. He agrees to meet me at the house after work to take a statement and look at the car. Quite what he's going to do about it is anyone's guess, but at least he's making an effort.

Once I've tidied up a little, the lunchtime trickle of customers begins. I've long since given up trying to understand why one day's trade is so different from the next, but today I take almost eighty pounds in just over two hours. I even manage to sell seven copies of *Fifty Shades*.

If it were not for the awful start to the day, I'd actually be feeling quite buoyed by now. However, I know a large bill for four new tyres is heading my way.

With more hope than expectation, I check my insurance policy and, as I feared, I discover I have to pay the first two hundred pounds of any claim. My fault for buying the cheapest policy I could find.

Disappointed, I file it away.

I then get a cloth from the staffroom and begin dusting the shelves. It's a tedious task but it keeps me busy.

My phone rings again just before three o'clock. It's Karl.

He begins in a grovelling tone.

"I'm really sorry about this morning, babe. I'm having the day from hell."

"Don't worry about it," I reply flatly. "I've sorted it anyway."

"Sorted what?"

"The damage to my tyres. I called the police, and a PC is popping round the house this evening."

"Why did you do that?" he asks, his voice spiky.

"What do you mean? What was I supposed to do?"

"The police won't help. Just call them and tell them not to bother."

"No, Karl. I won't. Whoever slashed my tyres needs to be caught and punished."

"Beth, listen to me for once — you're wasting your time. Just call them back and say you've changed your mind. I'll sort the tyres out when I get home."

"Don't tell me what to do, Karl," I snap. "I'm going to make a statement to the police, and that's that."

For a few seconds, all I can hear is his breathing.

"I gotta go. Sorry."

He hangs up on me for the second time today.

The veins in my temples begin to throb, and my fists become so tightly balled that my fingernails dig into my palms. Who the hell does he think he is, telling me what to do? And then he has the temerity to hang-up on me when I refuse. The utter, utter shitbag.

I am not happy with my fiancé. I am actually close to telling him he is no longer my fiancé. He can try his puppy dog stare on me but it won't work. Not this time.

Time, and two cups of camomile tea, take the edge off my anger. And, unfortunately, my motivation. Nothing constructive is accomplished for the remainder of the afternoon. My mind plays out all the things I'm going to say to Karl when he gets home, none of it good.

I lock the shop on the dot of five thirty and get a cab home.

I storm through the front door like a crazed harridan.

Karl isn't home.

He finishes at five o'clock and is usually home well before me. If he's gone to the pub, he's toast.

I slip my coat off and head into the kitchen to put away the washing-up from this morning. Another note has appeared on the table.

Really sorry but I had to go to Birmingham at short notice, for work. Be back in a few days. Love you xxx

I pluck my phone from my pocket and call him. It goes straight to voicemail.

"Call me back the minute you get this message. I'm not very happy with you."

I end the call and sit down at the table.

Karl has been sent away by his boss a few times, usually when they're working on a large project and need to pick the brains of planners from other councils. He's not usually sent at such short notice, though. But knowing Karl, he probably just forgot to tell me. Most convenient for him.

I toy with the idea of taking a long bath to calm myself, but PC Kane could turn up at any time. Instead, I decide to divert my pent-up annoyance towards some aggressive cleaning. I turn the radio on, don a set of yellow rubber gloves and set about my task.

A mindless hour passes and despite ending up sweaty and grimy, I've managed to thoroughly clean the inside of the fridge, de-scale the sink, and sweep the floor. I actually feel a lot better, at least mentally. I'm about to clean myself up when the doorbell rings.

I remove the rubber gloves and try to brush strands of hair away from my sticky forehead. I take a quick glance in the hallway mirror, and shudder. Oh well, he'll have to take me as he finds me.

I open the door to a policeman.

"Evening, Miss Baxter?"

His voice on the phone suggested he was middle-aged, but I'd guess PC Kane is in his mid to late twenties. He's tall, slim, with dark brown hair, cropped short. I really wish I'd found time for a shower and made myself look vaguely presentable.

"Um, yes."

"PC Kane. We spoke on the phone. Is this a good time?"

"Yes, yes...sorry. Come on in."

I lead PC Kane through the hallway and offer him a chair at the kitchen table.

"You'll have to excuse me," I gush. "I've just finished cleaning."

He returns a strained smile and pulls out his notebook.

"Do you live alone Miss Baxter?"

"No. My fiancé lives here too."

"Is he around?"

"Unfortunately not. He had to go away on business at the last minute."

"Okay. I might need to talk to him at some point."

"Really? Why is that?"

"Just routine. He might have seen or heard something."

PC Kane then proceeds to ask me a series of questions I struggle to answer. There really isn't much I can tell him and I start to wonder if maybe Karl was right. This does feel like a waste of everyone's time.

As he wraps up my statement, he fires a final question.

"Have you fallen out with anyone recently? Any problems with people at work, or arguments with family members?"

"No. I work on my own, and besides my mum and a few uncles I rarely see, I don't have any immediate family."

"And Mr Patterson?"

"He's a planning officer and from what I gather, his colleagues are fairly benign civil servant types. I can't imagine this would have anything to do with Karl's colleagues."

"And his family?"

"His parents live in Wales and he's got a sister living somewhere in London. I don't think they're a close family."

PC Kane closes his notepad and tucks it into his pocket.

"I think that's about it for now. I'll take a look at your car before I head back to the station."

"Thank you. What happens next?"

"If I'm honest, there's not really anything to go on. It could be kids or just a random act of vandalism by a disgruntled neighbour. Parking seems to be at a premium around here so I wouldn't rule that out."

"You think one of my neighbours did it?"

"Possibly. It's the only obvious motive. I'll knock on a few doors and gauge the reaction."

He stands and offers his hand.

"I'll do what I can, Miss Baxter."

I shake his hand and see him out.

I close the front door and bolt it. It never crossed my mind that a neighbour might be the guilty party. While the residents are not exactly close knit, I've always found my neighbours to be a pretty friendly bunch. I can't believe one of them would be so vindictive over a parking space. It's an unsettling thought. I'm probably being overly paranoid but I actually wish Karl was here.

I call him again but it goes straight to voicemail. I leave another message.

"Me again. Don't panic, I've calmed down now. Give me a call, please."

The house feels eerily quiet. Why do I suddenly feel so uncomfortable?

I go back into the kitchen, pour a glass of wine, and make another call.

"Mum, it's me."

"Hello, darling."

"I was just seeing if you fancied a natter?"

"That would be lovely, but can I call you back in twenty minutes? I'm just finishing my dinner."

I agree to call her back and head upstairs for a shower, but not before double-checking both the front and back doors are locked.

Fifteen minutes later, dressed in a pair of jogging pants and one of Karl's hoodies, I return to the kitchen and my glass of wine. I take a seat at the table and call Mum back.

She picks up almost immediately.

"Me again, Mum."

"How are you, darling? And how's your lovely fiancé?"

My mother thinks the sun shines out of Karl's backside. They actually have very similar personalities although Mum is a little more naive, and not so keen on motorbikes.

"We're both good, thanks. Karl is away with work at the moment."

I consider telling Mum about the incident with my car but decide against it. She'd only worry.

"So what have you been up to?" I ask.

"Oh, nothing exciting. Just the usual."

Despite being in her late sixties, Mum still has a fairly active, if not erratic social life. She's forever trying her hand at new hobbies and promptly giving them up after a few months. This year alone she's joined a dozen different classes at the local college; everything from yoga to basket weaving.

"Have you joined any new classes recently?"

"Now you mention it, I quite fancy trying my hand at being a vegan."

"Um, I don't think that's a pastime, Mum."

"No, but there's a lovely-looking chap who does vegan cookery classes."

"You never give up do you?"

"Even at my age, darling, a woman still has her needs."

"Eww, Mum. Too much information."

My mother's needs actually run a little deeper. I think she has spent the last twenty nine years trying to find a replacement for the love of her life — my dad. They were totally different characters but their relationship proved the theory that opposites attract. Mum was, and still is, a little scatty. She wears her heart on her sleeve and is too trusting for her own good. Dad was steadfast, pragmatic, and generally treated life with caution.

Mercifully, I've inherited more of my father's traits than my mother's. I love my mum dearly, but what goes on in her head sometimes confounds me.

There was no man in my mother's life for five years after she lost her husband. Eventually, a series of flaky, unsuitable suitors appeared during my teenage years. None of them could meet the standards my dad set. Then, in early 2010, Mum had a whirlwind romance with Stanley Goodyear and they married five months later.

It did not end well.

Stanley was as naive and dreamy as my mother. They decided to sell Mum's house and buy a pub together. To this day, I'm amazed they managed to last the four years they bumbled through. The bailiffs eventually arrived and the pub was repossessed. Stanley was made bankrupt and Mum only just managed to avoid the same fate, aided by the last of my father's inheritance money she'd squirrelled away and subsequently forgotten about. Typical of my dad to be the knight in shining armour, long after his death.

She now lives in a one-bedroom council flat and still hasn't given up on finding a man who might come close to my father. I'm not sure if I admire her optimism or pity her chances.

We chat for an hour, until my stomach begins to rumble.

"I should probably grab something to eat, Mum."

"Okay, darling, I'll let you go. Give Karl a kiss from me."

"I will. I'll try and pop over to see you at the weekend."

"That would be lovely."

"Love you, Mum."

"You too, darling. Bye bye."

I hang up and make myself a sandwich. I sit and eat it in the kitchen while reading a magazine, the radio playing in the background. Minutes turn into an hour and Karl still hasn't returned my call. I try again but only reach his voicemail.

My annoyance is fast becoming concern. Why the hell is Karl not returning my calls?

I head up to bed with a book and read for a while. It proves enough of a distraction until I fall into a fitful sleep.

5

The alarm on my phone shrieks at seven thirty. I stretch across and grab it from the bedside table. Once I've silenced the alarm, I check for messages — nothing.

My mind swings between annoyance and concern. Maybe Karl has lost his phone, or left it in the office. It would be typical of him to forget his phone so perhaps I shouldn't start worrying just yet.

On the upside, I enjoy a quiet breakfast in a tidy kitchen.

With the car still requiring a set of new tyres, I'm set for another walk to work this morning. Another taxi is a luxury I can ill-afford.

I slip my coat on and head out of the house, checking the car as I pass to ensure it hasn't suffered any further damage. Thankfully, it's exactly as I left it. Sadly, the tyres have not repaired themselves overnight.

The temperature this morning is some way below double digits, and a chill wind bites as I make my way to work. I turn my collar up and dig my hands deep into my coat pockets. I glare enviously at passing motorists, cocooned in their cosy cars. I don't like being hot, but I'm not so keen on freezing my tits off either.

I arrive at the shop and fumble in my bag for the keys. The search is particularly fraught, knowing I'll have to walk home if I've forgotten them. The crazy thing is, I've never forgotten my keys, not once. I'm glad not to have broken that run, today of all days.

I unlock the door and determine my priorities: fill the kettle, turn the heating on, and unlock the front door. I keep my coat on.

With the first two priorities sorted, I head out to the shop and unlock the front door. There's a pile of letters on the doormat. I scoop them up and shove them under the counter. Opening bills is pretty low down any list of priorities.

I head back to the staffroom and make myself a cup of builders tea; strong, with half-a-teaspoon of milk.

Tea in hand, I return to the counter and stamp my feet. It'll be at least thirty minutes before the heating system warms the air in the shop to a comfortable level.

While I wait for nothing to happen, as is usual most mornings, I try calling Karl. Voicemail.

"It's me. Again. Please call me back."

I finish my tea and fire up the computer. I find a mobile tyre fitting service and book the latest appointment available. I resentfully stab the keyboard as I enter my credit card details. The bill for four new tyres is a shade over two hundred pounds and paying it makes my blood boil. I hope the perpetrator burns in hell, the bastard.

It has to be classical music again today and I slip a CD of piano concertos into the player.

The four boxes of charity books are still on the floor. I can't put it off any longer and lift the first one onto the counter. With precious little enthusiasm, I pull back the tape and sigh at the pile of tatty paperbacks. I grab a handful and place them on the counter.

My system for selecting and cataloguing new stock is fairly simple. If a book isn't in saleable condition, it goes straight into the recycling bin. If it is in saleable condition, I scan the barcode and check if it's one I currently have in stock. From there, I decide whether it's worthy of a place on the shelves or if it's destined for the stockroom. It can be a painstaking task.

I get through the first box within an hour, almost a third of the books going straight to the recycling bin. Only a handful of the remaining books are worthy of a place on the shelves. The second box isn't much better. The third box is a complete write-off. I can only guess the books once lived alongside a heavy smoker as they're all tinged yellow and still carry a faint whiff of cigarette smoke.

I make a note to tell Eric he can forget payment for that box.

By the time I drop the fourth box onto the counter, the first few lunchtime customers trickle in.

I tear the tape away and open the box. On first inspection it looks as uninspiring as the other boxes. That is until I spot a red, leather bound spine tucked between two tatty paperbacks. I extract the book and smile; a King James Bible, and although it's in terrible condition, it looks old enough to have some value.

I delicately open the cover and check the publication date on the yellowed page — M DC LXXXIII. It takes me a few seconds to calculate the date as 1683. If there weren't customers in the shop, I'd probably whoop and do a little dance. Even in this state, it's probably worth a few hundred pounds; enough to cover the cost of my new tyres.

"Excuse me," says a voice. "Do you have any of the Jack Reacher books in stock?"

I look up from my prized find at the suited man on the other side of the counter.

"Sorry, yes. I'm fairly sure we've got most of them."

I put the bible under the counter and show the man over to the far side of the shop. I've actually got three entire shelves crammed with Lee Child's books. The man seems appropriately enthusiastic about my selection and I leave him to browse.

For the next two hours I'm run off my feet. I'm back and forth between the till and the stockroom, and by the time the rush subsides, my sales are well into three figures. On days like this I love my job. The problem is, days like this are all too infrequent.

With the shop empty, I find five minutes to scoff down a bag of crisps and a chocolate bar.

Hunger sated, I ring Karl again. I don't bother leaving yet another message when it diverts through to his voicemail.

I process the remaining books in the final charity box but my mind won't allow me to focus on anything other than Karl. It's now been over twenty four hours since I spoke to him and my concern is mounting.

I decide to ring his office.

Once I navigate through the automated telephone system, I'm connected to the planning department. I'm relieved when a familiar voice answers.

"Good afternoon. Planning."

"Toby?"

"Speaking."

"Hi, Toby, it's Beth, Karl's other half."

I wouldn't go as far as saying we're friends, but we've been out several times as a foursome with Toby and his partner, Donna.

"Hi, Beth. How are you?"

"I'm okay, thanks. Is Karl around? I've been calling his mobile since yesterday but he's not answering."

"Um, no...he's not here at the moment."

I don't need a polygraph to tell he's lying.

"Toby. Where's Karl?"

He flounders for a moment, clearly struggling to come up with an answer that doesn't drop Karl in it.

"He's...not in work this week."

"Where is he, Toby?" I growl. "I'm close to reporting him as a missing person so unless you come clean, expect a visit from the police."

A few seconds of silence are eventually punctuated by a deep sigh.

"He called yesterday morning and asked for the rest of the week off. Compassionate leave apparently. He said there'd been a bereavement in the family."

My mind spins and I struggle to keep my composure. Why is my fiancé lying to me and his colleagues?

"Did he say anything else, Toby?"

"Nothing. Sorry."

"Right. Can I ask you a question?"

"Erm, sure."

"Did he say anything to you on Monday, at the pub?"

"What? Monday?" he splutters.

"Karl said you called and asked to meet him at the pub on Monday evening."

"Oh, right, yeah."

"Toby. Don't lie to me. Did you meet Karl on Monday evening?"

"No," he eventually gulps.

This just gets worse.

"I'll be honest with you, Toby, I'm really worried about him. Clearly he's been lying to both of us but there might be a legitimate reason behind it. I need to know."

"Okay. I'll help, if I can."

"Has he been particularly stressed at work lately? Any problems?"

"Not that I know of. He's been working on a fairly complicated application for a large commercial development, but that went to the planning committee last Friday."

"What happened?"

"The application was unanimously refused by the committee, against Karl's recommendation."

"How did he take it?"

"Now you come to mention it, he was livid when he got to work on Monday morning and found out. Obviously it's part and parcel of the job that sometimes the planning committee go against our recommendations, but I think Karl took this refusal personally. I think he was particularly annoyed it even went to the planning committee in the first place."

"Couldn't he do anything about it?"

"No. It's frustrating, but it's just part of the job. After it happens a few times you let it wash over you."

"But Karl didn't with this one?"

"No."

"Thanks, Toby. Is there anything else? Anything at all?"

"Sorry, Beth. I wish I could tell you more but Karl always keeps his cards close to his chest, even with work projects."

"Alright. I appreciate your help. If you do hear from him, promise you'll let me know?"

"Sure, I promise. Look, Beth, I've, err, got a meeting to get to."

Toby appears relieved his interrogation is over, and quickly ends the call.

I lean against the counter and try to piece together Toby's revelations. Something is clearly going on in Karl's life that I'm not party to.

I run through a series of possibilities but they all feel like clichéd plots from one of my awful novels. All but one.

If Karl has been under so much pressure at work, and seemingly troubled by the latest project failure, could he have spiralled into a depressive state? Has he had some sort of breakdown and decided just to cut himself off?

I've only ever known Karl to display one of two moods. His default mood is happy-go-lucky, and boundlessly enthusiastic. But when he's down, he's really down, often sulky and withdrawn. Thankfully, he's rarely in anything other than a good mood, but could this setback at work have pushed him too far the other way?

I start to feel uneasy. A feeling resurfaces; one I've kept buried away for decades.

It was such a long time ago, but a man once left my life without saying goodbye. He was there, and then he wasn't. No opportunity to prepare, no chance to adjust. One minute that man is the centre of your life, the next minute he's gone, leaving nothing but a gaping hole behind.

I can only pray to God that Karl hasn't done something stupid.

6

For almost an hour I do nothing other than stare into space and imagine the worst. Six attempts to call Karl all end in the same way as I'm greeted by his bloody voicemail message.

I don't know what to do. Should I call the police and report him a missing person? Should I call Karl's parents? Or should I do nothing and hope he gets in touch?

I hate this feeling and I hate Karl for bringing it to my door.

In the end I decide I'll call the police if I haven't heard anything by tomorrow morning. I already feel guilty about wasting PC Kane's time and I'd rather avoid another, potentially pointless visit from the police so soon after the first.

I need to focus on something positive so I bend down below the counter to locate the King James Bible. My positivity is short-lived when I also find the pile of unopened post from this morning.

I reluctantly extract the wad of letters and drop them on the counter.

I open two brown envelopes first. Good news rarely comes in brown envelopes so I'd rather get it out of the way.

The first letter is just a circular from the local council about a change of parking policy in the town centre. Not interested.

The second letter is a reminder about my impending tax return. Already in hand.

Two letters are addressed to the occupier and obviously junk mail. Straight in the bin.

A large purple envelope is marked with the logo of a supplier I haven't used in years. Also in the bin.

The final piece of mail is a plain white envelope with no stamp or postmark. I can only assume it was delivered by hand before the postman arrived. My name is printed on the front in capital letters. If it's junk mail, I'll give them some credit for piquing my interest.

I tear the envelope open and extract the contents. I'm slightly taken aback by what I find.

There are three photographs, held together with a paper clip. The resolution of the top photo is grainy; almost like the photographer took a picture of a computer screen. Despite the poor lighting, I can just about make out two bodies — one male, one female, both naked. The woman is lying on her back, facing away from the camera, her legs spread wide. The man is lying on his front, his face buried between the woman's legs.

I feel a little sordid, looking at a scene so personal.

I pull the paper clip away and slap the first photo face down on the counter.

The second photo is of equally poor quality. I assume it's the same couple but in a different pose. The woman is on all fours, again facing away from the camera. The man's head has been cropped, the photo ending at his shoulders. He's knelt behind the woman with his hands on her hips, clearly going at her doggy style.

I feel my cheeks flush red. I'm no prude but I draw the line at unsolicited pornography being shoved through my letterbox. The second photo joins the first; face down on the counter.

The final photo is the final photo for a very good reason — I can clearly make out the faces, both facing the camera, probably unaware their liaison is being recorded.

The man is lying on his back and the woman is straddling him. His arms are outstretched, his hands cupping her breasts.

You utter, utter scumbag!

I stare at Karl's face in the photo. He appears to be enjoying himself, certainly more than his companion, Dakota, who looks bored stiff.

Realisation washes over me like a tsunami. Her visit to the shop on Monday was to toy with me. The title of the book she wanted, *Lies in Plain Sight,* and Karl's name. His reaction when I mentioned her name during the evening.

Oh, my God, how did I not make that connection?

Dakota must have delivered the photos, knowing full well they'd destroy my relationship with Karl. With me out of the picture, she could have him to herself.

You dumb cow.

It's not how I'd expect myself to react upon seeing photographic evidence of my fiancé cheating, but I start to laugh.

I can only put my involuntary mirth down to sheer relief. Suddenly everything makes perfect sense.

Karl is not currently on the edge of a cliff, ready to end his life. He's probably holed-up in some seedy hotel, banging his equally seedy girlfriend.

My relief quickly turns to something else.

When I was dating boyfriend number four, Andy, I found him screwing my best friend in the back seat of her car. I still recall their shock when they eventually realised I was on the other side of the glass. Before they noticed me, I must have watched them for a minute or two. Crazy really, that I'd torment myself like that, watching my boyfriend pummel my best friend in such a frenzied manner. Perhaps I just didn't want to believe what I was seeing, so I continued to watch in a state of self-denial.

And of course there was boyfriend number two, Danny. When I walked in and found him fellating his tutor, there were no hysterics. I calmly shook my head, turned around, and walked out, closing the door behind me.

Having caught two previous partners in the actual act of betrayal, seeing pictures of Karl doing the same thing doesn't quite deliver the same level of shock.

Even so, I don't think it's the shock of being cheated on that really irks, because I don't explode with fury as one might. It's more the shock of realising I'm so stupid for putting my trust in these men. It's more disappointment really. Every man in my adult life has let me down. Granted, for different reasons, but the net result is the same: crushing disappointment.

I hoped Karl might be different, but I think he has literally screwed the final nail in the coffin.

Fuck him. Fuck all of them. I'm done with men.

There is only one thing on my mind now — expunging Karl Patterson from my life.

It's still an hour before closing time but I can't face anyone. I lock the door, put my coat on and head home.

Two women stop me on the way back to Elmore Road, both concerned that I'm stumbling through the streets, a little dazed, and crying. I assure both of them it's just 'man trouble', and continue on my way.

Both women probably assumed my tears were of grief, when in actual fact they were tears of anger.

I arrive home, head straight up to the bedroom, and throw the wardrobe doors open. Every stitch of Karl's clothing is unceremoniously dumped on the bed. I pull out drawers and tip the contents onto the growing mound of clothes. Once every piece of furniture has been emptied of his possessions, and the mound is complete, I transfer it all into black sacks. When each one is full, it's tied, and thrown down the stairs.

Such is my determination to remove any semblance of that man from my life, it takes less than an hour to complete the pile of black sacks in the hallway. It proves to be a cathartic process and my anger subsides a little. I still feel bitterly disappointed though, and foolish for not spotting the obvious signs of Karl's infidelity.

As I stand and proudly examine my work, the doorbell rings.

I open the door to a skinny young man in dark blue overalls.

"Alright, Love," he grins. "I'm Luke, the mobile tyre fitter."

I take an exaggerated glance at my watch. "You're ten minutes late," I growl. "And it's Miss Baxter."

His cheeks glow pink and, seemingly unsure how to react, he goes for a feeble smile.

"Sorry. Miss Baxter."

Luke fiddles with a set of keys and looks everywhere but at me. I close my eyes for a second and let out a sigh.

"No, I'm sorry, Luke. I've had a bad day. Ignore me."

His cherub-like face brightens a little as I hand over my keys.

"The car is just down the road. You can't miss it; it's bright yellow. Can I get you a cup of tea or coffee?"

"Nah.You're alright, Love."

The second the word leaves his mouth, horror crosses his face.

"Sorry...Miss. Miss, erm, Baker."

"Baxter."

"God, yeah. Sorry. Sorry."

I chuckle at his fumbling, and with obvious relief, he scoots off down the road.

While Luke is busy replacing my tyres, I turn my attention to locating and bagging Karl's possessions from the kitchen and lounge. That process also involves extracting his Xbox games console from beneath the TV.

I spend five minutes blindly tugging at cables before I'm able to transfer the console and a dozen games to the sack mountain in the hall. In hindsight, the Xbox should have served as a warning. Any man willing to dedicate large parts of his weekend to shooting digital aliens in a make-believe world was never going to possess the emotional maturity I sought.

The doorbell rings again just as I'm putting the last of Karl's tat into a final black sack.

"All done, Miss Baxter."

Luke returns my keys and asks me to sign a receipt. I scribble on the grease-blotched form and hand it back to him.

"Thank you, Luke."

He turns to leave.

"Luke. Do you like video games?"

He spins around, his face puzzled.

"Err, yeah. I do actually."

I pick up the black sack containing Karl's Xbox and games, and place it on the floor at Luke's feet.

"There's an Xbox and a dozen games in there. Consider it a generous tip."

"What? Really?"

He tentatively opens the sack and stares wide eyed at the contents.

"Yep. All yours. Have a nice evening, Luke."

I give him a parting smile and shut the door.

Screw you, Karl.

I return to the kitchen and pour myself an overly generous glass of Merlot. I sit at the table, sipping at the wine and contemplating how I now move forward with my life. A dozen different thoughts cloud the horizon.

I snatch my phone from the table and compose a text message to Karl...

I've seen the photos of you and Dakota, so suffice to say we're done. Your stuff is bagged in the hall. Collect by the weekend or it goes to the tip.

As I make a start on a second glass of Merlot, I compose another text to Karl...

And if you even think about causing me any trouble. I'll tell your boss where you really were this week.

The second glass of Merlot is quickly consumed, and a third started. One final text I think...

And just so you know, I faked it most of the time.

I think a couple of threats and a fairly base attempt to undermine his masculinity are the least Karl deserves. I might regret my texts tomorrow, in the sober light of day, but for now I can bask in a self-satisfied glow.

I head to the lounge with another bottle of Merlot. Getting drunk on your own is a bad idea at the best of times. To do it after the day I've had is a terrible idea.

I don't care.

I turn the TV on and flick through the music channels. It's probably not the wisest choice, but I select a channel playing love songs. I curl up on the sofa with my wine glass in hand.

With no anger left to hide behind, I'm fully exposed to the reality of my failed relationship. The wedding date I had yet to decide upon, will never come around. There won't be any Mr & Mrs Patterson, nor will there be that perfect little family I had once imagined. That stings more than anything else. I can deal with the deceit and the betrayal, just, but the wider implications of that betrayal cut a much deeper wound.

Four years of my life — wasted. My biological clock ticks on relentlessly while my relationship clock resets to zero.

I think this was it. My final chance of motherhood, stolen away by a two-bit slag.

Bitch.

My mind swirls with thoughts of the two of them, together, at this very moment. Are they laughing at me? Do they know what they've taken from me?

The anger returns, as do the tears.

Where is my Edward Rochester, my Fitzwilliam Darcy?

It's not fair. I will never be a wife, or a mother, or an author for that matter. I will never be all the things I dreamt of being. For all the good my dreams did me, I might as well have wished for handsome princes, unicorns, and cats in hats.

The room begins to spin. I put my wine glass on the floor, close my eyes, and curl into a foetal position.

This is it. It's just you now, girl.

In reality, it always has been just me. And I fear it always will be.

7

At some point during the night I must have staggered from the sofa to my bed. I wake to the kind of hangover only red wine can induce.

It takes a moment for memories of yesterday to clamber through the fudge in my head. One by one, they all arrive, my fiancé's infidelity standing at the head of the line.

When a marriage breaks down and culminates in a divorce, you become a divorcee. I never made it that far so I don't know what I am now. Maybe the term is simply ex-fiancé. Semantics, I suppose. Today I have awoken as a single woman and that's all that really matters.

Bleary-eyed, I check my phone to see if Karl replied to any of my text messages. He's nothing if not consistent — not a peep. Should I even care now?

I take a long shower, get dressed and plod down to the kitchen. It's silent, tidy, and that's the way it will be for the foreseeable future. I'm not hungry but I force down two slices of buttered toast and a cup of green tea; the two empty Merlot bottles offer a reminder of why my head feels so thick.

Was it such a good idea to drink when my emotions were already raw? Maybe not, but an hour of alcohol-fuelled blubbing is surprisingly therapeutic. I'm still bitter about those wasted years, and my confidence in men is now at an all-time low, but I won't let Karl Patterson keep me down. Dakota is welcome to him, and his untidiness, his mood swings, and his premature ejaculation.

I ceremoniously drop the wine bottles in the bin, symbolic of my relationship going the same way. A couple of aspirin, a deep breath, and I think I'm ready to face the first day as a freshly-minted singleton. I'm hoping by the time I get to work

I've managed to ease both my headache and any lingering self-pity.

I step beyond the front door into a repeat of yesterday's frigid weather. A chill wind whips down the street to greet me. I scamper to my car and fall into the driver's seat, gratefully slamming the door behind me.

Just as I'm about to pull away, I pause for a second. Should I have checked my tyres are okay? Sod that, it's too cold out there and I'll find out one way or another in the next twenty yards.

I draw a deep breath and pull away. No rumbling noises and no errant steering issues. I breathe again.

The traffic is a little heavier this morning and it takes almost twenty minutes to get to the shop. I pull into the parking bay, unlock the door, and go through the same routine as yesterday: kettle, heating, front door.

By the time I'm behind the counter with a cup of tea in hand, the first customer of the day walks through the front door. I'm glad. I want to be busy today, I want to be distracted.

"Good morning, young lady," the man calls across the shop as he wipes his feet on the doormat. Most customers never bother.

"Morning."

The man gazes around for a moment. Judging by his thinning white hair and craggy face, I guess he must be in his seventies. His dapper attire is another clue to his age. A navy blue pinstripe suit beneath a tan-coloured camel hair coat — a look I haven't seen in a while. His aftershave is also markedly old-school too; the potent scent of musk and leather drifting across the shop.

"It looks like I'm your first customer of the day," he says in a clipped accent.

"Yes, you are."

"Splendid."

He moves confidently across the floor towards the counter, his hand outstretched.

He reaches the counter and smiles. "Miss Baxter, I assume?"

I shake his hand.

"David Sterling."

I try to recall if we've ever met or how he'd know my name. Mr Sterling notes my blank expression.

"We've never met, Miss Baxter."

"I did wonder. What can I do for you, Mr Sterling?"

"Now, that is quite the question."

He leans forward and rests one arm on the counter, the spotlights in the ceiling casting a shadow across his lined face. It's only then I spot the thin, crescent-shaped scar, running from the corner of his mouth up to his right ear. Coupled with his prominent, hooked nose, it's a face hard not to stare at.

"Motorcycle accident, when I was a young man," he casually remarks.

That explains the scar, but his beak-like conk must be a genetic curse.

"Oh...err, sorry, "I splutter.

"It's alright. I've become quite accustomed to strangers seeing the scar before they see the man."

I return a nervous smile, the awkwardness of the situation heightened as Mr Sterling's steely grey eyes bore into me.

"How is business, Miss Baxter? I'd imagine it must be challenging, what with most people purchasing books on the Internet these days."

He turns away and spends a few seconds casting his eye over the shelves.

Something clicks in my head and a strand of irritation suddenly flares. I've had quite enough of being pissed around by men.

"What was it you wanted, Mr Sterling? Are you selling something? If you are, I'm really not interested."

His face snaps back in my direction.

"I like a lady who gets to the point. And to answer your question, no, I'm not selling anything."

He stares at me but doesn't expand on his answer.

"Okay, so what do you want?"

"Not so much *what*, Miss Baxter, but *who*."

"Excuse me?"

"I'm looking for someone. Your errant fiancé."

"He's not my fiancé any longer," I snap. "In fact, he's no longer my anything."

"Well, well. That must have been a recent development. I do hope my photographs weren't the catalyst."

I feel myself shrink, my confidence draining away at the sight of Mr Sterling's knowing smile. It seems I now know the identity of the voyeuristic photographer.

"It was you..."

"I'm sorry you had to see those photographs, Miss Baxter," he interrupts. "Your fiancé and I had a deal. He reneged on that deal so I had to up the ante, see if I could shake him up a little. Seems I shook him a little too hard and he's now gone to ground."

What the hell has Karl got himself into? And why is this old man taking lurid photos of Karl and his floozy? More to the point, why is he sending those photos to me?

"I'm afraid I can't help you. Karl isn't returning my messages and according to his colleague, he's taken time off work. I don't have the first clue where he is."

"Oh dear. That is disappointing."

He puffs out his cheeks and takes a glance at an expensive looking wristwatch.

"Unfortunately, if that is the case I'm afraid it falls upon you to repay his debt, Miss Baxter."

"What debt? I don't think so," I bark. "I don't know why Karl owes you money, but it's his problem, not mine."

I move from behind the counter and stride purposely towards the front door. Mr Sterling stands motionless, his eyes following my path until I reach the door and pull it open.

"I'd like you to leave. Now."

"Close the door, Miss Baxter."

"If you don't leave, I'll call the police."

He takes half-a-dozen strides towards the door, and for a moment I think he's going to leave. He doesn't.

He grabs the door edge and yanks it from my grip with such force it slams into the frame.

"Calling the police would be a very bad idea," he says, his tone edging towards aggressive. "Slashed tyres can be replaced. A slashed face, not so easily, as I can attest to."

His thin smile returns as he waits for a reaction.

"You...slashed my tyres?" I stutter.

"Don't be silly. I'm far too respectable to be committing acts of petty vandalism. Fortunately, I do happen to know some fairly undesirable individuals who are more than willing to do my bidding."

He leans against the door and dips a hand inside his coat. He pulls out a piece of paper and hands it to me.

"Obviously a man in my position has to ensure all the legal bases are covered. This letter covers Mr Patterson's arrangement. Take a look."

I tentatively take the letter and unfold it. I scan the text but I'm drawn to the two signatures at the bottom — Karl's, and mine.

"I'll save you reading it, Miss Baxter. What you have in your hand is a copy of a contract which gave Mr Patterson a deadline to repay monies owed. That deadline has passed."

"I never signed this," I scoff.

"It's your signature, is it not?"

I look at the letter again. The signature certainly looks identical to mine, but I'm positive I never signed it.

I open my mouth to repeat my position, but Sterling snatches the letter out of my hand.

"This is a legally binding contract, Miss Baxter. It was given to Mr Patterson and he returned it, with both signatures. If you're claiming it's a forgery, you had better take that up with Mr Patterson. It makes no odds to me."

"This is ridiculous. I don't even know how much he owes you, or why?"

"The *why* is unimportant. The *how much* is twenty grand."

I stagger backwards and have to hold myself upright by leaning against a shelf.

"I...I...don't have that sort of money."

"Of course you do," he replies glibly. "You own a property in Elmore Road, and of course, there's this place. I think you could raise the money if you put your mind to it."

He steps towards me. I want to run but my legs don't cooperate.

"Seven days for you and Mr Patterson to get the funds together, Miss Baxter. Perhaps that deadline will help you focus on finding him."

He looks down his beaky nose at me before opening the door.

"I'll be back next Thursday afternoon. Don't let me down — that would not end well for you."

With that, he strides out of the shop, closing the door behind him.

My legs finally give way and I slide down the edge of the bookcase to the floor, my breathing ragged, my thoughts mashed.

For ten minutes I just sit there, trying to piece together what little I know. It isn't much. Karl has clearly got himself into debt, although I have no idea how he'd wrack up one of twenty thousand pounds. And for some inexplicable reason, he thought it an appropriate time to embark on an affair. Are those two facts connected? Has he borrowed money to setup home with that Dakota woman?

Why has he gone to ground though? And more importantly, how the hell did my signature end up on that contract?

Christ. What do I do?

My fear slowly ebbs away and anger replaces it. Even if I had the means to pay Karl's debt, which I most certainly don't, why the hell should I?

I clamber to my feet and stagger into the staffroom. With shaky hands I pull my phone from my bag and call Karl. Voicemail.

"Listen to me you little shit, I've just had a visit from David Sterling and he's not happy. If you don't call me back the minute you get this message, I'm calling the police and they can deal with his threats."

With my nerves still jangling, I try to find some calm, some resolve. I put the kettle on and make myself a camomile tea. I need a clear head to think, to plan.

Seven days.

On the basis Mr Sterling won't be paid by me, what possible consequences could there be? This is not the Wild West; we have laws, and punishment for people who break those laws. Sterling can't go around threatening people and damaging property without consequences, surely?

I have the law on my side.

But he has a signed contract.

Suddenly a thought crosses my mind. Karl's annoyance when I insisted on calling the police to report my slashed tyres. He must have known it was something to do with Sterling. No wonder he didn't want me to get the police involved. In hindsight, I'm glad I never listened to him.

I shouldn't listen to Sterling either. I don't even know who he is. Should I? I know so very little and that puts Sterling at an advantage.

I dart back into the shop and wake the computer. After a search for his name, and a little filtering, I find several results from the local newspaper website. I click on, and read four articles, all of which refer to a charitable donation made by Sterling's company, Guildale Developments. Three of the articles are accompanied by photos; all of David Sterling standing beside charity volunteers, proudly holding poster sized cheques. The sums displayed on the cheques are sizeable.

This makes no sense.

The man smiling in the photos appears to be a generous and patently successful businessman. The face is the same but it was no genteel, philanthropic pensioner who threatened me this morning.

I search for Guildale Developments and click through to their website.

A few more clicks and I locate a page displaying photos of their board members, with links to their respective profiles. I click the profile link for their Chairman, David Sterling.

The words paint a picture of a virtual saint. Having moved into the area forty years ago, Sterling built Guildale up from nothing. In that time, the company have constructed hundreds of homes, and have a sizeable portfolio of rental properties. Alongside Sterling's success in business, he's also forged a credible reputation in the local community with a string of honorary awards from numerous charitable organisations.

Why is a man with such obvious wealth, and good standing, risking it all over a debt he could chase through the courts? He has so much at stake, and that surely undermines his threats. If I go to the police, the publicity alone could damage his reputation.

Do I call his bluff or call the police? I need to give this some thought.

I steel myself and prepare to get on with my day while I consider the best way to deal with David Sterling.

Just as I reach the door, my phone rings on the table.

It's Karl.

8

I snatch the phone from the table and accept Karl's call. With so much anger built up over so many unreturned calls, I've given little thought to what I'm actually going to say to him.

I let loose with industrial-grade gibberish. "You bastard. You despicable, cheating little shit. You...you..."

I run out of expletives.

"I'm so sorry, Beth," Karl interjects, his voice calm but subdued.

I take a second to compose myself.

"I don't even know where to start so I'll give you thirty seconds to tell me what the hell is going on. And I want the truth, Karl. Every bit of it."

"Beth, I'm in deep shit."

"No kidding," I bark. "I worked that one out myself. But I'm the one getting my tyres slashed and pornographic pictures shoved through my letterbox. Where the hell are you, Karl?"

He pauses for a moment. All I can hear is a series of heavy breaths.

"Karl. I don't have the patience for this. Tell me what the hell is going on. Now."

"Alright. Alright."

The line goes quiet again and I hear a door close.

"Are you on your own?" he asks.

"Yes. Now get on with it."

"I guess there's no point trying to sugar-coat any of this but please save your screaming until I've finished. Alright?"

"Fine."

He begins, and his voice becomes a little more frantic.

"This all started about eighteen months ago. I...err...had a bit of a gambling problem. It spiralled out of control and before I knew it, I owed about five grand to a bookie. He then sold my debt to a loan shark. He ramped it up to eight grand within a month. The interest just kept being piled on and I couldn't keep up with the payments."

"For crying out loud, Karl. Why didn't you tell me?"

"Dunno. Shame, I suppose. Anyway, I met a guy in a pub who said he could offer me a way out. He introduced me to David Sterling."

"Why would Sterling help you out?"

"He runs a property development company."

"That much I know. So what?"

"He said he'd pay my debt off in full if I helped him see a planning application over the line."

"What? You took a bribe?"

"He said it was an incentive, not a bribe. The application was pretty sound anyway, so I didn't really have to do much to ensure it went through."

"But if you helped him, why is he now harassing me?"

The line goes quiet again. I suspect we've barely scratched the surface of Karl's misdemeanours.

"A few days after the application went through, Sterling and a few of his associates invited me for a night out to celebrate. We went to an expensive restaurant, then on to a casino. He gave me a grand to wager, which I blew in about two hours, and then we somehow ended up in a hotel suite."

"Go on."

"It all turned bad from that point," he sighs. "That's where those photos were taken."

I can almost feel his shame across the phone line.

"The photos of you and your new girlfriend?" I spit.

"She's not my girlfriend, Beth. She's an escort."

My stomach somersaults. "You paid her for sex?"

"I know it's no excuse, but I was drunk. And I never paid her anything. It was Sterling. He wanted the pictures as leverage."

"Ohh, that's alright then," I yell. "It makes it all the more palatable to know you never wrote the cheque."

"Beth. Please."

I try to calm myself. It takes some doing.

"I never heard anything from Sterling for about ten months. Then I got a call out of the blue to say he needed my input on another application."

"What did he offer? A whole troupe of whores?"

"No. Ten grand."

"You idiot. You took it didn't you?"

"It was such a simple application and I didn't really have to do much. It was easy money, and I really wanted a chunk of cash..."

"Oh no. Please, Karl," I interrupt. "Don't tell me you spent that money on what I think you spent it on."

"I'm sorry, Beth. There never was a winning scratch card."

"What the hell is wrong with you? What sort of man buys his fianceé an engagement ring with an illegal bung?"

"I...I...just wanted to make you happy."

"Happy? By implicating me in your corrupt little scheme? No wonder you didn't want me to go to the police. I'm wearing an engagement ring, and driving around in a new car, both bought with your dirty money."

"I know, I'm sorry." he whispers.

I take another deep breath.

"So why is he now chasing you for twenty grand."

"I accepted a much bigger bribe."

"What? Why?"

"You know how much I've always wanted to run my own business?"

"Yes. You tried, Karl, and failed several times."

"Thanks for reminding me," he huffs. "But this time was different. I wanted to set up my own planning consultancy and I know it would have worked. I just needed forty grand to get it up-and-running. And I thought once I'd left the planning department, I'd no longer be of use to Sterling and he'd leave me alone."

"Wait. If he gave you twenty grand, and you needed forty, where were you planning to get the rest of the cash?"

I already have a fair idea of his answer.

"I had a dead-cert bet on a horse. I put the whole twenty grand on the win. It lost by a nose."

"Jesus wept. You stupid, stupid man."

The line goes quiet again. I haven't smoked for years, but for some inexplicable reason I really want a cigarette about now.

"Notwithstanding your gross stupidity, Karl, you still haven't explained why I'm now being targeted by Sterling, and how my signature ended up on a contract I've never seen before."

"His latest planning application ended up going to the committee. That was bad enough, but it was declined last week. I told Sterling I was going to resign because I'd had enough. I thought that would be the end of it."

"Clearly it wasn't."

"No, he went nuts. He gave me until nine o'clock Tuesday morning to repay his money, or he'd involve you. He did give me another option, though. He wanted me to approve another application but it was so complex I'd never have got it through. I had no choice but to run."

More dots are connected.

"So Dakota's visit to the shop was a warning? And when you failed to heed that warning, that's why my tyres were slashed?"

"Yes. I went to see him on Monday evening, to plead with him, but it was a total waste of time."

"Monday evening? When you were supposedly at the pub with Toby?"

"Sorry, yes."

"And then you decided to disappear, so Sterling sent the pictures to me?"

"Yes."

"And my signature?"

"I, um, copied it from your mobile phone contract. It was his way of making everything look above board. I had no choice, babe."

"And now I'm being ordered to repay your debt, or face the consequences."

I realise I've been pacing up and down the staffroom for the entirety of our conversation. I take a seat at the table and work out how I can bring some order to this chaos.

"Where are you, Karl?"

"I'd rather not say."

"Don't play games with me. You need to get your backside back here and sort this mess out."

"I can't, babe."

"Don't ever call me babe again. And why can't you come back?"

"I'm scared. Sterling isn't the sort of man you want to owe money to."

"Grow up. From what I've seen, he's virtually a pillar of the community. He's just as guilty as you are so he's not likely to create any waves. I don't see what else he can do."

"He's not the man you think he is."

"Meaning?"

"He's originally from the east end of London. Rumour has it he was once part of an organised crime gang in the sixties, an enforcer of some sort. There's talk of him working with the likes of The Krays. Apparently, he's buried dozens of people who've crossed him, both figuratively and literally."

"You're being ridiculous. Whatever he may have been involved in, he's now a bloody pensioner."

"You think he amassed all that money and power by writing cheques for charity?"

This conversation is doing nothing for my headache.

"I give up with you, Karl. None of this is my fault and if you're too scared of Grandpa Sterling, that's your lookout. I'm going to call the police and tell them everything."

"Beth, please, think about it. What evidence is there against Sterling? There's no way to prove anything. Even if there was, it wouldn't just be Sterling going to prison. I've broken the law too."

"You should have bloody-well thought about that before you got involved with all this."

"I know, I know. But what can I do about it now? If I come back and face Sterling, he's only going to demand I fix more planning applications. It's too risky and I'm gonna end up getting caught, assuming he doesn't kill me first. The money and the contract are leverage to get what he really wants — a permanent patsy in the planning office."

"Just bloody do it then. If you have to be Sterling's bitch then so be it. That's your problem now and I want no part in it."

"But if you pay the money back then he no longer has any leverage. And he's played all his cards by sending you those photos."

"I'm not listening to any more of this. Just get yourself back here and face up to him."

"I can't do it, Beth. I just can't."

"So that's it? You run away and leave me to clear up your mess?"

"I know you must hate me, but you have choices. I don't."

"Choices? What choices do I have?"

The delay in his reply signals I'm about to receive a suggestion he knows I don't want to hear.

"You could remortgage the house."

"Are you kidding me? Absolutely not. Forget it."

"I'll pay you back, every penny, plus interest. I promise."

My phone is pressed so tight to my ear, I can hear my own pulse in the silence. I want to scream at Karl. Actually, I want to murder him myself. Slowly, painfully.

"Even if I was prepared to remortgage my home, which I'm not, who the hell is going to lend that amount of money to a woman barely scratching a living?"

"I...I...don't know. But there's bound to be some company out there who will."

"I'm not remortgaging my home. It's not going to happen so just forget it."

"Beth, if you loved me..."

"Oh. My. God. Don't you dare, Karl. Don't you dare."

"You don't love me though, do you?"

"What the hell has our relationship got to do with your debt?"

"If you truly loved me, you wouldn't think twice about helping me."

"And if you truly loved me, you wouldn't have shagged a bloody prostitute."

"I know, and I'm sorry. Please, just think about it."

"There's nothing to think about. I'm not remortgaging my home. Not for you, not for anyone."

"Then I'm not coming back."

I have to bite my lip to retain any sort of control. It only postpones my inevitable reaction.

"Fuck you then, Karl."

I hang up.

The temptation to throw my phone across the staffroom is almost too great. My cup makes the journey instead, splintering into a hundred pieces as it strikes the wall. I remain seated at the table, my head in my hands, breathing heavily.

Keep it together, Beth.

I consider calling him back and offloading my anger, but I suspect any further discussion will only stoke it further. What is there to say, anyway? The man I was going to marry is not the man I thought he was — not by a long chalk. The man I was going to marry is a liar, a fraud, and a coward. Perhaps I've had a lucky escape, but I feel a million miles away from lucky.

Pangs of anger continue to jab at me from different angles: Karl's deceit, Sterling's threats, and my own stupidity. How could I have been so blind? I think back over the last few years, searching for any signs that might have passed me by at the time. So easy with the benefit of hindsight.

I could probably sit and wallow in my indignation all day, but the sound of the shop door opening pulls me back to reality.

I get up and slope into the shop, taking up position behind the counter. One of my regulars, Miss Henderson, is browsing the aisles. She's a portly, grey-haired spinster with little in her life other than her cat and her love of romantic novels. It scares me that when I look at Miss Henderson, I could well be looking at my own future.

She waves at me and returns her attention to the shelves.

The silence is uncomfortable so I reach beneath the counter and switch the CD player on. *Grieg's Piano Concerto in A minor* provides a fittingly dramatic accompaniment to my thoughts. The anger continues to bubble away like lava in a volcano crater, ready to erupt without notice.

God forgive any customer who dares to complain today.

Miss Henderson spends thirty minutes browsing the shelves while I consider the many ways I'd like to murder Karl. She eventually waddles over to the counter and drops a paperback on the counter — *Lovers and Liars* by Josephine Cox.

A loud snort escapes my mouth. If there really is a God, I don't appreciate his inappropriate sense of humour.

I doubt if Miss Henderson understands the context.

"Is there a problem, Beth?"

"No...no...I'm sorry, Miss Henderson," I splutter. "It's just the title of the book. It's a little apt."

Her expression shifts and she eyes me with a look of concern. I assume my face isn't masking my feelings as well as I hoped.

"Are you okay?"

"I'm fine. Thank you. That's seventy five pence please."

I put the book in paper bag and pass it across the counter. She hands me the correct change.

"Are you sure you're okay? You look very pale."

"Honestly, I'm fine. I've just got a few problems with my ex-fiancé."

Miss Henderson picks the book up and drops it into her bag. She's about to turn and leave but hesitates for a second.

"You know what Eleanor Roosevelt once said?"

"Um, no."

"A woman is like a teabag — you can't tell how strong she is until you put her in hot water."

She reaches across the counter and pats my hand. "Better to be a teabag than a mug, my love."

With that, she turns and leaves.

Somehow, I find a smile. I've never thought of myself as a teabag but maybe Miss Henderson has a point.

For the next two hours, a steady stream of customers keeps my mind occupied. But all too soon the lunchtime rush is over and I'm left in an empty shop. It doesn't take long for my anger to resurface. I have to do something. I have to be strong.

I retrieve PC Kane's card from my purse and place it on the counter. There it sits for twenty minutes while I mentally play out the various ways a call to PC Kane might go.

There are two reasons why my phone remains in my pocket.

Firstly, I don't have any evidence of Sterling's threats. And secondly, that bloody contract. Clearly Sterling is a belt and braces type of businessman. If his threats don't work, he can turn to the legal system to recoup his losses. Either way, I'm screwed. The fact Karl made me a beneficiary of Sterling's bribe money also doesn't help.

Perhaps informing the police will be my last resort. For now, I need another plan.

I open the web browser on the computer and return to the Guildale Developments website. A few clicks and I'm back on David Sterling's profile page, with his email address at the bottom. They say that attack is the best form of defence, so I'll drop him an email with a few threats of my own.

I open Gmail and compose an email to Sterling...

Dear Mr Sterling

Further to our meeting this morning, I have now spoken to Mr Patterson and he's brought me up-to-speed on your business arrangement. I must say, it was quite an interesting discussion, and I can see why you wouldn't want details of your deal becoming public knowledge.

Suffice to say, I will not be repaying Mr Patterson's debt.

If you genuinely feel I am liable for that debt, I would recommend you go through the court system and we can see if they agree — I am confident they won't, but it's your right.

I would also like to make it clear you are not welcome at my place of work or my home. If I receive any further visits, from you or any of your associates, I will have no hesitation in contacting the police and reporting everything Mr Patterson told me.

I sign off and send it.

I will not be bullied or threatened by anyone, and I think Sterling will get that message loud and clear. With any luck, I'll never hear from him, or Karl, ever again.

9

Friday signifies the end of the working week for most people. But for those of us in retail, it's just another day.

I spend most of the morning nervously checking my email inbox for a reply from Sterling. As the hours pass, the only emails to arrive are junk, and I relax a little.

By the time the lunchtime rush arrives, I'm busy enough to almost forget about Sterling's threat, or at least bury it away.

Fridays are usually a good day in the shop, with customers keen to acquire new reading material for the weekend. Today looks like it'll be a good one.

By the time the rush peters out around half-two, the till reports sales of almost a hundred and fifty pounds. I allow myself a moment to bask in satisfaction, just before I check my email inbox again. Still nothing.

While the till might be full, my stomach isn't. I lock the door and nip to the newsagent to grab something to eat. I return five minutes later with some wholewheat crackers and a muesli bar. If I'm going back on the shelf, I'd prefer it not to creak.

I take a seat at the table in the staffroom to eat my late lunch. The wholewheat crackers are as dry as a nun's crotch, and the muesli bar reminds me of something I used to feed my pet hamster.

As I attempt to chew my way through the final mouthful, I hear the shop door open, followed by the sound of female voices. A bomb goes off in my head.

Shitting buggery and bollocks.

I never forget birthdays or anniversaries. I'm never late for appointments. If I say I'll be somewhere at a certain time, I will.

It is so rare I forget a commitment, when I do, it almost invokes a breakdown.

I'm about to have a breakdown.

I leap from my chair and stand in the doorway to the shop. It's just gone three o'clock and eleven members of the St Augustine's Ladies Book Club are milling around. They're waiting for tea and biscuits, and they're keenly anticipating my recommendation for this week's read.

There's no tea, no biscuits, and no recommendation. What with everything that's happened over the last few days, I totally forgot they were due in today. The only saving grace is their numbers are low today. Some days there can be as many as twenty of them.

Eleven elderly faces, topped with cotton wool hair, stare at me.

With remnants of the muesli bar cemented to my gums, I try to splutter a greeting. "After...noon...ladies."

"Good afternoon, Bethany," they all reply in unison.

A few of them glance around the shop like geriatric meerkats. There's usually a table setup in the middle of the shop, laden with a teapot, china cups, and most importantly, plates of biscuits. The lack of custard creams threatens anarchy.

"We're not early are we?" asks Vera, founder of the book club and ringleader.

"No...no, I'm running a bit late today. I'm so sorry."

There's a murmur amongst the crowd. I'm sure I hear a few of them tutting at the lack of bland tea, bland biscuits, and bland romantic literature.

"If you want to browse for a few minutes, I'll get everything ready."

I need this like a hole in the head. As much as I'd like to tell them to sod off, the shop needs their regular custom.

I spend fifteen frantic minutes setting up the table, arranging chairs, and scurrying around with cups and saucers. Despite all the huffing and the puffing, and the rolling of eyes, nobody offers to help. My angst simmers behind a withering smile.

Once the tea and biscuits are served, I leave them to mumble amongst themselves and dart into the stockroom. I scan the shelves looking for a title in sufficient stock to supply all eleven ladies. Typically, I'd spend a few hours carefully selecting a suitable title for this particular club. I've got a few minutes at best. I find a stack of a title by Barbara Cartland but there are only nine copies. Bugger.

I search on.

With time against me, I head to a rack of shelves I rarely visit. It's stacked high with remaindered books; overstock, sold cheaply by publishers, and for good reason. I went through a phase of buying remaindered books because they were cheap, but I quickly discovered they hung around like a bad smell. Alas, desperate times call for desperate measures.

I move along the Manhattan skyline of books, scanning the covers in search of a title suitable for a conservative, church-going audience. Dozens of titles from authors I've never heard of. It's the literary equivalent of Celebrity Big Brother. These authors have got as far as having their work thrust into the public domain, but they'll never bother the best sellers list or an awards ceremony.

A cream-coloured book catches my eye — *The Service of Venus,* by Kitty MacBride.

The cover depicts a handsome couple in the midst of an embrace; a pastiche of a movie poster for *Gone with the Wind,* featuring Clark Gable and Vivien Leigh. I quickly scan the blurb on the back. It's poorly written and cliché-ridden, but the plot appears suitably vanilla for my puritan audience. I'm past caring.

I grab a dozen copies, including one for myself, and head back into the shop.

"Are we ready, ladies?"

Cups are placed on the table and veiny hands snatch at the remaining biscuits. The eleven women all slowly take to their chairs, sitting in a tight circle.

The tortuous format of this particular book club involves us collectively reading a dozen chapters of our chosen book. They then take the book away to finish it at home before we reconvene to discuss it in two weeks' time.

With all eleven women seated, I hand them all a copy of my hastily chosen title.

"This week's book is *The Service of Venus,* by Kitty MacBride."

More mumbling and frowning.

"It's a hidden gem. I'm sure you'll enjoy it," I add confidently.

Each woman inspects their copy with obvious disdain. They don't like surprises, and my decision to choose a book by an unknown author is clearly an affront. They'll have to lump it this week.

"So, who'd like to read the first chapter?" I ask.

Come on you blue-rinsed crones, don't make me read it.

"I'll do it," pipes Beatrice.

I have to physically force the muscles in my face to form a smile. Beatrice has poor eyesight and reads out loud like a five-year-old to a teacher.

"Thank you, Beatrice. Ready when you are."

The twelve of us flick to the first page and Beatrice clears her throat.

It begins.

"My...mother...warned...me...about...men...like...Victor...Car michael..."

Her ponderous diction is akin to water torture. Every word, every syllable, painfully delivered in a monotone voice.

"He...was...handsome...but...he...knew...it..."

I try to tune Beatrice's voice out, and read the text in my head. It proves impossible.

"The...day...the...carnival...came...to...town..."

I can't do this anymore. My mind begins to drift away as Beatrice's voice fades into the background.

"He...won...a...teddy...bear...on...the...coconut...shy..."

What shall I have for dinner tonight? I can have whatever I like now. No need to worry about Karl's fussy tastes.

"Victor...took...my...hand...and...led...me...behind...the...old...oak...tree..."

I haven't had Thai green curry in ages. Yes, that sounds nice.

"He...ripped...my...panties...away..."

Or shall I go for something a little more exotic? They do some lovely Malaysian dishes in Waitrose.

"I...grasped...his...throbbing...shaft...and...lowered...myself...onto...it..."

And I need to get some more granola, and....wait. What was that?

"I...squealed...at...Victor's...impressive...girth..."

Ohh, shit.

My head snaps up and ten shocked faces stare back at me. The eleventh, Beatrice, continues her graphic narration, seemingly oblivious to what she's reading.

"Oh, gosh...sorry, Beatrice," I splutter. "Maybe we should leave it there for now."

Beatrice drops the book to her lap. The silence is deafening.

Just when I thought my week couldn't get any worse, I've now inflicted some fairly awful erotic fiction on my most active book group.

Vera eventually speaks. "Bethany, you said this book was a hidden gem. I assume you'd read it in order to draw that conclusion?"

Oh, Christ. Oh, Christ.

"Yes...well...I may have scanned it. Perhaps I didn't give it my full attention."

The silence returns.

"Look, ladies. I'm so, so sorry. Perhaps it wasn't the most appropriate of choices. Forgive me."

Peggy, a wizened eighty-year-old, slowly raises her hand, seeking permission to speak.

"Yes, what is it Peggy?" I ask with some hesitancy.

"We can still take it home?" she squeaks.

Glances are sent left and right between the ladies.

"Yes, can we?" Prudence adds.

"You still want to take the book away with you?" I say in disbelief.

A chorus of nods and approval. Apparently they do.

"Err, sure."

Without any prompt, Beatrice continues where she left off. The other ten ladies settle down and listen.

The following forty minutes are, without question, the most cringeworthy of my entire life. The awful writing, thin plot, and two-dimensional characters are bad enough, but that's not the worst part of the book. The protagonist, Ruby, is clearly some sort of post-virginal nymphomaniac and indulges Victor's desires in toe curling detail throughout the ten chapters we wade through.

By the time we finish, a cloud of musty oestrogen has formed above our circle of chairs. On the upside, I have never seen this book group so enthusiastic, so engaged.

As the group disbands, I take up position behind the counter to receive payment from the eleven ladies; all eager to get their new book home. Last in line is Vera.

"That was very brave of you, Bethany."

"Sorry?"

"I thought it made a refreshing change to read something with a little spice. Well done."

She shakes my hand and smiles.

"But you never read it, did you?" she asks while still clutching my hand.

"Um, I can't lie to you, Vera. I've been a bit distracted the last few days."

"Don't worry, dear. We might be women of God, but we're not nuns."

She gives me a wink and ushers the final few members from the shop. The deep breath I exhale once they've all left almost blows the window out. I don't know how I managed to busk my way through that, but they all left happy. Maybe it's another sign that my little spell of misfortune is now behind me.

It's gone five o'clock by the time I finish clearing up. I check my email to see if Sterling has replied but my inbox is empty. It appears his bluff has been called. I'm not willing to waste any more of my emotions on Sterling, Karl, or any other man for that matter.

Perhaps I can now focus on novel eighteen. It's enough for me.

I pop to Waitrose on the way home and spoil myself by purchasing a Malaysian ready-meal, together with a few other groceries.

I arrive home just after six-thirty. It's probably psychological but the house feels more empty than ever before. Of the ten years I've lived here, six of them have been on my own so it's not as though I'm entering uncharted territory. Somehow though, the post-relationship emptiness is different.

I felt the same when Stuart left. Perhaps it's the permanence; knowing nobody will be walking through the front door anytime soon.

As I pass through the hallway, I let my hand brush gently across the smooth plaster wall.

Just you and me again.

It's ridiculous to think of it as anything other than bricks and mortar, but this little house means so much more. It has been a rock in my life for the last decade; like a steadfast friend, always willing to provide assurance, to give comfort. It was here long before I entered this world, and it will be here long after I've left. There's something reassuring in that.

I throw my ready-meal in the microwave and head upstairs to change.

Sporting a pair of pink jogging pants and a fleece hoodie, I return to the kitchen just as the microwave pings. I slide the ready-meal container onto a tray, grab a fork and wander through to the lounge. With the TV switched on, I settle down on the sofa to eat.

As I pick at my beef rendang, I gaze around the room. The decor is long overdue a refresh. The regency red walls now feel a little dated, and sometimes the cosy space errs too close to being claustrophobic. Perhaps something brighter, a little more contemporary, would give the room a lift. I'll pop to the DIY store tomorrow and pick up some samples. It'll give me something positive to focus on.

I wish I had the money to give the whole house a facelift. It could certainly do with it. The romantic notion of living in a century-old home is somewhat tainted by the ongoing cost of the maintenance. I had the kitchen and bathroom re-fitted seven years ago, but the boiler needs replacing and the slate roof is nearing the end of its life. Maybe one day, when my yet unpenned eighteenth novel is a global best-seller, I'll be able to spend some of my royalties on remodelling the entire house.

I allow myself a wry smile.

Dream on, girl.

Once I've finished my meal, I toy with the idea of getting the laptop out and seeing if I can move forward with novel eighteen. I don't know if I can face the inevitable frustration and disappointment though. Maybe I'll give it a miss tonight.

I settle on watching a movie instead, and curl up on the sofa.

Half-an-hour into it, my phone starts ringing in the kitchen. I reluctantly clamber from the sofa and trudge through to the kitchen. I pluck my phone from the table and study the number on the screen. It's a local dialling code but not one of my contacts, nor is it a number I recognise.

I want to ignore it.

But it's eight o'clock on a Friday evening so it's unlikely to be a cold caller.

I take the call.

"Who is it?" I answer curtly.

"Miss Baxter?"

"Speaking."

"I'm Nurse Evans from St Mary's Hospital," she says, her tone sombre. "I'm calling about your mother."

10

"Mum?" I gulp. "What's wrong with her?"

"Honestly, there's no need to worry, but I'm afraid she was the victim of a street robbery, about an hour ago."

"Oh, my God," I gasp. "Is she okay? Is she hurt?"

"Nothing too serious, Miss Baxter. She's got a few grazes and a bump on the head. Obviously she's in shock and because of her age, we're keeping her in overnight as a precaution."

"I can't believe this. How did it happen?"

"I don't know the full details I'm afraid, but I think she was attacked by two youths and fell to the ground during the struggle. That's when she banged her head. Thankfully, a passer-by managed to scare them off."

"Thank heavens there are still some good Samaritans around. Tell her I'll be there in ten minutes, please."

"Will do."

I hang up. As awful as it feels, the relief Mum is okay is overwhelmed by a surge of anger.

What sort of pond life tries to mug a defenceless pensioner?

I slip my trainers on, grab my handbag, and storm out of the house.

The drive to the hospital is a blur of screeching tyres and aggressive gear changes. The journey only takes ten minutes but navigating the hospital car park takes almost as long. I eventually find an empty bay on the fourth floor and haphazardly abandon the Fiat.

I soon discover my visit to the hospital has coincided with general visiting hours. The reception area and corridors throng with people, milling around or trudging along. Some faces happy, others full of concern.

After a painstaking wait at the reception desk, I finally make my way through the maze of stairwells and corridors towards ward F9.

I crash through a set of double doors into the relative calm of the ward. Two nurses in dark blue uniform are sitting behind a desk directly in front of me.

"Nurse Evans called to say my mother had been admitted."

The woman on the left stands. She looks tired, her complexion grey, and her eyes haloed with dark circles.

"I'm Nurse Evans. And you are?"

"Beth Baxter. My mother is Elizabeth Goodyear."

"Ah, yes. This way, Miss Baxter."

I follow Nurse Evans along two further corridors, ending in another set of double doors that lead into an open plan ward. There are four beds to my left and four to my right, all occupied by female patients of varying ages. The furthest bed on the left is shrouded by a light blue curtain. Nurse Evans makes her way over as I follow a few paces behind. She pokes her head through a gap in the curtain, and after a few seconds, she turns and beckons me forward.

I slip beyond the curtain to find my mother propped up on a pillow, with a policeman sitting on a chair beside the bed.

Mum looks up at me; a forlorn sight. Her usually pristine silver hair is splayed across the pillow, and the happy colours in her patterned dress are a stark contrast to her pale complexion. She looks small, fragile, and confused. She looks like the last woman on earth anyone would want to hurt.

"If you need me for anything, I'll be back at the desk," Nurse Evans says before she scoots off.

I dart across to the bed and into my mother's arms. Oblivious to the policeman, I hold my mum tight and fight back the urge to cry. Such is the odd dynamic of our relationship, I have to be the strong one.

I eventually let her go and sit on the edge of the bed, holding her hands in mine.

The policeman coughs. My mum remembers we're not alone.

"Darling, this is Sergeant Stone. He's been talking me through what happened."

The forty-something, bald-headed Sergeant flashes me a weary smile. He looks almost as tired as Nurse Evans.

"Miss Baxter I assume?"

I return his smile. "That's right."

"Well, the good news is that your mother hasn't sustained any serious injuries, and the assailants fled empty handed."

"The nurse said a passer-by intervened."

"That's right. He's just gone to get a coffee so you'll be able to thank him personally when he returns. He's been a great help in providing us with a detailed description of both assailants. It's a good job he was there; otherwise it could have been a lot worse for your mother."

I turn back to my mum. She looks up at me; her pale blue eyes like beacons, lighting an almost apologetic face.

"What were you thinking, Mum, walking the streets in the dark?"

"I was on the way home from the college. Pam usually gives me a lift home, but she called in sick tonight."

"Oh, Mum. You should have called me."

"I'm sorry, darling. I don't like to trouble you."

I shake my head and turn back to Sergeant Stone.

"Was this just a failed mugging?" I ask, my levels of paranoia already high after recent events.

"Looks that way. Opportunists I'd guess. There's a squat about three hundred yards from where the attack took place, so it might have been a couple of smackhead residents desperate for a fix."

"Bastards," I mumble.

"Indeed," the sergeant concurs.

"Have they said when you can go home?" I ask my mother.

"I don't feel too bad so hopefully they'll let me go home tomorrow."

"They'll only keep you in as a precaution, Mrs Goodyear," Sergeant Stone interjects. "They tend to treat head injuries with caution but I'm sure you'll be right as rain by the morning."

Mum smiles at the policeman as she tries to stifle a yawn.

"I think you could probably do with a rest now, Mrs Goodyear," Sergeant Stone says as he gets to his feet. "I think I've got everything I need here, ladies."

"Thank you, Sergeant," Mum replies.

He gives Mum a nod and steps around the bed.

"I just need a final word with our witness, so I'll grab him on the way out. I'll be in touch when there's something to report."

I get up and shake his hand. "Thank you for looking after Mum, Sergeant. I appreciate you sitting with her."

"All part of the service, Miss Baxter. Look after her."

"I will."

He disappears back through the gap in the curtain.

I've managed to avoid police officers for all of my adult life, but I've now had a second conversation with a member of our local constabulary within three days. I hope it's the last.

I return my attention to my mother. Sergeant Stone's detection skills were certainly on point about one thing — she does look tired.

"You look shattered, Mum."

"They gave me some painkillers, darling. They've made me a bit woozy."

"I think you should probably get some sleep."

"What time is it?"

"Just coming up to nine o'clock."

"You should go home. There's no point in you sitting there watching me fall asleep."

"I don't really want to leave you, Mum."

"Don't be silly. Go home, darling. I'm not going to be much company."

"Okay, if you're sure, but I'll wait until you're asleep. I'll call in the morning and see when I can pick you up."

She pats my hand and closes her eyes.

Within a few minutes her breathing slows as she drifts off.

I sit and watch her for fifteen minutes until I'm sure she's definitely out for the count. She doesn't stir when I lean over and kiss her forehead.

I'm relieved she didn't want me to stay. I really hate hospitals. I know nobody *likes* hospitals, but I can't stand the smell, the sounds, and the constant reminder of our own fragile mortality.

It's with some relief that I finally depart my mother's bedside and duck past the curtain. It's only when I get back on my feet that I realise my mother isn't the only one who is shattered. This week has been exhausting. I like routine in my life but this week has been chaos. I can't wait for Sunday when I can lie in bed and read, with nowhere to be and nobody bothering me.

I wearily push open the door leading back into the corridor. As I turn and make my way towards the main entrance, I hear the sound of a male voice, followed by raucous laughter. I turn right into another stretch of corridor to find two men standing at the far end.

The first man is immediately recognisable as Sergeant Stone in his uniform. The second man is standing with his back to me, dressed in beige trousers and a red pullover. Both men appear animated, seemingly engrossed in their conversation.

I get within ten yards of the two men before Sergeant Stone notices me.

"Ah, Miss Baxter," he says with a broad smile. "Let me introduce you to the gentleman who came to your mother's rescue."

The other man turns. "Good evening."

"Miss Baxter, this is David Sterling," Sergeant Stone adds.

My legs almost buckle, arresting my forward motion. I stand motionless, staring at the man who was in my shop yesterday, threatening me.

My mouth twitches but no words form. Both men stare at me, both smiling.

Sergeant Stone's radio suddenly crackles, filling the silence. His smile fades in an instant as he presses a button on his radio.

"Two-one-six, all received. Show me dealing."

He turns to face David Sterling. "Sorry, Dave, I've got to shoot. I'll see you Saturday evening. I'm looking forward to it."

"Duty calls, Andrew," Sterling replies. "Don't forget, the first round is on you."

The two men chuckle.

Sergeant Stone looks back at me. "I'll leave you to chat with David, Miss Baxter. Be in touch."

He pats Sterling on the shoulder before he turns and barges through the door.

Sterling watches him leave, and then slowly turns his gaze back in my direction. He steps towards me until there is barely three feet between us.

"Well, well, Miss Baxter. What a coincidence."

I try to gulp but my throat is too dry.

"It's awful, what happened to your mother, just awful."

The words are soft, kind even. The thin smile on his face is neither.

"You...you orchestrated this," I reply, my voice barely a whisper.

"What a dreadful thing to say after I came to your mother's rescue. I just happened to be walking along, minding my own business, when I saw those two reprobates trying to steal your mother's handbag. I put my personal safety on the line and that's all the thanks I get? I'm hurt, Miss Baxter."

He leans closer to me, close enough I catch a whiff of his acrid breath.

"But not as hurt as I was when I received your email earlier," he adds in a hushed voice. "That really hurt me. I don't like being told my debts won't be repaid. Fortunately I have some very clever IT people who scrubbed your email from our servers. Now, it's like you never sent it."

A dozen questions tumble through my mind. I can't vocalise a single one. I want to run, to get away from this man. My legs have other ideas.

"What do you want from me?"

"I think you already know that. I want what is owed to me. Your fiancé's disappearance, and please excuse my language, has pissed me off no end. I'm not in the mood to be charitable. I hope you understand."

"I...I can't pay that sort of money. You're wasting your time," I whimper.

"That's the problem with your generation, Miss Baxter. Too defeatist. However, I might be willing to offer you a more amicable solution."

"What?"

"Your house."

"What about it?"

"I'll buy it from you."

"It's not for sale."

"Don't be silly. Everything is for sale at the right price."

He shuffles nearer, his face so close I can see every detail of the pale scar tissue puckering his leathery skin.

"And in your case, the right price is fifty thousand pounds less than the market value."

He remains silent, his head tilted slightly, observing me.

"What? No. Why would I do that?"

"Because unless you find twenty thousand pounds by next Thursday, it will be the only way to ensure your mother doesn't fall victim to any other unfortunate incidents, unless of course, Mr Patterson makes a return."

I don't want to feel this way: weak, helpless, alone.

I grasp what little resolve I can find, and the anger I felt when I first arrived here. I can feel the adrenalin build as my heart rate increases.

Fuck you, Sterling.

My hand balls into a fist, and before I can talk myself out of it, I swing my arm in an uppercut motion towards Sterling's jaw.

It doesn't reach its destination.

With the reflexes of a startled deer, Sterling snaps out a wiry hand and grabs my wrist.

"Now, that wasn't very sensible, Miss Baxter."

He tightens his grip on my wrist, pressing his thumb into the soft flesh at the base of my palm. The pain slowly builds, as does the smile on Sterling's face.

"Please, you're hurting me," I whimper.

He throws me a look of contempt before he eases his grip slightly.

"Did Mr Patterson happen to mention what I used to do for a living, back in London?"

"Eh? I don't know...yes, maybe."

"People have underestimated me my entire life. The vast majority of them lived to regret it. The rest, they never lived another day."

He slowly lowers his hand, pulling my arm into an increasingly awkward position. To anyone looking on, it must almost look like we're in some sort of affectionate clutch. There is nothing affectionate about Sterling's intentions.

He leans in further so he's almost whispering in my ear.

"I've hurt plenty of women in my life so don't think it's beyond me. Whether it's you, or your dear mother, somebody will pay if my debt isn't settled."

A stabbing pain shoots up my arm and I try not to squeal. I won't give him that satisfaction.

"We'll see what the police have to say about that, shall we?" I spit, trying to assert some defiance.

"Ah, yes. The police. I'm glad you brought them up. I'm attending their gala dinner on Saturday as an honoured guest. I was just discussing it with Andrew, Sergeant Stone. You see, Miss Baxter, I've been very generous to the local constabulary's benevolent fund over the years. I'm actually making another sizable donation on Saturday."

He eventually releases my arm and takes a step back.

"Think about it. You have no evidence against me, and I have spent years cultivating goodwill with the local police force. Do you honestly think they're going to believe your outlandish accusations, let alone act upon them?"

Karl's words float back into my head. For all his stupidity, the advice he offered about Sterling now seems pretty sage. I have no evidence, and no options.

All I can offer in reply is silence.

"I rest my case, Miss Baxter. When you agreed to marry Mr Patterson, you agreed to accept his liabilities, least that's the way I see it, and the contract backs that up. You have six days left, after which I expect you and that fiancé of yours to come up with twenty thousand pounds, in cash, or I'll require you to sign a memorandum of sale for your property. That sale will be at fifty thousand pounds less than market value."

"No. Bloody. Way," I growl. "I'm not selling you the house."

"I have a legally binding contract so don't mess me around," he spits. "I'm not renowned for my patience."

My only, and final resort, is to beg.

"I don't have anything other than that house. I bought it with my late father's inheritance money. Please, you can't do this to me."

"I can, and I will, but it's entirely within your hands. Get the cash by 5.30pm next Thursday and you can keep your home. I think that's a perfectly reasonable proposal."

I have never considered killing another human being, but if I had a gun in my hand I don't think I'd hesitate to use it. How can any person be so cruel, so unfair, and so utterly despicable?

My anger is pointless.

"Fine. I'll get your bloody money," I eventually mumble.

"Excellent. I knew you'd see sense. And for what it's worth, I'm truly sorry it's come to this. If Mr Patterson hadn't disappeared, we wouldn't be having this conversation. If I were in your shoes, I'd be doing everything I could to track him down."

"Whatever."

"But be under no illusion, Miss Baxter, I always get what I want so it would be unwise to cross me. If you contact the police, the debt doubles. If you try any funny business, the debt doubles. If you fail to pay on time, or don't agree to sell your property on my terms, your mother's wellbeing is on the line. Do you understand me?"

I can do nothing other than nod.

"Splendid. I'll pop by your shop at five-thirty next Thursday to collect. In the meantime, a couple of my associates will be keeping tabs on your home, just in case Mr Patterson decides to resurface in the interim, or you decide to join him."

He holds out his hand, inviting me to shake it.

"You've got to be kidding?" I snort.

"Fair enough. Have a pleasant evening, Miss Baxter."

He turns and walks away, whistling to himself.

I count to twenty in my head, and when I'm sure he's gone, I collapse to the floor. As much as I try to fight it back, my chest heaves and I begin to sob.

From the depths of my despair, a single question emerges from the darkness — why is this happening to me?

11

I'm not sure how long I sit on the floor in the corridor, but at some point a nurse finds me.

"Are you alright, madam?"

She's much younger than me, much prettier than me. Probably doesn't have a care in the world.

"Um, yeah, I'm okay. Thank you."

I get to my feet and take a sharp intake of breath.

"Were you visiting somebody?" the young nurse asks.

"My mum. She was hurt in a mugging."

"How awful. You're not suffering from shock are you? It's not uncommon among relatives of crime victims."

I probably am in shock, but not just because of my mother's misfortune.

"No, I think I'm fine. Just a bit overwhelmed. Can you point me in the direction of the toilets?"

She double-checks I am actually okay and offers directions.

With visiting time over, the hospital corridors and the toilets are quiet. I pad across the tiled floor and stand in front of a row of sinks, staring into a mirrored wall behind. I look horrendous. My face is ashen, my eyes bloodshot. In fairness, it is the look of a broke woman who has six days to find twenty grand.

What the hell are you going to do, Beth?

I have so few options it doesn't take long to discount them. I can't borrow the money from a bank since I barely earn enough to cover the business overheads. I don't have any close friends who might come to my rescue. I haven't seen most of my family in years so I can't ask them. And even if I could sell my car, my engagement ring, and all the stock in the shop, it wouldn't come remotely close to what Sterling wants.

I own nothing else of value — besides my home.

Even the thought of losing it summons more tears. It's not just the fact it's my home; it's my father's legacy. It was his money that allowed me to buy it in the first place, and in some tenuous way, it keeps his memory alive.

This is beyond any nightmare, beyond any wicked plot my own imagination could ever have conjured.

I want to scream. I want to vent the anger boiling within me. But more than anything, I want to dig my nails into Sterling's face and tear at his flesh. I want to ram my elbow into his freakish nose and watch it splatter across his disfigured face.

I want him to die. I want to dance on his grave.

Come to think of it, I want to dance on Karl's grave even more.

I snatch my phone from my handbag and ring his number.

An automated voice answers...

The number you are calling has not been recognised. Please check and try again.

Why does it not surprise me that the coward has cancelled his phone contract? The temptation to launch my phone through the air returns.

I bite my lip and snort deep breaths through my nose. This is utterly hopeless. I have nowhere to turn. I am alone.

I turn on a tap and splash cold water on my face. Despite the looming deadline, I can't ignore how utterly exhausted I am. I need to get home. Maybe I'll awake tomorrow to some inspired idea. Maybe my mind will work on the problem as I sleep.

In truth, my mind is so clouded with anger at the moment, I can't focus on anything, so it's all I can do.

I exit the toilets and plod wearily back through the corridors and stairwells.

The drive home is much more subdued that the outbound journey. I pull into my road and slowly cruise the entire length, searching for somewhere to park. I pass a space sixty yards beyond my front door. It's too tight to drive straight into, so I have to parallel park.

I pull up alongside a dark coloured BMW as I prepare to reverse back into the space. As I look across at my mirror, a flash of movement catches my attention. A man, sitting in the passenger seat of the BMW. He waves, and smiles. His companion in the driver's seat leans forward and does the same. Two men, both with shaven heads, both with menacing smiles. They want me to know they're here, and they're watching me.

I struggle to catch my breath as my heart pounds. Sterling's warning about his associates watching the house for Karl. It must be them.

I might be tired, I might be angry, but both are suddenly trumped by fear. The game has changed from theory to reality.

I slam the car into first gear and gun the engine. The little Fiat squeals away from the BMW and darts towards the junction at the end of the street.

I daren't look in my mirror as I make a series of random turns, passing through one dark street after another. A right, then a left, then another right.

I subconsciously weave my way through the back streets towards the town centre, adrenalin my co-pilot. That adrenalin is welcome as I can't think straight. The only thing I do know is that I can't stay in the house tonight. My skin crawls at the thought of Sterling's goons sitting outside.

But where do I go?

I take a right turn and make my way towards the only place I can think of — the shop.

I pull into the parking bay and scramble in my handbag for the keys.

Please, please, please. Be in here.

My panic eases a little when I hear them jingle at the bottom. I cautiously get out of the car and survey the area. The darkness is only broken by the glow of a single streetlight, some twenty yards away. There are no other vehicles parked up and no sign of anyone else around.

I open the back door, step into the staffroom and switch the light on. I lock and bolt the door, wedging a chair under the handle as an extra line of security. The cold air helps to clear my head and ease my fatigue, but I don't think the short-term benefits will outweigh the long-term discomfort. I switch the heating on. A few extra quid on my gas bill is the least of my worries.

Now I'm here, and feeling slightly less exposed, I need to think about what I'm going to do.

With few options open, it doesn't take long to formulate a plan.

I can sleep here for the night and then pick Mum up tomorrow. I can stay with her for a few days while I try and think of a way to raise Sterling's money.

However, my most immediate problem is avoiding frostbite. The radiator in the staffroom hasn't worked properly in years, and with no staff to warm, I saw no reason to get it fixed. Even with the heating on, it'll remain as cold as a fridge in here. The stockroom has no radiator at all, broken or otherwise. If I want to avoid freezing to death in my sleep, I'll have to crash out in the shop.

I enter the darkness of the shop, and rather than the main lights which would be too bright to allow sleep, I switch on a standard lamp in the corner. I slump down behind the counter where I can't be seen by passers-by on the street. In truth, it's not a huge concern. Very few pedestrians venture up our road during the day so it's not likely to be busy at night.

With my back against the wall I hug my knees, pulling them tight towards my chest in a futile attempt to retain some warmth. The silence is only broken by the occasional ticking of the radiator as the cold iron fills with hot water. There will be no sleep until that radiator shares its heat with the frigid air.

Minutes tick by as the silence, the cold, and the gloomy light slowly suffocate me. I have never felt so lonely. My mind races back and forth over the last few days, trying to find something positive to cling to; anything to provide respite from this nightmare.

Nothing comes.

Sitting inactive, and adrenalin spent, my body temperature continues to fall. Shivers arrive. How I long for my bed; to snuggle beneath my duvet. The promise of warmth is almost tempting enough to send me home, but not quite. As cold and despondent as I may be, I don't wish to trade it for warmth and fear.

I have to stick this out.

While I can only wait for warmth to arrive, I can address the deafening silence. I lean forward and turn the CD player on. The rich notes of a concert piano permeate the silence — *Haydn's Concerto No. 11*. If I wasn't so damn cold, I'm sure the familiar, comforting melody would lull me to sleep in minutes.

I lean back against the wall, bathed in a sickly green light from the digital display on the CD player. I watch the bars on the equaliser dance up and down in tune to the music. My eyelids begin to droop and I sense sleep isn't far away. Another cold shiver spasms through my body, bringing me back from the brink.

I continue to watch the bars dance as, little by little, the air temperature creeps another degree north.

The concerto draws to an end. The final track on the CD.

I lean forward and press the play button again. As I move, the slightest glint of green light reflects from the shelf next to the CD player. Curiosity prompts me to lean further forward in order to identify the source of the light. I squint at a dark rectangle shape, with gilded gold leaf on the spine — the King James Bible. In any normal week I'd already have put it up for sale. This is no ordinary week and I'd almost forgotten about it.

I pluck the bible from the shelf and hold it in my hands. Other than the monetary value of this particular edition, the bible no longer holds any meaning.

When I was a child, before I lost my father, it did mean something to me.

My dad was devoted to our local church. Every Sunday, without fail, the three of us would dress to the nines and clamber into his Austin Maestro. We'd take our position at the front of the congregation, sitting upon unforgiving oak pews. The grand organ would bellow out the accompaniment to hymns I rarely knew. I vividly remember the sheer gusto with which my father used to sing those hymns, as if keen to ensure every word was heard by the man upstairs.

When Dad left us, he took our faith with him.

Besides weddings, christenings, and the occasional funeral, the only reason I ever visit our local church is to lay flowers on my father's grave. I always offer a prayer that he's safe, that he's happy. With every passing year it feels more and more like I'm talking to myself.

Like much of everything in my life, my faith in God has been slowly eroded to virtually nothing.

Until now.

Truth is, I'll take comfort wherever I can get it. After all these years, surely one of my prayers has to be answered.

I open the bible and spend a few minutes haphazardly flicking through it. The English is from a period not long after the Civil War and in the dim light, the faded print is headache-inducing. Sadly, the few paragraphs I struggle through don't encourage me back along the path to righteousness.

Frustrated, I stop thinking about it as a route to salvation. I don't need salvation — I need a route to money.

Beyond the condition, there is one thing that can make or break the value of a collectible book — provenance. If you're able to trace the ownership back to a person of note, it can turn a hundred pound book into a thousand pound book. If you're lucky, there might be an author's signature. And if you're really lucky, there might be a hand written dedication. For a bible of this period, the holy grail would be to find a quilled message from a prominent figure of the time.

I check inside the front cover and first page. Nothing.

A quick scan of the internal pages brings the same result. Nothing.

I reach the final page opposite the rear cover, and lean forward, squinting.

My woes are briefly replaced with a twinge of excitement when I spot six lines of faint reddish text, beautifully scribed by hand.

It doesn't take long to determine the text isn't a dedication or a note. Too short to be a sonnet, popular in the period. A poem, of sorts?

I try to paint a picture of whoever wrote it. Where they were, who they were. Words conjured from a man, or woman, who lived in the reign of Charles II. Could they ever have imagined their words still being spoken centuries after their death?

I mumble those words under my breath...

O child of need, who shall be thy steed?
To carry thou on, tho hope be gone

The light to see, with words for thee
For once thou speak, thy steed thou seek
O Heavenly alchemy;
blessed thou shall be.

I've got no idea what it means. I do wonder, though, if it could be a known poem.

A sudden thought strikes me — what if I've discovered an unpublished poem by a famous writer? It would propel the value of the bible into the thousands.

I scramble to my feet and turn the computer monitor on. I'm about to start searching for the poem when, from nowhere, a voice booms across the shop.

"Alright, doll."

12

I did hear a voice. I know that because my heart is now somewhere in my throat, and I'm currently paralysed with fear. Even if I could, I daren't turn my head to the source of the voice. I can hear the tinkling of a piano from the speakers above my head. I can smell the books and the faint funk of damp from the cellar below my feet. I can also smell something else — tobacco, and a scent I vaguely recognise. Old Spice aftershave?

I move the only part of my body I can, and slowly roll my eyes to the left.

They meet a figure. A man, standing about twelve feet away.

No. No. No.

I squeeze my eyes shut and slowly open them again. He's still there. A figment of my imagination? Maybe, but didn't I hear him speak? If he is an illusion, he's a pretty convincing one.

He moves, tilting his head slowly to the left, then the right.

My paralysis comes to an abrupt end as a scream escapes me.

The man raises his hands, palms out. "Whoa! Calm down, doll. I'm not gonna hurt you."

Surely a bog-standard lie, as offered by all murderers' right before they rudely murder you.

Oddly, my murderer has chosen to dress in flared jeans, and a denim waistcoat over a salmon-orange t-shirt. Is he some sort of retro-themed murderer? Is that his 'thing'?

Beyond his quirky attire, the sheer size of the man is more of a worry — he is enormous. The bookshelves are six feet tall, and he stands maybe five or six inches taller.

My scream ends as my breath runs out. Confused thoughts scramble through my mind. How the hell did he get in here?

What does he want with me? And why is he wearing blue-tinted sunglasses at night?

It matters not. He's here, and I'm about to die. I'm sure of it.

He strides towards me, eating up the space in barely a second, and with it, any chance I have of escape. Even if I could fight my way past him, the front door is locked and the key is in my handbag, in the staffroom.

This must be that moment; the one where you know death is coming. I've read about people who've experienced it — a final culmination of all your fears and regrets. I was kind of hoping I'd drift away peacefully with neither, at some point in my nineties.

This is not how I imagined my end — throttled by a man in fancy dress.

He comes to a stop right in front of the counter.

Please don't soil your knickers, Beth. It'll look embarrassing on the autopsy report.

However, as I stare up at him, something in his facial expression doesn't correlate with a man seemingly intent on murder. There is no obvious menace, no scowl. He actually looks a little bewildered, curious even.

His head turns slowly left, then right, as if inspecting his surroundings. As his head turns, I study his features. Huge mutton-chop sideburns flow from a crown of dark hair, spiked upwards. A thick moustache frames his upper lip, dropping down either side of his mouth; a style reminiscent of Mexican bandits, and now popular amongst the hipster generation.

He speaks again.

"A bleedin' book shop. There's a first."

His voice is level, with a gravelly tone like a man who smokes too much.

I try to place his accent. London? Definitely. A working class area? Probably.

"You're quite the chatterbox, ain't you?" he adds.

Without warning, he stretches his arms above his head and yawns. I try to find another scream but I can barely inhale enough air to draw breath.

His t-shirt strains to contain his bulk. I don't know why, but I suspect that bulk wasn't forged in a gym. His arms are muscled, but not with the lean muscle earned through lifting weights day after day. A small paunch above his belt suggests this man doesn't spend much time in a gym.

Nevertheless, he looks like he could tear me in half without breaking sweat.

He leans forwards and waves his hands in the air, a few feet in front of my face. I try backing up, only to find the wall behind me.

"Hello. Anyone in there?"

I have to consciously force the words from my mouth.

"Who...are...you?"

"Thank fuck for that. I thought you were a mute. Clement is the name."

I gulp hard and find a tiny voice. "What do you want with me, Mr Clement?"

"Not Mr. Just Clement."

"What...do you want with me...Clement?" I stammer. "Did Sterling send you?"

"Who?"

"David Sterling."

"Never heard of the bloke."

I don't know if that's good news or not.

"Why are you here then?"

"You summoned me."

"Uh? I...I don't know what you're talking about."

"All that stuff about *child of need* and *heavenly alchemy*. I'm your steed, doll."

He grins. He needs a dentist.

"You're not making any sense, Mr...Clement. What has the poem got to do with you being here?"

"It's not a poem. It's...I dunno, a prayer, I suppose. You need help, and they sent me."

"Who sent you?"

"Dunno," he shrugs. "Just doing my job, doll. You read the bleedin' thing and here I am."

Maybe this man is not going to kill me, or at least he doesn't see it as a priority. My initial fear eases a little but I'm struggling to muster any patience.

"I don't wish to be rude, but I'm too tired for this. Can you just leave, please?"

"Not really."

"Why not?"

"Nowhere to go."

"You're homeless?"

"Suppose I am, in a way."

"Well, could you not speak to a charity?"

"If only it were that simple," he chuckles. "I doubt they'll be able to help me."

Every boyfriend has said it. I'm not good company when I'm tired. Fear becomes irritation.

"Look, I don't know what you want but I can't help you. Can you just go back to wherever you came from, please?"

"Can't."

"Why on earth not?"

"Because I wasn't anywhere. I was dead."

Okay, now I get it. He's obviously suffering from some sort of mental illness — it's the only explanation. I need to tread carefully.

"Oh, I see," I reply, trying to sound sympathetic. "You were dead were you?"

It sounds patronising rather than sympathetic.

"I was. Now I'm here to make penance."

"Okay. Penance for what exactly?"

"My previous life. I did some shit that I probably shouldn't have done."

"Are you taking any medication? If not, you probably should be."

He starts laughing. I'm now considering death as an attractive proposition.

"I like you," he snorts. "You're pretty funny, for a chick."

"Flattered, I'm sure."

"But I'm guessing you don't believe in miracles?"

"No. I don't."

"Maybe you should."

"Look — try and see this from my perspective. I'm having a *really* bad week and then you turn up, from nowhere apparently, claiming to be a dead man seeking penance. If I'm honest with you, I could do without it."

He strokes his moustache and sighs.

"I dunno what else to say, doll."

"And can you please stop calling me doll."

"Alright, Bethany," he says with a smirk.

"Thank you...hold on. How do you know my name? I never told you."

"Dunno. It just popped into my head when I arrived here. Bethany Louise Dusty Baxter."

I stare up at him, open mouthed.

Nobody, besides my parents, knows my middle name is Dusty. My dad was a huge fan of Dusty Springfield and my mum thought it would be a nice surprise to add it as a middle name when she registered my birth. Dad was delighted, and promptly gave me the nickname, 'Diddy Dusty'. I've always been a bit embarrassed about it, and never willingly shared it with anyone. I'm fairly sure my dad was the last person ever to use it.

"What do you mean, it just popped into your head?"

"I dunno. This gig doesn't come with an instruction manual."

It seems I'm not dealing with a murderer, but a crazed stalker. Either way, there is little chance of my physically ejecting him from the shop, and I'd rather not provoke him. It appears I have no option but to humour him.

"Okay, Clement" I sigh. "Can you at least tell me why, and indeed how, you came to be standing in my shop at this time of night?"

"Short or long version?"

"Short. Very short."

"Fair enough. Can we get a cup of tea though? I'm bloody parched."

I offer him a weak smile and cautiously move from beyond the counter. I hold my arm out, inviting him to take the lead.

"The staffroom is through that door. After you."

Clement slowly ambles towards the staffroom door and I follow a safe distance behind. For a fleeting second, I toy with the idea of running back across the shop and throwing myself through the plate glass window. Probably not a sensible move.

I turn the staffroom light on just as Clement perches his backside on the edge of the table, inches from my handbag.

Bugger.

I shuffle to the far side of the room and put the kettle on, trying not to turn my back on my unwelcome guest for too long. As I contort, I notice the chair is still wedged under the handle of the back door. How the hell did he get in here?

I turn my gaze to the man. He appears fairly nonplussed by the whole charade, casually gazing around the room.

I have no choice but to see this through.

"Go on then," I sigh. "Why are you here?"

"Right. Just prepare yourself, doll. This might seem a bit of a stretch."

"I'm listening."

"You asked for help, and I've been sent here to provide it. I can't go anywhere until I've made penance, and helped you."

"So, what are you? Some sort of guardian angel?"

"Do I look like an angel?" he scoffs.

"Erm, I'd say you look more like a seventies porn star. No offence."

"None taken. I dabbled, once."

Ewww.

The kettle boils. I turn around and quickly snatch a couple of mugs from the cupboard.

"Sugar?" I ask over my shoulder.

"Three."

That explains his paunch.

I pour boiling water into the mugs and drop a teabag in each. My mind flashes back to Miss Henderson's words — I hope Eleanor Roosevelt was right, and I'm stronger than the weak tea I'm about to serve.

I scoop sugar into one of the mugs, and add a splash of milk to both. I turn, and cautiously pass a mug to Clement, or whoever the hell he is.

"Cheers, doll."

I wish he'd stop calling me that. I guess it's the least of my problems though. I let it go.

I grab my mug and take a sip, hoping the caffeine will ease my tiredness.

"So, Clement. You're here to help me?"

"You got it."

"And to be clear, you're actually dead?"

"Since 1975."

"I guess that explains the hideous double denim outfit."

He looks down and studies his attire for a second. He looks back at me, indignant.

"What's the problem, doll? This garb cost a bleedin' fortune. Got it from Carnaby Street."

"In 1975?"

"Nah. '74, I think."

I nod, and take another sip of tea.

"And what did you do, in 1975, before you...err, died?"

"I was an odd job man."

"Brilliant," I groan. "I need a saviour and I'm sent somebody who can put up shelves."

"Not that sort of odd job man."

He takes a gulp of tea and places his mug on the table.

"I was a fixer."

"And what exactly did that entail?"

"People had problems and I fixed them. I did a bit of protection, a bit of debt collection, and occasionally I'd have to persuade the odd person to, shall we say, change their position on certain matters. It was varied work."

"Right. And if you don't mind me asking, how exactly did you die?"

"I banged my head."

"You banged your head?"

"Yeah — on a cricket bat. Didn't see it coming."

"You played cricket?" I say with no effort to hide my surprise.

"It was two in the morning. An alleyway in Camden. I wasn't wearing my whites."

"Oh."

I try hard to stifle a yawn. I need to extract myself from this ridiculous situation.

"Well, it's been interesting, but I've had a long day and I'd quite like to go home now."

"Great. It's brass monkeys in here."

He stands up.

"Sorry, Clement. I meant I want to go home on my own."

"Oh. But you need help, right?"

"Well, yes, but..."

"Then we can talk about it on the way. Where's your motor?"

He stares at me expectantly. There is no way I'm letting him into my car.

I then remember. The reason I'm here is because Sterling's henchmen are currently sitting outside my house. I won't be going home, but I have no desire to stay here either.

An idea strikes me.

"Actually, Clement. You might be able to help me with something."

"That's what I'm here for."

"I've been having problems with my front headlamp. Do you think you could check it's working okay?"

"No worries, doll."

My cunning plan is to get in the car, lock the doors while Clement is inspecting my headlamp, and drive off. Heaven knows where I'll go, but anywhere is preferable to being in the company of this nut job.

"I need a piss first, though," he proclaims. "That brew went straight through me. Where's your lav?"

I point him in the direction of the toilet and he lumbers off.

His weak bladder offers me an unexpected opportunity for a change of plan. I'll make a break for it while he's in the loo. I can head to the police station and ask them to come back to the shop and remove him. It's probably for his own good — he clearly needs medical help.

I grab my handbag and remove the chair from the back door. I delicately prise it open and step out into the cold night air.

As my heart hammers in my chest, I scrabble around in my handbag for my keys. Just as I locate them, a voice startles me.

"Evening."

My head snaps up and I'm greeted by the sight of a dark coloured BMW parked behind the Fiat, blocking my exit. The voice belongs to one of Sterling's goons, sitting smiling in the driver's seat with the window down. Shit, they must have guessed I'd come here.

He gets out of the car a second before his passenger joins him. The two of them slowly edge around the Fiat and stand side-by-side about ten feet away. I've got nowhere to go.

"Cold out here ain't it?" the shorter of the two says.

Both of them are wearing dark clothing, their bald heads like hardboiled eggs, floating in the darkness.

"You gonna invite us in for coffee then?"

"Just leave me alone," I whimper.

"Sorry, love. No can do. Mr Sterling's orders. No reason why we can't have some fun though, is there?"

They stare at me, both grinning.

"Perhaps we should introduce ourselves before we get fully acquainted," the shorter goon adds. "I'm Mr Black, and my colleague here is Mr Blue."

Black & Blue? Really?

Mr Black takes a few ponderous steps towards me. Mr Blue follows closely behind. My only possible escape is back into the shop, and back to the deranged giant.

A terrifying thought crashes to the front of my mind — they're working together. One man inside the shop, sent in to distract me, and two outside, preventing my escape.

I've walked right into a trap.

I scan my surroundings, praying I might spot a passer-by. Pointless. Why would anyone stroll up a dead-end street at this time of night? I'm alone. I'm in deep trouble.

Messrs Black & Blue continue to edge towards me. I shuffle backwards until my shoulder blades meet a brick wall. My mind begins to playout the next few minutes. I picture myself screaming, and Mr Black forcing his meaty hand across my mouth to silence me. I can see myself being bundled back into the shop. What happens after that is just too awful to consider.

I press my back tight against the wall in a futile attempt to add an extra inch of distance between myself and the approaching thugs.

They're barely six feet away, and still grinning.

A flash of movement to my left and the shop door slams shut.

My head twists to the side to see Clement standing in front of the door. Looks like he's come to join the party, and I'm the piñata.

"What's going on here then?" he says casually.

Mr Black turns to face Clement. "This is none of your fucking business. Do one."

Whatever is going on here, clearly Black & Blue have no idea who Clement is. I've got a horrible feeling my deranged visitor is about to discover who they are, and what their line of work is.

Black & Blue shuffle into position with Mr Black directly in front of Mr Blue.

"I'll ask again. What's going on?" Clement growls.

Mr Black turns and says something to Mr Blue. They chuckle between themselves, but the mirth is fleeting as Mr Black turns back to Clement with a scowl.

"If you don't fuck off in the next five seconds, you're a dead man."

Clement huffs a reply. "I'm already a dead man, mate."

He moves with surprising speed for his size. In four huge strides, Clement covers the ground between them. Mr Black appraises the threat and decides to meet it head on. He shifts his feet and throws a punch towards Clement's head. With a significant height difference between the two men, it doesn't meet its target; it meets Clement's open palm and immediately loses its momentum with a dull slapping sound.

"You really didn't want to do that," Clement spits.

What happens next is like a fight scene from an action movie, only very real, and terrifyingly violent. I have never borne witness to an actual fight before, and I wish I wasn't party to the one I'm currently watching.

With lightening reflexes, Clement thrusts a ferocious jab into Mr Black's face. I'm sure I hear the sound of bone crunching. Mr Black immediately falls to the floor with a high pitched yelp, his hands clutching his face.

Mr Blue is not impressed, and throws a punch of his own. Too slow, and Clement brushes it aside before returning a far more potent punch. It squarely meets Mr Blue's jaw and his head jerks violently. He staggers backwards a few steps but manages to stay upright by splaying his legs. As he tries to shake away the grogginess from the blow, Clement leaps forwards.

I watch in horror as Clement swings a leg and his boot makes contact with Mr Blue's right knee. His collapse is immediate, his scream chilling.

Despite both goons floundering helplessly on the floor, it appears Clement is not finished with them. He moves away from the now-crippled Mr Blue and raises his leg again, intent on laying a boot into Mr Black's ribs.

I find my voice and shriek. "Clement!"

He freezes in an instant, his left leg still angled behind him, ready to deliver a kick. He slowly lets it fall to the ground before assessing his victims. Judging by their groans, I don't think they'll be offering much in the way of retaliation.

Clement turns to face me. "I'm guessing these two clowns are part of whatever it is you need help with?"

I nod, speechless.

"I don't think they'll be bothering you for a while. Shall we get going then?" he adds nonchalantly.

Clement bends over and grabs Mr Black by the scruff of his jacket, mumbling something in his ear. I can't bear to look at his bloodied face and turn away. I hear a few muffled voices and the sound of car doors being opened and closed. I turn back just as the BMW squeals away.

"What...what did you say to them?"

"Nothing much. Just told them to be on their way before I really lose my temper."

"Are they okay?"

"Better than they would have been if you hadn't stopped me."

He brushes his hands together and strides over. "You alright, doll? You look like you're gonna puke."

"I...I don't know whether to thank you, or scream at you."

"I'd go with the first option. I don't respond well to screaming chicks."

I find a feeble smile. "Thank you."

"Do you wanna explain what they were doing here?"

"They were told to watch me."

"By?"

"It's a long story."

He folds his arms and leans against the car.

"They said they'll be back. I think they might be a bit annoyed."

"Great," I sigh.

"So, it's your call, doll. You can stop messing me around and we can deal with this, together. Or, you can take your chances on your own."

"Eh? How have I messed you around?"

"Faulty headlight," he snorts. "You must think I was born yesterday."

My plan has been spectacularly thwarted. One thing is clear though: this man, whoever he is, has just rescued me from a fate I still can't bear to consider.

The question is: what the hell do I do with him now?

13

I'm cold and tired. And I'm confused. Very confused.

I don't know what to do about the giant man who is currently staring at me.

I think it's fair to say that Clement could beat me to a pulp with one arm tied behind his back. But he hasn't. Quite the opposite, in fact.

"Come on, doll," he calls across to me. "I'm freezing my knackers off out here. Make a decision."

What do I do? Clearly he's barking mad, but surely if he wanted to harm me, I'd already be lying in a pool of my own blood in the shop.

"Just a minute...I'm thinking."

He shakes his head and thrusts his hands into the pockets of his jeans.

"Can't we discuss this inside the bloody car?" he groans.

"With respect, Clement, I don't make a habit of inviting complete strangers into my car. You could be a serial rapist for all I know."

"Don't flatter yourself," he jeers. "I've kicked plenty of better-looking birds out of my bed."

"I beg your pardon," I snap back indignantly.

"What? Just saying, you're not my type."

"And what exactly is your type, Clement?"

"Jesus," he groans as he looks to the sky. "Is this really helping?"

I stand with my arms folded.

"Apologise."

"Apologise? For what?"

"That comment. How rude."

"If it means getting out of the friggin' cold, fine. I'm sorry."

123

His casual misogyny is not my greatest concern — far from it. I am now stuck between a rock and a hard place. On one side I have Black & Blue, who are probably plotting their revenge this very minute. Then there is Clement; a clearly deranged man-mountain who, despite his delusions, is willing to put himself in harm's way to protect me.

If he is a stalker, he's unlike any of those I've ever read about. He's certainly odd, but he's not creepy, and seems to have a fairly indifferent attitude towards me. And then there are the two questions that I can't answer: how did he get into the shop, and how did he know my middle name? I'm intrigued enough to consider his offer. And I'm so cold, so tired, I actually don't care if he is crazy, as long as he murders me in a warm bed.

"Alright. Get in."

I unlock the car and Clement eases his huge frame into my tiny car.

I turn the engine on and ramp the heating up to maximum while Clement tries to make himself comfortable.

"Does Noddy know you've borrowed his car?" he mumbles, his head pressed up against the vinyl roof.

"Stop complaining, and put your seatbelt on."

"No thanks. Just don't crash."

"It's not optional, Clement. It's the law."

"Since when?"

"I don't know. Since forever. Just put it on will you."

I reverse out of the parking bay while he reluctantly puts his seatbelt on, much to his obvious annoyance.

I could probably tell him the seat is adjustable, but seeing my oversized passenger contorted into his seat does amuse me somewhat. In fairness, he doesn't complain, probably because he appears mesmerised by the glowing dashboard lights.

"Like a bleedin' Christmas tree," he murmurs to himself.

"Sorry?"

"The dashboard. All lit up like a Christmas tree. How does that work?"

"You're asking the wrong person."

He continues to stare at the dashboard with child-like wonderment.

"Where are we going?" he eventually asks.

"My house, but don't assume I'll be letting you in."

"Suit yourself. How far is it?"

"Not far, but there's time enough for you to convince me you're not a threat to my wellbeing."

"Anyone ever told you, you've got major trust issues?"

He's observant, I'll give him that.

"It might help if you explained what happened in the shop."

"What do you mean?"

"Both doors were locked. How did you get in?"

"I dunno. It just happens."

"What just happens?"

"There's nothing, like being asleep. Then I sort of snap into consciousness."

I'm none the wiser.

"You said *happens*, as if you've done this before."

"Twice."

"Care to explain?"

He mumbles something under his breath and adjusts his position for the fifth time.

"Don't ask me how any of this works cos' I don't have a clue. The first time scared the shit out of me. One minute I'm walking down an alley in 1975, and the next I'm in an office in front of some random bloke. There was all this noise in my head and the bloke's name just popped out. All I knew was that I was supposed to help him."

Don't encourage him, Beth.

"What happened?"

Well done.

"Don't ask me how, but I knew the year was 1989. That was a head-fuck in itself. Anyway, the bloke I was sent to help didn't take my appearance well. I think he had underlying mental problems."

"Do you want to expand on that?"

"He threw himself out of a sixth floor window, ten minutes after I arrived."

"Oh, that's just great." I groan.

"Not my fault, doll."

"You said it happened twice before. What happened the second time?"

"Good question. What year is it?"

"2017."

"In which case, the second bloke should be out of prison by now. I think it was 2003 when I tried to help him."

We reach a junction. I pull to a stop and turn to face Clement.

"Let me just get this straight. You've been sent back from beyond the grave to help people, in order to make penance for your wayward life. Correct?"

"About sums it up."

"And of the two people you've previously tried to help, one committed suicide, and the other spent over a decade in prison?"

"Sounds bad when you put it like that."

"And now you're here to help me?"

"Yep."

"Lucky me. And what happens if you can't help me?"

"Three strikes and you're out. If I screw this up, it's game over."

"Meaning?"

"I end up in a place so abhorrent, so terrifying, the human mind can't begin to comprehend it."

"Piers Morgan's boudoir?"

"Eh?"

"Nothing."

I pull away from the junction, shaking my head. How anyone can keep up this pretence is beyond me, but Clement appears to truly believe he's on some sort of celestial quest. I guess it's just a matter of time before he slips up. Maybe I'll help.

"What's the relevance of the fourteen-year period?" I ask.

"Eh?"

"You said you died in 1975, and then came back in 1989 and 2003, and it's now 2017. Fourteen years between each date."

"In the bible, the number fourteen represents salvation," he replies matter-of-factly.

Christ, he's good.

"I didn't know that."

"Neither did I. As I say, shit just pops into my head."

We continue the final mile of the journey home in silence, Clement staring out of the window at the dark scenery.

I pull into my street and find a space towards the far end. Every shred of my being is screaming at me to ditch my deluded companion. Two things are stopping me.

Firstly, I simply cannot explain how Clement got into the shop.

Secondly, and for the first time in days, the feeling of vulnerability has eased slightly. It's illogical, considering I'm currently sitting in a car with a man who could probably kill me with his bare hands, but his demeanour doesn't suggest he will.

It's not a matter of trust, more gut instinct.

"Right, Clement. If you're going to step foot in my house, there are conditions."

"Go on."

"Number one. If I feel uncomfortable and ask you to leave, you go."

"Not sure where I'll go, but fair enough."

"Number two. Can you please stop calling me doll?"

He puffs out his cheeks. "Can't promise that."

I close my eyes and use the silence to get my thoughts in some sort of order. It's a futile task. I exhale a deep breath and turn to face Clement.

"Can you at least promise not to murder me?"

"Give it up, doll. I ain't gonna murder you. If that's what I wanted, you'd be dead already."

He makes a valid argument.

"I must be insane, but come on then."

We clamber out of the car and Clement joins me on the pavement. He pauses for a moment, looking up and down the street.

"Those clowns back at the shop. Do they know where you live?"

"They were parked on the street earlier."

"Right. Walk on my left, doll."

"Why?"

"It's my job to be paranoid. Anyone jumping out of a car will have to pass me to get to you."

I don't question him and stand to his left. We walk down the dark street in silence, Clement vigilantly scanning every parked car we pass.

We arrive at my house and I unlock the front door. I'm about to enter when Clement puts a hand on my shoulder.

"Wait."

He slides past me and barges through the door into the dark hallway.

"What are you doing?" I sigh.

"Can't be too careful."

I shake my head and follow him in.

I switch the lights on and Clement follows me through to the kitchen. Without waiting for an invitation, he takes a seat at the table.

"Got any beer?"

I'm about to scold his poor manners when I remind myself that he did come to my rescue. It would be churlish not to at least offer him a beer.

The good host in me opens the fridge and extracts a can of Karl's lager. I don't think he'll be coming back for it. I pass it to Clement.

"Cheers, doll."

He cracks the can open and takes a long slug. He then fiddles with the breast pocket of his denim waistcoat and pulls out a packet of Marlboro cigarettes.

He flips it open and holds it towards me. "Smoke?"

"No, thank you. And I'd rather you didn't smoke in the house."

"Where then?"

I unlock the back door and hold it open.

"You can stand on the patio."

He reluctantly clambers to his feet and shuffles outside, lighting his cigarette with a Zippo lighter on the way. He stops a few yards beyond the back door as I lean against the frame. He flicks his wrist, closing the lid shut on the Zippo before dropping it back into his pocket.

"Those things will kill you," I remark.

He takes a drag and slowly exhales. "You can't kill a bloke who's already dead."

I don't contest his statement.

A cloud of cigarette smoke drifts across the patio, sparking a hundred memories. Like many men of his generation, my dad was a smoker. Most people hate the smell of cigarette smoke but

I find it strangely comforting, in short doses. I even smoked myself throughout college and university — a futile attempt to fit in. When I left, there was no need to fit in, and even less reason to continue smoking.

"So, doll. You gonna tell me why I'm here?"

"Because I don't want the house stinking of cigarettes for days."

"Fuck me gently," he mumbles. "No. I mean, why I'm *here,* as, in your life?"

"Oh, right. It's too cold standing here. Come back in and I'll give you the highlights."

Clement takes another deep drag and drops the butt to the ground. A huge Chelsea Boot stamps it out.

He follows me back into the kitchen and we sit at the table.

I put my head in my hands and try to work out why I'm about to offload to this stranger, and where to even begin.

Once I start, it pours out. I didn't realise just how much I needed to vent, to offload.

Clement sits and listens patiently, occasionally nodding or offering a murmured response, but otherwise silent.

I rant on for almost ten minutes, explaining every detail of the events since Karl disappeared on Monday. The whole exercise is exhausting, but almost therapeutic.

"...and that's why I was at the shop tonight," I sigh, concluding my diatribe.

He sits back in his chair and takes another gulp of lager.

"Seems there's an obvious solution here, doll."

"Care to share it with me because I can't see one."

"I pay this Sterling fella a visit, and beat the shit out of him."

"Nice idea, but this guy is apparently well connected, and a nasty piece of work. Rumour has it he used to be some big noise in gangland London, during the sixties."

"I was born and bred in North London, and I've never heard of him."

"I think he was from the East End."

"London's a big place. Maybe he was a name, but not one I've ever come across."

"Anyway, I don't think that's a viable solution."

"Why not?"

I can't believe I'm about to say what I'm about to say.

"Look, Clement. Let's just say for one moment, I'm prepared to indulge this fantasy of yours. Firstly, I don't think beating up a pensioner would help your quest to make penance. And secondly, unless you're planning on hanging around for the rest of my life, God forbid, what happens when you leave? I'll be the one who receives any retribution."

He slowly strokes his moustache; something he appears to do when he's thinking, or maybe it helps him think.

"Yeah, you're right. Can't afford for this to go pear-shaped."

"So? Any other bright ideas?"

"Nah. That was basically all I had."

"Brilliant. I'm going to bed. Close the door on your way out."

"You want me to go?"

"For somebody who has apparently been sent to help me, you're not bringing much to the table."

"I'll come up with something, doll. I just need a bit of time to think. I'm a fixer, and I can fix this."

He looks across at me, his expression earnest. "I'll kip on the sofa. And I'll keep an eye out in case those blokes come back."

I have a dilemma. If I kick him out I won't have to worry about being murdered in my sleep, but I'll still have Messrs Black & Blue to worry about.

"I think I should call the police and report what happened this evening."

"Yeah, you could do that, but what do you think they'll do?"

"Um, I'm not sure."

"I'll tell you, doll. They'll do bugger all. The might send a plod round tomorrow morning, and they might take a statement. Beyond that, you're on your own."

He makes a good point. And Sterling made it clear what would happen if I involve the police.

I hate to admit it, but I guess Clement is the lesser of two evils.

"Okay. I'll get you a duvet."

"Good girl."

"Don't call me...oh, never mind, I'm too tired. Wait here."

I traipse upstairs and pull the duvet from the spare bed. I drag it down to the lounge and deposit it on the sofa. I call Clement in.

"The rules are simple. You stay in here unless you hear anything that needs investigating. You do not come upstairs under any circumstances. Clear?"

"Crystal."

"I mean it, Clement. If I hear as much as a squeak on the stairs, I'll call the police."

I pull my phone from my pocket and open the camera app. As Clement looks on, I take a quick snap of his confused face.

"What the hell was that?"

"Just taking your photo, for potential evidence. It'll give the police something to go on."

"Jesus, doll," he groans. "I get it, alright. You don't trust me."

He appears genuinely offended by my paranoia. I feel just a little awkward.

"Erm, do you need the bathroom."

"Bit late for a bath."

"I mean, do you need to go the toilet?"

"Nah. I'm good."

His eyes drift around the room before his attention is drawn to the television.

"Is that a TV?"

"Yes, Clement, it's a TV," I reply wearily.

"Where's the rest of it?"

"Eh? That's it, all of it."

"Cool. What time does it start?" he asks.

"What do you mean, *start*?"

He looks down at me as if I'm the one asking stupid questions.

"What time do the channels begin broadcasting?"

"There is no time. There's always something on."

"Even now, at this time of night?"

"Yes, Clement."

"Can I watch it?"

Why does it feel like I'm dealing with an eighteen-stone child?

"Whatever."

I grab the remote control and switch the television on. Clement lowers himself onto the sofa, keeping his eyes fixed on the screen.

I pass the remote control to him. "Press this button to change channel up or down."

"How many channels are there?"

"I don't know. Over a hundred, I guess."

"No way," he replies incredulously. "Are you shittin' me?"

"Goodnight, Clement."

"Yeah. Night, doll," he replies dismissively, without shifting his attention from the screen.

Whether he's an errant saviour or suffering from a mental illness, he definitely has the attention span of every man I've ever known.

I close the lounge door and plod up the stairs to my bedroom. I stand at the foot of the bed for a moment. Am I being overly paranoid, or am I being stupidly naive? Surely it's better to be the former?

I put my pyjamas on, grab the duvet and pillows, and drag them to the bathroom.

The bathroom door is the only one in the house with a lock. It also has a window which offers an escape route on to the flat roof of the kitchen below.

I fold the duvet in half, lay it in the bath, and position the pillows at one end. I quickly brush my teeth and climb into my makeshift bed, my mobile phone tucked under the pillow. It's actually quite cosy, and more comfortable than I thought it would be.

Even a raucous chorus of concerned voices can't prevent me falling asleep within minutes.

14

Sunlight creeps above the window sill and spills into the bathroom.

It wasn't responsible for my abrupt awakening. No, that was due to a series of desperate thumps on the bathroom door.

"Doll! Doll! Let me in!"

I open my eyes to confusion. Why am I in the bath? Who's banging at the door?

One by one, memories fall into line. Panic quickly follows.

I clamber out of the bath and stumble towards the door. It takes a few seconds to force the stiff lock. I frantically pull the door open.

"Bloody hell, doll," Clement shrieks as he barges past me.

Is the house on fire? Are Messrs Black & Blue trying to break in? I'm still half-asleep and struggling to comprehend what's going on.

Clement, sporting nothing more than a pair of purple underpants and black socks, charges across the bathroom to the toilet.

"Sweet Jesus," he groans, as he empties his bladder.

Seconds pass and his flow continues, like a hosepipe being emptied into a bucket.

"You could have told me there wasn't a lav downstairs."

On and on it goes.

"And I didn't think you'd want me to piss in the kitchen sink."

It finally ends. He shakes himself, breaks wind and turns to face me.

"Sorry," he says with a broad grin. He doesn't look sorry.

I suppose I should be grateful he didn't murder me during the night. Saying that, the foul stench wafting across the bathroom has enough potency to kill.

I clamp my hand across my face. "You're disgusting," I mumble.

"What's for breakfast?" he asks.

I shake my head and beat a hasty retreat to my bedroom.

As I throw some clothes on, I hear Clement clumping back down the stairs. I return to the bathroom, flush the chain, and empty half a can of air freshener. I brush my teeth and attend to my own bodily functions, all the while wondering what possessed me to let Clement into my home.

I put it down to tiredness impairing my judgement.

A voice bellows up the stairs. "You coming down, doll? I could murder a brew."

Why me, God? Why me?

I count to ten and trudge down the stairs.

Clement is sitting at the kitchen table. Thankfully, he's now fully dressed.

"Alright?"

"I've had better mornings."

I put the kettle on and pull a box of granola out of the cupboard.

"What's that?"

"This, Clement, is breakfast," I reply as I place the box on the table.

He eyes it suspiciously. "Yeah, I think I'd rather have a bacon sarnie, if it's all the same with you."

"I don't have any bacon..."

My phone chimes the arrival of a text message.

"What was that noise?" Clement asks.

"Just my phone."

I pluck it from my pocket and breathe a sigh of relief when I see it's just a balance update from my bank.

"I thought you said that thing was a camera?"

I assume he's being sarcastic. The look on his face suggests he isn't.

"You don't have a smart phone?"

"A what?"

"Good grief, Clement. Have you been living under a rock?"

"I told you where I've been. Still don't believe me, do you?"

I don't answer him.

The kettle boils and I pour two mugs of tea. As I stir in Clement's three teaspoons of sugar, he presses me for an answer.

"Well?"

I place the mugs on the table and lower myself down on to a chair, keeping my gaze fixed on the big man. In the cold light of day, his delusional claims have morphed from ridiculous to irritating. While I was getting dressed, I considered the two questions I couldn't answer last night.

How did he get into a locked shop? It's obvious with the benefit of a clear head — he could have already been in there before I arrived. He could have picked the lock and hidden himself away in the stockroom.

How did he know my middle name was Dusty? It wouldn't be too tricky for somebody to get a copy of my birth certificate.

There is, however, still one question I can't answer — why he would bother?

Perhaps if I can find a few holes in his ridiculous claim, he might relent and come clean. Whatever his agenda is, I'd rather know the truth.

"I'm sorry, Clement, but I don't buy any of this. I don't believe you're here to make penance and I don't believe you died in 1975."

He shrugs his shoulders.

I refer back to my phone and open the web browser.

"Who was Prime Minister?" I ask.

"Harold Wilson," he answers without hesitation.

I google the question. He's correct. Another search pulls up a list of events from 1975.

"There was a major crash on the tube. It killed 43 people. Which station?"

"Yeah, that was bad. Moorgate."

"Which Monty Python film was released?"

"The Holy Grail."

"There was a referendum. What was it for?"

"Something to do with joining the European Economic Community, I think."

Right on all three. Bugger.

"How did that whole European Community thing pan out in the end?" he asks.

"Err, don't ask."

I drop my eyes back to the list and fire another question.

"Which hotel in London was bombed by the IRA?"

"The Hilton."

I drop the phone on the table. His answers don't prove anything, other than his delusion is fairly deep rooted.

We sit in silence for a long minute, Clement sipping his tea as if this is just a run-of-the-mill Saturday morning. I don't have the first clue what to say.

"Let's say, for the sake of argument, I'm bullshitting you," he eventually says. "What have you got to lose by letting me help you?"

A good question to which I don't have an answer.

"Well, nothing, I suppose."

"And do you think I'm gonna hurt you in any way?"

"I guess not."

He puts his mug down and sits forward, resting his elbows on the table.

"I get it, doll. Trust is a bit like money. It has to be earned, and only an idiot gives it away freely."

"And your point is?"

"You don't have to trust me; you just have to believe I can help you. Doesn't really matter if you think all the stuff about my previous life is bullshit as long as I do what I came here to do. I have to help you, doll."

For the first time this morning, I notice he's not wearing his blue-tinted sunglasses. The eyes that were hidden yesterday are as blue as those sunglasses. What is it they say? The eyes are the window to the soul? Clement's eyes offer a window to a broken mind; a deluded, broken mind. Whatever is going on in his head, I'm struggling not to feel anything other than sympathy.

"Okay," I sigh. "I'd appreciate any help you can give me."

"Fab," he replies with a grin.

"So, do you have any ideas?"

"Think so. Assuming I can't simply beat the shit out of this Sterling fella, the only option is to get his money. Correct?"

I nod.

"In which case, we just need to get our hands on twenty grand in the next five days. Correct?"

I nod again, fighting the urge not to roll my eyes.

"And to do that, we need to take a trip."

"Where?"

"London. How far is it from here?"

"About fifty minutes on the train."

"That's that sorted then. Ready when you are."

He plucks his sunglasses from a pocket and puts them on.

"What? I can't go gallivanting around London at the drop of a hat."

"Why not?"

"Firstly, I've got to pick my mother up from the hospital this morning, and secondly, I've got a shop to run."

"Time's running out, doll. It's up to you."

"Why do I have to come with you? Can't you go on your own?"

"Nope. Doesn't work like that."

Here we go again.

"Explain."

"If you're not with me then I can't protect you. If something bad happens, my final chance goes up in smoke."

"And they say chivalry is dead."

I sit back and sip my tea. I feel like I'm lost in a maze, with every exit bricked up. If I dismiss Clement's impractical plan, my problem remains. And quite apart from my other commitments, do I want to go on a wild goose chase around London?

An impractical plan or no plan. Which is it to be?

"Why London?"

"It's my manor. And I think I know where we can get our hands on your twenty grand."

"You think?"

"Nothing in life is certain, doll. Got any better suggestions?"

My silence answers his question.

"Alright, but I can't just drop everything and jump on a train. I've got to pick my mother up, and if I'm going to close the shop, I need to put a notice in the window."

"Better get your arse in gear then."

"Don't you want breakfast first?"

He eyes up the box of granola. "Nah. Think I'll pass."

I dash upstairs and take a quick shower. With my previous visits to London in mind, I scour my wardrobe looking for something practical to wear. I decide on a pair of stretch jeans, a lilac jumper, and a distressed-leather jacket. My choice of footwear is limited as I quickly discount anything with heels. I snatch a pair of Converse trainers from the floor of the wardrobe and slip them on.

Twenty five minutes later, we're back in the Fiat and heading to the shop. Clement continues his odd behaviour from last night's journey, gawping at the passing scenery with obvious fascination.

"What's a Starbucks?" he asks.

"It's a coffee shop."

A minute passes.

"What's a Nando's?"

"It's a chicken restaurant."

Another minute passes.

"What's a broadband?"

"Eh?"

"That bill poster we just passed. It said unlimited broadband for a tenner."

"Are you being serious?" I groan. "Broadband provides access to the Internet."

"What's the Internet?"

I no longer want to play his game and return a scowl. He correctly decides not to ask any more dumb questions and the rest of the journey passes in silence.

We pull up behind the shop and Clement insists on going in first. Once he's confirmed the coast is clear, I follow him in and head for the counter. I open Microsoft Word on the computer and create a poster to say the shop will be closed today, due to 'unforeseen circumstances'. Never a truer word has been printed.

I stick the poster in the window and ring the hospital to see if I can collect my mother.

After being pushed from pillar to post, I'm eventually put through to a nurse and she confirms Mum will be discharged in an hour or so. I tell the nurse to expect me.

I return to the staffroom to find Clement lounging in a chair with his feet up on the table.

"Right. I've got to go and collect my mother from the hospital and drop her home. I'll probably be a couple of hours and then we can head to London."

"I'll come with you."

"No, you won't. My mother might consider it a little odd I've brought a member of a Status Quo tribute band with me, don't you think?"

"But, doll..."

"Clement, I'm only going to the hospital. I couldn't be in a safer place. I'll be fine."

He shakes his head but doesn't offer any further protest.

"Alright, your call. But what the hell am I supposed to do for the next two hours?"

"Um, there's plenty to read."

"Great," he grunts.

"And there's tea and coffee in the cupboard, and biscuits if you get peckish."

"Any music?"

I point to a radio on the side.

"Feel free to change the channel. Do you need anything else?"

"Nah. I'm good."

I scribble my mobile number on a slip of paper and show Clement where the shop phone is located.

"Emergencies only. Understood?"

He nods and I double check he'll be okay on his own.

"Christ's sake, doll. I'm not twelve."

I mumble an embarrassed apology and leave.

The entire fifteen minute journey to the hospital is fraught with regret. I've just left a complete stranger alone in my shop. I try to ease my concern by reminding myself there is nothing worth stealing, and if Clement had any sinister intentions, he could have already acted upon them. Surely there's far less risk leaving him in the shop than letting him into my home. And he did behave himself last night, I suppose.

By the time I navigate my way through the hospital car park, my concern has rightfully switched towards my mother.

With significantly less urgency than last night, I make my way past the reception area and back through the stairwells and corridors.

As I push through a set of double doors, I'm greeted by the sight of an old woman in a wheelchair, being pushed by a porter. I hold the door open and let them pass. Judging by her frail body and wispy grey hair, the old woman must be well into her eighties. Her hollow eyes remain fixed on the corridor ahead, her expression suggesting she's not heading anywhere she wants to go.

I turn and watch them for a second as they continue their journey. It brings on a sudden shudder, knowing that woman might be my mother at some point in the not too distant future. It's no way for anyone to spend their twilight years.

An overriding need to hug my mum urges me on.

I reach the ward to find a solitary nurse stationed behind the desk. She greets me with a tired smile.

"Can I help?"

"I called a little earlier. I'm here to collect my mother, Elizabeth Goodyear."

"Ah, yes. Your father arrived about ten minutes ago. He's just helping her get ready."

"My father?"

"Yes. A friendly chap with white hair?"

I stare at the nurse, open mouthed.

The nurse has just described the last man I'd want anywhere near my mother — David Sterling.

15

It's not quite a run, more a frenzied waddle. My stumpy legs propel me along the corridor while my mind considers what revenge Sterling has in mind for Clement's attack on Messrs Black & Blue.

For a second, I wish Clement was with me.

I crash through the doors and look straight across at the bed in the far corner. My mother is sitting on the edge of the bed, fully dressed. The man with the white hair is sitting on the chair Sergeant Stone occupied last night.

I stomp across the ward and stare daggers at the man.

"Morning, Bethany," he chimes.

The man does have white hair, but it caps a plump, ruddy face. No beak-like nose and no scar.

"Stanley. What are you doing here?"

Embarrassed smiles are swapped between my mother and her estranged husband.

"Darling, I asked Stanley to drop by."

"You mother phoned me this morning," Stanley adds apologetically.

"Why?" I ask, turning to my mother and ignoring Stanley.

"Because he's my friend. And despite everything that happened, he cares about me."

Stanley looks up at me, his eyes like those of a scolded dog seeking forgiveness.

"Well, nice to see you again, Stanley. Shall we get going, Mum?"

She frowns at me. "Sit down, darling."

I huff like a sulky teenager and slump down on the edge of the bed next to my mother.

"What's going on here, Mum?"

"Stanley has offered to put me up for a few days, to look after me."

"No. That's my job," I protest.

"But, darling, you've got the shop to run and a fiancé to look after. You've got enough on your plate without worrying about me."

I look across at Stanley.

"Where are you even living? Last I heard you were in some grotty bedsit."

"I've got a mobile home now, Bethany. It's in a lovely spot out in the sticks. Plenty of peace and quiet."

I turn back to my mother.

"This is madness. Have you forgotten it was Stanley's *help* that almost bankrupted you?"

"That was then, and we were both to blame. He just wants to look after me, and it's only for a few days; a week at most."

"I'm not working now," Stanley interjects. "So I can be there if your mother needs anything. I'll take good care of her, I promise."

"See, darling? Stanley only wants to help. And it'll be nice to get away and recuperate in the country."

The two of them stare at me expectedly, awaiting my approval. This feels like it was already a done deal before I arrived.

To confirm my theory, Stanley hands me a slip of paper. "My phone number. Call any time you like, day or night."

If I can overcome my controlling instincts, this might actually turn out in my favour. My mother will be far safer holed up in the country and I can concentrate on finding Sterling's money without worrying about her.

But just because it happens to suit me, it doesn't mean I'm about to let Stanley off the hook.

"If anything happens to her, Stanley, I'll remove your testicles with a pair of blunt scissors. Clear?"

I turn to my mother. "And don't let him persuade you to invest in any more of his hare-brained schemes."

They both smile, probably with relief, and I give my mother an overdue hug.

"I'll call you tonight, okay?"

"Alright, darling. And please don't worry about me."

I'll never stop worrying about you, especially where Stanley Goodyear is concerned.

I say my goodbyes and traipse back to the car park.

By the time I'm back in the car, a gnawing guilt has set in. Perhaps I was too harsh on Stanley. Compared to the way Karl has treated me, he's a virtual saint. Stanley might be a hapless fool, but Karl was a conniving, devious, cheating shitbag. My mother was naive, but I also stood blissfully by and let a man destroy my life. I think I've lost the moral high ground now.

I make a mental note to apologise to Stanley when I call later.

The guilt follows me all the way back to the shop.

As I pull into the parking bay, I check the clock on the dashboard. Rather than the couple of hours I predicted, I'm back within an hour. With my inherent mistrust of men, I can't help but see this as an opportunity to catch Clement up to no good.

I quietly unlock the back door and open it.

Good God!

Clement is still sitting in the staffroom with his feet on the table, the radio playing in the background. His face is hidden behind a copy of *Fifty Shades of Gray*.

I cough and he drops the book to his lap.

"Of the thousands of books you could have read, you chose *that*?"

He grins back at me. "Have you read it? It's utter filth."

I suppose I should be grateful I didn't walk in as he was mid-wank.

"You're back early," he adds.

"Yes. It seems my mother doesn't require my babysitting service."

"You wanna get going then?"

"Shortly. I want a cup of tea first, and we need to discuss this plan of yours."

"Fair enough."

I put the kettle on and turn the radio down. I've lost count of the times I've done those two things in quick succession.

"I was listening to that," Clement protests.

"Listening to what?"

"The funny Irish fella."

I look across at the dial on the radio, set to Radio 2.

"Graham Norton."

"Yeah, him. I was trying to find Radio 1 but I think your set must be buggered."

"Eh?"

"I managed to find the right frequency but it was just a load of bleedin' noise."

"Ah, right," I snigger. "When did you last listen to Radio 1?"

"Long time ago."

I fill my mug with boiling water and turn to face Clement while it brews.

"So which DJ did you listen to on a Saturday morning?"

That's it, Beth. Embrace the madness.

"Ed Stewart."

I pluck my phone from my handbag and google the Radio 1 schedule from 1975. It lists Ed Steward in the breakfast slot.

"Is he still on the radio?" Clement asks.

"He's dead, I'm afraid."

"What about Fluff Freeman?"

"Dead."

"John Peel?"

"Dead."

"Jesus," he sighs. "That's bleedin' tragic."

"There are still some old DJs around though. There's Tony Blackburn, David Hamilton, Johnnie Walker…"

"Ooh, what about Jimmy Savile?" he interjects excitedly. "I used to bloody love his show on a Sunday afternoon."

"Seriously? Come on, Clement, the whole world knows about Savile."

"Well, I don't. What about him?"

"Erm, he's also dead. And if he wasn't, he'd be in prison."

"Eh? Why?"

I turn back around and remove my teabag from the mug. I add a splash of milk, take a sip, and sit down at the table opposite Clement.

"Savile was a paedophile."

"What? A nonce? Never," he replies in obvious disbelief.

"Afraid so, and quite a prolific offender as it transpires. There have been scores of allegations against him, over several decades."

"Well, bugger me. You'd never have guessed."

I almost choke on my tea. "Really? He never struck you as a bit odd?"

He strokes his moustache. "Now I think about it, he was always a bit touchy-feely with the kids on *Jim'll Fix It*."

"Indeed."

The room falls silent for a moment as Clement processes my revelation.

"There was a lot of that going on back then, you know," he says quietly.

"A lot of what?"

"Dirty bastards interfering with kids."

"So we're learning."

"They make my fucking flesh creep."

"You're not alone."

"I remember one bloke who used to hang out at my local — Tommy Four-Fingers. He was caught trying to take pictures of kids getting changed at the swimming baths. Unfortunately for Tommy, one of those kids was the nephew of a local gang leader. The kid grassed on Tommy."

"Did he go to prison?"

"Eventually, but not before he was taken to a warehouse where his thumbs were removed with bolt cutters."

"My God. That's awful."

"He never took another photo though, on account he couldn't use a camera without his thumbs."

"How very civilised."

"Maybe not, but I used to mix with some right evil bastards and there was an unwritten code of conduct — you never messed with women or kids. If you did, and anyone found out, you got what you deserved."

It's my turn to process. The way Clement regales this supposed life of his is quite convincing. His psychosis must be pretty acute.

I wonder if I'm doing him any favours by indulging him. Shouldn't he be receiving treatment in a psychiatric hospital?

It's a horribly selfish stance, but I need his help more than I care about his delusions. I'll balance my conscience by ensuring he gets medical attention once we're done. I can't do this on my own, and at least he *seems* willing. Besides, who else is going to help me?

"Anyway, tell me about this plan of yours."

He sits up and rubs his hands together. "It's a bloody long story, doll. Why don't we talk it over on the train, make better use of our time?"

"If I'm going to lose a day's trade, Clement, I'd quite like to know before I commit."

"Don't you have staff?"

"Um, no. But even if I could get somebody in at such short notice, it wouldn't be worth it after paying their wages."

"No money in books then?"

"Not since the Kindle."

"The what?"

"Never mind. Look, can't you at least give me the gist of your idea?"

He leans across the table so our faces are only feet apart, as if he's about to share some great secret.

"The plan is to find some lost gold," he says excitedly.

I sit back in my chair, incredulous. "How marvellous. I've got five days to find twenty grand and your plan is to go on a treasure hunt around London?"

He looks genuinely hurt that I don't share his enthusiasm. "You got any better ideas?" he grumbles.

Clearly, I don't.

"No, but I need a bit more than that, Clement."

He rolls his eyes and sits back. "Alright. You better make me another brew then."

I get up and skip across to the kettle, pausing momentarily to scold myself for being so subservient.

Like a good little woman, I make Clement's tea without complaint and place his mug on the table.

"That alright for you darlin'?" I say in my best Cockney accent.

He peers into the mug. "Bit weak, but it'll do," my sarcasm clearly wasted on him.

"Okay," he begins. "Back in '71, a gang broke into the vault of Lloyds Bank on Baker Street. They tunnelled in from the cellar of an empty shop two doors down, and then used a thermic lance to cut a hole in the steel floor of the vault. They broke through on a Sunday and bagged the contents of hundreds of safety deposit boxes."

"Okay. Still not seeing how this helps us."

"Just getting to that. There were four members of the gang, and because some idiot rented the shop using his real name, the old bill arrested him pretty sharpish. Then it was just a case of rounding up his known associates. All four of them were eventually caught and sent down. Now, none of the loot was ever found, and neither of the two lookouts were named. They both got away scot-free."

"And?" I interrupt impatiently.

"I heard on the grapevine that one of those lookouts was a bloke called Harry Cole, and he was paid off with a bar of pure gold they pulled from one of the safety deposit boxes."

"And that's the gold you want to find?"

"It is, but the story don't end there. I never knew him, but apparently this Harry fella was the nervous type. As soon as the other gang members were arrested, he would have needed to hide his cut. Make sense?"

"I suppose so."

"Unfortunately for poor old Harry, he had a dodgy ticker and dropped dead in the street. The stress of the old bill sniffing around probably finished him off. Sometime later the old bill heard rumours Harry was involved and they turned his gaff inside out. The gold was never found."

"But how do you know this Harry character hadn't already sold it?"

Clement looks at me like I'm a complete idiot. "Because every bleedin' copper in London was on the lookout for it. No fence would touch it, so he had no choice but to sit on it for a few months and then get rid. Standard form after a blag like that."

"So how much is a bar of gold worth?"

"Depends. They came in all sorts of sizes but the largest were about four hundred ounces. Back in my day, you'd get about fifty quid an ounce on the black market."

"Twenty thousand pounds? In, what? The early seventies?"

"Yep."

I grab my phone and check the value of gold today.

"Christ. It's now just under a thousand pounds per ounce. That bar could be worth four hundred thousand pounds."

I drop my phone on the table as I work out the myriad ways I could spend that sort of money. Reality quickly kicks back in.

"I'm hoping you have some idea where this bar might be?"

"We'll talk about that on the train. And don't think for one minute you'll get four hundred grand for it."

"Why not?"

"Firstly, we don't know what size the bar is — it could be four hundred ounces, or it could be a hundred ounces. And secondly, it's scrap gold, so you won't get market value."

"Alright. How much less than market value could we get?"

"Knock about a third off for scrap value, then maybe another ten to twenty percent as an incentive for somebody to buy it without asking any awkward questions."

"So, all in all, it's worth about half the market value?"

"Yeah, about that."

I quickly calculate the possible numbers in my head — a four hundred ounce bar could be worth as much as two hundred thousand pounds.

"I could pay off Sterling, and my mortgage."

"Not such a crazy idea then?"

"I'm warming to it," I reply nonchalantly.

I'm actually trying hard not to show my excitement. However, I need to remain calm, and I need to process what, on the face of it, seems a pretty ludicrous plan.

"I'm just going to the loo."

Clement nods and returns his attention back to *Fifty Shades of Grey*.

I grab my phone from the table and head to the toilet. As soon as I'm sitting down, I google the Baker Street robbery of 1971.

There are pages of results and I'm relieved to see it was a real event and not a figment of Clement's broken mind. I tap a link to a Wikipedia page. As I scan the text, all of the information checks out, all except the part about Harry Cole and his gold bar. That would make sense, but it doesn't mean Clement isn't making it up.

I google 'Harry Cole stolen gold'.

The first page of results are totally irrelevant to my search. I click through to the second page, and more irrelevant results. I'm about to click through to the third page when the last result catches my attention. It's a link to an obscure chat forum I've never heard of, but the page title at least appears relevant. I tap the link.

There are just four posts in the thread. The first asks if anyone had heard about Harry Cole's alleged involvement in the Baker Street robbery. Two of the replies acknowledge the rumour, but offer nothing to corroborate it. The fourth, and final post, offers a little more. It cites a member of the gang, and his relationship with Harry Cole. A few theories about the missing gold are offered, but then discounted for a variety of reasons. Whoever posted the final message seems to imply that Harry Cole might well have been in possession of stolen gold, but concludes by saying that after such a long time, there is little chance of it ever being found.

Interesting.

I flush the chain and consider if this really is as crazy as it sounds. For two hundred thousand pounds, it's got to be worth a trip to London, hasn't it?

I wash my hands and stare at my pale, jaded face, reflected in the mirror above the sink.

Do you have any idea what you're doing, Beth?

I don't, and I've only ever felt like this once before in my life.

I must have been six years old and we went on holiday to a caravan park in Dorset. On the second day, Dad took me to the indoor swimming pool where they had this brightly coloured flume slide, snaking up to the roof like a twisted beanstalk. I think my dad was reluctant to let me have a go, but I begged him, and he eventually relented.

I remember clambering excitedly up the steps and staring down this dark hole. With a dozen kids waiting impatiently behind me, it was too late to change my mind. I climbed in and sat down. Before I knew it, I was lying on my back and hurtling down the tube. As the coloured sections of the slide flashed past, I quickly learnt what it was like to have no control and nothing to cling to. No matter how much I wanted it to stop, and I really did, I had no choice but to put my trust in gravity and pray I wouldn't be splattered against the curved walls. It was my first experience of being totally and utterly helpless.

After what seemed an age, I was spat out into the swimming pool. Noting the fear on my face, Dad quickly fished me out and wrapped me in a towel. Safety. Comfort.

As much as the slide scared the living daylights out of me — enough to stop me going back for another turn — there was a faint undercurrent of excitement to the experience. I didn't understand it, and I haven't felt it since — until now.

Here I am with no control, little to cling to, and putting my trust in something, or someone, almost as incomprehensible as gravity. Despite my fears, that tinge of adrenalin-fuelled excitement is lurking beneath the surface once more.

I give an encouraging smile to the woman in the mirror, dry my hands, and return to the staffroom.

"I think you've got post," Clement mumbles without looking up from his book.

"Sorry?"

He looks up. "Postman just shoved some letters though the door. You still have post these days?"

"Err, yes."

"Never know, doll, there might be a cheque from the pools company. All your problems solved."

I'm not sure anyone does the football pools these days, and I certainly don't, so it's unlikely. I traipse through to the shop.

On first inspection, the pile of letters on the doormat looks like just another batch of junk mail. All except the plain white envelope with my name printed on the front, just like the one containing the photographic evidence of Karl's dirty secret.

I snatch the envelope up and tear it open.

There are no photos, just a single piece of plain white paper containing a few lines of printed text...

Dear Miss Baxter

Just a courtesy reminder that you have five days before your debt is due for collection.

Whilst writing, I understand you may have secured protection, and the gentleman in question assaulted my associates without provocation. They are both currently in hospital, undergoing treatment for their injuries. Suffice to say, they are keen to catch up with you on their discharge.

I managed to convince my associates to stand down until your deadline on Thursday. However, I would stress that if you fail to settle the debt at the agreed date and time, I can no longer be responsible for the actions of my associates. They are very protective of their reputation, and therefore keen to put matters right.

I trust that fact provides sufficient motivation for you to focus on finding the cash, and Mr Patterson.

I look forward to seeing you on Thursday — D

I read it three times, each time adding a different ingredient to a simmering pot of emotions: anger, fear, hatred. I'm so caught in my negative thoughts, I don't notice Clement ambling up behind me.

"Not a pools cheque then?" he says, startling me.

I draw a calming breath and hand him the letter. He takes it in a pan-sized hand and scans the text.

"Bin it," he snorts.

"But it's evidence. If I have to involve the police, this could be crucial."

"You reckon Sterling's dabs will be all over it? Don't be naive — it's not gonna help you."

Maybe he's right. Why would Sterling be so careless with so much at stake?

I scoop up the pile of mail from the doormat and place it under the counter, together with Sterling's letter.

"You wanna get going, doll?"

"I suppose so."

The truth is, I don't really want to go. I don't really want any of this. The tinge of excitement I felt only five minutes ago has fizzled out. This is no great adventure — it's a nightmarish hole I can't climb out of, as Sterling's letter has just reminded me.

My only hope is an insane treasure hunt, concocted by a denim-clad whacko who thinks he's been dead since the seventies.

What I wouldn't give to be wrapped in a comforting towel about now.

16

The train station is only a mile away, so I decide to leave the car parked outside the shop. I thought a walk in the autumn sunshine might help to clear my mind and bolster my flagging enthusiasm.

It might have done, if I wasn't accompanied by an inquisitive, part-shaven Yeti.

Praying I don't bump into anyone I know, I walk as quickly as I can through the town centre. Clement has no trouble keeping up, or firing questions every few minutes.

"What's Santander?"

"It's a bank. I think it's used to be Abbey National."

"What's Ann Summers?"

"They sell lingerie and...um, marital aids."

"What's Carphone Warehouse?"

"They sell phones, like the one I used to take your photo."

Clement ponders this. "What's it got to do with cars then? Don't look much like a warehouse, either."

"I...err, don't know."

By the time we reach the paved forecourt at the front of the train station, I'm questioning my own sanity as much as Clement's.

We pass the main entrance and I head towards an automated ticket machine.

"Have you got any money, Clement?"

"Nope."

"So I'm supposed to fund this expedition am I?"

"You do realise I usually charge people for my help? There's bugger all in this for me, so you can at least pay the expenses."

"How convenient your misogynistic principles don't stretch to letting me, a mere chick, pay for everything."

"I have no idea what you're on about, doll."

"Misogyny is...never mind," I sigh.

It's senseless arguing with him, and I suppose he does have a point.

With Clement looking over my shoulder, I stand in front of the ticket machine and prod at the screen to order two London travel cards.

"What the hell does that thing do?" Clement asks as I slip my credit card into the slot.

"It's a ticket machine and most stations have them now. I guess they're cheaper than staff."

"British Rail got rid of all their darkies then?"

"British Rail doesn't exist anymore, and what is a..."

Oh. My. God.

I spin around and scan the forecourt, praying nobody is close enough to have overheard Clement. Thankfully, there are only a handful of people milling around, and they're loitering near the main entrance, thirty feet away.

"For God's sake, Clement," I hiss. "You can't say that word."

"What word?"

"The dark word."

"Darkies?"

"Clement!" I snap, glancing nervously over my shoulder. "Stop saying it."

"Why?"

"Because it's highly offensive. It's a horrible word."

I expected a defensive reaction but his expression is one of confusion.

"When did that happen?"

"When did what happen?"

"When did that word become offensive? I had plenty of coloured mates and they never seemed bothered by it."

"And that's another one. You can't say coloured."

"Are you taking the piss?"

"No, I'm not. Those words have very negative connotations and they're considered racist."

He shakes his head and mutters something under his breath.

Praying he'll keep any further racial remarks to himself, I grab the tickets from the machine and head towards the station entrance. Clement trudges along behind.

We enter the main ticket hall and squeak across the polished floor towards the platform.

"Here, you'll need this," I say, handing Clement one of the tickets.

I slide my ticket into the automated barrier and the gates clatter open, allowing me to pass onto the platform. I take a dozen steps forward and turn, expecting to see Clement behind me. He's still on the other side of the barrier.

"What are you doing?" I call across to him.

He stares at the barrier, and then at the ticket in his hand.

"What the hell do I do with this?" he calls back.

I traipse back to the barrier and point at the ticket slot. "Slide it in there, and grab it when it comes out of the top. The gates will open automatically."

Clement does as instructed, and the machine snatches his ticket. "Fuck me," he yelps, snapping his hand away as if he'd been scalded.

"Grab the ticket. Grab the ticket," I yell.

He snatches the ticket and barges through the gates at the precise moment they begin to close. After some impromptu contortion, and colourful language, he passes through the barrier.

A group of teenagers are on the other side, nudging one another and giggling at Clement's antics. In fairness, there's a lot to laugh at.

Despite his street cred being in tatters, Clement appears otherwise unscathed after his ordeal.

"Never thought I'd say it, but I preferred the British Rail system," he grumbles.

I don't know whether to laugh or throw myself onto the track.

Keen to avoid any further embarrassment, I lead Clement up to the far end of the platform where we're as far away from the other passengers as possible.

"Good timing. Our train will be here in three minutes."

He nods as he pulls the cigarette packet from his waistcoat pocket.

"You can't smoke here."

"Says who?"

"It's the law. It's illegal to smoke in all public buildings."

"But we're outside."

"I don't make the laws, Clement. You can't smoke here."

"What the hell has happened to the world?" he mumbles as the cigarette pack is returned to his pocket.

We stand in silence as we wait for the train. I don't know if Clement is sulking or if his default setting is moody, but I'm just grateful he's stopped asking questions.

Our train finally emerges from beyond a curve in the track, rattling towards us until it squeals to a halt alongside the platform.

I move toward the end carriage, offering silent thanks it's empty. Clement looms up beside me just as the automatic doors hiss open.

"Neat," he remarks.

I ignore his comment and step into the carriage, taking a seat by the window. Clement joins me and collapses onto the seat opposite, his trunk-like legs stretched out into the aisle.

"I'm guessing there isn't a smoking carriage?"

"You guess correctly."

I look at my watch. Fifty minutes before we reach Waterloo. Why do I get the feeling it's going to be the longest fifty minutes of my life?

The doors close with another hiss, much to Clement's fascination.

We settle into an almost comfortable silence. It lasts barely six minutes.

"What do you call them?" he asks.

"Them?"

"Yeah, people who...aren't white."

"Um, I think the correct term is people of colour."

"Not so different from the word I used."

"The latter one maybe, but that first word you used is definitely not acceptable."

Clement strokes his moustache and gazes out of the window.

"I'm not a racist," he eventually says.

"I never said you were, Clement. Those words are racist though."

"Are they?" he says, still gazing out of the window.

"Yes. Definitely."

"Not the racism I knew."

"What do you mean?"

He turns to face me. "I used to know this black fella, Felix Tomblin. A decent bloke was Felix."

He waits for my reaction to the word black. I don't correct him.

"He came over with his family in the early sixties, from Jamaica," he continues. "Loads of families came over from that part of the world, looking for work and a better life, I suppose. Anyway, there was Felix, his parents, and his kid sister, Lorna. They lived in a crappy terraced house, a few streets from my local — that's where I first met him. The whole area was a right shit-hole back then. Christ knows why they wanted to live there, but they seemed happy enough. Good people they were."

Fearing Clement is about to regale me with another tale involving bolt cutters, I try to feign a lack of interest. He doesn't notice.

"People didn't take too kindly to Felix and his family living in a white area. They used to get spat at in the street, dog shit shoved through their letterbox, and they lost count of how many times poor Lorna came home from school with cuts and bruises. In the end, Felix took up boxing so he could defend his family. He took plenty of kickings over the years, but eventually dished out a fair few too."

I'm genuinely appalled.

"That's terrible."

"Nah. *That's* racism. Hatred of another man just because his skin is a different colour. For me, those fuckers who tormented the Tomblins are right up there with the nonces."

Clement shifts his legs and leans towards me.

"You see, doll, I'm no racist."

I slowly nod as Clement maintains eye contact over the top of his sunglasses.

Even if I felt like arguing the point, which I don't think I'm qualified to do, Clement's tale has left me a little fazed. He paints a vivid picture of a past I never knew. So much so, it *feels* credible. Some of the greatest authors I've read have that same skill; the ability to drag you away from reality and seamlessly drop you into an unreal world.

"And if you want references, I've shagged a fair few black chicks over the years," he adds, his casual sexism destroying my admiration in a heartbeat.

"Thanks, but I'll take your word for it."

The train slows as it approaches a station. I turn my gaze to the rear gardens of the houses sidled up to the track. I'm minded of the novel, *The Girl on the Train*. The girl on *this* train would probably swap a life of mild alcoholism and obsessive jealousy for my current one. I'd certainly settle for even a sliver of the author's success.

As the train slows to stop, I keep my fingers crossed that nobody ventures into our carriage. I don't know how long Clement will remain silent, or what will come out of his mouth next.

Nobody joins us, and a minute later we're on our way again.

As the train reaches speed, Clement continues with the questions. "How old are you, doll?"

"Why do you ask?"

"Just making conversation."

"I'm thirty six."

"You never married? No kids?"

"No, and no."

This is a line of conversation I definitely don't want to pursue. I turn Clement's question back on him.

"How old are you?"

"Roughly?"

"Most people tend to know precisely how old they are. We have these things called birthdays every year to remind us."

"Don't know what date I was born. I can tell you the month, and the year. Not the date though."

"How can you not know your own birthday?"

"Because my mother dumped me outside The Royal Free Hospital in Holloway, some point after I was born. Dunno if she did that the day I was born, or days, or weeks later."

I offer a sympathetic smile but there's not much I can say in response.

"But as you asked," he adds. "I was born in November, 1935. You do the maths."

"Right. I must say, you're in good shape for a man in his early eighties."

"Yeah," he huffs. "But not such good shape for a man in his early forties."

Drop this line of conversation, Beth.

We both stare out of the window.

As we get nearer to London, the open fields and thickets of woodland have been replaced with an urban sprawl of tightly packed houses and industrial buildings. Concrete tower blocks loom in the distance; the ugly sisters of the modern, glass-clad buildings occupying the same horizon. As vistas go, it's as depressing as it is enticing.

I turn back to Clement.

"Don't you think it's time you shared a few more details about this plan of yours?"

"Probably," he replies wistfully, still staring out of the window.

"Clement?"

He snaps out of his malaise and with no explanation, gets to his feet. He then strides down the carriage, glancing left and right at each set of seats as he passes. When he reaches the end, he turns around, and returns to his seat.

"What on earth was that in aid of?" I ask, bemused.

"Just checking there was nobody earwigging. Don't want anyone getting the jump on us."

"Just get on with it."

"Right. Where to start?"

He drums his fingers on the window while staring at his feet.

"Clement."

"Alright, alright."

166

Despite the fact the carriage is empty, he leans forward and talks in a low voice.

"One evening, back in '75, I'd just finished a job and decided to have a pint. I happened to be in Camden; Harry Cole's patch, although I didn't give that any thought when I strolled into this boozer. Anyway, I was standing at the bar, just minding my own business, when this old timer wanders up and orders a drink. As you do, we got chatting and Harry's name came up. Turns out that pub used to be his local, before he, you know, snuffed it."

"Why would some random old man bring up Harry's name?"

"Cos' by that point, Harry and his missing gold had become local folklore. Everyone knew about it, and half of London had looked for it. There were all sorts of crazy theories about what he'd done with it. Over time, people gave up looking but the theories kept coming. Four years after Harry carked it, Cole's gold had become a...what's the term?"

"An urban legend?"

"Yeah, something like that."

"So, I'm guessing you have a theory of your own?"

"I do, and I reckon mine is sound."

"Go on."

"This old fella in the pub used to play dominoes with Harry. I don't think they were best mates or anything, but he knew Harry well enough to attend his funeral. He was wittering on about it, and I was half listening, but mainly wishing he'd just piss off. I was just about to down my pint and leave when he starts going on about how lovely the church bells were."

"Church bells? At a funeral?"

"Yeah, and not just a single bell, but the full works, like at a wedding."

"How odd."

"That's what I thought. I mentioned it to the old fella and apparently, Harry was into bell-ringing."

"Campanology."

"Eh?"

"People who study bells and bell-ringing are called campanologists."

"Right. Anyway, he said the bells were rung by some of Harry's fellow ringers, as a mark of respect I suppose. That got me thinking. If Harry was a regular bell ringer at the church, he'd have access to the bell tower — the perfect hiding place for something small, like a bar of gold. I doubt anyone would have reason to go in there very often, and it's not as though the old bill would raid a church is it? Think about it, doll."

Clement's tale sounds so plausible, I can't do anything other than think about it.

"But surely someone else would have made that connection?"

"We're talking about Cole's gold here. If somebody had found it, there's no way they'd have been able to keep it a secret. They'd have needed a fence to get rid of it, and all the fences I knew would never have kept their traps shut. There'd have been whispers around the manor, and everyone would have been talking about it within days. It would have been like finding Lord Lucan."

"Okay. So we just go to this church and somehow take a look around the belfry?"

"Ah, that's the only snag. I don't know which church."

"You didn't think to ask the old man?"

"By the time I'd made the connection, he'd already left the pub. I was planning on going back the next day to ask him."

"And why didn't you?"

"On account I was dead the next day," he replies matter-of-factly. "It was the same night I got whacked, in the alley."

In a split second, his plausibility is shattered.

"I do wish you wouldn't keep saying that."

"Saying what?"

"That you died. You do realise how ridiculous it sounds?"

"Says the woman who writes unbelievable tosh."

"What?"

"While I was watching TV last night, I found a notebook down the side of the sofa. Now, what was it, written on the front? *Novel Ideas & Concepts,* or something like that?"

"You had no right to read that," I snap.

"Bit touchy aren't we? To be frank, doll, the shit I read in that notebook was a damn sight more ridiculous than anything I've told you."

I feel my cheeks burn red. Partly in embarrassment, partly in anger. As my embarrassment is greater, I swallow the anger and move the conversation on.

"Can we get back to the plan?"

I hate losing an argument and I suspect Clement is taking pleasure in my defeat, his lips curling into a faint smile.

"Whatever you say, doll."

"There must be hundreds of churches in North London alone. Where do we even start?"

"I suppose we just hop on the tube to Camden, find the first church, and go through them one by one."

"Or we could use the Internet?"

"Second time you've mentioned it, but I still don't know what the hell you're talking about."

I delve into my handbag and pull out my phone. A quick search on Google maps reveals the magnitude of our task. I hold the phone up so Clement can see the screen.

"There's about a dozen churches in the Camden area."

Clement appears more interested in the phone than my revelation.

"You got a map on that thing?"

"Yes."

"And it's a camera, and a phone?"

"Yes."

"What else can it do?"

"All sorts. I can watch movies, listen to music, read a book."

He leans back in his seat. "That's just crazy, doll. There's not even any wires."

This feels like a conversation I had with my mother, a few months ago. She was trying to remember the name of the band who sung *Ventura Highway*. I opened Spotify on my phone, found the track, and played it, all within about thirty seconds. My dear mother thought it was some sort of witchcraft.

"Tell you what, Clement, If we find that gold I'll buy you one."

"And if we don't, no magic box of fuckery is gonna help either of us."

"Yes, right. So, do we just go through the churches one by one?"

"Guess so, unless that thing can tell us which ones have a bell tower, and which don't?"

"Actually, it might."

Clement shakes his head as if his comment was only meant in jest. I open the list below the map to view tiny thumbnail photos of each church.

"Well, we can strike at least half of them from our list as they're not traditional churches."

"Just the half dozen then," he grunts.

"It's not the number that worries me, Clement, it's how we're going to physically check the belfry of each one."

"Only one way, doll. We bullshit our way in."

"We lie to the priests?"

"Yeah, put it down to God's will."

I doubt God will see it that way but in lieu of not being able to ask him, I suppose I have no choice but to follow Clement's lead. That thought prompts a niggling concern: lying to members of the clergy probably won't be the worst thing we do today.

Forgive me, Father. I think I'm about to sin.

17

The train clacks to a standstill beneath the cavernous roof of Waterloo station.

Clement is already on his feet, standing in front of the carriage doors. I get up from my seat and join him. The doors hiss open and Clement takes one huge stride onto the platform. He turns to me as I step down from the carriage.

"Can you smell that, doll?" he asks as he sniffs the air.

To me, the air smells dirty but there's no discernible odour.

"Smell what?"

"The smell of London," he confirms proudly. "Greatest city on God's earth."

I'm not such a fan, but keep my opinion to myself. I've visited our capital city scores of times, but I've got mixed feelings about the place. Somehow, London feels bewilderingly vast, and yet claustrophobic at the same time. I know some people love the general hustle and bustle, but I hate the crowds, and I hate the constant din.

Despite my general ambivalence for our crowded capital, I visit fairly frequently because it also happens to house some of the best book shops on the planet. Amongst the noise and the dirt and the throngs of faceless humans, there are these calm oases. Quaint little shops, hidden away in back streets, and serving only those who have the desire to find them. To bibliophiles such as myself, those shops are like a peaceful corner of nirvana.

I doubt I'll be visiting any today, though.

Clement lifts his hand to the pocket of his waistcoat. I throw him a frown and his hand drops back to his side.

"I need a fag, doll, and something to eat. I think better on a full stomach."

I have no craving for nicotine, but my rumbling stomach reminds me I didn't eat anything for breakfast.

"Alright. We'll grab a bite to eat first."

We make our way along the never ending platform, Clement striding purposefully as I scurry along in his wake.

"Can you slow down a bit," I puff.

Clement comes to a halt and turns to me. "Sorry, doll. Wanna piggy-back?"

I assume he's joking, although the offer is tempting. He chuckles to himself and continues towards the ticket barriers at a slower pace.

We make our way through the barriers, with no great drama this time, and into the cathedral-like concourse.

This is the London I hate. I couldn't begin to estimate how many people occupy the vast space, but it's too many for my liking. Some are just loitering, others scampering across the tiled floor, hauling bags or dragging wheeled suitcases. Some people don't seem to know where they're going. Those that do aren't looking where they're going.

Clement chooses to join those who are loitering.

He stands with his hands on his hips, casting his gaze from left to right, high and low.

"Christ, this place has changed," he murmurs.

Dozens of shops and kiosks line the perimeter, and Clement studies the names, one by one.

"What's a...."

"Don't, Clement. Just don't."

"Suit yourself," he replies with shrug. "Where do you wanna eat then?"

There's no shortage of options.

"Starbucks. I could do with a caffeine boost."

It's my turn to lead and we carve our way through the crowd towards Starbucks. Unlike our earlier walk from the shop, no heads are turned by Clement's attire. Only in London would his bizarre outfit be deemed perfectly normal.

With Clement at my heels, we enter Starbucks and join the short queue.

"What do you want?" I ask.

"Do they do a full English?"

"No."

"Alright. I'll just have a couple of bacon sarnies then."

"This is not a greasy spoon, Clement. Can you please choose something they actually sell?"

Clement's eyes follow my finger as I point to the menu above the counter. He studies it for a moment, his face suggesting he's not enamoured with the choice of fare.

"What's pesto?"

"Just choose something you recognise."

"Ham and cheddar toastie then," he grumbles.

The queue edges forward and an enthusiastic young woman asks for our order.

"One ham and cheddar toastie. One tuna baguette. A medium Americano, and..."

"Clement. What do you want to drink?"

"They got Tizer?"

"No."

"Tea then."

I turn back to the young woman and confirm Clement's beverage choice. She taps away at the screen on the till and I pay with a credit card. I've got a horrible feeling it won't be the last time it leaves my purse today.

With Clement standing by the entrance like a nightclub bouncer, we mill around in silence for a few minutes until the young woman calls our order. I grab the tray, and a handful of sugar sachets, and we head upstairs to the seating area.

Typical of most coffee shops, the scene is a sea of ghostly faces fixed to a variety of digital devices.

I place the tray on the nearest empty table and take a seat. Clement falls onto the chair opposite, his attention focused on our fellow diners.

He eventually turns to me. "Reminds me of a movie I saw at the flicks once."

"Sorry?"

"*Night of the Living Dead.* You seen it?"

"Um, no, don't think I have."

"Look at them," he says, nodding his head towards a twenty-something couple sitting at a table against the far wall. Both are holding phones and staring blankly at the screens. The fact they're at the same table is the only reason you'd assume they're together.

"That's our digital society for you, Clement."

"Has everyone got one of those things then?"

"Yep."

He shakes his head as he removes the lid from his tea. Five sachets of sugar are deposited in the cup before he takes a sip.

"Can you hear that, doll?"

I pause for a second and listen. I don't hear anything untoward. "Hear what?"

"Fuck all, that's what I mean — nobody is talking. Every cafe I've ever been in, people sit and natter."

"Yes, well, people communicate in different ways now."

"What? You saying people don't talk?"

"No, it's just that people tend to say things using social media, or by texting."

"Well, whatever those things are, you're living like bleedin' zombies."

I let my gaze drift around the room. I guess Clement has a point.

We join the massed silence as we eat, sipping quietly at our overpriced drinks. Now Clement has mentioned it, the lack of conversation around us is hard to ignore. If it wasn't for the barely audible background music and the ambient noise from the station concourse, the silence would be uncomfortable.

A prolonged belch breaks through the muted atmosphere.

"Pardon me," Clement booms.

A dozen heads snap in our direction, accompanied by a chorus of loud tuts.

"Christ. They're alive," he adds.

Clement stands up and the dozen heads quickly snap back to their original position. It doesn't appear anyone is keen to challenge his lack of social grace.

My leather jacket suddenly feels like a cloak of shame.

I grab my handbag and dart towards the stairs, keeping my head low to avoid contact with the eyes following me.

My legs don't stop until I'm at least thirty yards across the concourse and partly hidden behind a ticket machine. Clement appears a few seconds later, and strolls across to my hiding place.

"You alright, doll? You need the lav?"

"No, Clement. I do not," I snap. "Nor do I need your appalling manners or embarrassing comments. What the hell were you thinking?"

"Wasn't thinking anything."

"No, you weren't. Wherever the hell you were dragged up, it's a shame they never taught you any manners. You're so uncouth."

"Calm down, doll. I was just trying to lighten the mood. That lot seemed like they could do with it."

In any other circumstance I'd have stormed off in a huff. Now, I have no choice but to front this out.

"Before we go any further, I want your word you'll behave yourself. Honestly, Clement, I'd expect that sort of behaviour from a ten year-old. Grow up will you."

My rant over, he stands motionless, staring down at me. I don't know him well enough to determine what's going on behind those blue eyes. Perhaps he's contemplating hell as an appealing alternative to my company. Or perhaps he's considering the various ways he'd like to kill me.

As the seconds pass, it dawns on me that antagonising this huge man was probably not wise, especially after witnessing the brutally efficient way he dealt with Messrs Black & Blue.

Maybe discretion is the better part of valour in this instance. I'm about to swallow my pride and apologise when a smile breaks on his face.

"You're a feisty little thing, ain't you?"

"Um, sometimes."

"You always get your own way?"

"Eh? No, it's nothing to do with getting my own way. I just..."

"Like everyone to dance to your tune?"

"No. That's not fair. I don't..."

"If you say so, doll," he interrupts, again. "I need a smoke."

Conversation over.

Clement turns and heads towards the nearest exit. He gets a dozen yards away before I follow.

The steps down from the concourse lead out to the rear of the station. It's almost as chaotic, with the added delight of suffocating fumes from the idling buses and taxis buzzing past every few seconds.

Clement leans up against a stone pillar, lights a cigarette and stares off into the distance. The view of a brick viaduct is nothing to write home about.

Time to offer that apology.

"I'm, um, sorry, Clement. I overstepped the mark."

He puffs a cloud of cigarette smoke into the air, and then looks down at me.

"No need, doll. You are who you are."

"Yes, well, I didn't mean to be so judgemental."

"Forget it. You weren't so far from the truth."

"Sorry?"

"I *was* dragged up. And when I wasn't being dragged, I was being kicked, shoved, or generally battered. Twelve years in boys' home might account for my uncouth behaviour."

Nicely handled, Beth. Real sensitive.

"I'm so sorry, Clement. I didn't think."

"Seems the way of the world now, from what I've seen. People talking too much without thinking, or thinking too much without talking."

He stamps his cigarette out on the floor and steps away from the pillar.

"And just so you know, I prefer the less talking option."

He turns and walks away.

18

I catch up with Clement and we make our way across the station concourse towards the Underground entrance. If I did offend him, he appears to have got over it pretty quickly as he hums a tune I don't recognise.

He also appears to have mastered the automatic barriers, and we pass seamlessly through the main ticket hall and down the escalator towards the Bakerloo Line platform. I assume it's the correct line for our destination, Camden, but my knowledge of the Underground is sketchy at best. All I can do is follow Clement as he bulldozes through the crowds.

For a woman of my diminutive stature, the Underground is usually a hellish experience, but this time I'm able to follow the path cleared by my bulky travel companion. However, the one aspect of travel on the London Underground I still have to suffer is the halitosis of hot, stale air that engulfs you at the bottom of the escalators. Within seconds I'm craving a shower and full body scrub.

As we descend the crowds thin and we're able to navigate our way through the tubular walkways down to the northbound platform, without the usual weekday stampede I've experienced on previous visits.

We're eventually spat out onto the platform alongside a gaggle of other passengers awaiting the next northbound train.

I follow Clement as he wanders twenty yards down the platform, passing a group of men in football shirts, a young couple holding hands, a family with two excitable kids, and numerous lone passengers who all look like they'd rather be somewhere else.

We find a few square yards of empty platform and Clement leans up against the wall, his thumbs hooked into his jean pockets. I take up a position alongside him.

A digital sign, hung from the curved ceiling, confirms the next train will arrive in four minutes.

No words are exchanged for a minute or so, until Clement makes a confession.

"I thought we'd make a slight detour before we go to Camden. Shouldn't take more than half hour."

"A detour to where exactly?"

"Not far. Somewhere special I visited a few times a month as a kid," he says solemnly. "Suppose you'd call it a place of refuge."

I assume he's talking about a church or maybe some quiet spot on the banks of the River Thames. Either way, I'm wary of saying the wrong thing again so I just agree with a nod. It's clear that Clement had a troubled childhood and perhaps this is an opportunity for some sort of closure.

With our detour confirmed, we both stare silently at the advertising posters opposite. I suspect neither of us has any great need for a budget flight to Amsterdam or a half-price colonic irrigation treatment.

Another minute passes and a low whine leaks from the tunnel, followed by a wave of warm air.

A flash of red zooms past followed by the red, white, and blue carriages. The train quickly loses speed and grinds to a halt with a set of red doors conveniently opening opposite our position.

We wait a moment for the departing passengers to clear the doors. Clement then takes three strides and stoops into the carriage before I've moved off the wall. Like a clingy child, I scuttle across the platform and join him. Unusually, there are seats available so we sit next to each other, opposite the young couple from the platform. With inadvertent eye contact near impossible to avoid, I hate the awkwardness of sitting directly opposite a stranger.

As the train pulls away, my concerns are eased as the couple stare longingly at each other, whispering in hushed tones. Clearly a couple in the exciting first throes of a new relationship.

Don't believe a word he says, girl. They're all full of crap.

I lower my gaze and keep my eyes fixed on my trainers.

We're about to make our third stop when Clement clambers to his feet.

"We need to change here," he says, as the train pulls into Piccadilly Circus.

Both the platform and walkways are much busier than Waterloo and I struggle to keep up with Clement. We follow the signs for the Piccadilly Line and emerge onto the crowded platform for northbound trains. Both the heat and the tight crowd contribute to my growing sense of claustrophobia. Clement, on the other hand, seems at home as he casually casts his gaze above the sea of heads.

Although the digital sign suggested it would only be a two minute wait, I'm sure an entire hour passes before our train arrives.

Ignoring the poor souls trying to escape the carriages, the crowd shuffles towards the doors. Clement is standing a few feet to my right, nobody keen to invade his personal space. I feel like half of London is pressed up against me, with somebody's hot breath on my neck, and a clumsy idiot stepping on my foot. Unsurprisingly, no apology follows.

Like herded cattle, we eventually squeeze into the carriage and I try to force my way across the packed aisle towards Clement.

A thirty-something guy in a cheap suit takes umbrage at my efforts to pass, and stands his ground.

"You want to get in my pocket?" he barks, scowling down at me.

"Sorry, I just need to get to the far doors."

"Tough. You'll just have to wait," he snaps back.

A low, rumbling voice passes over my head.

"Oi, dickhead. Let the lady through."

I crane my neck and spot Clement's face beyond the man's shoulder. It's not what I would call a happy face.

The man in the suit, clearly agitated, turns to challenge his aggressor. His challenge is short-lived once he identifies the owner of the voice, and he shuffles to his left, allowing me to pass.

I squeeze past and offer him a smile, or more a smirk if I'm honest. "Thank you."

He doesn't smile back.

Two more passengers step out of my way without a word. Clement is standing with his right arm raised, holding on to the ceiling rail. I position myself next to him, directly under his armpit. It's not the most fragrant of havens but I'll take it.

He looks down at me and winks.

I've always believed it's perfectly acceptable for a father to wink at his young children. But men winking at women sits somewhere between sad and creepy. I can't put my finger on the reason why, but I didn't find Clement's wink to be either sad or creepy. Without thinking about it, I smile back at him.

The train rattles through the darkness and we stop at several stations. Some of the names I recognise: Leicester Square, Covent Garden, and King's Cross. Others, I don't think I've ever passed through, let alone visited.

As more stations come and go, so does the number of passengers in our carriage. By the time we depart from Holloway Road station, there are even a handful of empty seats.

"Shall we sit down?" I ask.

"We're getting off at the next stop."

Barely a minute later, the platform of our destination station fills the windows.

"Ready, doll?"

I nod as the doors open.

Whatever sacrilegious site he's come to pay homage to, Clement is obviously keen to get there. I have to gallop along behind him to keep pace as we navigate another series of walkways and escalators towards the exit. We're in such a hurry, I don't even notice the name of the station, not that it matters as I'm well beyond the parts of London I know.

We eventually exit the station onto a residential street that isn't too dissimilar to the one I live on. Clement pauses for a moment and slowly looks up and down the street, seemingly reacquainting himself with the area.

"It's just a few minutes away."

"What is?"

"You'll see."

He turns to his left and strides away.

We get barely thirty yards before I have to call out to him.

"Can you slow down? Please."

He stops and waits for me to catch up.

"Sorry, doll."

We continue at a more leisurely pace, past rows of Victorian terraced houses. Clement shows a passing interest in a few of the cars parked on the street, occasionally slowing to stare through the windows. I'm not sure what his fascination is, and like each of the cars, the street itself is nondescript, ordinary. We could just as easily be in Liverpool or Leicester as London.

We stroll along in silence. I don't think Clement is one for small talk, and that suits me. Although our surroundings are ordinary, I can't ignore the niggling fact that my reason for being here is extraordinary. This time yesterday I was busy in the shop with customers. I thought all my problems were behind me. Now, I'm wandering through the back streets of London, on some ridiculous quest, with the oddest of strangers for company.

I've read some outlandish plots in my time, but now it seems I'm living one.

After several hundred yards of what feels like aimless traipsing, we cross the road and turn into another residential street. The road sign, fixed to the side wall of a house on the corner, tells me we're now in Avenell Road. Utterly meaningless to me.

We pass more terraced houses, and just as I'm about to ask how much further, Clement breaks into a jog. The paving slabs between us increase as he jogs further away. Twenty yards. Thirty yards. Forty yards.

He stops. So do I, primarily because Clement's mood has changed. His hands are clamped to his head, and he's yelling obscenities. For the first time since he barged into my life yesterday evening, he's displaying some emotion. Clearly something has upset him, but as there isn't another soul on the street, it's obviously not a person.

I tentatively move forward to within twenty yards, and his mood changes again. He appears to have spent his initial anger and his head is now stooped, his hands on his hips.

I move closer.

"Clement? What's wrong?"

He keeps his head bowed and slowly shakes it.

I'm only a couple of feet away when he finally looks up at me.

"What the hell happened here?"

I look around, trying to identify what he could possibly be talking about. To my left there are just more terraced houses. To my right there's a railed fence with a gate opening onto the communal gardens of what looks like an apartment block.

"I don't know what you mean, Clement."

He suddenly turns and darts across the road. Once he reaches the other side, his hands return to his head and he stares up at the facade of the apartment block.

I let out a sigh and slowly cross the road, trying to suppress my growing agitation. I sidle up to him and follow his gaze.

The front facade of the apartment block is part brick, part stone; very much in the Art Deco style. Standing opposite, I'm able to gauge the full scale of the building, and it's huge, stretching at least a hundred yards down the street. I'm still none the wiser as to what Clement's problem is.

"What is it? Is this the place you were talking about?"

He doesn't answer, but points up at a series of large red letters, fixed to the stone part of the building — EAST STAND.

I realise what I'm looking at.

"Ohh, this used to be a football ground?"

"No, doll. This was *the* football ground."

He strides off down the street without further explanation. I trudge after him for another forty yards until he stops again. He looks up at the building and I mirror his action. More red letters - ARSENAL STADIUM.

At some point last year, I unearthed a book about the Highbury Stadium from one of the charity shop boxes. It actually sold pretty quickly, to one of my regular customers. I know this because he bored me witless on the subject the next time he came in.

The house behind us has a two-foot high wall to the front, separating it from the pavement. Clement perches himself on the edge and stares up at the former home of Arsenal Football Club.

"When did it die?" he asks, his voice low.

"Die? What are you on about?"

"The club. Arsenal. When did it die?"

"It didn't. They moved to a new stadium."

"There's still a club? A team?"

"Yes, not far from here I believe. This building is actually listed, which is why they converted it into apartments rather than knocking it down."

He shakes his head and mumbles to himself.

I can feel my irritation bubbling below the surface. This isn't what I had in mind when I agreed to this detour.

"When you said you wanted to visit a place of refuge, I thought you meant a church or something. I didn't realise you wanted to reminisce over a bloody football ground."

Clement turns to face me, clearly riled. "Listen, doll. I've said more prayers and offered more thanks in that stadium, than any bleedin' church. Shit, it *was* my church, for almost thirty years, man and boy."

"Yes, well, it is just a football club though. I don't understand why you're so upset about it."

The moment the words leave my mouth, I'm already wishing I could retract them.

"Don't get it, do you, doll?" he growls. "It's not just a football club, not to me, anyway. The other fans, they were my family, and the terraces were more of a home than the house I grew up in."

I've think I've just put my foot in it again.

"Sorry," I mumble.

My irritation gives way to guilt. No matter how ridiculous this whole episode may be, and despite Clement's questionable motives, I really need to work with this guy.

Clement puffs his cheeks and closes his eyes. I resist the urge to say anything else and wait for him to speak.

It takes almost a minute.

186

"That's twice in the last hour," he says, his voice now calm.

"Twice what?"

"You've had to apologise."

"Fair point. I'm afraid sometimes I don't think before I open my mouth."

"You're not alone there, doll. But in my experience, you achieve more by keeping your mind open and your mouth closed."

Noted.

"I know, and I'm sorry. There's your hat trick."

A rueful smile breaks on his face. "Last hat trick this place will ever see."

We sit in silence for a few minutes. I'd love to know what Clement is thinking, but I daren't ask. Probably best to let him work through his memories while I try to fathom out why he's so willing to put up with me.

In the end, I decide a conciliatory gesture might be in order.

"I think we can look at the grounds, through that gate, if you wanted to?"

The moustache receives a stroke or two.

"Nah. You're alright, doll. Think it'd break my heart to see it now."

"Sure?"

He stands and takes a final glance at the building. "Yeah, let's get going."

19

My record is four days.

Boyfriend number four, Stuart, once forgot to record Coronation Street, despite two reminders. I didn't speak to him for four days. There have been countless other occasions where I've sent a boyfriend to Coventry after an argument. Once you get past the first hour, it's surprisingly easy to keep it up. I see it as a point of principle — he who has sinned, shall be ignored, at least until I've calmed down.

For this reason, I am intrigued by Clement's ability to move on so easily after a disagreement.

Despite my efforts to bitch him out, he is currently humming a tune as we walk back toward the tube station. No hint of latent resentment, no snide comments, and no period of enforced silence. He just draws a line, and moves on. I have to admit it's an admirable quality, and one I wish I could adopt.

"What's that tune?" I ask.

"It's called *Wielder of Words*."

"Never heard of it."

"It's by some band I used to do a bit of minding for, back in the late sixties. They gave me a copy of their first album as a thank you."

"The late sixties?"

He looks down at me, and without a flicker of hesitation, repeats himself. "Yeah. The late sixties."

I'm sure he's not lying, but he's patently not telling the truth either. Either way, I'm curious enough to look past his claim.

"What does minding a band involve then?"

"A lot of hanging around pubs and clubs, doing sod all until some drunken dickhead in the audience decides they've heard enough. The money was shit 'cos they were always skint, and soon as they started making a few quid, they hired proper security."

"Any bands I might have heard of?"

"Doubt it. They were all fairly small time. Some of them did okay though, one or two even got into the charts, but The Stones and The Beatles they weren't."

He lights a cigarette and pulls a deep drag. "Better than the shit I heard on your radio, though."

I can't argue with him.

By the time we reach the tube station, Clement has sucked the life out of his cigarette and flicks the butt into the gutter.

"You can get a fine for that, you know?"

"For what? Flicking a fag end?"

"Yes. I think it's sixty pounds if you get caught."

"Gotta catch me though, don't they? And if I'm good at anything, it's breaking rules and not getting caught."

That's a statement I can well believe.

We descend back into the Underground and down to the southbound platform.

"How far is it to Camden?" I ask as we wait.

"We take the line down to King's Cross, then hop on the Northern Line to Camden Town. Fifteen minutes I guess."

A minute later we're sitting on the train to King's Cross, watching the standing passengers wobble gently back and forth to the motion of the carriage. Even if I felt like a chat with Clement, it's too noisy, and there are too many people within earshot. While I'm willing to humour him, I don't think I could bear the embarrassment of anyone else overhearing his outlandish anecdotes, let alone his outdated views on certain subjects.

We arrive at King's Cross within six minutes and make our way through the crowds towards the Northern Line platform.

For the first time since we arrived in London, Clement appears to have lost his bearings.

"This is nothing like I remember," he grumbles.

"When were you last here?"

"Not sure. October '75 I suppose."

Let it pass, Beth. Let it pass.

"It's like a different station now," he adds.

"It probably is a different station. I'd imagine there's been a lot of changes here over the years, not least because of the fire."

"What fire?"

I point to two slate plaques, fixed to the wall across the walkway. Clement squints as he tries to read them, but apparently can't. He wanders over to take a closer look and I join him.

"There was a huge fire here, in the late eighties. How can you not have heard about it? It caused a lot of damage, and as you can see, cost thirty-odd people their lives."

He looks down at the lower plaque, listing the names of all the victims.

"Shit."

"And, Clement, can you guess how the fire started?"

"No idea."

"Somebody lit a cigarette and dropped the match on the escalator. It slipped through a gap and set fire to all the rubbish below. That's why you can no longer smoke down here."

"Seems you can't smoke anywhere, doll."

"And for good reason. Can we get on now?"

He presses his fingers against the top plaque and lowers his head a fraction. "Yeah."

Following the signs, we find our way to the Northern Line platform. Another crowd, another crush, and my craving for a shower surpasses the level usually reserved for camping weekends.

I'm grateful the journey to Camden Town is only five minutes, albeit five long minutes. However, I'm conscious it's already early afternoon, and we haven't achieved anything. I'm not convinced we're likely to, but even the cynic in me can't ignore the sliver of chance that Clement might not be leading us on a wild goose chase. It's madness, of course, but I suspect most people would be willing to search a few haystacks for such a valuable needle.

I'm no exception.

We exit the station into muted sunshine and the hustle of Camden High Street. Just an ordinary Saturday afternoon on a fairly ordinary High Street. There are plenty of people around, some even more ridiculously dressed than Clement. I've been to Camden twice before: once to see a Kings of Leon gig at the Electric Ballroom, and once to visit a book dealer. Both my previous visits proved worthwhile, and I desperately need that run to continue.

"Where shall we start?"

Clement looks up and down the road, frowning.

"Don't recognise much."

"Maybe you will, as we wander around. Where do you think we should start?"

"You're the one with the magic map, doll."

"Right, yes."

I pull my phone out and open the Google Maps app. My previous search is still on the screen and I wait for our location to update.

"First contender is only a few minutes away, in that direction," I say, nodding to our right.

Clement sweeps his arm out to indicate I should lead on. "After you, ma'am," he says mockingly. "You can tell me your plan on the way."

"Plan?"

"To get into the bell tower."

"That's my responsibility now, is it?"

"Yeah. It's called delegation."

"I'll think about it."

I plod ahead and we make barely forty yards when Clement stops abruptly. He turns to the building on our right; one of the two places I've visited in Camden.

"It's still here," he says excitedly, looking up at The Electric Ballroom.

As legendary music venues go, it's a pretty understated building: mid-terrace, three storeys high, and the Victorian brickwork painted black.

"You know The Electric Ballroom?" I ask.

"No, but this place used to be called The Carousel. I had some crazy nights in there, doll."

"Right. I had a pretty crazy night myself in there too, a few years back."

I intended my response to sound nonchalantly cool. I failed. It sounded lame, even to me.

Clement turns to face me, his eyebrows arched. "Really? Who'd you see?"

"Kings of Leon."

"Any good?"

"They were fantastic. Do you like anything of theirs? *Sex on Fire*? *Use Somebody*?"

Step into my trap, Clement.

"Never heard of them."

"Oh."

Foiled again.

"Who did you see here then?" I ask.

"Christ, dozens of acts, but I was pretty wasted most of the time. I remember some, though. Led Zeppelin was a top night."

"Gosh, that must have been quite something?"

"Yeah, it was, and then there was Wings, with Paul McCartney, the bloke from The Beatles."

"Yes, Clement, I know who Paul McCartney is."

"Is he..."

"Yes, he's still alive. Unfortunately, the same can't be said for John Lennon or George Harrison, I'm afraid. Ringo Starr is still around though, but he doesn't seem to do much these days."

"Sounds about right," Clement huffs. "Seems some things don't change."

We both stare up at the building for a moment, reflecting on our respective memories, and then walk on.

We pass Camden Market and Clement slows his pace, studying the wares on offer. He stops to inspect a leather jacket and the stall holder, a middle-aged woman in a hijab headscarf and full-length dress, approaches him.

"Very nice," she says, gesturing at the jacket.

Clement appraises the woman for a few seconds. A sudden sense of panic engulfs me.

"How much is it darlin'?" he says.

"To you, my love, just seventy quid," she replies in a strong London accent.

For a man who claims not to have any money, he ponders her answer a little too long.

"You mind if I ask you a question?" he eventually says.

Oh, Jesus.

Would it be inappropriate to run away at this point? I won't discount it as an option just yet.

"Why are you dressed in that garb?" he asks.

"Garb?" she replies, puzzled.

"Yeah, the scarf and the dress, like an Arab."

This could go one of two ways.

"I'm a Muslim," she replies, thankfully with a smile.

"Right, ta. I'll have a think about the jacket."

He gives her a nod and walks away. The woman turns her attention to another prospect browsing the rails.

I skip up alongside him. "What was that all about?"

"Nothing. Just curious about that woman's garb. I thought it was some sort of fashion statement."

"Why on earth would you think that?"

"Take a look around, doll. Loads of woman wearing something similar. Never saw it in my day."

I glance up the road, and he's right. But with London being so multi-cultural, it's not something I consciously notice, or give any thought to.

"Well, you're lucky she didn't take offence."

"Not every bird is as uptight as you, doll."

I stop dead in my tracks and grab his arm. "What's that supposed to mean?"

He looks down at my hand, still fixed to his forearm. A quick stare over the top of his sunglasses is all it takes for me to remove my hand.

"Just an observation, doll. Shall we get on with finding this church?"

I throw him a frown before consulting my phone.

"Next turning on the right."

We walk in silence down Buck Street.

Our first target is the Trinity United Reformed Church, at the end of Buck Street and on the corner of Kentish Town Road. It takes barely half a minute to locate.

I'm no expert on architecture, but the brick-built church looks sternly Victorian. The masonry and brickwork are heavily soiled with a layer of carbon residue, courtesy of the busy road on which the church sits. If I were to imagine a quaint, picturesque church for my dream wedding day, this one would be about the furthest I could get from it.

We cross the road, and from the pavement opposite, stare up at the church roof for evidence of any bells.

"I can't see anything that looks like a belfry, can you?"

"Nah. It's too modern, I think."

"Shall we cross this one off the list then?"

"Yeah. Where's the next one?"

I check the map, and the location of our next target. "St Michael's. Not far from here."

We head up Kentish Town Road, past a number of independent shops that probably can't afford the rent on Camden High Street. Many of them look as down on their luck as Baxter's Books.

We take a left turn into Camden Road and quickly cover the few hundred yards to St Michael's.

First impressions don't bode well. The same style of architecture and the same grubby facade as the last church. Another contender for the church I'd least like to get married in. However, there does appear to be a bell, set in an alcove just below the roof ridge.

"Don't look like you'd need a bell ringer for that," Clement remarks.

"I think you might be right."

"There's a first."

"What?"

"You think I'm right about something."

I ignore his comment.

"I think we should go and check, just to be sure."

There's no entrance on the front elevation so we head down the left flank of the church, and find the main door set within an imposing stone archway. The door is wide open so we step inside.

I'd guess I've probably been in a few dozen churches over the years, and I have to admit they all look the same to me. St

Michael's appears to follow the same template as every other church, with rows of wooden pews to the left and the right, and a central aisle leading up to the altar. The still air is tinged with the familiar scent of aged paper, probably from the dozens of bibles and hymn books tucked behind the pews.

We edge across the stone floor towards the aisle, the silence a stark contrast to the noise beyond the thick walls.

"These places give me the willies," Clement whispers.

"Ironic, considering your claim."

He's about to argue my point when a door creaks open, somewhere off in the far left corner.

The sound of footsteps echo through the quiet and a figure appears from beyond one of the stone columns.

"Can I help you?"

The priest is young, certainly younger than me. He has the same butterscotch-coloured hair as Karl, although it's neatly trimmed and clearly more familiar with a hairbrush than Karl's mop.

"Oh, hi, yes...hopefully you can," I stammer.

The priest offers a patient smile, waiting for me to expand. A thousand words flutter through my mind like confetti, but my mouth is unable to collate enough of them to produce a coherent sentence.

"We...um..."

"We wanna get hitched," Clement interjects.

I turn and look up at him in disbelief.

"Don't we, doll?" he adds, smiling down at me.

Damn you, Clement.

"Yes, we want to get married," I confirm through gritted teeth.

The young priest must meet some fairly odd couples in his line of work. His expression suggests we might be the oddest, but he does a reasonable job of sounding sincere.

"Congratulations to you both. And were you hoping to get married here at St Michael's?"

"Yeah, maybe," Clement says. "But my fianceé here is dead keen on having a traditional wedding with all the trimmings. You know, choir, flowers, massive organ, and bells — definitely lots of church bells."

Clement places a hand on my shoulder and grins at me. "You just love a good ding-dong, don't you, doll?"

"Yes, love it," I laugh nervously.

The priest's face washes with relief, as if he's just plucked the *Get out of Jail* card in a game of Monopoly.

"That's a pity. We only have a single bell here, I'm afraid."

Clement frowns. "Ahh, that's a bitch. Still, suppose it saves you hiring bell ringers?"

"Erm, yes. The warden usually rings it."

"Well, thank you anyway, Father," I hurriedly interrupt. "We'll leave you in peace."

I turn to leave but apparently Clement hasn't finished. "Wait one sec, doll."

He throws a final question at the priest. "Father, are there any other churches locally that have a full set of bells?"

There must be times when a priest really wishes they could tell the odd white lie. I think this is one such instance.

"I've not been here long so I don't know all the local churches that well," he offers. "But you might want to try All Saints, or maybe St Jude's in Kentish Town. I think they're probably the closest."

"Cheers, Father. And I'm sorry we can't get hitched here, but Beth here is a demanding girl, used to getting her own way."

I suspect Clement's closing statement was followed by a wink. I don't know because I'm already cringing my way back down the aisle.

I continue through the doorway and don't stop until I'm back on the pavement at the front of the church. Clement appears a few seconds later, smiling as he approaches me.

"That didn't go too badly. Least we know where to go next."

I have other concerns.

"Did you have to embarrass me like that?" I snap.

"Eh?"

"Why did you tell him we were getting married?"

The smile is gone. "Oh, I'm sorry," he says sarcastically. "But you were standing mumbling like an idiot, so I had to say something."

"You could have said something more believable. Honestly, Clement, that was humiliating."

He reaches for his chest pocket and pulls out the crumbled cigarette packet. After a peek inside, he crushes the packet in his hand.

"Fucking great. What a time to run out of fags."

"Maybe this is a good time to give them up," I venture.

"You know what I'd like to give up, doll? *This*. You're doing my bleedin' nut in."

"What have I done?"

"You never stop whinging. If you won the pools, you'd complain about the cost of the stamp to send the coupon in."

"That's not fair."

"Ain't it? For somebody who needs help, you're pretty bloody ungrateful. Honestly, doll, do you think I really wanna be schlepping around town with a prissy-knickered brat?"

Ouch.

This isn't an argument I can win. Actually, this isn't an argument I really want to win. I shouldn't care what he thinks of me, but I can't deny his words don't sting, and I'm not keen on hearing any more. What is it they say? Truth hurts?

I think it might be better to sidestep this one.

"Um, can I buy you some more cigarettes?"

I hope Clement's need for nicotine is greater than his pride.

"Yeah, ta," he eventually sighs. "But if we're gonna carry on with this, you've gotta drop the attitude, doll. Clear?"

I offer a feeble smile. "I'll try."

Game, set, and match to Clement.

20

True to its name, there's a convenience store directly opposite the church. We cross the road and Clement follows me in.

A sour faced woman with bottle-blonde hair is standing idle behind the counter, picking at her nails.

"A pack of Marlboro please."

Without a word, she turns to slide the door across the cigarette cabinet behind her. I can almost sense Clement's mind questioning why the cigarettes aren't on open display. He doesn't ask though.

A pack of Marlboro are slapped on the counter.

"£10.50, please," she says wearily.

"How much?" we both choke in unison.

"£10.50. If you want to save fifty pence, go to a supermarket."

I pull a twenty pound note from my purse and begrudgingly hand it over. The price some people are prepared to pay for their addiction.

I take my change and grab the pack from the counter. "Thank you."

The woman returns to her nail picking.

We step back outside and I pass the cigarettes to Clement.

"More than ten quid for a packet of smokes?" he grumbles. "Un-fucking-believable."

"You're telling me. You'd better smoke those sparingly because I'm not made of money."

He removes the cellophane wrap and examines the packet, specifically the picture of a diseased lung on the front.

"What the hell is that? Looks like a Scotsman's breakfast."

"It's a smoker's lung. I think it's supposed to deter you from smoking."

He shrugs his shoulders and lights up a cigarette. "Didn't work."

With Clement puffing away, I check the location of the two churches the priest suggested.

"All Saints is a fifteen minute walk, and St Jude's six minutes on from there."

"Alright. Let's get going then."

I double-check our route, which is fairly straightforward, and we set off in a northerly direction along Camden Road.

For the first few minutes we walk in silence, but I'm keen to avoid any more of Clement's little surprises and question the specifics of our plan.

"So, how are we going to get into the belfry?" I ask.

"Thought you'd have come up with something by now."

"Erm, I'm still thinking."

"No need. We'll use the marriage line again."

"Do we have to?"

"Can you think of any other reason a bloke and a woman would want to chat to a priest?"

I can't, and my expression gives me away.

"It's easy enough, doll. We chat to the priest, and I'll ask to use the lav. You keep him occupied so I can take a look around."

"Will that give you enough time? There's only so long I can keep him chatting for."

"Maybe you can do a confession while you're there. That'll keep him busy."

"I doubt it. I'm a good girl, Clement."

"Yeah, thought as much," he snorts. "Anyway, how many places are there to hide something in a bell tower? It's just four walls and the wooden parts that hold the bells in place."

"Okay. If you're sure."

"I'll be in and out in five minutes."

We continue along Camden Road, passing an eclectic range of independent shops, restaurants, takeaways, coffee shops, and a surprising number of estate agents. The one consistent is the traffic; a never ending stream of vehicles pumping exhaust fumes in our direction. I do wonder whether, if people could actually see pollution, like a cloud of red smog, they'd be so ambivalent about it.

I'm dragged from my environmental concerns when Clement stops abruptly outside a Thai restaurant.

"What's the matter?" I ask.

"This was it," he gasps. "The pub where Harry Cole used to drink."

"Really? You sure?"

"Yeah, hundred percent. Can't believe it's a bloody chinky now."

"It's actually Thai, and that's another word you probably shouldn't say."

"Chinky?"

"Correct."

"Right. Sorry."

His apologetic response surprises me, especially after the last time I corrected his use of politically incorrect language. We appear to be making progress.

Clement then turns and surveys our surroundings as if he's looking for something.

"What's so interesting?" I ask.

"It was over there I think. The alley."

"What alley?"

"*The* alley, doll."

So much for progress.

"Oh, the alley where you...died?"

No answer. He continues to stare off into the distance.

I wait a long moment for him to answer. "Yeah. Sounds like bullshit when you say it, though."

"Does it? Sorry."

"Don't apologise, doll. I know how it sounds and I wouldn't believe me either."

He blows out a lungful of air and turns back to the pavement ahead of us.

"Let's get out of here. It's making my balls itch."

He takes a few strides and I gallop up beside him. I don't have anything to say in response to his itchy balls so I wait for him to speak again. It doesn't take long.

"You know what I find odd, doll? You don't believe what I said about being whacked, and I get why, yet here we are — you and me, strolling through the streets of London looking for a gold bar that hasn't been seen for decades."

"Okay. And your point is?"

"Blind faith."

"Sorry?"

"When the reward is big enough, people are prepared to believe anything. It's a bit like religion, I suppose."

"What do you mean?"

"People who believe in God. You're promised eternal life and all that jazz, and despite there being absolutely no reason to believe any of it, people do."

"Never thought of it like that."

"So, is that what you have, doll? Blind faith?"

"Um, I guess so."

"Not the same as trust though, is it?"

This is getting a little deep, and uncomfortable.

"Where are you going with this, Clement?"

"Nowhere. Just passing the time."

I have no interest in pursuing this subject and check the map on my phone.

"We take a right turn, about fifty yards ahead."

Clement nods and we continue onwards.

We turn into Murray Street and it's a far cry from the urban sprawl of Camden Road. It's a wide avenue lined with grand, semi-detached townhouses, painted a variety of pastel shades.

"Some money round here, doll."

"All Saints is just around the corner, so let's hope so."

We turn left and the scenery becomes greener. There's a small park to our right, dotted with mature trees and planted borders. Beyond the wrought iron railings, a handful of the local residents are taking advantage of the open space: a father and his young son kicking a plastic football, a couple sitting chatting beneath a tree, and a few loners perched on benches, reading.

"According to the map, the church is at the end of this road."

Nerves arrive, and I'm now that little girl again, standing at the top of the water flume and staring down a dark hole. I have the same fears about what comes next, but circumstances dictate I have no option but to face those fears. The only difference is I have a man at my side this time, rather than one waiting at the end with a towel.

"You alright, doll?"

"I'm okay," I mumble with little conviction.

"You don't look it. You shitting yourself?"

"A little nervous maybe."

"Don't be. What's the worst thing that could happen?"

"I dread to think. I'm a terrible liar and I'm worried the priest will see right through me."

"Don't lie then. Just play a part."

"Eh?"

"Think of your favourite film, your favourite actor. They're just pretending to be somebody else. Roger Moore pretends to be James Bond in *Live and Let Die*. Sophia Loren pretends to be

Anna Jesson in *Brief Encounter*. You're just playing a part in there, doll."

It's not the worst bit of advice I've ever received. I've spent most of my adult life acting out my role as a bride-in-waiting, so it won't be that much of a stretch. It's a shame the role of an actual bride has always eluded me.

"Thank you, Clement."

"Anytime."

We reach the end of the wrought iron railings, and the spire of All Saints Church comes into view beyond a cluster of trees.

With my heart beating a little faster, we turn into a narrow lane and pass under the lychgates.

Clearly much older than the two Victorian churches we visited earlier, All Saints is far more in keeping with the sort of church I'd want to be married in. Beyond the softer architecture, the walls are constructed of sandy-coloured blocks and intricately carved stonework, rather than carbon-stained brick. Most impressive of all is the bell tower, with a black and gold clock face positioned just below the belfry.

It's a beautiful little church, and we are not the only ones there to admire it.

"Shit. Who are this lot?" Clement grumbles.

He's referring to a group of a few dozen people, loitering just outside the main doors. Tailored suits, hats, and some gorgeous dresses — the attire of choice for wedding guests.

"It's Saturday, so I guess it's a wedding."

"Great. Guess we're gonna have to wait till they've cleared off."

"Let's sit down. My feet are killing me," I say, pointing to a bench in front of the stout holly hedge, screening the church from the road.

We cross a patch of scrubby grass and sit down.

From our position we have a clear view of the main doors, some thirty yards away. The crowd are all facing the doors, chatting and laughing as they presumably wait for the bride and groom to make their grand exit as husband and wife.

On cue, the bells begin to toll.

"Well, that's one thing we know for sure," I shout. "They definitely employ bell ringers."

Clement rolls his eyes and shuffles across the bench so we can hear each other above the chimes.

"Yeah, and let's hope this is where Harry Cole did his thing."

We sit back and wait.

Amongst the greenery, it feels good to be away from the noise and the grime of central London. I still feel filthy, and my feet are throbbing, but our unplanned break is welcome.

I tip my head back and close my eyes, the sun's tepid rays warming my face. My heart rate slows, and as I try to put all my worries to the back of my mind, I begin to relax a little.

I should have known better.

"Bloody hell. Doll, did you see that?"

My head snaps forward and I squint at Clement.

"What? What is it?"

"You didn't see them?"

"See who?"

"The groom and the best man. They walked out of the church and..." His voice drops to almost a whisper. "They only kissed each other, doll. A proper, full-on kiss."

He turns to face the church doors and points, open mouthed. "Look! They're at it again. What the hell is the bride gonna make of that? And why is everyone cheering?"

"Clement, there is no bride," I chuckle.

"What? It's not a wedding?"

"No, it's a wedding, but there's no bride. And that's not the best man, it's the groom. I don't know if there's a specific term but both men are grooms."

"I don't get it."

"They're a gay couple."

"Poofs? Getting married? No way."

"Yes, way, and don't use that word. It's offensive."

"Jesus wept," he groans. "Who gets to decide which words are offensive nowadays?"

"Typically, people on Twitter."

"Who?"

"It's complicated."

He shakes his head. "What do you call them now then? You know...men who prefer a bit of cock?"

His terminology throws me for a second. I can't decide if it's offensive, or just brutally factual.

"Erm, nothing. They're just men who happen to be gay. It's no big deal, Clement, and neither is the fact those two have just got married, so stop staring."

Clement's earlier words, about playing a part, clatter to the front of my mind. If he himself is putting on an act, his shock at seeing the couple kiss was worthy of an Oscar. He did appear genuinely shocked.

He continues to stare at the happy couple, now surrounded by well-wishers, smiling and swapping kisses.

"Clement, you're still staring. Have you never seen a gay couple before?"

"Jesus, doll, course I've seen poof....sorry, gays before," he fires back. "I lived in London, not in bleedin' ignorance. Some of the blokes I did jobs for were gay — suppose that's why they hired me. Some folks weren't so tolerant of gays back then, and they dished out a shitload of grief. Maybe that's why the closet seemed a safer option."

"Okay. It's just you seem a little shocked."

"Not shocked, just surprised how normal this all seems to everyone. It's like blokes have always married other blokes, as if it's nothing new."

"I guess it's not really new, well, not in this country."

Clement doesn't answer and we sit in silence as the crowd sees the couple to an awaiting car. With the two grooms on their way, the guests quickly follow. Within five minutes we're alone in the church grounds.

Knowing our challenge is now imminent, my nerves return.

"I suppose we should head on in then?" I sigh.

"Not yet. Need to wait for the bell ringers to leave. Can't really check the place out if they're still messing around with their bells."

"Of course. Good point."

It's only postponing the inevitable but I'll take another five minutes of sitting here doing nothing. Clement appears equally content just to sit in silence and soak up our surroundings.

The minutes tick by and my nerves get the better of me. I feel compelled to distract myself with small talk.

"Where in London did you live, Clement?"

"Grew up in a boys' home, Kentish Town way."

"That's where St Luke's is, isn't it?"

"Yeah."

I don't think Clement really wants to chat, but I persist.

"Can't have been much fun, growing up in a boys' home."

"Not really."

"If you don't mind me asking, why didn't they find you a foster home, or a family to adopt you?"

"They did try, but somebody messed things up for me."

"Who?"

"Adolf Hitler."

"Hitler? What did he do?"

"Directly, nothing. Indirectly, the second world war kicking off when I was a nipper didn't help."

"You grew up during the war?"

"Told you. I was born in 1935, so yeah."

"What was it like?"

He turns to face me. "Are you shittin' me? What do you think it was like?"

"Sorry. I'm just curious."

He runs a hand through his hair and stares up at the clock tower. My nerves build, but not so much I want to question Clement any further.

Another minute passes and he puffs his cheeks out, exhaling a long breath. Keeping his gaze fixed on the church, he mumbles two words.

"Tommy Baker."

"I'm sorry?"

"Tommy Baker. He was my best mate at school."

"Okay," I reply hesitantly, unsure where he's going with this.

"It was his seventh or eighth birthday, can't remember which. His mum organised a party at their house and Tommy invited every boy in our class — except me."

"I thought he was your best mate?"

"He was, but his mum didn't like me — thought I was a bad influence on him. She didn't want me at Tommy's party."

"That's harsh."

"Maybe. Anyway, I remember the day of the party. All the boys in our class were excited, talking about it all bleedin' day. I sat at the back of the classroom and just kept my head down. Didn't talk, didn't listen. Shed a few tears though, couldn't help it."

I feel a lump bob in my throat.

"The moment the bell rang, I was out of that classroom like a rat up a drainpipe. Couldn't stomach hearing any more about the bloody party. I went back to the boys' home and picked a fight with one of the toughest kids there. He gave me a right battering; only stopped when an air-raid siren went off."

"Jesus, Clement. Why?"

"Distraction. Better to feel the pain of a good hiding than feeling sorry for myself about Tommy's party."

"I honestly don't know what to say."

"Some things happen for a good reason, doll."

"How so?"

"I was gonna bunk off school the next day but I was on a final warning. I was a pretty bright kid and didn't mind school. Certainly didn't wanna get kicked out. So, I walked in the next morning, thinking how I'd have to listen to the other boys harping on about how great the party was. As it turns out, I didn't have to worry about it."

"Why not?"

"There was just me and one other kid at registration."

For the first time since he began his tale, Clement turns to face me.

"The Luftwaffe delivered their own birthday present to Tommy's house. Direct hit. The only reason I wasn't alone at registration that morning is because the other kid had thrown up an hour before the party and his mum wouldn't let him go. All the other poor sods were blown to bits."

Over the years, I've read many novels with unexpected twists. The end of Clement's tale is in a different league.

"I...that's awful."

"Yep. Does that answer your question, doll?"

"My question?"

"You wanted to know what it was like, living through the war."

I suddenly feel foolish. Such a glib question in hindsight, like I'd asked Clement what his ham and cheddar toastie was like. But beyond my foolishness, I'm struggling to reconcile Clement's seemingly genuine recollection of such a tragic event and the simple fact it can't possibly be true.

There really isn't anything I can say, so I don't.

We sit in silence again, until we hear chatter from beyond the church door.

"Heads up, doll."

Three men and a woman, all pension age, wander out of the church and make their way across the lawn towards the car park.

"That's gotta be them, don't you reckon?"

"I think so."

"Right. Time to go to work."

Clement slowly gets to his feet, but my legs are less cooperative and I remain seated.

"Come on, doll," he says, looking down at me.

From my seated position, his sheer size reminds me of the giant in *Jack and the Beanstalk*, least the way I once imagined him. One thing I can't imagine is *this* giant ever being a fragile little boy, sobbing his heart out in a wartime classroom. But I guess if he can move on from that, real or otherwise, I can deal with a minor act of subterfuge.

I get to my feet.

"Ready when you are."

21

The interior of All Saints doesn't deliver much in the way of surprise. Rows of wooden pews, stone columns, stained glass windows — a cookie-cutter church, in almost every respect. It does feel much grander than the interior of St Michael's, though. Might be down to the money in the local neighbourhood. Maybe the poorer areas get budget churches, and the wealthy get a scaled-down version of Westminster Abbey. I'm not sure how these things work.

A figure dressed in black is mindlessly collecting hymn books from the pews as we step towards the aisle.

Clement coughs to signal our presence and the figure turns around, a warm smile breaking on her face. The black top is actually a cassock, complete with white dog collar.

"Oh, hello there," she chirps. "Sorry. I was miles away."

She eases herself from behind the pew and strides down the aisle towards us.

"I'm Reverend Claire," she says.

In my head, I had imagined spinning my lies to a man. Now I'm facing a different challenge — a woman, not much older than me. This changes the dynamic slightly.

I take a breath to steady my nerves but I still have to physically force the words out. My first lie, and possibly the biggest stretch, certainly in my mind.

"Good afternoon, Reverend. I'm Beth, and this is my fiancé, Clement."

I read somewhere that people tend to avoid eye contact when lying. I do the opposite, and stare straight into her pale green eyes. There's not a flicker to suggest she doesn't believe me.

"No need for titles, Beth. Most of my parishioners just call me Claire."

"Right, okay...Claire. You have a lovely church here."

"It's quite something isn't it? I've been here four years and it still fills me with joy every time I walk through the door."

To prove her point, she lets her gaze drift above our heads. A few seconds of awkward silence ensue.

"So, what can I do for you?" she asks, snapping back to reality.

I wait for Clement to explain our fictitious marriage plans.

Silence.

Claire continues to smile at us, tucking an errant strand of auburn hair behind her ear.

I flick my elbow a fraction, barely noticeable, but enough to nudge Clement into action.

"You're...a woman," he eventually booms, his voice echoing around the empty church.

"Well, I have a uterus, breasts, and I'm quite partial to shoes, so I suppose I must be," Claire retorts, an undercurrent of sarcasm in her voice.

"But...women..."

"Sorry, Claire," I interject. "Clement has been...um, away for a while. He's still acclimatising to life in modern Britain."

"Okay, so it's not a problem, me being a woman?"

Clement doesn't answer. I look up at him and frown, willing him to look at me, but his eyes are fixed on Claire.

I flick my elbow again.

"Yeah, no. It's...err, all good darlin'," he finally splutters.

"Splendid. So, what brings you to All Saints this afternoon?"

Clement clears his throat and finds some composure. "We've just moved into the area and we wanna tie the knot, don't we, doll?"

I nod, and flash Claire what I hope is a sincere smile.

"That's great news. Congratulations, and welcome to Camden," she replies enthusiastically.

"What we need to do is pop into the vestry and book an appointment for you to come in. I've got to be somewhere else within the hour, otherwise we could have gone through the process now."

"No, an appointment is fine, Thank you," I squeak.

"Let's get you booked in then. Step this way."

Claire turns and leads us down the aisle. As we follow, Clement grins at me and offers his arm, as a father might before walking his daughter down the aisle. I'm sure he meant it in jest, but to me it feels more like a cruel taunt. I shove his arm away.

We reach the end of the aisle and Claire steps through a low doorway to the left of the altar.

"Mind your head," she calls over her shoulder, presumably to Clement.

He stoops through the doorway. I don't.

We enter a narrow corridor which leads to the vestry; to all intents and purposes an office. We follow Claire into a ten-foot-square room and the claustrophobia I felt on the Underground returns with a vengeance.

She takes a seat behind a solid oak desk which dominates the cramped space.

"Please, pull up a chair," Claire says, waving at two leather-bound, oak chairs, positioned in front of the desk.

We sit, Clement's chair creaking in complaint at the sudden load.

Claire opens a sleek Apple laptop and stares at the screen while tapping the touchpad.

"Give me a moment to open my diary. This is a new machine and I'm still finding my way around."

While we wait for Claire, I cast my gaze around the room. It reminds me of my headmaster's office at primary school. I only visited it twice, both occasions for praise rather than punishment. Two of the walls are lined with shelves, straining under the weight of books, coloured binders, and stuffed document trays. Feeble light is provided by two tiny windows above Claire's head, supplemented by a desk lamp.

"How long have you guys lived in Camden then?" she casually enquires, her eyes still on the screen.

"Few weeks," Clement answers.

"And why have you decided you'd like to get married at All Saints?"

"Beth wants a proper wedding with all the trimmings. Choir, big organ, bells — don't you, doll?"

"Um, yes, especially the bells. My father was a campanologist."

I don't know where it came from, but I feel a sudden buzz of excitement at my totally plausible lie.

Claire looks up from the screen. "Was?"

"He passed away when I was seven."

She eyes me, her face awash with sympathy. "How awful. I'm so sorry to hear that, Beth."

I stare down at the desk and shuffle awkwardly in my chair. "Thank you," I mumble.

Detecting my discomfort, Claire wisely decides to move away from the subject of my father. "You'll be glad to know we have bells again though."

"Again?" Clement interjects.

"Yes. Up until last year, we'd been without bells here at All Saints for a long time."

"Why?"

"There was a storm, maybe seven or eight years ago, before I arrived. It brought down a large tree in the grounds, and unfortunately, it fell into the bell tower, half-destroying it. The wooden structure supporting the bells also collapsed and they crashed through the belfry floor. Sadly, they couldn't be salvaged."

Clement looks across at me and frowns. I feel my shoulders slump.

Wrongly interpreting our body language as concern for safety, Claire tries to put our minds at rest.

"Don't worry. The whole bell tower was rebuilt six years ago, and it's regularly inspected, as are the trees in the grounds. The only reason it took so long for the bells to be replaced is because of a rather protracted legal wrangle with the insurance company. They said the damage to the bells was an 'Act of God', and therefore not covered by our policy."

Claire chuckles at that irony. I offer a half-hearted snort but Clement remains silent.

"And of course, the church is a grade one listed building, which didn't exactly help," she adds. "English Heritage insisted we use all of the original stone to rebuild the tower. Every piece of stone had to be extracted from the mound of debris and meticulously catalogued. I'm told there were four skips full of it. The restoration company did an incredible job though, and you'd never guess anything happened. Our beautiful tower, restored to its former glory."

I smile, but inside I'm crushed. If there was any gold hidden in the belfry here, there's no way it would have been missed when they catalogued the debris.

"Right, I've got a slot free on Thursday evening at six," Claire chirps. "How does that sound?"

Clement suddenly gets to his feet and looks down at me. "Sorry, doll, but you and me — it ain't working. I can't marry you."

With that, he stoops through the doorway and out of the vestry.

I watch him leave, then slowly turn to Claire.

"Did he really just do that?" she says, clearly stunned.

"Err, he can be...a little unpredictable," I laugh nervously. "I'm sure it's just nerves."

"Sounded more than just wedding jitters to me, Beth. Are you sure he's the right man for you?"

"Is anyone ever sure?" I offer in defence. "I'd better go after him. Sorry, Claire."

I don't wait for her to reply.

I bolt from the vestry and scurry back down the aisle. I glance over my shoulder, hoping Claire isn't in pursuit, ready to administer spiritual guidance. I'm relieved to see she isn't.

As I step through the main door, I raise my hand to my forehead to shade my eyes from the bright sunlight while I scan the church grounds. I spot Clement, leaning against the lychgates, smoking a cigarette. I canter over to him, frowning.

"Well, that was humiliating. Thank you, Clement. "

"Sorry, doll. Just wasn't working," he says, a slight smirk on his face. "It's not you, it's me."

I have to bite my lip to prevent a laugh escaping. "Well, you could have warned me."

"What can I say, doll? I'm an impulsive sort of bloke. You'll find someone else."

I deploy my terrible Cockney accent again. "But who's gonna buy ya fags now, darlin'?"

Clement chuckles and I allow myself a wry smile as I lean up against a wooden pillar, opposite him.

"Ignoring the fact you dumped me in front of the vicar, at least we got a definitive answer, I suppose. Harry clearly didn't hide his gold here."

"Nah. They'd have found it when the tower toppled over. Didn't see much point hanging around once she told us that. And while we're on the subject, when did they start allowing women to be bloody priests?"

"Years ago. Do you have a problem with it?"

"Not really a churchy sort of bloke, so it's no skin off my nose."

"Perhaps you should have spent more time in church. You wouldn't be stuck with me now if you'd led a more virtuous life."

"Easy, doll. That would suggest you believe why I'm here."

I don't think I believe anything anymore, but at least Clement's lies are easy to separate from the truth. The worst kind of lies are those that creep up and slap you around the face — the lies you should have seen coming. Conversely, this particular lie has slowly drawn me in, much like the plot of a good book: you absorb it, you live it, and you *want* it to be true.

Clement flicks his cigarette butt away. "Let's get going then."

I pull my phone out and plot the short walk to St Jude's. Six minutes to get there, and maybe another ten minutes until we know if this exercise has been a monumental waste of time, or otherwise.

22

As we wander through the northern fringes of Camden, towards Kentish Town, Clement spends an inordinate amount of time stroking his moustache.

"Penny for them," I casually remark.

"They're not worth a penny, doll."

"Perhaps I can be the judge of that?"

"It's nothing. Don't worry yourself."

"Come on, Clement. A problem shared and all that."

"Jesus, doll. You're like a dog with a bone."

"Well, excuse me for showing concern."

We pass a sports ground where a six-a-side football match is in full swing. Men who look grossly unfit shout instructions at one another: 'pass', 'switch it', and 'away'. Most of them appear unable to follow said instructions.

Still deep in thought, Clement finally relents.

"Alright, if you must know, I was thinking about what you said, to the vicar."

"Which part?"

"About your dad."

"Oh."

"What happened?"

"He died. Not much else to say, really."

Twenty strides and another stroke of the moustache.

"Suppose that explains why you turned out the way you are."

"And what *way* am I?"

"You know…controlling, defensive, cynical."

"Don't hold back, Clement" I scoff. "That's some character assassination considering you barely know me."

"I doubt many people know you, doll."

We reach the end of the path and turn into a leafy residential street.

"Next left," I murmur.

We cover another twenty yards and turn into a road lined with redbrick terraced houses. In most towns, these would be considered modest homes, but I guess in this location they carry a price tag close to a major lottery win.

It seems Clement isn't great at reading body language, and continues his psychoanalysis.

"What do you reckon then? You think losing your old man screwed you up a little?"

"Who knows," I sigh wearily. "Why are you so interested, anyway?"

"I like to know what makes people tick. Helps me do my job."

"Is that what it is? A job?"

"Suppose it is."

"And what does that make me?"

"The hardest part of the job, doll."

As the spire of St Jude's appears above the rooftops ahead, I replay Clement's words in my head, trying to determine if his views were profound or puerile. Either way, it's perturbing that I'm actually giving them any thought at all.

Why should I care what he thinks of me? It annoys me to think that I might.

We round a slight bend in the road and St Jude's creeps into view on our right.

"This is it, doll. Last chance saloon."

St Jude's is like an amalgamation of the three churches we've already visited. It's another redbrick Victorian church, but on a much grander scale than the United Reform Church, or St Michael's. Sited in a quiet residential area, St Jude's isn't blighted with a grimy veneer of pollution like its urban siblings. It's far more imposing than All Saints, but not as pretty.

"Right. Same plan as before?"

Clement nods and pushes open a wrought iron gate which leads onto a tarmacked area, stretching the full width of the church. I assume it's an area for the congregation to gather before and after a service. A bit like the church itself, it's stark, functional, and not the most picturesque location for wedding photos.

We make our way towards the vestibule, jutting out from the front of the building on the left, and housing two heavyset doors positioned within a stone arch. Even beneath a backdrop of bright blue sky, the entrance to St Jude's looks foreboding rather than welcoming.

We approach the doors, the silence suggesting there isn't anyone around. I, perhaps naively, hadn't considered the implication of finding the church locked up. It matters not though, because in a few seconds we'll know for sure if the last chance saloon is open for business.

Each door has a wrought iron handle. Clement grasps the handle on the right-hand door and pushes down. It doesn't budge.

He switches his attention to the left-hand door and repeats his action. Same result.

Clearly frustrated, Clement then grasps both handles and shakes them hard. Even with his obvious strength, the doors steadfastly refuse to budge.

"Bollocks."

"Now what?"

He turns and surveys the street. An end-terrace house, fronting onto an adjoining road, sits directly opposite our position. There are a few small windows and an overgrown rear garden offering limited views of the church. The only other houses with any type of view are at least forty yards away.

"We look for another way in."

"Are you kidding?" I hiss. "You're not suggesting we break into a church?"

"It's God's house, doll, and I'm sure he won't mind, considering the bigger picture."

"I'm not worried about God. I'm worried about the police."

"You worry too much," he says with a shrug of his broad shoulders.

He then steps away from the doors and looks left, then right. "Let's go and have a nose around the back."

"Clement, this is a really bad idea."

"We're just gonna have a look, alright?"

He doesn't wait for permission and sets off across the tarmacked area towards the far end of the building. Frustratingly, it appears I have little option other than to follow.

I scamper up behind him, paranoid we're being watched. A quick glance at the street allays my fears a little, but my primary concern is what Clement intends to do next.

We reach the end of the tarmacked area and find a narrow path leading down the right flank of the church. There's no gate and no warning sign to indicate we aren't allowed to follow it, not that I suspect either would have deterred Clement.

We edge down the path, trapped between the church wall and a hedge. My claustrophobia is tempered by the fact that at least nobody can see us.

We emerge onto a small lawn at the rear of the church, hemmed in with a five-foot panel fence. Beyond the lawn, more tarmac, and a path that disappears around the left flank of the building.

I follow Clement as he moves along the rear of the church, scanning the walls as he goes. Apart from breaking a window, there doesn't appear any other way in. We get half way along when he stops.

"Look at that, doll."

I stare down at a wooden grill fixed into the brickwork, a few inches off the ground. It's maybe twenty inches high and about three feet wide.

"I reckon that's a vent for the cellar."

"Churches don't have cellars, Clement. They have crypts."

"Not a church this age."

"Semantics. I don't think you'll fit through there anyway."

"No, but you will."

I stare up at him. "Oh, no. Absolutely not."

"All you've gotta do is drop into the cellar and let me in. Where's your sense of adventure, doll?"

"Clement, this is not a bungee jump. This is breaking and entering."

"Do you want that money or not?"

"Not so much I want to risk a few years in prison."

He slumps against the wall and shakes his head. A few choice expletives are mumbled but I don't care — there is no way I'm going along with his crazy idea.

We reach an impasse and silently glare at one another. Just as I'm about to suggest we simply come back when the church is open, a booming voice breaks the peace.

"Hey, you there. What are you doing?"

I spin around in the direction of the voice.

A man is striding towards us. I'm slightly relieved he's wearing a tweed jacket and brown slacks, rather than a police uniform.

He gets within ten feet and asks us again. "I said...what are you doing?"

"We're having a row," Clement replies nonchalantly.

I don't know what possessed Clement to say that, but as I'm standing mute, I guess it was better than nothing.

Clement's reply appears to throw the man and he stops in his tracks. We all stare at one another. The man is short, stocky, and has a face like a dried prune. I'd guess he must be close to pension age and clearly doesn't present a physical threat — not that Clement ever seems worried by such things.

"Why are you rowing out here?" the old man says.

"She ran off, in a huff," Clement replies. "I chased her down the path, trying to reason with her. You know what they're like though."

Clement moves towards the old man and holds out a hand. "I'm Clement, and this is my other half, Beth, but I'd give her a few minutes to calm down."

The old man looks at me, and then, almost with a glint of sympathy in his eyes, shakes Clement's hand.

"Yes, well, this part of the church is out of bounds to the public. And I'm Father Norris, by the way."

"Oh, great. It was actually you we came to see, Father, before Beth had her tantrum."

"What did you want to see me about?" Father Norris replies.

I feel like a spectator at a tennis match, watching two men bat a conversation back and forth while my presence appears incidental.

"Um, excuse me. I am here you know."

Both men turn to face me. Neither says anything. Clement then turns back to the priest and wheels out our now-familiar lie.

"We want to tie the knot, Father. Hoping you might be able to help us with that.

The priest tries, and fails, to hide his surprise. "Oh, really? It's quite a commitment, marriage. If you don't mind me saying, most couples don't turn up at my door on the back of a row."

"Yeah, what can I say, Father? I'm a glutton for punishment."

"Right, well, I've got five minutes free if you want to come inside and book an appointment. There's a bit more to it than simply turning up with good intentions."

"Understood, Father. Thank you."

Clement then turns to me. "Beth, apologise to Father Norris for making a scene."

"What?"

I look at the priest and he looks at me. From the corner of my eye, I can just about see Clement's smug face. This is the third time he's put me in an embarrassing situation, and I'm starting to wonder if he gets some perverse enjoyment from it. However, I also have to begrudgingly admit he has a real knack for thinking on his feet.

"Sorry, Father," I mumble.

"It's quite alright, young lady. If you'd like to come with me."

We follow Father Norris along the rear of the church towards a glossy blue door, set beneath a limestone lintel.

"The vestry is just in here," he says, pushing the door open.

We enter the vestry, remarkably similar to that in All Saints. The key difference is the bulky computer monitor on the desk. The computer itself, on the floor next to the desk, is adorned with a Windows XP logo. If we have to wait for the priest to boot up his archaic machine, we could be here a while.

Father Norris invites us to take a seat. Much to my relief, he opens up a diary and thumbs through the pages.

"Sorry, Father," Clement suddenly rasps. "My guts are giving me jip. Don't suppose I could use your lav?"

This is it. Three churches discounted and we finally get to implement our plan.

The priest looks up and makes no effort to hide his annoyance. "If you really have to, but please make it quick."

He reluctantly gets to his feet and steps towards a doorway. "It's this way."

Clement leaps up, winks at me, and follows the priest out of the door. I hear the clump of his boots fade away and distant voices. Thirty seconds later, the priest returns to the vestry and slumps behind his desk.

"We may as well make use of the time whilst your fiancé is busy," he says as he squints at a page in his diary.

Time to deploy my delaying tactics.

"How long have you been priest here, Father?"

It's a great question, even if I say so myself. Whenever I ask my mother a question about the past, she spends at least five minutes arguing with herself about dates.

"Too long, some might say," he replies curtly.

Damn.

"Right. Are you married?"

Not such a great question. Can priests even marry? I have no idea.

He scours the desk, looking for a pen presumably. He answers without looking up. "No."

Double damn.

"Did you go anywhere nice on holiday?"

Really?

He continues to scowl at his diary, flicking from page to page. "I've got a slot a week Tuesday, at five o'clock."

Maybe he had a terrible holiday. Best not pursue that line of questioning.

"Um, yes, that would be good for us."

He clicks his pen, and finally looks up at me. "Your full names, please."

Oh dear.

"Erm, Bethany Louise...Smith."

He scribbles my name in the diary.

"And your fiancé?"

"Clement."

"His full name."

"Um, Clement...Jones."

Clement's name is added to the diary and the priest checks his watch. "Your fiancé is taking his time."

"Yes, sorry. We had prawn madras for dinner last night. I don't think it agreed with him."

For an improvised answer, I'm quite pleased with it.

Father Norris sits back in his chair and clicks his pen a few times. I think we're now testing his patience.

I try to think of some more questions, but he gets one in first.

"You live in Kentish Town I assume?"

"Yes, we do."

"Whereabouts?"

Ohh, Christ.

I search every corner of my mind, trying to recall any of the streets we just walked along. I'm conscious that every passing second makes my answer less credible. Nobody has to think that hard about where they live. I have to say something.

"The High Street."

"The High Street? In Kentish Town?"

"Yes, number...fourteen."

He throws the pen on the desk and clambers to his feet.

"Wait here," he snaps as he moves from behind the desk and makes his way towards the door.

This is not good. By my reckoning, I've only kept the priest occupied for a few minutes; certainly not long enough for Clement to have conducted a search of the belfry.

I grab my phone, intent on warning Clement with a text. It quickly dawns on me that he's the only man in the country without a mobile phone.

"Shit."

I get to my feet and pace the floor. What should I do?

Seconds pass and my anxiety grows. I consider the implication of the priest discovering Clement snooping around the belfry. My concern is not so much for Clement, but for the priest. What if Clement decides to silence him?

The reality of my relationship with Clement suddenly becomes apparent. I simply don't know him well enough to guess how he'll react. I've seen what he's capable of, and it isn't pretty, but would he really hurt an elderly priest?

I can't stand by and do nothing.

I dart through the vestry door into a dark corridor. An open door to my right looks the best option.

I tentatively step through the doorway and find myself at the rear of the church, opposite the vestibule doors. All is quiet and there's no sign of either man. I don't know if that's good or bad.

A lone voice suddenly echoes from the far end of the church. Loud, but not clear enough to determine what was said, or who said it.

I stand motionless, paralysed by indecision. Should I just run, and leave Clement to clear up this mess? Nobody would know I was here and there's nothing to link me to any potential crime being committed.

Can I really do that? It's not exactly fair to abandon Clement, is it?

As I let shame and fear battle away in my head, a door slams.

My head snaps in the direction of the sound, towards the rear of the church. Clement suddenly appears from behind a stone column. He strides down the aisle, his thumbs tucked into the pockets of his jeans as if he's out for a stroll.

His casual manner is similar to that he displayed after the fight with Messrs Black & Blue. This does not bode well.

As he gets within twenty feet, I catch a glimpse of tweed behind Clement. I breathe a sigh of relief upon seeing Father Norris waddling down the aisle. The look on his face suggests my relief will be temporary.

Clement strides up to me and mumbles a single word. "Rumbled."

The priest has far more to say and shouts down the aisle. "One of you had better explain what the hell is going on here, before I call the police."

I turn to Clement.

"Sorry, doll. He caught me coming back down the belfry stairs. No bleedin' gold in there either."

Father Norris pants up to us, his face now a blotchy shade of crimson. "Well?" he bellows.

Clement turns and raises his hands in surrender. "Alright, Father, you got me. I was looking for something. No harm done so we'll be on our way."

The priest shakes his head. "God help me, I'm getting sick and tired of you people."

"What people?" Clement asks, a second before I do.

The priest chuckles to himself. I don't think it's a joyous mirth.

"Do you think you're the first?" he roars. "Fools, the lot of you."

I swap a puzzled look with Clement.

"Sorry, Father. Not with you."

"You were looking for that bloody gold bar weren't you? What is wrong with you, cheating and lying your way into God's house?"

"Other people have been here looking for it?" Clement says hesitantly.

"Yes, just before they tried to find Father Christmas and the Tooth Fairy. Idiots."

I'm not sure if it's possible to look dumb and sheepish at the same time, but I give it a go. It feels like I've just read a huge spoiler in a book review. The basis of our quest, exposed for what it is.

"Shit," Clement groans as he looks to the rafters.

"Did you seriously think you were the first to think it might be here?" the priest repeats.

"Yeah," Clement mumbles.

From the moment we first met Father Norris, we've been lying to him. It's clear from our body language that neither of us is now lying; our disappointment obvious.

Faced with our confession, the priest's anger subsides a little. "There is no gold hidden here," he says flatly. "And to be frank with you, I find the implication there was, a little disrespectful."

My growing guilt compels me to say something. "I'm really sorry, Father. We're really sorry," I declare, as sincerely as I can. "We got a bit carried away with the whole tale. I know it sounds silly, but we didn't mean any harm, honestly."

"Apology accepted, but in future, you might want to consider the wider implication of your actions. You're both old enough to know better."

"Understood."

"Now, if you don't mind, I need to get away."

He holds his arm out towards the door leading back into the vestry. I keep my head low and take a few steps but Clement stays where he is, and shoots a question at the priest.

"Sorry, Father. One question and then we'll be out of your hair."

"Make it quick." the priest reluctantly agrees.

"You said it was disrespectful that people thought there was gold hidden here. Disrespectful to who?"

"You clearly haven't researched that well, have you?"

"Eh?"

"Disrespectful to the memory of my uncle."

"Your uncle?"

"Yes, the man you all incorrectly assume was in possession of stolen gold — Harry Cole."

23

The fact I'm standing with a confused expression on my face suggests I didn't see that one coming. And I didn't.

I'm assuming Clement didn't either. "What? But your surname is Norris," he says.

"Yes, it is," the priest confirms. "Uncle Harry was my mother's brother."

Clement looks at me. I look at Clement. We both turn to the priest. "Ohh."

"And he was a good man," Father Norris adds. "I can't believe for one moment he would handle stolen property. People want to believe fairy tales about hidden gold, but after more than four decades of searching, nobody has found it, and that tells you something — my uncle never had any gold. And besides, he would never have hidden it in a church. It would be sacrilegious, and Uncle Harry had too much respect for the church."

Sermon delivered, and his uncle's reputation defended, the priest checks his watch.

Taking the cue, Clement holds out his hand towards Father Norris. "Fair enough, Father. I'm sure Harry was a good man."

The priest shakes Clement's hand and nods an acknowledgement.

With our plot derailed and the priest's confirmation there was never any gold here, I just want to get away.

"I think we should be going now, Clement."

I turn to the priest. "Please accept our apologies, Father. I'm afraid I've had a bit of bad luck recently, and when you're out of options, you're prepared to believe just about anything. Silly really, in hindsight."

The priest quietly eyes me for a moment, possibly to determine if I'm genuinely repentant.

"I do understand," he eventually replies, his expression softening a little. "When we think our prayers are going unanswered, it's easy to fall into temptation, to stray from the path of righteousness. But if you keep your faith, The Lord will show you the way."

"Thank you, Father. I'll try."

"I'm only sorry I never got to the chance to offer Uncle Harry the same advice," he wistfully sighs. "It would have stopped all this nonsense right from the outset."

Clement pushes his luck and asks a question. "Do you mind me asking, Father, why Harry? Obviously we're not the only idiots to put two and two together, and come up with five. If he had nothing to do with the Baker Street job, how did his name get dragged into it?"

"I don't know for sure, I was only a teenager at the time."

"But there must have been some reason. Perhaps if we knew, we could put the word out, make it clear that Harry had nothing to do with it. Might stop anyone else turning up here looking for gold that doesn't exist."

The priest appears to ponder Clement's offer for a few seconds. If I'm honest, I'd like to know why we wasted our time.

"I suppose so," he mutters. "But purely on the understanding I never see you, or any other treasure hunters, here again. Agreed?"

"Yeah, agreed."

The priest folds his arms and leans against the nearest pew. The lines on his ruddy face deepen as he appears to dredge his memory.

"From what my mother told me, Harry became a little desperate after he was made redundant. He would have been in his fifties by then, and his job options would have been limited. I think he started hanging around with some rather unsavoury characters who paid him to do small jobs. Nothing serious and he only did it to put food on the table you understand, but one of those characters was eventually sent to prison as an accomplice in the Baker Street hoist. People probably knew Harry did some work for him, and as you say, put two and two together. He was down on his luck, but I'm positive he wouldn't have taken stolen property as payment. The police never found anything because I'm certain there wasn't anything to find."

He takes another exaggerated look at his watch. "Anyway, that's Harry's story, and why you've had a wasted trip this afternoon. Now, I really do need to get away. I hope you manage to sort whatever problem led you here."

Clement decides to test the priest's patience by asking another question.

"Sorry, Father. You said Harry was made redundant. What did he do?"

The priest edges towards the vestry in an attempt to drag us in the same direction.

"He worked on the Underground. Best part of thirty years, I think."

We follow the priest and Clement fires yet another question. "He drove a tube train?"

"No. He ran the ticket office at Wood Lane until it closed. Then they moved him to Tower Hill."

"Right. Thanks."

We're finally ushered out of the church and Father Norris ensures we're well beyond the gates before he stops watching us. He's wasting his time as there's no reason for us to return, and we walk away at a brisk pace.

It's now clear we've wasted an entire day, and almost fifty quid, chasing a fool's errand. I feel gutted, not about the wasted day, or even the money, but because the flicker of excitement I felt when we left the shop has been snuffed out. Once again, I've allowed myself to believe in something, believe in someone, and once again, I've been left disappointed.

I should probably be tearing a strip off Clement by now, but his pensive expression suggests he's probably as gutted as I am. Maybe he really did believe we were going to strike gold. In hindsight, I should have realised it was just one of his many delusions. On that basis, I should be more angry with myself than Clement. Truth is, I wanted to believe him. Maybe I just wanted to believe in *something*.

We silently retrace our steps back towards Camden, neither of us seemingly keen to dissect our failure. Even if I felt like talking, what's there to say?

We get as far as All Saints before I feel compelled to fill the silence.

"Are you okay, Clement?"

"I'm thinking," he replies.

"About?"

"What the priest said, about Harry's job."

"What about it?"

"Still thinking. Give me a minute."

We reach the park we passed earlier, now deserted. Clement points to the gate and a bench twenty yards beyond.

"Let's go grab a seat. Got a theory I wanna run by you."

I don't argue, and follow him into the park. The grass looks, and smells, like it's been freshly cut. It's quiet, and with a gentle breeze ruffling the tree branches above us, it would be easy to forget where we are.

We sit down on the bench, and I wait for Clement to announce that his train of thought has arrived somewhere.

"Tower Hill tube station," he says, somewhat randomly. "The priest said Harry was made redundant."

"Okay."

"I'm guessing he worked there in the sixties. If I remember, there were real staff shortages on the Underground back then. That's why they started bringing in immigrants."

"Right. So what?"

"Why would they make Harry redundant if they were already short of staff?"

"I don't know, but didn't he say Harry worked in the ticket office? Maybe they started using automated ticket machines?"

"Nah. That wasn't it."

"Okay. What about line closures?"

I know what he's about to do before he does it. A hand comes up and strokes his moustache. A long moment and a dozen strokes pass before he speaks again.

"We need to check something. Where's the nearest library?"

I pull out my phone. "We don't need a library. What do you want to know?"

"Christ. Is there anything you can't do with that thing?"

"Print money, unfortunately."

"Shame."

"So?"

"Right, yeah. I can't say for sure, but I think they might have shut Tower Hill station down, and maybe that's why Harry got the boot."

"I don't need to check that. I saw it on the map at King's Cross, so we can discount that theory."

"Just check for me, doll."

"What's the point? I clearly saw it on the tube map, and I'm sure I've been past it on previous trips to London."

"Doll..."

"Alright," I huff.

I open a web browser and search 'Tower Hill tube station'.

As I expected, a location map and an image pop up in the search results. I hold the screen towards Clement.

"See. It's still very much open."

"Can you check the history?"

I shake my head and jab at the screen, scrolling through the results. A link to a Wikipedia page rolls into view. I tap the link and the page loads. I scan through the text, unsure what I'm looking for."

"What does it say?" Clement asks, becoming impatient.

"Nothing. Just information about the location and...hold on."

I almost miss it — a single line in the second paragraph. I read it in my head twice before I read it aloud.

"The present Tower Hill station opened in 1967 and replaced a nearby station with the same name."

"I bloody knew it," Clement booms triumphantly.

I have no idea why he seems so pleased at this news.

"Sorry, Clement. Am I missing something here?"

"Harry lost his job because the station closed. I don't know why they didn't give him a job at the new station, but think about it, doll."

"Think about what?"

"Harry would have known the original Tower Hill station like the back of his hand. And by the time of the Baker Street job, it had been closed for four years. No staff, no passengers, and no reason for anyone to go down there. Can you think of a better place to hide something?"

"You're saying he might have hidden the gold in the old Tower Hill station? Is that even possible?"

"Yeah, course it is. There's loads of disused stations on the Underground, and they just locked them up and forgot about them."

He stares at me, expectant, enthused.

"Wait. Just hold on a minute. Are you seriously suggesting we search a disused Underground station for a gold bar?

Notwithstanding the fact it'll be locked up, and dark as hell, where do you even start looking? It would take forever with just the two of us."

"But we know exactly where to look — in the ticket office, obviously."

I close my eyes and draw a deep breath as I try to expunge a growing sense of deja vu.

I'm tired, dejected, and I feel disgusting. What I really want is to go home, take a long shower, and then hide under my duvet for a month. What I don't want is to have my hopes raised and then dashed again. I can't keep doing it. I can't keep ceding my dwindling faith; there's so little left as it is.

I open my eyes and turn to Clement. "I'm sorry. I'm done."

"What?"

"I can't do this anymore."

"But, doll, this could be it. Everyone was looking at the church angle, but how many people knew Harry worked on the underground? And how many would have known he worked at the old Tower Hill station? None, I reckon. We only found out cos' the priest told us, and Harry was given the boot years before the Baker Street job. Forget the church stuff, this makes far more sense."

"I appreciate your efforts, Clement, but I'm tired, and I just want to go home."

"And then what? How are you gonna get twenty grand together in five days?"

"I'll have to speak to a loan company on Monday."

"If you really thought that was a realistic option, we wouldn't be here, would we?"

We wouldn't, I know that. It's just a feeble excuse to avoid any more of this madness.

"Doll, look at me."

I slowly turn my head and do as instructed. Clement removes his sunglasses, his blue eyes fixing on mine.

"I came here to do a job. I don't care what you think about me, if you think I'm bleedin' crazy, I only care about getting the job done."

"I appreciate that, Clement, but..."

"But nothing," he interrupts. "I might be wrong about the tube station, but it's gotta be worth a look ain't it? And if I'm wrong, we find another way. I'll keep looking until I draw my last breath, but you have to trust me, doll. I need you to believe I can do this."

Over the last eighteen years, five men have declared their love for me. Subsequently, all five men left me questioning the sincerity of that declaration. I'm sure they meant it at the time, and I probably believed them at the time. Not one of them ever displayed the intense sincerity currently burning in Clement's eyes.

"If you need to know anything about me, doll, know that I never give up. Ever."

For a fleeting moment I bask in Clement's sincerity, happy to believe almost anything he says. Unicorns are real, the moon is made of soft cream cheese, and not all men are complete shits — I'd willingly believe it all.

Like most good things in my life, the moment soon passes.

"I don't know, Clement."

"Tell you what, why don't we just go and have a look at the old station, see how the land lies?"

He puts his sunglasses back on and pulls out the Marlboros. I watch him as he flicks the Zippo open and lights it in one fluid action, like he's done it a thousand times before, which he probably has, come to think of it.

He takes a long drag before slowly exhaling a plume of blue-grey smoke. It drifts over my head, close enough for me to catch a whiff of the pungent odour. Coupled with the smell of freshly cut grass, I'm suddenly seven-years-old again, standing at my father's side in the garden as he puffs on a cigarette while tinkering with the lawnmower. A time when I was untainted by the lies and perpetual disappointment life would eventually throw my way.

"Just a quick look?"

"Honestly, doll, just a quick look."

"And no breaking and entering?"

"Scout's honour."

"I must be crazy. Come on then."

"Good girl. You won't regret it," he beams.

"Please don't patronise me, Clement. I'm a woman, not a girl."

He gets up and crushes the cigarette butt under his boot. He then looks down at me, a wry smile on his face. "Sometimes, you're still a girl."

He turns and strides towards the gate.

I'm left on the bench, trying to answer a question — did he just say that?

24

As we stroll back up Camden High Street towards the tube station, it dawns on me that we could have simply gone to Kentish Town, only a five minute walk from St Jude's.

"Why didn't you say we could have used Kentish Town?" I ask Clement.

"Fancied the walk. Besides, it gave us a chance to chat."

On reflection, I suspect our little detour to the park was all part of his plan.

Whether it was planned or not, his pep talk has prodded my motivation back into life. And despite my skin feeling like the floor of a kebab shop, maybe a teeny part of me is secretly pleased our quest isn't quite over yet; not that I want Clement to know that.

"What happened to all the pubs?" he randomly remarks as we stroll along.

"Eh?"

"That's the fourth building we've passed that used to be a pub."

"Oh, I'm afraid it's a pretty similar story across the whole country. There was something on the news about it, last week. Apparently three pubs close down every day."

"People don't drink so much?"

"Maybe, but it's probably more to do with supermarkets selling cheap booze, and the smoking ban of course."

"No, don't tell me..."

"Afraid so. You can't smoke in pubs either."

"Shittin' hell. A pint and a fag is a British institution, like fish and chips."

"You can still have a pint and a fag; you just have to stand outside."

"That must be fun in the winter — freezing your bleedin' knackers off just to have a smoke."

"Well, it's one reason people stay at home and drink, and why so many pubs have closed."

He shakes his head and looks genuinely saddened. Another masterful piece of acting, or chronic delusion? I really can't tell which.

We pass Camden Market and The Electric Ballroom, and then enter the tube station.

"Do you know where we're going?" I ask.

"Yeah. Northern Line down to Bank station, then a short walk to Monument. Tower Hill is one stop from there."

"Are you sure?"

"Yeah."

We head down to the Northern Line platform and three minutes later, we're on a train down to Bank.

The first leg of our journey takes thirteen minutes. Our carriage isn't overly crowded and I'm relieved we're able to secure seats. A gaggle of new passengers hop on at every stop, many of them eyeing the empty seat next to Clement. None of them take it.

We pull into Bank station a little after four o'clock. As we shuffle away from the platform, I spot a sign for Monument station.

"Clement, it says this way."

We then follow a confusing maze of walkways and escalators that wind between the two stations.

"What's the DLR?" Clement asks as we pass a sign.

"The Docklands Light Railway. I don't really know too much about it, other than it connects all the new developments to the east of the city."

"Have you been on it?"

"Once or twice. I think we used it a few years back when we went to the O2 Arena."

I regret saying it within a second of finishing my sentence.

"What's…"

"It's a big entertainment venue. They hold concerts there."

I look across at Clement. His frown is like that of an overly inquisitive child who puts his hand up too often in class, and is eventually overlooked by the teacher.

"If we find what we're looking for, I'll take you on a limousine tour of all the sights."

"Promises, promises," he replies, his frown fading away.

We emerge from the tunnel and take the Circle Line for the short journey to Tower Hill. The train arrives, and barely a minute later, we reach our destination.

As we emerge back into daylight, I remind Clement this is purely a reconnaissance exercise.

"Yeah, alright. Trust me, doll."

Hmmm…

I google the location of the old Tower Hill station. It's just a few hundred yards away.

We follow a path away from the station entrance, and head towards the main road which leads to our destination. We turn right and I check the map again, to ensure we're heading in the right direction.

"Christ on a bike," Clement bellows.

I snap my head up. "What? What is it?"

"Look at that."

I assume he's talking about the Tower of London, directly opposite our location. I went there once, on a school trip, and while I recall being vaguely impressed at seeing one of London's most famous landmarks, I'm surprised at Clement's reaction.

"Surely you've seen the Tower of London before?"

"Course I have, but not that bloody thing."

He points a few degrees to the right of the Tower, at the Shard — the latest addition to the London skyline.

"Ohh, you mean the Shard?"

"What is it?"

"It's the tallest building in Europe, if my memory serves me correctly. I think it was built a few years ago."

Clement continues to stare at it as we wander along the road.

"It's bleedin' massive," he murmurs.

I'm more interested in Tower Bridge, which comes into view as we pass the Tower of London. It's a bridge so distinctive, so iconic, not least because its picture adorns every bit of tourist gift tat, from tea towels to fridge magnets. Despite my frequent visits to London, I rarely get to see any of our famous landmarks. I take a few seconds to admire the impressive structure, much like the scores of tourist taking photos on the opposite side of the road.

We pass the Trinity Square Gardens, home of the grand Trinity House, and I check our location on the map.

"It's just up here on the right."

With only the point of the Shard now visible above the buildings across the street, Clement regains his focus.

"Just think, doll. We could be within fifty yards of that gold."

We reach the entrance to the old Tower Hill station, and it becomes clear we won't be getting any nearer.

A steel scissor gate stretches across the entrance, secured by a cylinder lock within a sturdy frame. Beyond the metal latticework, there's a tantalising view of the stairs down to the old station. Unfortunately, the stairs take a ninety degree turn so it's impossible to see more than seven or eight yards beyond our position.

"Shit," Clement mumbles.

"Now what?"

He turns around and stares at something on the opposite side of the road.

"Look over there, doll."

I do as instructed, but besides an old red phone box, I see nothing of note.

"What am I supposed to be looking at?"

"There's another entrance over there. I bet there's a subway below the road."

"You reckon?"

"Yeah. Lots of tube stations on busy roads have more than one entrance. We ain't gonna be getting in this way, so we might as well check it out."

We wait a few seconds for the lights to change and the traffic to stop. We then scoot around the back of a stationary double-decker bus, straight into a fog of diesel fumes belching from its exhaust. The west-bound traffic is still buzzing along and we have to choose our moment to cross.

If you didn't know it was there, the second entrance to the old Tower Hill station would be easy to miss. A waist-high brick wall surrounds a stairwell, protected by a gate that even I could hop over. Beyond the gate, the stairs lead down to a pair of steel mesh doors. From the street, it would be near impossible for anyone to see those doors unless they stood next to the wall and deliberately looked over.

"This looks a better way in. Wait here a sec, doll."

Before I have chance to argue, Clement clambers over the gate and disappears down the stairs.

Keen to distance myself from anything illegal Clement has in mind, I slowly edge away from the wall. Behind it stands an ancient-looking church; All Hallows by the Tower, according to the sign adjacent to the door. I might have had some interest in its history, if I hadn't already had my fill of churches today.

Nevertheless, it gives me a reason to loiter in the middle of the pavement.

I become just another tourist, drinking in the architecture, but all the while keeping one eye out for the police car I fear will arrive any second.

Barely a minute passes before Clement emerges and clambers back over the gate.

"Good news," he shouts above the noise of the traffic. "The doors are locked with a run-of-the-mill padlock."

"Do you want to shout a bit louder," I hiss. "I don't think somebody in Leicester Square quite heard you."

"Keep your knickers on, doll" he says dismissively.

"So why is that good news?" I whisper, somewhat pointlessly as another bus rumbles past.

"With the right tools, I reckon I could have it open."

"And what are the right tools exactly?"

"Quickest option would be a decent set of bolt cutters. Failing that, just a couple of hair pins, but that might take a while."

"Well, forgive me for not checking, but I'm fairly certain I don't have either in my handbag."

Clement lets his gaze drift over my head and across the street, as if pondering our next move.

"Don't think there's much we can do then. Not now, anyway."

"So, what do you want to do?"

"Head back to your place and regroup. Work out a plan, and what we need."

I'm slightly relieved at his pragmatism. As much as I want to find out one way or another if we're chasing another wild goose, today has been just a tad too much for me.

"Good idea. What's the quickest way back to Waterloo?"

"Via that pub over there."

"Eh?"

"Go on, doll. Shout me a pint. I'm gagging, and I need a piss."

It's actually one of his better ideas. I don't think I've ever needed a glass of wine more than I currently do.

"Okay. Just a quick one."

We cross the road and wander twenty yards along the pavement to the pub. A variety of meal and drink offers are advertised on garish posters outside, suggesting it's a typical chain pub similar to thousands across the country.

The decor inside is suitably generic; all light oak veneer and faux brass. I guess it's somebody's idea of a traditional British pub, geared towards the hordes of tourists visiting the Tower.

Clement heads off to the toilets while I make my way to the bar. It's reasonably busy but I think we've arrived before the early evening dinner rush.

As I wait to be served, it strikes me that I have no idea what his idea of 'a pint' actually is.

It matters not, as I'm still waiting to be served by the time he returns.

"What did you want to drink, Clement?"

"A pint."

"Of what?"

"Lager."

"Which lager?"

I point to the array of pumps lined up behind the bar. "Take your pick."

He studies each pump, his frown deepening. "Suppose I'll have a Heineken. Never heard of the others."

A chirpy barman eventually takes our order and furnished with our drinks, we take a seat at a table next to the window. After three large gulps of white wine I relax a little, knowing our quest for the day is over. The alcohol also helps.

"Don't suppose you could stretch to some fodder too?" Clement asks. "I'm starving."

I suppose a toasted sandwich isn't enough for a man of his size to survive on. I take a quick look at the menu and I'm pleasantly surprised how inexpensive their meals are.

"Go on then. Keep it under a tenner though."

"Cheers, doll."

Clement grabs a menu and eyes it hungrily. His enthusiasm quickly wains once he realises that, even in here, a tenner isn't going to get him a banquet.

"Guess I'll have the steak and kidney pudding."

"Right. I need to order at the bar so try not to get in any trouble while I'm gone."

He nods, and continues to study the menu.

I head back to the bar and place our order. The barman is good enough to advise me that I can save money by ordering another round of drinks with our meals. It seems churlish not to take advantage, and I return to the table with another pint and another glass of wine.

"You're not a cheap date, Clement."

"I'm not a cheap anything, doll."

We sup our drinks and stare out of the window at the passing traffic. Clement seems perfectly happy to do nothing and say nothing. I, on the other hand, feel obliged to make conversation.

"Can I ask you a question, Clement?"

"Sure."

"You never said. Is Clement your first name or your surname?"

"Neither. Both. It's just a name."

"Surely it has to be one or the other? What does it say on your birth certificate?"

"Dunno. Never seen it."

"Okay. What about your passport?"

"Never had one."

"I don't understand how you can go through life without a proper name."

"Why do I need one?" he shrugs. "I've never paid taxes and never claimed anything. Never got called up for national service, and never had a bank account."

"So your name isn't listed on any government database?"

"Nope."

"But what about...," I can't believe I'm about to say this. "...your death certificate."

"Funnily enough, I never got to see it. But I'd guess it says, *John Doe.*"

"Right, of course. But your, err, previous line of work. Didn't you ever get arrested?"

"Never."

"So no criminal record, and no fingerprints or DNA on file?"

"Dunno what DNA is, but no."

Seemingly bored with my questioning, Clement returns his attention to the scene beyond the window. I take a sip of wine and quietly ponder his revelation.

I can't imagine anyone being able to slip through the system in this day and age, let alone be able to function. I mean, without any official identification, how do you open a bank account? And without a bank account, how do you get a line of credit? And with no line of credit, you couldn't even get a mobile phone contract, let alone a tenancy agreement or a mortgage.

Of course, he could just be lying, and that actually makes far more sense. If I don't know his full name, I can't use the Internet to check up on him.

I'm about to probe a little deeper when we're interrupted by somebody shouting from the bar.

"Clem! Clem!"

We both turn our heads in the direction of the voice. We're greeted by the sight of an old man, slowly shuffling across the floorboards towards our table. Dressed in a navy overcoat and crumpled grey trousers, he looks frail and gaunt.

He gets within ten feet and slowly raises his hand in the air. He calls out again. "Oi, Clem! You bugger."

I look at Clement but his eyes are now fixed to the table, as if he's deliberately ignoring the old man.

"Fuck," he mumbles under his breath.

Before I get a chance to question Clement, the old man finally completes his journey, stopping a few feet from our table.

"I thought it was you," the old man wheezes. "How you doing, mate?"

Clement doesn't move, steadfastly ignoring the old man. I can't.

"Hello there," I chirp.

"Ello darlin'," he replies in a strong London accent. "What's the matter with him?"

"You know him do you?"

"Course I bloody do. Me and Clem are pals, ain't we?"

He smiles down at Clement but the smile isn't returned. No acknowledgement. Nothing.

"How do you know Clement?" I ask.

He ignores me and continues to address the top of Clement's head.

"She's a nosey tart ain't she, Clem? Where'd you find her?"

Old man or not, I'm not having that.

"How dare you," I snap. "Show some respect."

He ignores me and throws another question at Clement. "She ain't another barmaid from the Flamingo Club is she? Thought you'd learnt your lesson after the last one. Do you remember her, Clem? Bleedin' mental, that one, but a smashing pair of knockers."

He chuckles away to himself; strangely oblivious to the fact Clement is blanking him.

I have no idea what's going on here, but I've had enough of it.

"Clement, will you deal with this man, please."

My turn to be ignored.

I turn to face the old man, intent on asking him to leave, when a middle-aged man in a maroon sweater scoots up beside him.

"Christ, Dad, don't slope off like that. You nearly gave me a heart attack."

The old man's son looks like a man more accustomed to wearing a pinstripe suit. His brown hair has a stern side parting and sits above horn-rimmed glasses. His accent is more home counties than London.

"Is he with you?" I ask the son. "Because his language is highly inappropriate.

He looks visibly shocked. "I'm so sorry."

The younger man shuffles a little closer to our table and leans towards me.

"He's suffering from dementia," he says in a low voice. "I'm afraid he still thinks it's the 1960s and some of his language is, well, a bit outdated shall we say."

"Oh, right. I'm sorry."

"No need to apologise," he sighs. "Unfortunately this is not the first time he's done this today. He gets confused, thinks he knows people that are probably long dead. He grew up in London, you see, so we bring him up here every now and again. Initially, it seemed to help him with his memory, but I think this will probably be the last time."

The man offers me a weak smile. "I hope you'll forgive him."

"Yes, of course."

The man digs his hand into his pocket and pulls out a wallet. He extracts a twenty pound note and places it on the table.

"Please, let me pay for your meal."

It seems an over-the-top gesture considering his father's illness. Maybe he just fancies me, or more likely, maybe he's concerned Clement will beat the crap out of him.

"Honestly, that's very kind but there's really no need. We couldn't take your money."

"No, I insist. And thank you for your understanding."

Before I can argue any further, he turns and drapes his arm around the old man's shoulder.

"Come on Dad. Let's leave these good people in peace."

"Seeya tonight at the Flamingo, Clem," the old man calls over his shoulder.

I wait until they're out of earshot. "What the hell was that all about? And who was that old man?"

Clement finally looks up from the table. "Dunno."

"Bullshit, Clement. He knew you."

"Nah. Think he got me confused with someone else. You heard his son — his head is messed up."

"You expect me to believe he guessed your name? It's not exactly common is it?"

"Just leave it, doll."

He picks up the menu again and stares at it blankly. It seems this conversation is over.

If Clement won't tell me what the old man was on about, I'll dig around myself. I pull out my phone and google 'Flamingo Club London'.

Wikipedia once again proves the source of information. I click on a link and scan the page. According to the article, the Flamingo Club was a somewhat notorious nightclub in Soho.

Some years after it opened, it was relocated to Wardour Street, before it finally closed in 1967.

However, the one question Wikipedia can't answer, and the one which puzzles me the most, is why Clement totally ignored the old man?

25

After two glasses of wine, I'm currently standing on that narrow patch of ground located somewhere between sober and tipsy.

As we wait for our overdue food, Clement necks the dregs of his first drink while I consider the acquisition of a third. It's not a good idea, but it would be in good company with the other bad ideas I've embraced in the last twenty four hours.

Sod it.

"Another pint, Clement?"

"Yeah, please," he mumbles.

"Great. And when I get back, you can tell me all about the Flamingo Club."

I skip off to the bar and return a few minutes later with our drinks, and possibly too much alcohol-fuelled bravado.

"So, the Flamingo Club. Did you ever go there?"

"Now and again."

"And you went with the old man, whose son paid for these drinks?"

"Sometimes."

"And you used to be friends?"

"Yeah."

"Why did you ignore him then?"

Clement takes a slow swig of his lager. He then places the glass on the table and continues to stare at it.

"Well?"

"Why do you think, doll? His head is messed up enough without me confirming I've returned from beyond the friggin' grave."

Maybe it's the alcohol impairing my judgement, but I can't untangle the truth in all of this. Did the old man simply mistake

Clement for an old friend he used to hang out with? Or did his dementia convince him he was back in the 1960s; chatting to Clement like it's just another Saturday afternoon?

"If he hadn't been suffering from dementia, how do you think he'd have reacted?"

"Stupid question. How would I know?"

"Don't you think he'd have been a bit freaked out, seeing you sitting there looking exactly the same as you did over forty years ago?"

"Suppose so. Or more likely, he'd have just assumed it wasn't me."

"You're quite, err...distinctive though."

"Yeah, well, so what? I don't see where you're going with this."

"Just chatting, Clement."

"Can we chat about something else? Like, where's our bleedin' food?"

"What was his name, the old man?"

Another slow swig of lager and another long pause before he answers.

"Freddy Markham."

"Were you close?"

"Honestly, doll. I really don't wanna talk about Freddy."

I know I'm pushing my luck with all these questions, and I was kind of expecting him to close me down. But rather than agitation in his response, there's more than a hint of sadness. It sounds familiar, like when people ask me about my father. It's not that I don't want to talk about him, it's just that it rekindles feelings I've spent my life trying to suppress.

"Okay. Sorry. We'll talk about something else."

"Good."

Before we get a chance to move onto another subject, our food finally arrives.

We eat in silence. Clement devours his steak and kidney pudding in minutes, while I pick at my chicken salad. Drinking on an empty stomach is never a good idea as it kills my appetite.

With an empty plate and an empty glass, Clement appears keen to leave.

"Let's get out of here, doll."

I'm not fussed about finishing my salad, but neck the remainder of my wine.

"I'm just going to pop to the loo. Give me five minutes."

"Alright. I might join you."

"What?"

"I need another piss."

"Oh. Right."

He follows me towards the toilets, but thankfully doesn't join me in the ladies.

We reconvene five minutes later, Clement leaning against the wall outside the gents. He already has a cigarette and Zippo in hand.

"You fit?" I ask, now feeling just a little tipsy.

He nods, and we make our way towards the exit. As we reach the door, I feel a little guilty about not leaving a tip, but it doesn't weigh so heavily I return to the table. I'm sure lots of wealthy tourists will make up for the few quid I didn't leave.

It could be the alcohol, but back on the street the noise of the traffic and the chatter of the crowds seem to have intensified. I think I really want to go home now. Clement finishes his cigarette by the time we reach Tower Hill.

Three tube trains and a route march later, we finally arrive back at Waterloo. I check the departure board and inwardly groan when I see we have a forty minute wait until our train departs.

We find a couple of empty seats opposite WH Smiths. With nothing else better to do, we sit and stare at the posters in the window, promoting a best-selling novel from a debut author I've never heard of. Out of interest, I look it up on Amazon. The reviews are mixed, but overall, it seems the book has left its readers underwhelmed. Maybe the book was just over-hyped, as is often the case these days.

Still, what I wouldn't give to see my name on those posters. I think I'd happily take the underwhelming reviews.

I let my mind drift to novel eighteen, hoping some inspiration might bite. Not even a nibble. If there's anything in my head, it's clouded in a fog of alcohol and tiredness.

"I need a piss again. That beer went straight through me."

Clement's statement pierces the fog.

"Eh? Oh, right. Again?"

"Joys of middle age."

He climbs to his feet and wanders off towards the toilets.

I toy with the idea of popping into WH Smith and reading a few pages of that best-selling novel. Perhaps it will show me where I'm going wrong. More likely though, it'll just induce pangs of jealousy.

I revert to my phone and browse Facebook. I'm not surprised to see Karl hasn't updated his status for almost a week. I let my thumb hover over the message icon as I consider the rationale of sending him a message.

There's nothing to say.

I remove him from my friends list and block him. It's a small but cathartic gesture.

As I return to my news feed, two twenty-something men, dressed in football shirts and jeans, flop down in the seats next to me. They stink of booze.

"How you doin' sweetheart?" the nearest one slurs.

"Fine. Least I was," I reply, without taking my eyes from my phone.

"I'm Lee, and this is Davey."

I ignore him.

"You fancy joining us for a few drinks?"

"No. I'm waiting for my friend."

"That's alright, darlin'. She can come too."

"I don't think *he's* your type."

Lee thinks this is hilarious. "We're definitely not arse bandits, are we Davey?"

"Fucking queers," Davey mumbles.

I finally lift my gaze from the screen and stare at Lee. "Can you take your homophobic views somewhere else, please?"

"Wassa matter? You a lezza?"

I'm about to give the scumbag a piece of my mind when two shovel-like hands descend on Lee's shoulders. I look up at Clement, standing behind the seats.

He leans forward and speaks slowly, measured. "Five seconds to hand it back. Five...four...three..."

Lee squirms in his seat but Clements hands are like clamps, holding him firmly in place.

"Da fuck you talking about?" Lee spits. "Let me go or I swear, we'll fuck you up bad."

He clearly can't see the giant man standing behind him, as otherwise I suspect his reaction would be a little different. Davey, on the other hand, can see Clement, and his face suggests he wants no part in Lee's threat.

"Two...one..."

Clements hands depart Lee's shoulders and encircle his scrawny neck. "Last chance, dickhead," he growls as his knuckles whiten.

Lee slips his hand down the side of the seat and pulls out my purse. I snatch it from him; now wise to the reason Clement is currently throttling the little shit.

"Now, apologise."

"Sorry," Lee wheezes.

Clement then lifts him to his feet and shoves him forward like a rag doll. Lee's legs can't move fast enough and he staggers a few steps before face-planting the floor.

Clement then turns his attention to Davey, feigning a sudden movement towards him. Davey's eyes almost pop out of his head before he scampers away, collecting his fallen comrade on the way.

"Check your bag, doll."

I do as I'm told and check nothing else has been pilfered.

"It's all here."

"Good. I need fifty pence."

"Eh?"

"That's why I came back. They charge fifty bleedin' pence to take a slash. Robbing bastards. "

I open my purse and hand him a fifty pence piece.

"Cheers, doll. You do tip then?"

Before I have a chance to thank him, he turns on his heels and strides away.

It's probably the alcohol, but I feel a warm glow, not too dissimilar to when my father wrapped me in that towel. The same safe haven where nothing can harm me.

Shame Clement isn't as fluffy as the towel, though.

I decide to wait for him in WH Smith. I loiter just inside the entrance and pluck a random magazine from the rack. It's only when I start flicking through the pages I realise it's one of those celebrity gossip mags. No, thank you.

I slip it back in the rack and grab an interior design mag. I might as well have read that best-selling novel as the glossy pages summon pangs of jealousy for beautifully designed rooms, all beyond any budget I can afford.

Unless.

An insignificant word of just six letters, but all my hopes are pinned on it.

"Oi, bookworm. You coming?" Clement calls from outside.

I slip the magazine back and skip outside.

"You disappeared before I got the chance to thank you. We'd have been screwed if they'd taken my purse."

"All part of the service, doll. I knew they were up to no good the moment I clapped eyes on them."

"Really? How? I just assumed they were a couple of drunken idiots."

"Obviously they weren't chatting you up so just a process of elimination."

"They might have been."

"Yeah, right," he snorts. "I don't think you're their type, doll."

I'm not sure if I should be offended or flattered. I choose to assume the latter.

We check the departure board again, and with only five minutes before our train is due to leave, make our way to the platform.

We find a relatively quiet carriage and settle in for the journey home. A few minutes after we leave Waterloo, Clement spots another famous landmark, just beyond the office buildings and graffiti-ridden bridges.

"What's that, doll?"

"The London Eye."

"What does it do?"

"It just goes around like a giant Ferris wheel," I say, pointing up at the transparent pods dotted around the circumference. "The views are quite something."

It quickly disappears from view and Clement settles back in his seat. Five minutes later, his head lops to the side and his breathing slows. Seems I'm not the only one who's tired.

I take the opportunity to call Stanley and check on Mum. It's not a particularly long call and I lose connection three times, probably due to their rural location and the fact I'm on a moving train. Mum sounds happy enough, though. They've been for a walk in the woods this afternoon, and are just about to visit the local pub for dinner. It's enough to put my mind at rest sufficiently so I can join Clement in the land of nod, or at least I can try.

I don't sleep, but I manage to slip into a semi-conscious doze. My paranoia that we'll miss our stop prevents me falling any deeper.

We get within five minutes of our destination when the train comes to a juddering halt. The guard announces there's a slight delay due to emergency engineering works at our station. Fantastic.

That slight delay turns out to be ten minutes.

The train sets off again and I attempt to wake Clement. Repeatedly saying his name doesn't work, so I'm forced to gently shake his shoulder.

"Wassup?" he mumbles.

"We're nearly there."

He stretches out his huge frame and expels a yawn.

"I feel better for that, doll."

"Good for you. I still feel horrendous."

Concern for my well-being apparently has its limits, and he just stares out of the window.

The train rattles into the station and we get up. As we move towards the doors, Clement's attention is suddenly focused on something beyond the window. He cranes his neck to the right, staring back towards the end of the platform.

The train comes to a standstill and we wait for the doors to open.

"Got a little job for you, doll."

"What job?"

"One sec."

The doors hiss open. Clement steps onto the platform and positions himself behind a vending machine. I follow him out and we wait for the dozen other passengers to pass.

"See that guy in the orange work outfit?" he says in a low voice.

He points to a man in hi-viz orange clothing and hard hat, standing at the far end of the platform. Judging by the collection of tools around him, I assume he's a track engineer, sent to fix whatever problem caused our delay.

"What about him?"

"I need you to distract him."

"Why?"

"Cos' he's bound to have a pair of bolt cutters we could borrow."

"No way, Clement. You can't just steal his tools."

"Fair enough. You gonna buy some then?"

"Erm, how much are they?"

"A decent pair costs an arm and a leg."

I face a moral dilemma. My dwindling bank balance can't take another significant expense. But stealing?

"We're only borrowing them, doll. We'll drop them back as soon as we're done."

"Do I have to?" I groan. I sound like a whiny teenager.

"No. I could just wander over and knock him out. Your choice."

"Alright," I sigh. "What do I say to him?"

"Tell him you've spotted something on the track, and lead him up the platform away from the tools. I only need half a minute."

It sounds so simple, so easy. My quickening pulse and a flush of adrenalin suggests otherwise.

"Go on then," Clement prompts.

I take a deep breath and pad down the platform towards the workman. Thankfully his attention is focused on some sort of digital device, a little larger than a mobile phone. I get within five feet and he continues to prod away at the screen with a sausage-like finger.

"Excuse me," I say, my voice scratchy.

He looks up from the screen. I feel a little better when a youngish face stares back at me.

"I, err, spotted something on the track and thought I should let somebody know."

"What is it?" he replies curtly.

"I don't know...a metal thing. It's probably nothing, but better safe than sorry, eh?"

He doesn't try to hide his annoyance as he slips the digital device into his pocket.

"Suppose you'd better show me." he grumbles.

I don't like his attitude, and my initial guilt about liberating his equipment eases a little.

I turn and walk as slowly as I can back along the platform. I pass Clement, leaning casually against a wall. There's only a handful of other passengers loitering around, all of them distracted by mobile phones or chatting to one another.

"It's just up here."

I shuffle another dozen steps, coming to a stop by the platform edge. The workman stands beside me and we both stare down at the track.

"Where is it then, this thing?"

I scan the shingle in search of something, anything. Besides the rails and the wooden sleepers, there's absolutely nothing down there.

"That's odd. Maybe it's a bit further up."

I don't wait for the workman to argue. I shuffle slowly along the platform edge, keeping my eyes fixed on the shingle bed. Tiny, tortuous steps.

I count to sixty in my head, stopping every ten seconds to focus on another part of the track. It all looks the same, nothing out of the ordinary.

"I think you're seeing things," the workman grumbles.

"No, wait. Look," I splutter, pointing at a shiny object nestled next to a sleeper.

"It's a beer can."

"Really?"

"Are you having me on? It's a bloody beer can."

I lean forward and make an exaggerated attempt to inspect the object; so obviously a beer can.

"Oh, so it is."

I turn to the workman. "Silly me," I giggle, offering my best impression of an airhead. "What must you think of me?"

He's clearly not impressed and shakes his head. I'm actually quite proud of my performance and continue to smile at him.

An obvious conclusion strikes the workman a millisecond before I draw the same conclusion.

Ohh, crap.

"Ahh, I get it," he says. "This is some sort of ruse, so you could talk to me."

"Oh, um...err."

"So, you fancy a drink sometime then?"

"Well, I'm not sure..."

Clement's voice booms across the platform. The sweetest sound.

"You coming, doll'?"

I look over the workman's shoulder. Clement is standing a dozen yards beyond.

"Sorry. I've got to go. My fiancé is here to pick me up."

264

The workman, clearly annoyed at this rejection, turns to eye up his competition. His shoulders slump when he sees Clement.

I join my partner in crime and we scuttle out of the station before the workman realises he's been played.

Fifty yards beyond the station forecourt, Clement stops and unbuttons his denim waistcoat, inviting me to take a peek. A pair of heavy-duty bolt cutters are nestled against his torso, supported by his thick leather belt.

I shouldn't, but I can't help myself. I grin up at him. "You're a bad influence on me, Clement."

"Funnily enough, you're not the first person to say that."

In truth, I'm beginning to wonder if Clement's influence on me is anything but bad.

26

Three glasses of wine, the last of which was consumed over two hours ago.

Am I okay to drive?

As we stand behind the shop, Clement leans against the car and argues the case for the defence.

"You sound sober enough to me, doll."

"I'm not sure. I don't feel sober."

"You'll be fine."

I really want to get home, but not so much I want to risk a driving ban.

"You'll have to drive, Clement."

"Yeah, but I've been drinking."

"Come off it," I scoff. "I doubt three pints would even register on a man your size. And besides, being a fraction over the drink drive limit would sit pretty low on your list of misdemeanours."

"Fair point."

Clement opens the driver's door and attempts to get behind the wheel. He quickly gives up.

"Can you move the bleedin' seat? I can't even get in."

I ease into the passenger side and slide the driver's seat back as far as it will go. Clement clambers in as the suspension groans.

"There's a lever on the right if you need to adjust the seat any further."

With his head pressed up against the vinyl roof, I guess he probably does.

After a few adjustments, he eventually finds an acceptable driving position. I hand him the keys and point out the ignition barrel.

A thought crosses my mind. "You can drive, can't you?"

"Yeah, course I can. Bit out of practice, mind you."

Five hundred yards later, I realise just how out of practice he really is.

"Jesus, Clement," I shriek as he overtakes a cyclist, almost meeting a lorry head on. "How on earth did you pass a driving test?

"I didn't."

"What? You've never passed a driving test?"

"Don't worry. I've never failed one either."

He slips into third gear and floors the accelerator, racing to beat an amber traffic light.

"It's got some poke, ain't it?"

"For Christ's sake, slow down," I screech, stamping my right foot on a brake pedal that isn't there.

After eight long minutes of screaming directions, and pleading for my life, we finally turn into my road and park up.

"Thank you for that, Clement. Suffice to say, I'll be doing the driving from now on."

"I did say I was a bit out of practice."

"As what? A getaway driver?"

I grab the keys and peel myself from the seat. Clement collects our borrowed bolt cutters from the boot and we stroll back down the street to my house.

I've never been so glad to step through the front door.

"Right. I'm going up for a shower. There's more beer in the fridge if you want one, and you can make yourself useful by pouring me a glass of wine."

"Yes, ma'am."

I traipse up the stairs and flop down on the edge of my bed. Removing my trainers is almost orgasmic; the smell less so.

With a pair of joggers, a hoodie, and clean underwear in hand, I head to the bathroom and scrub my skin raw in the shower for ten minutes. London might be a great city, but it penetrates every pore, every hair follicle. I'm not sure how people live there. I suppose they just get used to it — I never could.

I head down to the kitchen feeling human again, and I'm pleased to see a glass of wine waiting for me. Clement is sitting at the table supping beer from a can.

"Thank you."

"No worries, doll. You mind if I grab a shower? I smell like a badger's arse."

"You've no clean clothes, have you?"

"I travel light."

"I gathered. Come with me a sec."

I lead Clement back into the hallway where Karl's clothes are still bagged up on the floor. After a few minutes of delving, I locate some items that might help my stinky companion.

"Karl's mum always sent him socks and pants for Christmas, and they were always the wrong size, but they should fit you. And he bought this sweater in the sales but it was way too big for him. Never got around to returning it."

"Cheers, doll."

Clement takes the clothes and disappears up the stairs.

"There's a towel in the airing cupboard," I call after him.

I hear the bathroom door close. As I take a seat at the kitchen table and sup my wine, the bathroom door opens again and Clement calls down the stairs.

"You got any soap, doll?"

Who the hell still uses soap?

I reluctantly get up and shuffle through to the hallway.

"No I haven't," I call up the stairs. "But there should still be some of Karl's shower gel up there. It's in a green bottle."

"Shower gel?"

"Yes. It's like liquid soap."

"Right. Ta."

I hear the door close again. I give it a few seconds and return to the kitchen.

For three or four minutes, all I can hear is the gentle hum of the shower pump. My chilled white wine is exquisite, and I wallow in that contented, post-shower feeling as I ease back towards tipsy.

I should have known my contentment wouldn't last.

Clement screams from the bathroom above. "Jesus...fucking...Christ."

Strangely, this is not the first time a man has screamed from the bathroom. I once left a razor in the shower tray and Karl stepped on it. He made a similar commotion. Seeing as Karl's foot bled for an age, I'm seriously hoping Clement hasn't done the same thing.

I put my glass down and traipse up the stairs.

Having already witnessed Clement parading around in his underpants, I have no desire to see the full reveal. I knock on the bathroom door and stand back.

"You okay in there, Clement?"

A few more expletives are offered in reply, and I think he asked me to wait a minute.

I'm about to return to my wine when the shower pump stops. I hear the slap of wet feet on the tiled floor and the bathroom door opens. Clement is standing with a towel wrapped around his waist, and a green bottle in his hand.

"What the bleedin' hell is this?" he wails, thrusting the bottle towards me.

"Shower gel," I reply, puzzled.

"You sure, doll? Feels like I've washed my knackers with Epsom salts."

I lean in and look at the bottle.

"Ohh."

"What? What is it?" he says, a hint of panic in his voice.

"Mint and tea tree. It does have a bit of a tingle."

"Tingle? Are you shittin' me? Why would anyone wash their jewels in this stuff?"

I can't help but laugh. Clement doesn't see the funny side and slams the door.

I'm still chuckling to myself five minutes later when Clement enters the kitchen.

"You smell nice."

"Sod off."

He grabs another lager from the fridge and slumps down at the table. The navy jumper I gave him, which I think was extra-large, clings to his upper body like Lycra. When Karl tried it on, he looked like a child who'd ransacked his father's wardrobe.

"You're not sulking are you?" I ask.

"Bleedin' stuff," he grumbles. "It's like napalm. I can still feel it."

"Karl said it was invigorating."

"Karl said a lot of things that were bullshit, didn't he?"

"Touché."

I refill my glass and move the subject on. "So, what's the plan for tomorrow?"

"I think we'd be better off heading up there in the evening, when it's dark. Fewer people around and less chance of being spotted."

"I agree."

"And we need a few tools, and a decent torch."

I get up and open the cupboard under the sink. After a bit of rummaging, I locate Karl's toolbox.

"This do you?"

Clement takes the toolbox and unclips the lid. It's a fairly basic kit with spanners, screwdrivers, pliers, and a hammer.

"Yeah, that'll do. What about a torch?"

"I think I've got just the thing. One minute."

I dart up the stairs and head into the spare bedroom. I find what I'm looking for in the bottom of the wardrobe. My loft doesn't have a light, so I bought a rechargeable halogen lamp to aid the annual search for suitcases and Christmas decorations.

I pad back down the stairs with the lamp in hand. As I enter the kitchen, I switch off the light and turn the lamp on.

"Light enough for you?"

"Perfect."

I switch the light back on and plug the lamp in to charge.

"The battery is good for about four hours."

"Christ, doll. I bloody hope we're not down there that long."

"You and me both."

We sit for a while and finalise our plans for tomorrow evening. With the toolbox, the bolt cutters, and the lamp, it makes more sense to drive up to Tower Hill rather than lug everything on the train and tube. I wouldn't normally dream of driving into central London but it should be fairly quiet on a Sunday evening.

With the plan settled, the finality of tomorrow's foray begins to sink in.

"If you were a gambling man, Clement, would you bet on us finding it?"

"I might wager a fiver."

"That doesn't fill me with confidence."

"Lots of things we don't know for sure, doll. It's definitely worth a punt though, and we've got sod all to lose, have we?"

"We have if we get caught."

"What they gonna do? Charge you with trespassing? You'd get a fine and a slap on the wrists."

"I can't afford a fine."

"Best we don't get caught then."

I take a sip of wine and ask the question we've both been avoiding.

"What am I going to do if there's nothing there? I'll only have four days until Sterling wants paying."

"You still don't like my plan-A?"

"To beat him up?"

"Yeah."

"Oh, I like it, Clement. Nothing would give me greater pleasure than to see that creep get his comeuppance."

"Then why bother looking for the gold? Tell me where he lives and I'll pay him a visit."

"Because he's an old man, Clement — chances are, you'd kill him. And even if you don't, I get the feeling he doesn't like losing. He still has that bloody contract with my forged signature, and no doubt, a team of expensive lawyers who could ruin me financially if I contest it."

"So plan-A is still definitely a non-starter?"

"Afraid so."

Clement gets up and retrieves another can of lager from the fridge.

"The best way to think is with a drink," he says. "More wine?"

"Go on then."

Clement empties the bottle into my glass. I'm beginning to wish I'd finished my chicken salad.

"Shall we go and sit in the lounge?" I suggest. "It's a bit more comfortable and we can listen to some music."

"Are you trying to seduce me, doll?" he replies with a grin.

I almost spit my wine across the kitchen. "Good God. No, I'm not."

"Just checking. Wouldn't wanna disappoint you."

"You wouldn't be the first."

We head through to the lounge and Clement flops into an armchair. I turn on the TV and connect the Spotify app on my phone.

"I thought you said we were gonna listen to some music?"

"We are. I can stream music from my phone app through the TV surround system."

"Explain that again, in English."

"I'll show you. What's your favourite song?"

"Don't have one."

"Alright, a song you really like then."

He ponders for a moment. "The Troggs, *A Girl Like You*."

Perhaps the only positive legacy of Karl's time living here is the home cinema system he set up last year. With five speakers dotted around the room, and a big base unit beside the TV, it makes an impressive noise.

I jab away at my phone and barely ten seconds after Clement has made his request, the first notes peel from the speakers. Once the vocals kick in, I recognise the song.

Clement sits forward, his foot tapping away. "That's bloody clever. What else can it play?"

"Pretty much anything. I think there's something like thirty million tracks available."

"You're shittin' me?"

"No. You name an artist and I'm fairly sure they'll be in here."

"Any artist?"

"Yep, except Taylor Swift."

"Taylor who?"

"Forget it. You wouldn't like her anyway."

"So let me get this right. I can name any song by any artist, and you reckon you can play it straight away?"

"Yep. Let's try."

"Alright. Queen, *Seven Seas of Rhye*."

"Got it."

As Freddie Mercury's voice echoes around the room, Clement's smile broadens. "He's got some voice, ain't he? I bloody love Queen."

I don't have the heart to tell him Freddie Mercury died over twenty five years ago.

"Okay. Next?"

"Let's have some Deep Purple. *Strange Kind of Woman.*"

"No problem."

It takes me twenty seconds to establish I'm not a fan of Deep Purple, least not this track.

"Something else?"

"Yeah, a song that's quite apt," he grins. "Gary Glitter, *Hello! Hello! I'm Back Again.*"

He's right inasmuch that it's apt. Inappropriate, but apt.

"Err, slight issue with that one."

"What?"

"Didn't Gary Glitter also have a song about being in a gang?" I ask.

"Yeah, think it was called, *I'm The Leader of the Gang.*"

"Right. As it turned out, Glitter was in the same gang as Jimmy Saville."

"No way," he groans. "Gary Glitter is a nonce?"

"Afraid so. He's currently in prison, so he won't be *back again* anytime soon."

Clement shakes his head. "I need a smoke."

He slopes off to the patio while I select some music a little more to my liking. I skip through my playlists and decide on an album from my university days, *No Angel,* by Dido.

Clement returns after five minutes and stands motionless for a moment.

"What's this song?"

"It's called, *Here With Me.*"

"It's good."

"You've never heard it before?"

"Nope."

"I used to play this album all the time when I was at university. Seems such a long time ago now."

He sits back down in the armchair and continues to listen intently. As the track ends, he makes another request.

"Can you play *Misty* by Johnny Mathis?"

"Sure. Give me a sec."

It appears to be a song covered by a number of artists. I scroll down the results and find the version by Johnny Mathis, and press the play icon.

A piano, accompanied by the gentle brush of drums, and the stroking of a harp. The vocal begins and my skin tingles. It's such a timeless classic, rendered in crystal clarity through the expensive speakers.

For three minutes and forty four seconds, Clement sits and stares into space. He doesn't move or say a word. This continues for seconds after the song ends and silence fills the room.

"I've never really listened to that song before. It's beautiful, Clement."

"First heard it in the sixties," he says wistfully. "A...friend played it to me, on a Dansette record player. We played it over and over again."

"Friend?"

"Yeah. A good friend."

"I'm guessing that friend was of the female persuasion?"

He strokes his moustache and his head drops, just a fraction. "Yeah. Was," he sighs.

"Do you want to talk about it?"

"Not really."

He snaps out of his malaise and grabs his can. "Stick something a bit more cheerful on, doll."

I pick a random playlist and turn the volume down so it's mere background noise. We still have a twenty grand problem that needs addressing.

"If we don't find anything tomorrow, we still don't have a backup plan, do we?"

"I'm working on it."

"Anything you want to share?"

"I don't think you wanna know, doll."

"It's something illegal, isn't it?"

"Maybe."

"Can you not come up with something that doesn't carry the risk of a prison sentence?"

"I can only help you with what I know, and most of what I know is...a bit dodgy."

"Great. Why didn't they send me a multi-millionaire with a briefcase full of cash?"

"Don't think it works like that, doll."

"It was a rhetorical question."

"Eh?"

"Never mind. I suppose a dodgy plan is better than no plan."

"That's the spirit. Want another drink?"

I've lost track of how much wine I've consumed, but it's probably too much.

"No, thank you. I think I might hit the sack. It's been a long day."

"Right. You gonna sleep in the bath again?"

I feel my cheeks flush. "Um, no, not tonight."

"That's good. I think I might need the lav during the night."

"Do you want to sleep in the spare bedroom?"

"Up to you, doll. I'm alright on the sofa."

It's only been twenty four hours since Clement burst into my life, and without even thinking about it, I've invited him to sleep in the room next to mine. There's no bolt on my bedroom door, no chance of a quick escape through the window.

That should bother me, but it doesn't.

Despite my instincts telling me not to, I'm slowly beginning to believe in Clement. What I don't believe is his reason for being here, or his fanciful tales of a previous life, a generation ago. But if I can continue to separate the two, there might be a happy ending to all of this.

I only hope the lines don't blur any further.

27

It's just gone nine in the morning.

It wasn't my alarm that woke me. No, it was the family of warthogs that appear to have taken up residency in the spare bedroom.

Even if I wanted to lie in any longer, there's little chance of sleeping through the barrage of grunts echoing across the landing.

I get up and head into the bathroom. I make no attempt to be quiet as I take a shower and stomp back to my bedroom to get dressed.

And still the grunting continues.

I rap on the door to the spare bedroom.

"Clement. It's nearly half past nine. You awake?"

No response.

I wrap on the door a little harder. "Clement!"

The grunting stops.

"Hope you're decent. I'm coming in."

I open the door and slowly peer into the dark room.

Very quickly, I wish I hadn't.

I clamp my hand over my nose. "Good God, Clement. It smells like fetid cabbage in here."

"Sorry, doll," he coughs. "It's the beer. Gives me wind."

I retreat a safe distance back onto the landing. "Open the windows before you come down."

With my appetite ruined, I trudge down the stairs to the more fragrant surroundings of the kitchen and put the kettle on. As I prepare the cups, I hear the bathroom door close, followed by a series of grunts and groans. The radio is immediately switched on.

Once I've made a cup of tea, I sit down at the table. Clement breezes in after a few minutes.

"Morning, doll."

"Did you open the bedroom windows?"

"Yeah, and in the bathroom. I'd give it ten minutes if I were you."

"That is so gross. I shouldn't have to ask, but you have washed your hands?"

"Yeah, course I have. Wanna smell?"

"No, I'll take your word for it."

I nod towards the side. "I made you a cup of tea."

"Cheers."

Clement grabs his cup and joins me at the table.

"I'm guessing we're not having a cooked breakfast."

"You guess correctly. But as we'll be occupied at dinner time, we can have something substantial for lunch."

"What day is it?"

"Sunday."

"A roast then?"

"Erm, probably not. I was going to go and see my mum for an hour, so I can pick something up from the supermarket on the way home."

"You gonna break in?"

"What?"

"The supermarket. It's Sunday. It'll be closed."

"No, Clement. Supermarkets are open on Sunday these days. And so are shops, and so are pubs."

"Really? Do pubs still close after lunch?"

"Eh? No. Most of them are open all day, every day."

"That sounds a good way to spend a Sunday."

"Shame you're skint."

"Guess I'll wait here then. Can I watch TV?"

"Yes, Clement. Actually, I think Karl set *Match of the Day* to auto-record if you want to watch that?"

"I can watch *Match of the Day*, from last night?"

"Yes."

"Cool. Does Jimmy Hill still present it?"

"No, I think it's Gary Lineker."

"Who?"

"Big ears. Likes crisps."

He looks at me blankly as I get up and retrieve a loaf of bread from the cupboard.

"Do you fancy some toast?" I ask.

"Got any baked beans?"

"I think baked beans are the last thing you should be eating. Don't you?"

"Spaghetti hoops?"

"Toast with margarine is all I can offer. Although, I might have some marmalade."

"Nah. You're alright. Three rounds of buttered toast will do."

I drop three slices of wholemeal bread into the toaster and slide the lever down.

"Is there anything in particular you want for lunch?"

"I'm easy, doll. Not keen on faggots though."

"Faggots? Ohh, you mean those little meatball things?"

"Yeah. I think they're made from pig's arseholes, or something."

"Right. Noted."

While I wait for the toaster, I grab a couple of plates from the cupboard.

"You got a newspaper?" Clement asks.

"No. I don't have one delivered as there's not much point these days. I get my news from social media or the BBC news app."

"Great," he mumbles.

The toaster pops and I drop the slices onto a plate before spreading a nob of margarine across each one.

I pass the plate to Clement. "Enjoy."

"Cheers," he says, with little enthusiasm.

I slide a couple more slices of bread into the toaster and sip tea while I wait. To think, I was standing here this time last week, going through the exact same motions with my fiancé. What a difference a week makes.

By the time I sit down with my plate, Clement has already demolished his toast.

"Can you get some bacon from the supermarket, doll? Don't fancy toast again tomorrow."

"I suppose so. Anything else sir desires?"

"Eggs, mushrooms, and some decent pork sausages wouldn't go amiss. Oh, and some soap. "

How quickly the surreal becomes the mundane.

"I'll see. I'm not exactly flush with cash at the moment."

I finish my toast and Clement follows me through to the lounge so I can show him how to use the Sky box.

Painstaking doesn't cover it.

It takes almost twenty minutes for him to get to grips with the remote control and on-screen menu. I can only compare it to training a chimp to use an iPad.

He eventually settles down to watch the football.

"I'm off then. I'll be a few hours but there's plenty on there for you to watch. Help yourself to tea but don't go stuffing your face with cake or biscuits."

"Yeah, alright," he says dismissively.

"Oh, and no alcohol. We need clear heads for tonight."

"Shh, doll. Arsenal are about to kick off."

I roll my eyes and leave him to it.

I grab my handbag and leave the house. As I close the door, I quickly scan up and down the road, conscious that Messrs Black & Blue might have returned to their post. There's no sign of them.

I hop into the Fiat and check the route to Stanley's mobile home. It should take no more than twenty minutes but I'm in no great hurry.

The roads are relatively clear and it's another glorious autumnal day, the watery sun glinting against a vivid blue canvas. As the miles slip by, the grey and brown scenery slowly gives way to shades of green.

I take a turning off the main road and head along a country lane. The tight bends and narrow carriageway were made for the Fiat, and I savour the thrill of throwing it into the tight bends. For a brief moment, I forget all about David Sterling. I forget about Karl, and I forget about the trip to London later.

And I almost forget about Clement too, that is until I see him standing in front of a five-bar gate, forty yards ahead of me.

I slam my foot on the brake just as a shard of bright sunlight bursts over a hedgerow, temporarily blinding me.

The tyres squeal and the smell of burnt rubber drifts through the heating vent.

The car comes to a standstill and through squinted eyes, I lower the sun visor.

I stare straight ahead, my heart thumping. Hedgerows, grass banks, and a metal gate. There's nobody there, let alone the man I left back at my house a little over fifteen minutes ago.

I slip the Fiat into first gear and slowly crawl along the lane. I reach a tight bend, and pass the gate on my right where I thought I saw Clement. Not a soul around.

Christ, I must be going crazy, seeing things.

I edge the Fiat around the bend before I work through the gears and pull away, keeping my speed below thirty. Every few seconds I glance in my rear view mirror, but the scene just shrinks away, never changing.

I suddenly become conscious I'm drawing sharp, shallow breaths, and I can feel the blood pulsing through a vein in my neck.

I pull into a pass point and try to steady my breathing. My left eyelid begins to twitch, and my knuckles whiten as sweaty palms grip the steering wheel.

I know these symptoms. I've seen them before.

My mother suffered from anxiety throughout my early teenage years. She'd lock herself in her bedroom for days on end, leaving me to fend for myself. When she wasn't crying or mumbling gibberish, she was listless and uncommunicative.

Then one day, it just stopped. I was relieved, until she confided in me that my dead father had appeared at her bedside, and told her everything was going to be okay.

As much as I wanted to believe my mother, the doctor provided a more rational explanation. Apparently, victims of acute anxiety can experience hallucinations. It's rare, but it does happen. I just wanted my mother to be well again. If it helped her to function, I didn't care what she believed.

I have to ask myself — has that same susceptibility to anxiety been passed down through my mother's genes?

Is it now happening to me?

I have every reason to be suffering from anxiety, but I'm stronger than my mother. I've had to be.

As unwelcome as a bout of acute anxiety might be, at least it offers a rational explanation for what I thought I saw. Cold comfort, but it calms me slightly. Maybe I just need a holiday, or at least a week of doing nothing.

Yes, that's it. Once I've put this mess behind me, I'll take a break. I'll be fine.

I close my eyes and take several long, deep breaths.

You're in control, Beth. Keep it together.

It takes a few minutes for my composure to return before I drive the final two miles like an octogenarian.

28

I have to admit, it's not what I expected.

Two brick pillars stand abreast of the entrance, with a black granite sign affixed to the left pillar. Gold letters form the name 'Grange Park'; the location of Stanley's home. A tarmac road cuts through the centre, with neat little mobile homes lined up either side and dense woodland beyond. There's no more than forty homes, each with a parking space and decked patio area to the front. Every one of them is impeccably kept, not a blade of grass out of place.

I reach the end of the road and pull into the visitors' parking area. As I step from the Fiat, I question my decision to turn up unannounced. I guess old habits die hard and I can't help but fear the worst where Stanley Goodyear is concerned.

I lock the car and walk back up the road towards number twelve. It's every bit as peaceful as Stanley claimed. I imagined something more like a scrap yard. I pictured a grotty caravan on bricks, a choking bonfire, corrugated iron fencing, and a couple of barking Alsatians.

Begrudgingly, I have to concede my mother is better off convalescing in Grange Park than in her council-owned flat.

Stanley's mobile home is about half way along the road, on the left. A silver Honda Civic is parked outside, and a paved pathway leads up the side of the car towards the front door.

I follow the path up to the door and rap the brass knocker, twice.

Seconds pass but there's no reply. I rap the knocker again, and wait. Still no movement from within.

With my innate mistrust of Stanley, the only conclusion I can draw is that something is wrong.

I thump the door hard, several times.

Long seconds pass and all I can hear is birdsong. My concern mounts, and I'm just about to thump at the door again when it swings open.

"Bethany!" Stanley blusters. "Why...what are you doing here?"

Clearly he got dressed in a hurry. His light blue shirt is unbuttoned to the navel, and one of his trouser legs is rolled halfway up his shin.

"Where's my mother?" I growl, overlooking his dishevelled appearance.

My question is immediately answered as my mother appears behind Stanley.

"Beth, darling...what a lovely surprise."

She's wearing a skimpy, silk dressing gown, and little all else.

"You had me worried, Mum. Why didn't you answer the door?" I bark.

"We were...asleep," she replies coyly.

"At this time of the morning?"

My mother looks at Stanley. He looks back at her, his eyes wide.

"Yes, well, we fancied a lie in."

Two pink faces look at me, a faint glint of sweat on Stanley's forehead.

Realisation dawns, along with a crushing awkwardness.

"Ohh, right. Shall I, erm, come back in ten minutes?" I ask.

Ten minutes? Why not twenty minutes, or thirty? Christ, what is the socially acceptable period of time one should allow two pensioners to conclude a shag?

It's a question that brings no answers, but a cold shudder.

"No, don't be silly," my mother chirps. "Come on in."

Stanley forces a smile on his face before he disappears, presumably to deal with his attire.

I step through the door into a lounge area. The interior of the mobile home is surprisingly pleasant, styled with a palette of natural tones to complement dashes of plum and turquoise blue. A stone-coloured sofa faces an Adam-style fireplace, with two matching armchairs either side.

"This is really nice, Mum."

"It is, isn't it? Stanley chose all the furnishings."

We take a seat and chat idly until Stanley reappears.

"Tea, Bethany?"

"Please."

He heads through an archway into an equally pleasant kitchen, and puts the kettle on.

The three of us then sit for an hour, sipping tea and talking about nothing in particular. I catch Stanley's eye a couple of times, and I wonder if he's hoping I'll bugger off so they can resume their shenanigans. That doesn't bother me quite as much as the fact my pension-age mother is getting more bedroom action than I am.

The conversation eventually peters out but I'm satisfied everything is well with my mother. I get to my feet, much to Stanley's relief.

"I'll give you a call tomorrow, Mum. Is there anything you need?"

"No, thank you, darling. Stanley has everything in hand."

I'm sure he has, or did.

"Good. I'll leave you to, err..."

"Goodbye, darling."

They edge me towards the door and Mum plants a kiss on my cheek. Stanley cautiously pats me on the shoulder, as if petting an unpredictable terrier.

Once I'm on the opposite side of the door, they stand side-by-side and wave me goodbye as I edge backwards down the path. I'm sure Stanley mumbles "just piss off," through a gritted smile.

I plod back to the car, trying to purge the image of Stanley's ruddy sex face from my mind. As I cruise back past number twelve, I have to force myself to keep looking straight ahead.

Look away, Beth. Don't think about what's going on in there.

Notwithstanding the interruption of a scene I'd rather not dwell on, at least my mother appears in good spirits. She's safe, and that's all I really care about as I drive away from Grange Park.

I pass the same five-bar gate and I'm relieved there are no hallucinations this time. I seem to recall my mother's doctor once saying the first step in dealing with stress and anxiety is acceptance — you can't fix a problem if you don't accept you have one. Maybe I've done that now, and my little episode earlier was a warning; a signal that I could follow the same path as my mother if I'm not careful.

And that brings me to the object of my hallucination — Clement. Is he alleviating my stress levels, or adding to them? Would I now be in a better place if he hadn't gatecrashed my life?

It's an interesting question — where would I be?

Would I have been any less stressed if I'd spent yesterday in the shop, trying to figure out how to get Sterling's money on my own? I doubt it.

Would I now be at home, pacing up and down, still trying to come up with a solution? Probably.

Either way, I'd be on my own.

For all Clement's faults and delusions, he has stood by me. Maybe I should return the favour and stick by him, at least until this evening's foray is over.

The fields and hedgerows soon give way to brick and concrete as I get closer to the town centre.

I arrive at Waitrose and spend five minutes trying to find a parking space. Then, with a basket in hand, I head towards the ready meals aisle — sadly, a section of the supermarket I'll be frequenting more often now I'm single again.

There's a fairly eclectic choice of meals from around the globe. However, I suspect Clement favours more traditional fare. With that in mind, I plumb for lamb hotpot with herby dumplings.

I grab some milk and bread, and for a moment I consider the other items on Clement's shopping list. I compromise and buy a box of eggs to scramble for breakfast tomorrow.

Finally, I head down the toiletry aisle, looking for Imperial Leather soap. I have the option to buy a single bar, or a four-pack. Thinking about it, I assume Clement will be long gone before a second bar is ever opened so I grab a single bar.

I hadn't, until this moment, really considered what happens to Clement once this is all over. It's funny how the most innocent of decisions can suddenly prod your thoughts in an unexpected direction.

It's a question I'd rather brush away though, but it does play on my mind all the way through the checkout, and the journey home.

I walk through the door just after one o'clock. Judging by the noise coming from the lounge, Clement has finally got to grips with the volume on the TV.

I put the shopping away and wander through to the lounge.

"Is that loud enough?" I yell above the TV.

"Eh?" he shouts back.

I grab the remote control and lower the volume. I'm pleased to see there's no evidence of Clement having helped himself to food or drink.

"That's better. How was the football?"

"Terrible."

"Really? Why?"

"Because it was just a load of bloody foreigners falling over every five minutes."

"Ahh, you've discovered the joys of modern football, and the Premier League."

"Yeah, that's another thing. What happened to Division One?"

"I think it's one and the same now. It was re-branded."

"Load of poncey nonsense if you ask me," he grumbles. "They've ruined football."

"Never mind. I've got you something nice for lunch. I hope you like hotpot and dumplings."

"Yeah, perfect. I'm bleedin' starving."

"Great. It should be ready in ten minutes."

"Ten minutes? How are you gonna knock up a hotpot in ten minutes?"

"I'm...erm, not. It's a ready meal so it just needs to go in the microwave."

"The what?"

"Really?" I groan. "Did you not question what that shiny silver box on the kitchen side was?"

"That thing? Thought it was a TV."

"It's not. It's an oven, of sorts."

"Right. And it can cook a hotpot in ten minutes?"

"Well, less actually."

"Can I watch?"

"You want to watch a hotpot cook in the microwave?"

"I just watched West Brom play Watford. It can't be any less interesting."

"Right."

Clement follows me out to the kitchen where I retrieve our ready meals from the fridge. As instructed, I pierce the film lid several times and place the first tray in the microwave. Clement watches on intently as I set the timer to five minutes and press the start button.

I wash my hands as the aroma of lamb hotpot drifts across the kitchen.

"Oh, Clement, that reminds me — I bought you a present."

I dry my hands and retrieve the bar of Imperial Leather from the cupboard.

"As requested," I say, handing him the soap.

He unwraps the packaging and holds the bar to his nose, inhaling deeply.

"Ahh, that's what a man should smell like, doll."

"Unlike my spare bedroom."

The microwave pings and I retrieve the first tray, sliding the second one in and resetting the timer. Although I can't imagine Clement really caring, I serve his meal in a bowl rather than the depressing plastic tray.

To my surprise, he waits until my food is ready before he starts, and we tuck into our hotpots together at the kitchen table.

"We gonna get everything together after lunch?" he asks.

"Yep. I've checked the route and it should take about ninety minutes to drive, so I was aiming to leave around half five."

"You want me to drive?"

"Absolutely not."

He shoots me a frown while stabbing a dumpling with his fork. "Suit yourself."

"There is something else you might be able to help me with, though."

"Go on," he grunts.

"Something crossed my mind while I was in the supermarket. I was thinking, when this is over, where will you go?"

"Depends."

"On?"

"Whether this works out well, or not."

"Do you want to expand on that?"

"Not really."

"But when you first arrived, you said you'd end up somewhere horrible if you failed."

He chews slowly on a mouthful of lamb as he appears to consider my point.

"It's not your concern, doll. Don't worry about it."

"Well, it kind of is my concern. I...um...want you to be okay."

"Careful, doll. Next you'll be telling me you actually care."

"I do care, Clement."

"Then half my job is already done."

"Eh? I'm not with you."

He nudges the final dumpling around the bowl with his fork before slicing it in two. Half the dumpling is transferred to his mouth without an answer.

I give it a few seconds before pressing him. "Well?"

"What's for pudding?"

"Forget pudding. Are you going to answer my question? What do you mean about half the job being done?"

He forks the second half of the dumpling and devours it. I don't think he intends to answer my question so I pose another.

"Okay. Where will you go if everything works out and we solve the problem with Sterling?"

He drops his fork into a now empty bowl.

"Honestly, doll? No idea," he sighs. "Lap of the gods."

He gets up and takes his bowl to the sink.

"Doesn't that concern you?"

"What's the point in being concerned about something I can't change? I'll do what I can to help you but beyond that, what will be, will be."

"That's a very philosophical view."

He rinses his bowl under the tap and places it on the drainer.

"Not a view, doll. Just a fact."

With another line of questioning closed, I finish my lunch while Clement disappears outside for a cigarette.

Once our bowls are put away, I crack open a packet of apple pies and put the kettle on. Clement steps back into the kitchen and we return to the table for tea and cakes. Just one solitary apple pie is left in the packet, much to my shame.

Fully fuelled, we then get everything ready for our trip. It doesn't actually take long, despite Clement requesting we add a flask of tea to our inventory.

By two thirty, everything is laid out on the kitchen table, ready for our departure.

"Now what?" Clement asks.

"We could watch a film?"

"At the cinema?"

"No. There's more choice on Sky, and it's a damn sight cheaper."

We head into the lounge and I pull up the movie menu on the TV.

"What's your favourite film?"

"Easy. *Treasure Island*. First film I ever saw at the cinema."

"When did that come out?"

"I saw it when I was a teenager, so some time around the early fifties, I guess."

"Hmmm. Maybe something else then."

"You choose."

I dismiss dozens of movies before I spot something that might appeal to both of us.

"I'm guessing you used to watch Star Trek?"

"Yeah, I did. Now you mention it, you remind me of one of the characters."

"Really? Lieutenant Uhura?"

"Nah. Spock," he sniggers.

I frown, but as I have a soft spot for Spock, I'll take it as a compliment.

"I think you'll like this," I reply, ignoring his jibe.

I download the 2009 Star Trek movie; the one with a new cast playing the original characters. I've seen it before, but the geek in me is happy to watch it again.

It proves to be a good choice as Clement is glued to the screen for the entire two-hour duration. While he's absorbed in the action, I take the opportunity to scour Google on my laptop, trying to find any plans of the old Tower Hill station. It proves fruitless so it looks like we'll be going in blind. I do, however, manage to locate a cheap car park fairly close to our destination.

Unfortunately, neither the movie nor the research distract from the knot of anxiety, slowly growing in the pit of my stomach as our departure time looms closer.

All too soon, the movie ends and we return to the kitchen. We go through a final checklist before loading it all into an old rucksack I acquired for my one and only camping expedition.

"Right. I think we're good to go," I announce, trying my best to appear calm.

"To boldly go where…"

"Stop, Clement," I interrupt. "You're not going to do that all evening are you?"

"Do what?"

"Quote lines from *Star Trek*."

"Maybe."

I roll my eyes as Clement grabs the rucksack. "Let's go."

He raises his hand and salutes. "Aye, Captain," he replies in a passable Scottish accent.

God knows how he can be so jovial. My nerves are already on edge and we've not even left yet.

I fear there will be nothing bold about this journey.

29

"Shit! It bloody speaks," Clement gasps, referring to the sat nav.

"Sort of."

"How does she know where we are?"

"It's not really a *she*. It's just a computer generated voice."

"Alright. How does *it* know where we are?"

"A signal is sent to a satellite every few seconds and it reports our position back to the device."

"That's bleedin' amazing. Do you have to buy your own satellite?" he asks.

"Um, no. That would be a bit impractical."

Clement continues to study the sat nav, fixed to the windscreen, with child-like fascination.

By the time we hit the M25, Clement has turned his inquisition from the sat nav to the motorway itself. When did it open? How long is it? Where does it go? Despite my mild incredulity at his questions, they do keep my mind distracted.

The decision to make the trip in the early evening proves wise as the traffic is light, and we reach junction seven within forty minutes. We can either leave the M25 for the M23 northbound, until it becomes the A23, or we can continue around the M25 towards Dartford and take the westbound A2. The Dartford option is marginally quicker but almost twice the distance. Time is not as valuable as petrol so we leave at junction seven and head north on the A23 — the road that will take us right into the heart of London.

For the first five miles we trundle along quite happily, and I even have to slow down as we pass the numerous speed cameras dotted along the road. Every few minutes, Clement stares intently out of the window and passes comment on a building that is either no longer there, or has changed. I give up responding by the fifteenth time.

We pass by Croydon and the traffic continues to build. Fifth gear becomes a stranger as I continually shift between second and third, or sit stationary at a never ending succession of traffic lights.

We reach Brixton, and still with almost five miles to go, the balls of my feet begin to ache from the constant pressing of pedals. It's so tedious, I'm almost tempted to ask Clement to take over the driving. Almost, but not quite.

After another thirty minutes of stop-start traffic, we eventually reach Tower Bridge Road, and my hope that the city would be quiet on a Sunday evening is dashed. It feels like we're nearing a giant hive, with hundreds of drones buzzing haphazardly from every direction while revving engines and blazing horns. I'm not the most confident of drivers and I think I've just entered my own personal driving hell.

It's just after seven o'clock by the time we pass over Tower Bridge, and I'm approaching meltdown. An already stressful drive is made worse as daylight ebbs away and dusk arrives.

"God, this is horrendous," I whimper. "I hate driving in London."

"I noticed," Clement jeers. "And I can't believe you had the nerve to criticise my driving."

What is now clear is that Clement's aggressive driving style is exactly how everyone in London drives. In my home town, lunatic drivers are a rare exception. Here, they rule.

"Please don't, Clement. I'm crapping myself enough without your input."

The sat nav chimes yet another instruction but I'm too focused on switching lanes, and miss it.

"I think you were supposed to turn right there," Clement mutters.

Another horn blares from behind us as I dither over my next manoeuvre.

"Turn around where possible," sat nav woman suggests.

"Fuck off," I scream in reply.

Clement chuckles to himself.

"Pull over, doll."

"Where? I can't."

He points to a drop off lane for coaches delivering tourists to The Tower.

"Just pull in there."

I guess I'm probably not supposed to, but I'm past caring. I pull up behind a coach and try to control my breathing.

"You want me to take over?" Clement asks.

It's an invite I'm only too happy to accept.

We both exit the car simultaneously, and as I climb into the passenger seat, I push the driver's seat back so Clement can squeeze his legs beneath the steering wheel. He clambers in and fights with the seatbelt. Once he locks it in place, he looks across at me.

"You alright, doll?"

"I think so."

He removes his sunglasses and puts them in the door pocket. A quick check of the sat nav screen and he rams the Fiat into gear.

"I'm in charge now, you bossy mare." he growls.

"I beg your pardon."

"I was talking to your robot friend."

"Oh. Right."

I'm thrown back in my seat as we dart from the drop off lane, Clement keen to see if the Fiat can do warp speed.

Five yelled expletives, two indecent hand gestures, and three minutes later, we arrive at the car park. I then have to give

Clement instructions on passing through the automatic entry system which dispatches our ticket and raises the barrier.

We circle around and find an empty bay at the far side of the car park. Clement turns sharply into it and cuts the engine.

I can finally breathe again.

"Well, that was horrific on just about every level."

"Never mind, doll. We're here now."

"And now all we have to do is break into a disused tube station, and find a small bar of gold that may, or may not, have been hidden there over forty years ago."

"That's the spirit. Piece of cake."

"I was being sarcastic."

We clamber out of the car and retrieve the rucksack from the boot. Clement throws it over his shoulder as if it weighs nothing, and we stride purposefully in the direction of an exit sign.

The exit leads out to a quiet backstreet. We turn left, and under darkening skies, make our way towards Byward Street.

I really hoped the walk would take longer, but we turn onto Byward Street barely two minutes after leaving the car park. Even at this time of day, the traffic is relentless.

"I thought there would be less passing traffic. It's not ideal is it?"

"Doesn't matter, doll. We just walk straight up to gate and hop over."

"What if somebody sees us?"

"This is London, not some quiet backwater. Nobody will give us a second glance."

I wish I had his confidence.

We approach the original entrance we inspected yesterday and wait for the traffic lights to change. Clement takes the opportunity to glance casually up and down the street. If he has any concerns, they don't show on his face.

"Soon as we get across, don't stop and don't look around. Just follow me. Clear?"

"Clear."

As the lights change, the traffic grinds to a halt. Clement moves off the kerb and I follow.

We reach the other side and he suddenly stops, bending down to tie a lace on a boot that has no laces.

"What are you doing?" I ask.

"Just buying a few seconds until the traffic moves on."

I fight the overwhelming urge to look around. I guess Clement is right in that it's a tell-tale sign you're up to no good.

The lights change and the traffic begins to flow again.

"Let's go," Clement orders.

Almost as if he's on a stroll in the country, he approaches the gate and steps over it, disappearing down the stairwell a second later.

Oh, crap. My turn.

I can feel a hundred pairs of invisible eyes staring as I approach.

Do not turn around.

Even though the gate is low, I clamber over it with all the grace of a heavily pregnant hippo. Once I'm on the other side, I waste no time in scampering down the stairs, out of sight of the invisible eyes.

By the time I reach the bottom, Clement's arm is already buried in the rucksack and he pulls out the bolt cutters. A weak bulb glows from behind a plastic casing above the door. Probably a health and safety measure, rather than a convenience for those up to no good in the dark recesses of the stairwell.

"Once these are open, it's plain sailing, doll," he says, nodding towards the wire mesh doors.

"You reckon?"

He doesn't reply but turns his attention to the padlock. He carefully locks the jaws of the bolt cutters around the steel loop of the padlock.

"I hope these are up to the job," he mumbles.

He draws a deep breath and positions his hands on the rubber grips. With his elbows jutting out to the side and a string of veins bulging in his neck, he begins to squeeze the handles together.

I'm surprised how little resistance is offered by the steel, or maybe I underestimated Clement's brute strength. The metal loop snaps and the padlock falls to the floor with a dull clunk.

"That was easier than I imagined," I whisper.

"Decent bolt cutters, doll. You could do some serious interrogation with these."

My mind conjures up an image of David Sterling, tied to a chair as I snap away at his bony fingers.

"Maybe we'll hold on to them until Thursday, just in case."

Clement smiles down at me as he tucks the bolt cutters back in the rucksack.

"We'll need the lamp from here on in. You okay holding it?"

"Let's save the battery, just in case we're in there for a while."

I activate the torch on my phone. "This will do for now."

"Bleedin' hell. That thing does more tricks than a two-bob whore."

"I'll take your word for it."

He pulls one of the doors open. "After you."

"No, I insist."

He bends down and snatches the broken padlock from the floor. "Best not leave any evidence behind."

The rucksack is then hoisted back onto his shoulder and he steps beyond the door. I follow him in and he pulls the door closed behind us.

"The actual station entrance is the other side."

I hold the phone out, illuminating the subway walls and dark floor stretching ahead of us. We move slowly, the noise of the traffic above us fading away with every step. The air becomes increasingly stale, tinged with an undercurrent of damp and vintage urine.

With no point of reference, it's hard to say how long the subway stretches, but the torch eventually catches a bright red 'No Entry' sign directly ahead of us. A dome mirror, fixed to the wall at head height, reflects weak light from a stairwell to the left. I presume it leads up to the main entrance on Byward Street.

"That's got to be the door into the station," Clement suggests.

The door is solid wood, painted black, with several warning notices fixed to it. There can be no doubt that unauthorised personnel should walk away, backed up by the fact the door is secured with a mortise lock, and a steel clasp fixed with another padlock.

Clement puts the rucksack down and retrieves the bolt cutters. The padlock receives the same treatment as its counterpart at the other end of the subway, and falls to the floor with a metallic thud that echoes around us.

"One down," Clement says to himself as he returns to the rucksack.

My contribution is limited to torch holding as I try to follow Clement's movements through the darkness.

"Should we use the lamp now?" I suggest.

"Nah. It'll bleed too much light up the stairs. Anyone passing by up there will see it."

He removes the toolkit from the rucksack and extracts two screwdrivers and a pair of pliers.

"I need light on the lock, doll."

I oblige and move closer to the door.

There are four screws holding an aluminium plate to the front of the mortise lock. Clement methodically unscrews each one before switching to a smaller screwdriver. He appears to undo a screw at the base of the handle before tugging it away, leaving a metal shaft in its place.

The metal plate is removed to reveal the inner workings of the lock mechanism.

"I can see why they added a padlock," Clement mutters. "This lock is as basic as they come."

"That's good, right?"

"Very."

It's tricky to see what he's doing as he sets about the lock mechanism with a pair of pliers and a screwdriver. It doesn't take long, and he then stands back from the door and twists the metal shaft with the pliers. With his free hand, he forces the screwdriver into the gap between the door and the frame, prising it open.

A wave of musty air bursts from the darkness.

"I'm impressed, Clement. Where did you learn to do that?"

"Misspent youth."

He puts the screwdrivers and the pliers back in the toolkit, and returns it to the rucksack.

"Think we'll need this now, doll."

He extracts the lamp and places it on the floor, just inside the door, facing into the darkness.

"Switch her on doll. Let's see what we're dealing with."

I lean over and switch the lamp on.

"Shittin' hell," Clement groans.

30

A metal staircase leads down to an empty space, and as best as I can tell in the limited light, it's about thirty feet square. It reminds me of a derelict house we used to play in as kids; bare brick walls, exposed rafters, and a complete absence of any features to hint at what purpose the space once served.

It's safe to say it's not what I imagined, nor Clement, judging by his reaction.

"This used to be a tube station?" I ask in disbelief.

"It was."

"What happened to it?"

"No idea, but it looks like they've stripped everything out."

"Surely that's not good? What if they inadvertently removed the gold?"

"Then we won't find it. But this place was closed long before the Baker Street job so if Harry did stash the gold down here, it was probably like it is now."

"So, we've got to search every corner?"

"Yeah, but it would make sense to start where the ticket office was located."

"And that was where?"

"Can't tell from here. Grab the lamp."

Clement plucks the rucksack from the floor and we step onto a steel platform. He pulls the door closed, entombing us in the dank, airless chamber.

I grab the lamp and direct it towards the metal staircase in front of us. It looks worryingly makeshift, bolted together God-only-knows how long ago. The guard rail, if you can call it that, is a single scaffolding pole, fixed to the treads with rusty brackets. From our position, it's easily an eight foot drop to the concrete floor below.

"Be careful, doll," Clement advises as he tentatively takes the first few stairs.

A tumble down a set of rickety stairs would nicely sum up my fortunes over the last week. I heed Clement's advice and take them one at a time, each step greeted with a metallic creak.

Slowly and steadily, we make our way down.

The magnitude of our task becomes all too apparent once we reach the bottom.

"Where the hell do we start?" I murmur.

"Process of elimination."

"Eh?"

"Give me the lamp."

I hand it to him and he moves towards the centre of the space. He holds it up, and slowly scans the beam from right to left across the far wall.

"There. Look."

I edge over to where he's standing and look up at the wall.

"See those?" he says.

"Ohh, yes."

There are two advertising posters fixed to the wall; both heavily faded and beyond tatty. It's impossible to make out any detail, or colour, but the text on both posters is still just about readable. The left poster advertises an Irish whisky, from a company called Jameson & Son. Beyond the title text, the rest of it is too faded to read. The poster on the right is slightly more legible, with *Julie Andrews* printed in white letters along the top, above the word *Hawaii*.

"Is that a movie poster?" I ask.

"Yeah."

"I've never seen it. Have you?"

"I saw the trailer, and trust me, that was bad enough."

"Well, as interesting as the posters are, they're not going to help us establish where the ticket office was located."

"They are, doll. They wouldn't put posters in a ticket office would they? So, it can't have been positioned against this wall."

"No. I suppose not."

He continues to scan the beam across the wall until it meets a dark, square aperture in the far corner, about seven feet wide. A set of iron scissor gates stretch across the void.

"Must be the stairs down to the platform."

He moves the beam onto the adjacent wall and scans nothing but bare brickwork.

"Don't think it could have been here as it would have been too close to the stairs."

"So, excluding the section where we came in, it must have been here," I suggest, pointing to the wall on our left.

"Yeah, I reckon so."

A low rumbling noise suddenly leaks from beyond the gates in the corner. It quickly builds into a symphony of grinding, squealing, and clacking, gaining in volume. A wave of warm, stagnant air bursts from the darkness, followed by rapid flashes of light like paparazzi outside a West End nightclub.

"Jesus, Clement. What is that?"

He shakes his head, as the ground beneath us vibrates.

Seconds pass and the performance peters out.

"Using my powers of deduction, and seeing as we're in a bleedin' tube station, I'd guess that was a train."

"Yes...erm, of course. Sorry, I'm a bit jittery."

"Shall we get on?"

"Right. Where do we start?"

"Good question."

Clement casts his gaze up the high wall, bordering the left side of the space. His moustache receives a couple of strokes before he picks up the lamp and heads towards the corner. He places it on the floor, about four feet from the wall, angled upwards.

"If I were in Harry's shoes, and seeing as there's no obvious place to hide anything in here, I'd have removed a couple of bricks, chiselled a space behind them, then stashed the gold in there. Once you put the original bricks back, nobody would notice unless they were really looking."

I stare at the wall, thirty feet long and about sixteen feet high. I then turn my stare to Clement.

"You have got to be kidding me? There's almost five hundred square feet of bricks — it'll take all night to check them all."

"No it won't. I doubt he brought a ladder with him so it can't be above head height. That's half the wall we can forget about."

"Oh, that's alright then," I groan. "Just a thousand-odd individual bricks to check then."

From the very moment Clement suggested we go in search of Harry's fabled gold, I knew it was a long shot. Perhaps I've allowed myself to get carried away in the excitement of the hunt, and reality has taken a back seat to fantasy.

But now, standing in this dark, musty void, staring at a wall of damp bricks, reality is firmly back in the driving seat.

"You just gonna stand there, doll?"

Weighed down with negativity, I let out a deep sigh and reluctantly shuffle across to Clement.

"God, this is ridiculous," I groan. "Even if there is a bar of gold in here, we'll never find it."

He folds his arms and frowns down at me. "What were you expecting? Did you think we'd waltz in here and find it sitting on a little table in the corner?"

"Well, no, but this is hopeless."

"Fine. We'll call it a day then. We don't have to do this."

"Don't we?"

"Course we don't. We could just give up and be back in the car within ten minutes."

I don't know how to respond to that statement.

"Strikes me, doll, you're pretty good at giving up."

"Sorry?"

"All those books you never finished."

"What's my writing got to do with anything?"

"You fancy the idea of writing a book, but when it comes down to it, it's just too much like hard work ain't it?"

"If you're trying to make a point, Clement, I'm not getting it."

"Same problem. You like the idea of finding Harry's gold, but you don't wanna put the graft in."

"That's not fair," I protest. "It's just..."

"Just what? Look, doll, this is no different from your problem writing a book. You start at the beginning and keep going until the end. Head down, keep moving forward. Nothing complicated about it."

I fidget with my fingers, grateful Clement can't see my cheeks reddening in the gloomy light.

"Or, you give up and look for an easier way; one that probably ain't there. Nothing worth having comes easy, doll."

Another passing tube train breaks the uncomfortable silence. Clement leans up against the wall, waiting for the din to end, and to see if I pick up the gauntlet.

Clement possesses a number of traits which annoy me, but I must admit I do admire both his determination and pragmatism. They're traits which have sadly been lacking in all the men in my life. Well, at least my adult life.

The sound of the tube train ebbs away and the silence returns.

"Shall we get started then?" I chirp, doing my best to sound enthusiastic.

"Sure?"

"Positive."

Clement hands me a screwdriver which I stare at blankly.

"All you gotta do is work along the line of bricks, jabbing that into the mortar every few inches. If Harry did remove a couple of bricks, there won't be any mortar, or he'll have probably packed it out with dirt. Either way, you should notice a difference when the tip of the screwdriver hits it."

I stare at the wall and try to calculate how many linear feet of mortar we'll need to work along.

"Doll, don't," Clement chides, as if reading my mind. "Let's just get on with it."

Perhaps I'd feel more positive if there was a definitive answer waiting for us at the end of our arduous task, but there isn't. All we have to go on is Clement's theory, and that itself is based on another flimsy theory. Nevertheless, it looks like we're set to search a haystack for a needle that might not even exist.

"I'll start at the top and you start at the bottom," Clement suggests. "We'll switch around half way so neither of us ends up with a buggered back."

I inwardly groan and squat down, screwdriver in hand.

"Here we go. Page one," Clement says.

"Yep. Page one."

We get to work.

There are some domestic chores I loathe. Ironing is probably the worst. But after five minutes of jabbing a screwdriver into brickwork, I'd happily swap my ironing nemesis, a basket of cotton blouses, for this task. It's back-breaking, tedious work, not helped by the fact I keep hearing scratching noises.

"You think there are rats in here, Clement?"

"Probably."

"Great. Thanks for putting my mind at rest."

We reach the half way point and switch positions, Clement squatting down while I get to stand. It's scant consolation but at least I'll be a few feet further away from any rats.

We reach the end of our respective lines and switch over again. I start one line up from the bottom, and Clement one line down from the highest position he theorised Harry would have stashed the gold.

Mindlessly, we push on. Jab, jab, shuffle. Jab, jab, shuffle. Over and over again; every completed line ramming another nail into my coffin of dwindling hopes.

Inevitably, I can't resist the temptation to check my watch — fifty five minutes. We reach the end of another line and I suggest we stop for a breather.

"Yeah, good call. I could do with a cuppa."

I could do with a bottle of gin and an intravenous drip.

Clement retrieves the flask from the rucksack and unscrews the two plastic mugs from the top.

"Did you put sugar in this?"

"Sorry. I forgot."

I didn't forget. I just chose not to make it undrinkable.

"Suppose it'll have to do," he grumbles as he pours out the tea.

Clement hands me a mug and we face the wall we've become intimately familiar with.

"What do you reckon, doll. Just over half way?"

"I think so."

I'm tempted to ask what our plan is if, or more likely, when we don't find anything. I don't though, as I can't stomach having my motivation brought into question again. Besides, one of us has to stay optimistic.

We drink our tepid tea as the umpteenth train passes by. The noise and the dust are preferable to the small talk I suspect neither of us are in the mood for.

Clement is the first to finish and screws his mug back on the flask.

"Tea break over."

I'm not enjoying it anyway and pour the remaining tea on the floor.

We return to the wall and resume our positions, Clement's turn to squat. I get back in my rhythm, jabbing away at about three feet of brickwork before I shuffle a step to my right. While it's easier on the legs to stand, it takes its toll on the shoulders and I have to continually switch hands.

We complete another two rows and switch position, my turn to stand again. Limbs begin to ache and joints groan in complaint. My nails are scuffed to hell, and I dread to think what the damp has done to my hair.

We reach the halfway point and I prepare to resume the squatting position but Clement stops. He continues to jab away at the same spot.

"Got something, doll."

He doesn't clarify what the *something* is, but it's enough to make my heart skip a beat.

"What? What it is it?"

"Dunno, but the mortar is shot around this brick."

I squat down and inspect Clement's find.

The brick in question is nine rows up from the bottom and his screwdriver is buried in the mortar, up to the handle.

"There's still a load of crud in there," he grunts.

He continues to lever the screwdriver back and forth, moving steadily along the top of the brick.

"You wanna try and clear that end?" he suggests, nodding to the right hand edge of the brick.

I comply and jab my screwdriver into the gap between the two bricks. It sinks straight in with little resistance.

"Oh, my God, Clement," I coo breathlessly. "This could be it."

I continue to jab away enthusiastically. Most of my jabs sink into nothing, but every fourth or fifth jab meets resistance. However, a little forceful wiggling of the screwdriver quickly clears each blockage. I guess the gap around the brick has been filled with dust; blasted at the wall over the decades by millions of passing tube trains. Add a little moisture from the damp bricks and you've got a natural cement.

"How you getting on there, doll?"

"Nearly clear this end."

I look across and Clement is working on the gap below the brick.

Just four inches to clear and I can scarcely catch my breath.

Is this outlandish folly about to bear the most impossible of fruits?

Don't let us down, Harry. Not after we've come this far.

31

I was thirteen years of age when the National Lottery launched in the UK, and I can vividly remember the public fervour surrounding the first draw. Accordingly, most of the adult population, including my own mother, dashed to the shops to purchase what they believed would be the winning ticket.

I also remember watching the first draw, live on TV. I don't recall much about the programme itself, but I can still picture my mother's face as the balls popped from the lottery machine, and not one of them matched any of her numbers.

All that anticipation, the hope, the unwavering belief she would be a winner. In the end, I think she just felt cheated.

In hindsight, I can look back and see it for what it was — clever marketing to mask impossible odds. Everyone who purchased a ticket was convinced they'd win. Many, many millions were probably left with the same feeling as my mother.

But they came back for more, and still do.

While I've never purchased a lottery ticket, I can imagine how it must feel as you watch those balls roll from the machine. One ball matches, then two, then three. By the time the fourth ball matches, the tension must be almost unbearable.

As I squat in the dark, I think my fifth ball has just been matched.

"Nearly there, doll."

Clement jiggles the screwdriver and the final blockage gives way, the brick dropping a fraction.

"Gotta be honest with you," he adds. "I'm a bit nervous about this."

For me, nervous doesn't even come close to covering it.

I have to remind myself of the reason I'm actually here, and that Karl's debt is still due for repayment in four days. But wouldn't it be the sweetest irony if, while trying to fund that debt, I received a bonus large enough to unshackle myself from another long-term relationship — the one with my mortgage company.

Ball six is tantalisingly close.

Clement grips the brick in his fingertips and gives it a tug. It slips forward, maybe half an inch, but then appears to stick.

"I think it's caught on your side, doll. Jam the screwdriver in there and lever it a bit while I pull."

The rumble of yet another tube train fills the pin-dropping silence but I'm so focused on the brick I scarcely notice it.

I force the screwdriver into the gap and apply horizontal force as Clement regains his grip on the brick.

"Easy, doll," he murmurs.

I ease off a little, and the brick edges forward in juddering movements as Clement rocks it left and right.

Fraction by fraction, more of the brick is exposed.

"It's coming. Pull the screwdriver out."

With almost half the brick now jutting out of the wall, Clement continues to rock it left and right; his big fingers encouraging tiny movements.

"Nearly there," he whispers, as if the full volume of his voice might scare the brick back into its hole.

Another half inch, and then he stops.

"I think it's ready. One tug and she should pop out."

"Really?" I wheeze.

"Christ, I can barely force myself to look. This is it, doll."

I offer him an encouraging smile. "Do it."

With enough of the brick now exposed, Clement is able to secure a firm grip. With both ends pincered in his hands, he repositions his feet, just in case it pops out with no further resistance and he's sent sprawling backwards.

"Here goes."

He pulls the brick, and it cleanly departs the home it has occupied for over a century. He then unceremoniously lobs it over his shoulder.

It's too dark to see more than a couple of inches into the gaping hole left behind.

"Got your torch, doll?"

I pull my phone from my jacket pocket and activate the torch.

"Do you want to do the honours?" I ask, offering Clement the phone. "The only reason we're here is because of you."

"Nah. You put the graft in, you get the reward."

We both turn to the wall and I move the torch beam towards the void, slow enough to savour the moment.

All these years, hidden away, and we are seconds from unearthing Harry's hidden gold.

The beam hits the void.

Half-a-dozen tiny lights glint back at us.

I'm not sure how long it usually takes for the brain to send a message, but I'm certain it's quicker than my current reaction time.

I suspect it's because my brain is busy piecing together the images being sent by my eyes. The six glinting lights are now three pairs of tiny black eyes, above twitching snouts with wiry whiskers.

"Fuck!" Clement barks as he crabs backwards. "Rats!"

My ears eventually join the party and relay Clement's statement. Everything comes together and realisation slaps me around the face.

"Oh my God! Oh my God!"

My brain sends the message it should have sent five seconds ago. I lurch from my squatting position while simultaneously stumbling backwards, arms flailing. Momentum continues to drag me backwards until I trip over my own feet.

Weightlessness arrives, and with it, acceptance that I'm about to pay a jarring visit to the filthy concrete floor.

As I await the impending impact, two huge hands reach out and grab me around the waist, arresting my fall.

"Easy, doll."

We find ourselves in a position akin to a scene from *Dirty Dancing* — or at least a poorly choreographed re-make. I'm leant backwards with Clement supporting my weight. My left foot is planted on the floor at an uncomfortable angle, and my right leg thrust outward.

It would be fair to say I am not having the time of my life.

Clement lifts me into a standing position as I lower my right leg. I turn around and stare sheepishly at the floor.

"Umm...thank you."

"No sweat. I'm not so keen on rats either," he replies. "Filthy little shits."

We take a second to regain our composure, and for the awkwardness to ease a little.

"Sorry to say, doll, I don't think Harry chiselled that brick out. I reckon the rats ate their way through the mortar."

"They can do that?"

"They can eat their way through almost anything. There's probably a nest behind the wall and they've chewed through to get at the crap blown in here from the tracks."

"Great," I sigh. "Back to the drawing board then."

"Afraid so."

Clement picks up the discarded brick and pushes it in the void; the one remaining rat scurrying away into the darkness. With the heel of his boot, he hammers it back into place until it's flush with the surrounding bricks.

He turns to face me. "Shall we crack on?"

There's only about five lines of mortar left to check but I'm not sure I can face it. As horrid as it was, the unearthing of a rat's nest is not the reason for my reluctance. No, the overpowering sense of disappointment is why I can't bring myself to move.

Six lottery balls. Six matching numbers. I've lost the ticket.

"I can't do it," I croak.

I try so hard but my resilience has been beaten into submission. So many knocks so much disappointment.

I bite my bottom lip and squeeze my eyes tightly shut. A convulsion builds in my chest. I swallow hard, trying to force it back.

It's not enough.

A fat tear escapes my left eye and meanders its way down my cheek. Another follows, and before I can stop myself, I'm in the midst of a full-scale sobbing episode.

Clement shuffles over and I turn away. I hate myself for showing weakness, for fulfilling the stereotype.

"Doll? You alright?" he asks, his voice not much more than a whisper, almost gentle.

"I'm sorry," I sniffle. "Just ignore me. I'll be okay in a minute."

I wipe my eyes on the inside of my jacket while pulling shallow breaths.

A hand moves through the gloomy light and rests on my shoulder.

"Nothing to apologise for."

"Don't be nice to me, please. I'll start blubbing again."

"You sure you're alright?"

"Not really."

Another convulsion builds. I don't know where this is all coming from, and I wish I could stop it.

I can't, and another wave of sobbing begins.

"Come here," he orders.

The hand on my shoulder steers me towards him. I don't resist and suddenly his arms are wrapped around my shoulders. I lean my head against his chest and cry myself dry.

Clement, to his credit, doesn't offer any pointless platitudes or hollow sentiments. He doesn't have to; his bear-like embrace is comfort enough. I can feel his heart beating through the lambswool sweater, like a metronome ticking slowly back and forth.

A minute passes and my breathing slows, almost matching the rise and fall of Clement's broad chest.

He remains silent, and that's fine by me. I'm content where I am, probably because I can't face the embarrassing post-mortem of my breakdown.

Inevitably, that choice is taken out of my hands.

"How you doing down there, doll?"

Clement unwraps his arms. I shuffle backwards and look up at him.

"I'm okay."

"Sure?"

"Yep, and sorry about that. I don't know what came over me."

"You've had a lot of shit to deal with."

"I know, but still, I shouldn't have let things get on top of me like that."

"Don't beat yourself up about it. We all have a breaking point, me included."

I find a weak smile. "I can't imagine much gets to you. When was the last time you broke down in tears?"

"The FA Cup final in 1952. Newcastle scored six minutes before time and we lost one-nil."

"You know something, Clement? For once, I can quite believe that."

He plucks the Marlboro packet from his pocket and flips it open.

"I'm gonna have a smoke and then I'll finish checking the wall. You go and sit on the stairs until I'm done."

"I can't ask you to do that."

"You're not asking. I'm telling."

He slides a cigarette from the packet and lifts it to his mouth, flicking the Zippo open with his other hand.

"Can I have one?" I ask.

He lights the cigarette and plucks it from his lips. "Really? Never took you as a smoker."

"I was, a long time ago. The hankering for a cigarette never goes away though, especially when I'm stressed."

"Help yourself," he says, offering me the packet.

I extract a cigarette and place it between my lips. Clement hands me the Zippo.

I press down on the wheel and sparks fly towards the wick, a yellow flame emerging. I lift it to the tip of the cigarette and drag hard.

The rush of nicotine is sublime.

I slowly exhale and flick the Zippo shut, holding it to the light to examine the decoration etched into the metal.

"Nice lighter."

"Thanks."

I examine it a little closer, and notice the words engraved on the front. The metal is well worn, the text faint, but just about legible. I mindlessly read the words out loud.

"*For the dark times — Annie.*"

I pass the Zippo back to Clement.

"Who's Annie?"

"The friend that was."

"Oh, the same friend you played *Misty* with?"

"Yeah," he replies, his tone dismissive. "Anyway, I should get on."

Before I can question him about the words on the Zippo, he tucks it back in his pocket and makes his way over to the wall. I stand and smoke my cigarette while watching Clement as he silently jabs away at the brickwork.

The injection of nicotine, while initially welcome, has left me feeling light headed. It's been a long time since I finished a cigarette, and my body appears unable to process the flood of chemicals as efficiently as it once did.

I really should be helping Clement, but perhaps a few minutes sitting on the stairs might be sensible, at least until the wooziness passes.

I gingerly shuffle across the floor, the light fading as I move further away from the lamp. As my legs turn to jelly, I begin to question whether the cigarette was really such a good idea. I stop for a second and shake my head in an attempt to clear the giddiness.

A deep breath and I continue towards the stairs.

I make another five or six steps.

As I swing my left foot to the floor, it connects with a piece of debris, immediately arresting the forward motion. Every other part of me continues forward and I stumble into the darkness.

I remain on my feet for one final step before sprawling head first across the filthy concrete floor.

This week has been the gift that just keeps on giving.

As I lie on my stomach amongst the dust and the debris, I hear the clomp of Clement's boots approaching.

"Shit, doll. You hurt?"

My pride is on life support, but I don't think I've suffered any major physical damage.

"No, I think I'm okay," I grunt, slowly moving onto all fours.

Clement grabs my arm and helps me up. "You probably don't wanna look in a mirror anytime soon."

I turn towards the lamp and look down. "Jesus Christ."

My clothes are caked in a fine dust, as are my hands, thrown out to cushion my fall.

"What happened?" Clement asks.

"I tripped."

I think it must be instinctive, but whenever anyone trips, they immediately look to the floor in search of the offending trip hazard. I glare at the floor in search of something to kick. I don't care if it hurts, if I break a toe. I've had enough and want to vent my rage.

There is no debris on the floor, just a ten-inch square grate, embedded into the concrete but slightly proud along one edge — enough for me to trip over.

"And this is the bloody culprit," I yell, stamping on the grate with all my might.

I stamp on it five times before the futility becomes all too apparent.

"Feel better for that?" Clement asks.

"No."

"Do you wanna go home?"

"Yes."

He stares back at the wall, screwdriver in hand.

"Give me one minute."

Like a man possessed, he barrels along the length of the wall with the screwdriver scraping along the mortar. He reaches the end and moves to the next line down. Again he storms along the wall with the screwdriver trailing behind.

He runs out of wall and comes to a stop. His head drops, and the hand holding the screwdriver falls to his side.

He stands there, staring at nothing.

I take a dozen steps towards him. "Are you done, Clement?"

"Totally. Been a complete waste of bloody time, ain't it?"

"We tried."

"Yeah, and we failed."

It seems I'm not the only one with a limited supply of optimism.

"I think it's time we call it day, don't you?"

He looks across at me and nods. "Guess so."

He takes my screwdriver and packs it away in the toolkit. The toolkit is then thrust into the rucksack, which he hoists over his shoulder.

"You wanna grab the lamp and we'll get the hell out of here?"

I do as instructed and pick the lamp up. With the battery more than fifty percent depleted, the light is shining far less brightly than when we first arrived — a suitable analogy for our optimism. Lamp in hand, I move slowly towards the stairs, careful not to trip arse over tit again.

I reach the stairs and turn to check Clement is close behind, just in case I finish my perfect day with a backwards tumble. He's not there. He's standing ten feet away staring at the floor.

"Clement?"

"Here a sec."

Curiosity trumps irritation and I shuffle back across the floor.

"What is it?"

"Shine the lamp on that will you."

His boot scuffs across the metal grate I tripped over.

"Why?"

"Just humour me."

I place the lamp on the floor, a foot away from the grate. Clement pulls the rucksack from his shoulder and extracts the toolkit.

"What are you doing?" I ask.

"Ensuring no stone is left unturned."

"Eh?"

"Best I can tell, there is absolutely no place in here Harry could have hidden a bar of gold without it being found."

"That we know."

"Except, beneath this grate," he adds.

"Are you mad? God only knows how many rats are lurking under there."

"Maybe, probably, but I can't leave without checking, doll. It'll bug me if I don't."

He places a screwdriver against the edge of the grate and taps the top of the handle with a hammer. Several more taps are administered before he levers the screwdriver downward. The edge of the grate pops from the concrete by half an inch.

"Do you wanna stand on the stairs in case more of our furry friends appear?"

Yes I do, but my curiosity is now piqued. "No, it's okay. I'll leg it at the first sight."

Clement stands up and edges the welt of his boot beneath the grate. With a quick flick of his foot, the grate lifts and falls to the side, revealing a square black cavity in the concrete floor.

I was half expecting a re-enactment of The Pied Piper of Hamlin; hundreds of rats pursuing us up the stairs, but there's no obvious sign of life.

"Now what?" I ask.

Clement picks up the lamp and guides the beam into the hole. I'm tempted to look but I'd rather wait for confirmation it's rat-free.

He squats down and rests the lamp against his thigh.

"There's something down there, doll."

"Really?"

Have I found that winning lottery ticket? I edge towards the hole and peer down.

"What is it?"

"Not sure. Guess there's only one way to find out."

Clement slowly lowers his arm into the hole, down to his elbow. Tortuous seconds pass until he pulls his arm out, clutching a Tupperware container; the usually opaque white plastic smeared with grime.

I'm not impressed, and draw an immediate conclusion. "I bet you a fiver that's a workman's lost lunch."

Clement looks up at me and smiles. "I'll take that bet. Here."

He passes the container to me, and I flinch, not wishing to handle the filthy plastic. But with my hands already caked in dust and rat piss, I guess it doesn't matter now. I take it in my right hand.

"Both hands," Clement orders.

"I'm not that much of a wimp."

I indignantly snatch the container, and my wrist immediately buckles. Thankfully, Clement still has a grip and stops it falling to the floor.

"Shit! What's in there? It weighs a ton."

"Not a ton. About ten pounds, I reckon."

He places the container on the floor and peels the lid away. Whatever is in the container, it's wrapped in newspaper.

Clement carefully prises the package out of the container and lays it on the floor. He then grips the newspaper in his fingertips and slowly tears it away.

"Holy shit," he murmurs.

32

As Clement tears away at the newspaper, the content of the mystery package slowly reveals itself.

It's definitely not a round of cheese and pickle sandwiches.

I fall to my knees, no concern for my already filthy jeans.

No matter how closely I examine the now-exposed object, I cannot believe my own eyes.

"Is that...?"

We look at one another, and then back at the object — a bar of solid gold. Actual, real gold.

Clement begins to chuckle, quickly building into raucous laughter. It's infectious, and I can't help but join him.

Relief, joy, shock — an explosion of emotion fuelling our hysteria.

My abdominal muscles ache and I can barely see through the tears. Our laughter echoes off the walls, booming back at us.

It takes several minutes before any sense of composure returns.

"We bleedin' did it, doll."

I remain speechless, unable to vocalise any of the thoughts tumbling through my mind. Within ten minutes I've travelled from the depths of despair to the very heights of elation. I can barely take it in.

All I can do is stare dumbstruck at my giant companion, and the block of gold sitting on the floor. To think how far we've come, together, a team. Incredibly ridiculous. Ridiculously incredible.

There really aren't any words I can offer to suitably convey how I feel, so I do the next best thing — I throw my arms around Clement.

"Thank you," I whisper. "I...I..."

"Don't tell me you love me, doll," he chuckles. "That'd put a dampener on the evening."

I break away and playfully slap his arm. "No. I was going to say…"

"Beers are on you?"

"Shut up for a minute, will you," I chide. "I was going to say, I am incredibly grateful for what you've done."

"You're welcome, but we've still got work to do, doll. And we should really get out of here sharpish."

"Why?"

"Because of the noise we've been making for the last five minutes."

An image suddenly floats into my mind — a squad of police officers bursting through the door. Then the horror of watching them confiscate our gold while we're slapped into handcuffs.

"Time to go."

"Yeah, like now."

Clement returns all the tools to the rucksack. He then re-wraps the bar and places it carefully in the container before it joins the toolkit.

I collect the lamp from the floor as Clement hoists the rucksack onto his shoulder. Even with the additional weight, he makes it look effortless.

"Lead on, doll. And try not to trip over this time."

I keep the lamp low to highlight any further trip hazards, and we make our way to the stairs. Another train conveniently passes, masking the creaky staircase and squeal of the door as Clement pulls it open.

As soon as we're back in the subway tunnel, Clement suggests we lose the lamp and it's added to the rucksack.

We make our way back along the tunnel courtesy of my phone torch.

The final challenge is climbing the stairs to the street, or more specifically, the gate at the top of those stairs. As unlikely as it is, the last thing we want to do is pop back over the gate just as a police patrol passes. Every action is now high risk and we simply cannot afford to take any chances.

Clement leads, and crouches down as he reaches the top of the stairs. He takes a quick peak over the retaining wall, scanning left and right.

"Traffic is flowing. Let's move," he orders.

In a flash, his right leg is over the gate, quickly followed by the rest of him. I'm left alone, two-thirds up the stairs, clutching a redundant torch.

I make my move, but ninja-like I am not. My little legs hurry up the final steps and I clamber over the gate, trying my utmost to look inconspicuous.

Clement is already standing by the kerb, cigarette in hand. I scurry over while glancing nervously up and down the road.

"Shit, doll. You look like you've been mud wrestling."

"What?"

"Your clothes."

I look down. Under the bright street lights I can see his point. I am ninety percent woman, ten percent dust.

"It's not a good look, is it?"

Clement chuckles and shakes his head. "I was gonna suggest a quick pint, to celebrate, but maybe not."

As much as I like the idea, my need for a shower and a change of clothes is far greater than my need for wine.

"No. Maybe not."

We wind our way back to the car park where I feed the ticket machine as Clement deposits the rucksack in the boot. Once we're seated in the car, I scrabble through the glove box and locate a pack of wet wipes. I manage to remove most of the grime from my hands, but my clothes will need a couple of cycles in the washing machine.

I could not care less.

I turn to Clement, beaming like a child on Christmas morning. "Tell me this isn't a dream."

"You want me to pinch you?"

"You could punch me and I'd still be smiling."

"I doubt that," he chuckles.

As my euphoria eases, a crucial question begs to be answered.

"How much do you think the bar weighs?"

"Rough guess, I'd say about a hundred and fifty ounces."

It's significantly less gold than I initially hoped for, but still worth the best part of a hundred thousand pounds. That leaves me with eighty thousand once Sterling is paid — enough to make a huge difference to my life.

"You alright driving?" Clement asks.

"It's a lot quieter out there now. I'll be fine."

I set the sat nav to take us home and reverse the Fiat out of the parking bay.

Five minutes later, we're trundling across Tower Bridge, sticking vehemently to the twenty mile an hour speed limit.

"She's quite the sight, ain't she?"

"She?"

"London at night."

I shift my gaze from the road and take a quick glance out of the side window towards the Thames. Even taking into account how much I hate driving here, I can still appreciate the picture postcard expanse of coloured lights stretching far into the distance, mirrored against the shimmering black water.

"I have to admit, it's a stunning view."

"Yeah, shame I'll never see it again," he replies matter-of-factly.

My head snaps from the window to Clement.

"What do you mean by that?"

"Exactly what I said."

"I'm not with you. Why wouldn't you see it again?"

"We're nearly done, doll. As soon as we've converted that gold into cash and you've paid that arsehole, the job is over. Dunno where I'll end up, but it won't be London."

"Here we go again," I mumble under my breath.

"Just saying, doll."

We navigate through the streets in silence for a couple of miles, but I'm not inclined to let the subject rest on this occasion.

"I hope you don't take this the wrong way, Clement, but had it crossed your mind you might be suffering from some sort of mental illness?"

"You think I'm a nutter," he snorts. "Suppose that makes sense."

"No, I never said that, and mental illness is not funny."

"I'm not a nutter."

"Don't use that word. It's not nice."

"Alright. I'm not mentally ill."

"But the thing with mental illness is that you don't necessarily know you're suffering from it."

"I dunno what you want me to say."

"Would you consider seeing somebody?"

"What? Like a shrink?"

"No, a psychiatrist."

"That's what I said. And no, I wouldn't."

"Why?"

He turns and stares out of the window, clearly not interested in pursuing the conversation.

"Clement?"

"Just leave it, doll. There's no shrink that can help me."

"I'm only saying this because, well, I care what happens to you."

"Do you?" he grunts.

"Yes."

And there the conversation ends. Apparently.

We reach Brixton and the traffic builds. It's nowhere near as frenetic as earlier, but enough to slow our progress. As we sit at a red traffic light, I make one final attempt to resurrect the conversation.

"I know you don't want to talk about it, but will you promise me one thing?"

"I'm not big on promises."

"Okay, will you keep something in mind?"

"What?"

"I know somebody who works as a counsellor for a mental health charity. Would you be willing to have a chat with her? No strings, nothing formal, just a chat."

"And what good would that do?"

"I'm not sure, but it can't do any harm, can it?"

"You assume the decision is mine to make."

"Well, isn't it?"

He turns to face me. "This may come as a shock, doll, but nobody has control over their ultimate destiny. Not you, and certainly not me."

"I don't understand."

"Join the club."

Frustration begins to simmer. I don't know why I should care — Clement has almost served his purpose. What does it matter to me where he ends up once I've got my hands on the cash?

Perhaps my frustration is partly due to the fact he has made himself matter, to me. One thing is clear though — he is not a man to be coaxed anywhere he doesn't want to go. If I'm to convince him he needs help, I might need to play the long game.

"Perhaps we'll just see how things go." I suggest.

"That's all we can ever do."

We've clearly reached the boundaries of Clement's commitment. I don't press him any further.

We pass Croydon and soon enough, we hit the M25.

"I'm starving," Clement suddenly pronounces.

My stomach has been spinning like a washing machine since we left home but now he's mentioned it, I'm pretty peckish myself.

"We'll stop at the next services and grab something."

Over the twelve miles we cover before the service station exit appears, a bizarre craving develops. I suppose it's the closest I'll ever get to experiencing pregnancy.

By the time we pull into the car park, I'm salivating over the imminent acquisition of scotch eggs and jam tarts.

"Would you mind going in on your own, Clement?"

"Why?"

"Well, firstly, I look like I've been pot holing, and secondly, I don't like the idea of leaving the gold in the car."

"Yeah, alright."

I give him a twenty pound note together with my order.

"And Clement, try not to get into trouble."

"Me? Never."

He flashes me a grin and climbs out of the car. I watch him stride across the car park towards the main entrance before he disappears beyond the doors.

For the first time since we left home almost five hours ago, I can relax a little. I close my eyes and sit back in my seat. I can just about make out the distant thrum of traffic on the motorway, but it's otherwise quiet.

Inevitably, my mind turns to the various ways I'll be able to spend my impending windfall.

Maybe the first priority, after I've paid Sterling, is to take some time off. I haven't had a proper holiday in years, and that can't have helped my stress levels. Paying somebody to manage the shop for a week shouldn't be a problem so all I have to worry about is the choice of destination. A spa break at a country retreat might be a relaxing way to spend a week. Or maybe a lodge on the lakes in Switzerland.

As long as it's relaxing, and not too hot, I don't really care. I just want to put all of this behind me and move on with my life. And if anyone deserves some pampering, and a daily massage from a hunky young masseur, it's me.

That particular thought hangs around in my mind for a while. Possibly too long.

I'm deep into my daydream when the car door suddenly opens. The fantasy bubble I was occupying with Antonio, the masseur with busy hands, pops.

"Were you nodding off there, doll?"

Clement clambers into the car, a carrier bag in hand.

"No, I was...err, just thinking about a holiday."

Once he's seated, he delves into the carrier bag and withdraws a two-pack of scotch eggs.

"Dinner is served," he says, tossing the package into my lap.

"Thanks."

His hand returns to the carrier bag, and he pulls out a jumbo sausage roll. Then another. And a third.

"Partial to sausage rolls are we?" I enquire.

"My only vice," he replies. "Well, apart from alcohol, and loose women, and cigarettes, and..."

"Okay, I get it."

The conversation ends and we both set about demolishing our unhealthy snacks. It doesn't take long to go from starving to stuffed.

Hunger sated, we set off on the final leg of our journey.

As we bowl along the motorway, my mind turns to the issue of converting our gold into hard cash. It's not something I had seriously considered, primarily because I didn't want to tempt fate, but also because I wasn't convinced we'd ever find it.

"I was wondering, Clement, how are we going to sell the gold?"

"What do you mean?"

"Well, where do you sell a whole bar with, shall we say, dubious provenance?"

"Back in my day, we'd just offer it to a local fence and they'd find a buyer."

"A fence? That's like a middle-man isn't it?"

"More or less. If you wanted to dispose of hooky gear, you'd offer it to the fence with the right connections."

"I'm guessing that's not really an option now?"

"Nope."

"So, what are our options?"

"Dunno. The people I used to work with are probably long gone by now. I thought you'd have some ideas."

"Seriously? You thought I'd know the best place to sell a stolen gold bar? I run a book shop, Clement, not a crime syndicate."

"Plan-B then."

"Which is?"

"There are still pawnbrokers around?"

"Of course."

"That's where we start then. For every ten pawnbrokers, there'll always another one willing to take moody gear if the money is right."

"And how do we find the one in ten?"

"We make up a back story about how we got our hands on the gold, and ask."

"Simple as that?"

"Money talks, doll, so as long as we leave a decent profit in it for them, there's bound to be interest."

"And why do we need a back story?"

"Cos' we obviously can't tell them the truth about where we found the gold. It might raise too many questions."

I'd rather not ask my next question, knowing full well what the answer will be. I ask anyway.

"And what back story will we use?"

Clement shakes his head. "Jesus, doll," he groans. "Can't you come up with something?"

"Um, let me think about it."

A succession of ideas flash through my mind, each one less credible than the last.

"Don't over-think things, doll," Clement suggests, noting my perplexed scowl. "Just take a real situation, and give it a twist."

"What do you mean?"

"If you're gonna bullshit someone, stick as close to the truth as possible."

"How does that help?" I huff.

"All you need to do is take the truth — you found the gold bar in a tube station — then change the location to somewhere you're familiar with."

"Okay. Maybe my house?"

"Perfect. Now, where in your house would somebody hide a bar of gold? Somewhere you never look."

A light suddenly ignites in my head.

"Under the floorboards."

"There you go. Not so hard, was it? You found the gold under the floorboards at your house. If you wanna push it a bit further, ask yourself why you'd be nosing around under your floorboards. Suppose you could say you had a leaky pipe or something. You just pulled up the floorboards, and there it was."

The light is now shining so brightly, I can feel my brain sizzling with inspiration.

"That's genius, Clement," I coo.

"Is it? I thought that's how all stories were told. I ain't read many books, but they were all just a variation of somebody's truth."

"What books have you read?"

"Like I said, not many. I read *Animal Farm* when it first came out."

"In 1945?" I scoff.

"Yeah," he replies dismissively. "And wasn't that based on the Russian Revolution, or something?"

"Yes, it was. I'm impressed, Clement."

"Don't be. My point is, Orwell just took the truth and spun it into a story — a political uprising, but with farmyard animals instead of crazy Russians."

"Any other books?"

"The only other one I vividly remember is *Casino Royale*."

"Ian Fleming. His first James Bond novel."

"Yeah. And did you know Fleming used to serve in the Navy as an intelligence officer?"

"Yes."

"Well, there's another one for you. He invented Bond as this suave, playboy spy, and sent him on the same adventures Fleming probably experienced. No doubt he sexed the details up a bit, but the core story was based on Fleming's truth."

Clement levers his chair back and stifles a yawn.

"So you see, doll, when it comes to spinning a lie, it pays to stick to the truth. It don't take much creativity, and it's far more believable."

"Right. I see."

And with his words of wisdom delivered, he decides to take a nap.

As Clement snoozes, my mind whirs as I apply his technique to the plot of novel eighteen. One by one, the various mental roadblocks become passable. The story itself is still weak, but at least I can see the road ahead. Then, as we pull off the motorway, I experience something of an epiphany — novel eighteen can stay on the shelf because I have an amazing idea for a nineteenth novel.

And when this is all over I'm going to start writing it, and I'm going to finish it, come hell or high water.

33

I awake to the pattering of rain on the window, and a squally wind whistling through the gaps in the softwood frame.

When I first started house hunting with Stuart, I insisted our new home had to have character. I wanted an authentic, period property, brimming with original features. However, that character came at a price.

Sash windows are lovely to look at but they're a pain to open, they require frequent painting, and they aren't particularly efficient when it comes to keeping the cold out. On mornings like this, chunky plastic frames do hold some appeal.

It's a concession I might have to consider once my windfall is realised.

I sit up in bed and stretch. Monday morning — exactly one week ago, I awoke next to my fiancé, blissfully unaware of the shitstorm heading my way.

Now I have a different man in the house, and hopefully, calmer waters ahead. But first, there's the slight issue of liquidising my new found asset.

I slip my dressing gown on and head for the bathroom.

By the time I'm showered and dressed, Clement is awake, and is stomping around the spare bedroom.

He eventually emerges, wearing nothing other than the oversized underpants I retrieved from Karl's possessions. They're anything but oversized on Clement.

"You finished in the bathroom, doll? I'm desperate for a shit and a shower."

"Too much information, Clement. And yes, I have finished."

He gives me a thumbs-up with one hand while simultaneously scratching his arse with the other.

"Can you not walk around the house in your underwear, please?"

My request is met with a grin. "Worried you might get a bit hot under the collar, eh?"

"I think I'll manage to contain myself, but a little modesty wouldn't go amiss, would it?"

"You want me to get dressed, walk ten feet, and then get undressed?"

"I'll find you a dressing gown."

He shrugs his shoulders and strolls into the bathroom, closing the door behind him without another word.

Conversation over, I plod down the stairs and head for the kitchen in dire need of caffeine. While our weekend was ultimately worthwhile, it was both mentally and physically exhausting. I can't say I slept particularly well last night, either — too many thoughts pinging through my mind saw to that.

I make myself a cup of strong tea and start prepping breakfast.

By the time Clement strides into the kitchen, the toast is ready and the eggs almost scrambled.

"Something smells good, doll."

"It'll be ready in two minutes. Do you want tea?"

"Don't worry. I'll sort it."

He clatters around and then spends a long moment staring into the fridge.

"Where's the milk, doll?"

"Are you blind?" I call across the kitchen. "I can see it from here. Second shelf down, next to the tomatoes."

He leans in and plucks the dumpy carton from the shelf.

"Gotcha. I was looking for a bottle."

"Not in this house."

It's been many a year since I last poured milk from a glass bottle. It must have been when I was a child, and the milkman delivered tepid milk to our doorstep every morning.

I transfer the scrambled eggs and toast to plates and place them on the table. Clement sits down, mug in hand.

"Nice one, doll. I'm bleedin' famished."

"You're always famished."

"There's a lot of me to fuel."

"Tell you what, as soon as we've found a buyer for the gold, I'll treat you to a slap-up steak dinner."

"Deal," he splutters, his mouth already full of scrambled egg.

It doesn't take long for Clement to clear his plate. I offer him a slice of my toast which he promptly accepts, folding it into his mouth in one piece.

"You'll get indigestion."

"Nah. I've got the constitution of an ox."

I finish my breakfast as Clement slurps his tea.

"What's the plan then, doll?"

"I need to go to the shop and we can work out a plan from there."

"Fair enough."

"And, I think there's a pawnbroker in town. We could see if they're interested?"

"Bad idea."

"Why?"

"Too close to home. It's not a good idea to try and flog dodgy gear on your own patch."

"Right. Scrub that then. I'll google some places in other towns."

"You'll do what?"

"Google pawnbrokers in other towns."

"What's a google?"

"It's a search engine, you use it...never mind. I meant search, on the Internet."

"If you say so. I'll leave that one in your hands."

With that settled, I start to clear the table.

"If you wash up, doll, I'll dry."

"I'm sorry?" I remark, somewhat taken aback.

"I'll dry up."

"Yes. I thought that's what you said. I just assumed you weren't domesticated."

"Cheeky mare. I used to do all my own cooking and cleaning. Even darned my own socks."

"I take my hat off to you, Clement. Sock darning is an impressive, if not redundant skill."

"Are you taking the piss?"

The smirk on my face provides his answer.

I pass him the tea towel and crack on with the washing up, chuckling away to myself at the thought of Clement darning socks.

Once the kitchen is spic and span, Clement heads up to the spare bedroom to retrieve the rucksack containing the gold bar. After we sat and stared at it for half an hour last night, he insisted on stashing it under his bed for safe keeping.

And this morning, he's equally insistent on keeping it with us, wherever we go.

"What if you lose it?"

"I won't lose it."

"But what if you do?"

"Doll, just relax. It's safer with me than not."

Decision made, we leave the house just after eight thirty and head for the shop.

The relentless wind and rain has forced most of the town's residents into their cars this morning. The journey is a drag, not helped by Clement's insistence we discuss the decline of brown-coloured cars on the road.

We pull up behind the shop five minutes before opening time and no closer to determining why nobody buys a brown car these days.

Although it's far from a typical Monday morning, the opening routine remains the same: lights on, heating on, kettle on, front door unlocked.

I make us both a cup of tea and we sit in the staff room with the door to the shop open; not that I'm expecting a rush of customers.

"You wanna get on with your goggling then, doll?"

"It's googling, and yes, I will."

A quick search on my phone reveals there are eleven pawnbrokers within a ten mile radius. I narrow down the results by discounting any with a flashy website, or those which are clearly franchise operations; neither likely to be interested in a suspect gold bar.

We're left with four contenders.

"The nearest one is six miles away, and then there's another three slightly further afield."

"We better crack on then, doll."

"Now?"

"Why not? Not exactly busy in here is it?"

I almost object to closing the shop again, but it's a nonsensical argument. At most, I might lose fifty or sixty pounds of trade if I close for a few hours; a drop in the ocean compared to the small fortune heading my way once we find a buyer for the gold.

"Okay. Let me just print off a sign for the window."

Five minutes later, we're back in the car with the sat nav set to our first port of call — Powell & Partners Pawnbrokers.

Thankfully, Clement is less inquisitive on our outbound journey and the miles pass quietly by.

We follow the sat nav instructions until we turn into the road on which Powell & Partners is located. It's certainly not the most salubrious part of town. We pass rows of tatty terraced houses, interspersed with soulless apartment blocks, takeaway joints, and a bookmaker with a gaggle of unsavoury-looking characters standing outside. Waiting for opening time I assume.

"Quite the shit-hole, ain't it?" Clement remarks.

It certainly isn't the sort of area I'd choose to wander around on my own.

The sat nav counts down the final hundred yards until we reach a row of shops, set slightly back from the road with parking bays out front.

I turn into a bay and kill the engine.

Powell & Partners is the last shop in the row, next to a laundrette, an off licence, a kebab shop, and a tattoo parlour.

"I'm not sure about this, Clement. It's not exactly an affluent area, is it?"

"Well, we ain't gonna find a buyer in a legit area, are we? I'd say it looks exactly the right place for our purposes."

Before I can argue, Clement gets out of the car, grabbing the rucksack from the footwell.

It looks like we're going in, whether I like it or not.

I pull the sat nav from the windscreen and drop it into my handbag. After a quick scan to check no other valuables are in plain sight, I hop out of the car and join Clement on the pavement.

"Ready?" he asks.

"Nope, but let's just get on with it."

We make our way along the parade of shops towards the far end.

The exterior of Powell & Partners is certainly in keeping with the neighbourhood. The murky windows are covered in wire mesh, with very little visible beyond. The sign above the door is well weathered, the paint flaking and patchy.

If the proprietor does have money, he doesn't appear keen to invest any in his premises.

Clement pushes open the door and I follow him in, a bell ringing above the door to sound our arrival.

I've never had cause to visit a pawnbroker before, but I kind of expected it to look like a jewellers. Powell & Partners does not look like a jewellers.

The dull grey walls are bare, with the exception of a sign listing their terms of business, and a large circular clock. A partition wall has clearly been erected to split the shop into two sections. The front part, in which we're standing, has a counter at the rear, with a sturdy-looking door behind. I can only surmise the owners don't wish to display any of their merchandise to those who would prefer to steal rather than buy.

We cross the threadbare carpet towards the counter.

A doorbell has been fixed to the top of the counter, with a hand-written sign to indicate we should ring for assistance. Clement presses the button and a bell shrills beyond the door.

We wait.

"I don't wish to judge," I whisper to Clement. "But I can't see this place having the money we're after."

"Maybe, but don't go on first impressions. I don't think this is the kind of area where it pays to be flashy."

"I hope you're right."

We turn to face the counter again, and just as Clement is about to press the bell for the second time, the door opens.

A scrawny man, easily in his sixties, appears from the doorway.

"What can I do you for?" he asks, his voice as thin as his frame.

"We're looking to sell something," Clement informs the man. "But it might not exactly be legit. You interested?"

"What is it?"

"A solid gold bar. Hundred and fifty ounces."

The man tilts his head slightly, a wisp of white hair flopping to the side as his eyes narrow.

"Stolen?" the man asks.

"Nah. My friend here will explain."

I clear my throat and try to look sincere. I tell the man how I found the gold under the floorboards while attending to a leaky pipe.

I finish with a smile, relieved my scripted explanation sounded vaguely plausible.

"That was some stroke of luck," the man says, a slight undertone of suspicion in his voice.

I don't know how to respond to his statement, but thankfully Clement interjects.

"Yeah, it was, and we're willing to share that luck, Mr..."

The man holds out a bony hand. "Powell. Oswald Powell."

Clement reaches across and shakes Oswald Powell's hand. "I'm Cliff, and this here is my friend, Louise."

Of all the false names Clement could have offered, Cliff feels the least appropriate. However, I'm pretty sure I'd have given our real names, which would have been a mistake given the legality of what we're up to. Proof enough I'm out of my depth.

"How much are you looking for?" he asks.

"You know the current price of gold, so make us an offer," Clement replies.

"I need to see it first."

Clement nods, and removes the rucksack from his shoulder. The gold bar is extracted and placed on the counter.

"There she is — a hundred and fifty ounces of pure gold."

Mr Powell's eyes suddenly widen. He leans forward and slowly runs his hand across the bar while inspecting the hallmarks, embossed on the top.

"I need to test the purity. Can I take a small shaving?"

"Help yourself," Clement replies.

Mr Powell ducks below the counter and returns with a scalpel-like knife in his hand. He turns the bar over and runs the scalpel along the bottom edge, covering less than an inch.

With his miniscule sample shaved, he stands up straight and presses his thumb over the blade, presumably to stop the sample from falling off.

"Give me a minute."

He turns and disappears back through the door.

Clement doesn't waste any time in returning the bar to the rucksack.

"And you say I have trust issues," I scoff.

"Considering what we went through to find it, I'm not about to take any risks, doll. Anyone could wander in and grab it from the counter."

No matter how valuable the prize, I doubt anyone would be brave enough, or stupid enough, to take on Clement. Still, better to be safe than sorry, I guess.

"Okay. Point taken."

We continue to wait as the clock on the wall ticks away the seconds and minutes.

Mr Powell eventually emerges.

"It does indeed appear you have a block of pure gold. Congratulations."

"Good. Now, you interested in buying it, or not?" Clement replies.

Mr Powell rubs a hand across his bristly chin, perhaps contemplating his opening gambit.

"I'm interested, at the right price."

"And that price is?"

He drums his fingers on the counter and looks to the ceiling.

"I'm assuming you want cash?" he confirms.

"Correct."

"And no paperwork?"

"No paperwork. We take the cash and walk away. You never see or hear from us again."

"In which case, I'll give you fifty grand."

I really want to vent my opinion of his lowball offer, but as I look up at Clement, his stony expression suggests our response is in hand.

"Nah. Forget it. We're not idiots, mate. It's worth double that, even on the black market."

Mr Powell's mouth puckers, as if he's sucking on a lemon. "I'll go to sixty."

Clement picks the rucksack up and drapes it over his shoulder. Ignoring Mr Powell, he turns to me. "Let's go try that other place, shall we?"

I nod, and Mr Powell, sensing his opportunity to make some easy money is about to walk out of the door, throws his hand wide open.

"Alright, alright," he pleads. "Ninety grand, final offer. I can't get my hands on any more cash than that, so take it or leave it."

Clement stares down at Mr Powell, and even I don't know what he's going to say, such is his poker face.

"Give us a minute."

He makes his way over to the door, waving his hand to suggest I should follow.

We reconvene on the pavement. Clement doesn't waste any time in getting to the point.

"You wanna take his offer, doll?"

I am so conflicted I don't really know.

On the one hand, ninety thousand pounds is a ridiculous amount of money, and a windfall very few people would turn their nose up at. However, a greed gremlin is now whispering in my ear. While there's no disputing it's a lot of money, what if somebody is willing to pay an extra ten thousand? Or twenty even?

"Um, I don't know. What do you think?"

"Does ninety grand solve your problem with that Sterling bloke?"

"Yes, comfortably."

"There's your answer then. My job was to help you, and with him paid, I've done what I came to do."

"But, we might be able to get more for it."

"Yeah, we might. Or we might not."

Not the most helpful of answers.

I need more time, but I sense Clement is growing impatient with my indecision.

"Look, doll. If I'd turned up at your shop last week and offered you ninety grand in cash, would you have accepted it?"

"Yes, of course I would."

"Why?"

"Err, because no sane person would turn an offer like that down."

"Yet here we are now, and you're dithering over it."

"But..."

"Let's not push our luck, doll. We've squeezed the bloke to his maximum price so let's just quit while we're ahead. That's my advice."

He's right. While there is a chance we could get more, I've had enough stress over the last week to last me a lifetime. The emotional cost of trying to secure a better price might well outweigh any financial gain.

"Okay. Let's do it."

"Good call."

I can't believe we're nearly there. I draw a deep breath and follow Clement back into the shop.

34

Mr Powell is standing behind the counter, anxiously awaiting our decision judging by the pensive look on his face.

Clement approaches and holds out his hand. "Alright, you've got a deal. Ninety grand."

Mr Powell enthusiastically shakes Clement's hand. "Very sensible. It's a good offer."

"I'm sure it is," Clement grunts. "Shall we do this then?"

"I'll need a little time to get that much cash together, you understand?"

"How long?"

"Twenty four hours?"

Clement frowns, and applies a couple of strokes to his moustache.

"Alright. We'll come back tomorrow at ten."

Mr Powell assures Clement the cash will be waiting.

With that, I assume our business is done for the day, but Clement leans on the counter and fixes a stern gaze on Mr Powell.

"Just so we're clear, I don't like being dicked around. If you can't get the money, or you try to haggle us down on the agreed price, I'll be mightily pissed off. And you really don't wanna piss me off."

"It'll be here," Mr Powell confirms, his thin smile betraying the panic in his eyes.

With a final nod, Clement turns and I follow him out of the shop.

Back outside, I get a belated chance to offer my opinion. "Was that a good idea? Giving him time to get the money?"

"Nobody is gonna have that amount of cash kicking around. Another day doesn't matter does it?"

"No, I suppose not."

"It'll be alright, doll. I'm pretty sure he'll come good."

Considering the less-than-subtle threat Clement left with Mr Powell, I suspect he might be right.

"So, I suppose we might as well go and open the shop. No sense in losing a day's trade."

"We?"

"Um, yes, unless you had other plans?"

"Honestly, doll. I'd rather stick pins in my eyes than hang out in a book shop all day."

"What do you want to do then?"

"Drop me back at your gaff. I'm quite happy watching TV."

I'm actually quite relieved he'd rather not come back to the shop. I've got enough to do without keeping him occupied all day.

"Sure. And assuming you don't destroy my home while I'm out, how about we go out and celebrate later? Dinner and drinks on me."

"You're on."

"Excellent, and thank you again...Cliff." I snigger.

"What's so funny?"

"The thought of you being a Cliff Richard fan."

"Eh? I bleedin' well ain't."

"Why did you tell Mr Powell your name was Cliff?"

"Remember what I said about bullshitting people? Keep it close to the truth."

"Right. So why Cliff?"

An obvious conclusion strikes me. "Oh, my God," I shriek. "Is your first name Cliff?"

"Is it hell," he snorts. "When I was a kid, kicking a ball around with my mates, I pretended to be Cliff Bastin."

"Who?"

He stares at me in disbelief. "You telling me you've never heard of Cliff Bastin?"

"No. Should I?"

"Christ, he was an Arsenal legend, and our record goal-scorer. I'll never forget old Cliff so I use his name when needs must."

"Alright, I believe you," I giggle. "Cliffy."

"Piss off."

We get back in the car, which, to my mild surprise, still has all four wheels.

I drop Clement back home and leave him in front of the TV, furnished with instructions on how to use the phone if he needs me. I then drive back to the shop and open up, still early enough for customers wishing to browse during their lunch break.

For a few hours, I'm busy enough not to think about the pile of cash heading my way tomorrow. But by three o'clock, the shop is empty and my spending plans begin to take shape. While I might not have enough to completely pay off my mortgage, I can certainly put a significant dent in it. And I can also afford to deal with all the long overdue repairs to the house, and maybe get the lounge redecorated.

With my plans sorted, I'm ready to take a break for ten minutes.

I head into the staff room and make myself a cup of tea. I then grab a John Grisham novel, *The Racketeer,* and sit down at the table, content to wallow in a rare moment of quiet.

It's a challenge, trying to focus on the plot rather than interior design ideas. I reach chapter four and regain my focus, until a particular term leaps from the page and stops me dead in my tracks — money laundering.

Crap.

I snatch my phone from the table and google it.

It only takes a minute to determine I have seriously underestimated the practicalities of filtering ninety thousand pounds into my bank account.

I do a bit more googling, and the full extent of my problem becomes clear. I can't take the cash to the bank, or buy anything over ten thousand pounds without providing identification, and offering proof of how the cash came into my possession.

Double crap.

I slap the book on the table and curse my naivety.

However, there might be a solution, or more specifically, I might know someone who can offer a solution.

I call my home number and Clement picks up after six rings.

"Clement, it's me."

"Alright, doll. What's up?"

"I need you to have a think about something for me."

"Go on."

"I need to know how money laundering works, and how I can disguise the cash we're picking up tomorrow."

"You want me to explain now?" he groans. "I'm in the middle of a cracking film."

"No. Just have a think about it, please. We'll discuss it later, over dinner."

"Right, sure. Anything else?"

"No, that's it, thanks. What film are you watching?"

"*Frozen.*"

"Oh, okay. Is it...wait. Did you say *Frozen*?"

"Yeah."

"The animated kids film, with Anna and Elsa?"

"Yeah."

I'm tempted to ask why, but I don't think I want to know.

"Um, okay. I'll see you in a couple of hours."

"Alright, seeya."

He promptly hangs up. That man is an enigma.

I chuckle to myself and return to the shop.

Although I'm not feeling particularly motivated, there are still two tasks left for me to complete this afternoon. I need to restock the shelves, and I need to get the King James Bible photographed and listed online. Last week, the potential value of that book was all I had to hang my hopes upon. Now, it's almost inconsequential compared to the fortune heading my way in the morning. Still, it should provide a reasonable contribution to the cost of replacing my boiler.

I spend an hour restocking the shelves and serving the sum total of two customers.

With the shelves restocked, I delve below the counter in search of the bible.

I expected to see it sitting on the shelf, next to the CD player, but it's not there. Puzzled, I begin to remove all the detritus I've discarded under the counter.

After five minutes of searching, it's clear the bible isn't there.

I stand and scratch my head, trying to visualise the moment when Clement first appeared in the shop on Friday night. I remember sitting on the floor, holding the bible in my hands. I stood up to check something on the computer and that's when I realised I wasn't alone.

But then what?

I spend a few frustrating minutes replaying the scene in my head. Did I drop it on the floor? Did I leave it on the counter?

I just don't know.

The only thing I do know is that it isn't here, and the only person who might be able to recollect what happened to it, is Clement.

If he can't recall seeing it, the only other plausible explanation is that it's been stolen, although the shop has been closed up until this morning. Maybe I did simply drop it on the floor and some light-fingered tosser picked it up.

That thought annoys me more than the loss of the money. I don't know why I should expect more from my customers, but it riles me that anyone would steal from a struggling independent business.

I suppose I really shouldn't let it bother me. On the balance of good and bad fortune, I'm still well in credit.

I see another three customers before closing time arrives. The day's takings are barely into three figures; a depressing statistic which counters any guilt I might have felt for another delayed opening time tomorrow. I print off a sign and tape it to the door.

With another work day over, I lock up and endure a tortuous drive home under dark, rain-filled skies.

The one benefit of the wet weather is that many residents in my road have taken to their cars and parking spaces are in plentiful supply. I park up and dart the twenty yards to my front door. Such is the ferocity of the downpour, I'm half-soaked by the time I barge into the hallway.

I throw my jacket and handbag over a coat hook and kick my shoes off. Half-expecting to hear the TV blazing, the silence suddenly strikes me.

"Clement?"

No reply.

I poke my head around the door to an empty kitchen.

He's probably having a nap.

I wander through to the lounge, expecting to see Clement sprawled out in the armchair.

He isn't.

A sickly feeling begins to rise from the pit of my stomach.

I dash from the lounge and scrabble up the stairs. The bathroom door is open, as is the door to the spare bedroom.

"Clement?"

I'm met with silence, and the sickly feeling reaches nausea status.

With almost apoplectic panic, I charge into the spare bedroom and fall to my knees. I lift the duvet and look beneath the bed. I'm greeted with a clear view of the skirting board on the far side of the room.

There's no rucksack, ergo, no gold bar.

Fuck, no. Please God, no.

I clamber to my feet and cast my eyes around the room, for what I don't know.

Where the hell are you, Clement?

I sit on the edge of the bed and consider where he might have gone. As much as I want to believe he's just popped out for a walk, every shred of evidence suggests I'm deluding myself. It's pissing with rain for starters, but that fact is pretty inconsequential when coupled with the absence of the gold.

Have I just been the victim of some convoluted scam?

My mind spins with questions and half-baked conclusions. Nothing makes any sense. How can this possibly be a scam if I was nothing more than a passenger? It was Clement who orchestrated the hunt for the gold. Did he even need me? Besides funding our food and travel expenses, my contribution was minimal.

Am I missing something here? Am I really so dumb that I still can't see the obvious, even when it's staring me in the face?

But wait — what if something bad has happened to Clement? Could Sterling have sent round half-a-dozen goons, and they've overpowered him? Maybe they've taken him and the gold?

No, I'm clutching at straws. There would be signs of a struggle, and I can't imagine even half-a-dozen goons faring well against Clement.

Face it, Beth, he just walked away.

Through the haze of questions, two conclusions collide.

Without the gold, I have no money to pay Sterling.

Yet again, I've let my defences down and been royally shafted.

One catastrophic explosion of anger, disbelief, and shame.

You stupid, stupid, woman.

I'm torn between throwing a screaming fit, or slumping down on the bed and crying. I feel like one of those women, hoodwinked by an online scammer, offering love in return for large sums of money to help them out of a fictional predicament.

I can scoff at their naivety, their stupidity. Yet, here I am. No better.

The doorbell rings.

I suck in a lungful of air and take a moment to compose myself.

I stomp down the stairs, getting halfway before the doorbell rings again.

"I'm coming, for God's sake."

I flick the latch and swing the door open, ready to vent at my unwelcome visitor.

"Jesus, doll, what took you?" Clement huffs as he eases past me. "It's comin' down cats and dogs out there."

He's soaked to the skin, his denim now a dark shade of blue. The only thing that doesn't appear soaked is the waterproof rucksack over his shoulder. He removes it and lowers it to the floor. As it makes contact with the floorboards, I hear a dull thump.

I slam the door closed and slowly count to five in my head.

I get to three and can't hold back. "Fucking hell, Clement," I scream at him. "Where the hell have you been?"

He wipes his forehead with his sleeve, unfazed at my outburst.

"I asked you a question," I growl.

"Yeah," he mumbles. "I heard."

"Well?"

"Fags."

"What?"

"I ran out of fags. Went to get another pack."

"Why didn't you leave a note?"

"I dunno, didn't think I'd be that long. What's your problem?"

"I thought..."

"Ohh, I get it. You thought I'd done a runner with the gold."

My head drops and anger gives way to shame.

"Bloody charming," he adds.

I wish I could, but I can't let it go, not least until I've covered every angle.

"But how were you going to get back in?"

He opens the breast pocket of his sodden waistcoat and plucks out a key.

"Back door."

"Um, right, so why did you knock on the front door?"

"I saw your car in the street and didn't want to scare you by coming round the back of the house."

The scenario I pictured in my head is falling to pieces. I grasp the last straw.

"But you said you don't have any money."

"I don't. You've got a pot of shrapnel in the kitchen so I borrowed a tenner from there. Didn't think you'd mind, considering."

Of course — the car parking pot. I'm always running out of change for parking so I throw all my loose change in there once or twice a week.

"Is that it then?" he barks. "You finished with the interrogation?"

What have I become? My trust has been eroded to such a degree I now automatically assume the worst of people.

"I'm sorry, Clement," I murmur. "You didn't deserve that."

"No. I didn't," he snaps.

We stand in silence for a moment, the odd droplet of rainwater falling from Clement's hair and splatting on the floorboards.

"Do you still want to go out for dinner?" I ask, sheepishly.

"Too bleedin' right I do. And I think you owe me three courses, don't you?"

"Yes, and several pints," I reply. "And you know what I'm going to have for dessert?"

"Go on."

"Humble pie. A double portion."

35

To make amends for my neurotic outburst, I offer to wash and dry Clement's clothes.

I had to dig through Karl's clothes once more, but I managed to find a pair of bright red, elasticated jogging pants. The only top which looked like it might fit was a pale pink polo shirt. Admittedly, it's not a great combination of colours.

"I'll put these through a quick wash," I say as he hands me a pile of damp clothes. "They should be ready in an hour."

"Cheers," he replies as he stares down at his new outfit. I don't think he's impressed.

"I look like a right mug."

"I wouldn't leave the house dressed like that, but it's better than sitting around in your underpants."

"Better for who?"

"Well, me."

We retreat to the lounge while we wait for the washing machine to run through a cycle.

"So, Clement. Shall we talk about *Frozen*?"

"What about it?"

"Seemed an odd choice. Of all the films you could have watched, why that one?"

"Dunno really. I hit a few buttons and it was on a list of most-watched films."

"Still, I wouldn't have thought it was your cup of tea."

"Never seen a film like that before. It was like a cartoon, but sorta real. I watched the first ten minutes and just got into it."

"Right. We'll have to watch *Toy Story* at some point. That'll blow your mind."

"Stick it on then."

"What? I was joking, Clement. It's a kids' film."

"I didn't get to see many films as a nipper, so I kinda like watching kid's films."

There's a hint of sadness in his statement. I can't think of anything to say in response, so I attempt a kindly smile and search for *Toy Story*.

For the next hour, Clement watches intently, chuckling away at the antics of Woody and Buzz Lightyear. I spend more time watching him, rather than the film. It's hard to believe he's the same man who so violently dispatched Messrs Black & Blue. Then again, it's so hard to believe much about the man.

The washing machine beeps away from the kitchen. Clement frowns at the interruption.

"You carry on watching. I'll go and sort your clothes out."

"You sure?"

"Yep, I know what happens."

"Cheers, doll."

I climb up from the sofa and head into the kitchen. My combination washer-dryer isn't particularly efficient with the drying part of its job, but Clement's denims feel dry enough. I fold them up, along with the navy sweater, and carry them back into the lounge.

"Here you go."

"Ta."

"I'm just going up to shower and change. l should be ready by the time Buzz reaches infinity."

Clement stands and begins to peel himself out of the pink polo shirt. I make myself scarce and scoot upstairs to the bathroom.

By the time I clack back through the door, showered, and dressed in jeans and heels, the closing credits are rolling.

"Bloody good that was."

"Glad you enjoyed it. Shall we get going then?"

He clambers to his feet as I switch the TV off.

"You don't scrub up too badly, doll." he remarks. "For a bird who never wears a dress."

"Thanks. I think."

"So, where we going?"

"There's a pub called The Slug & Lettuce, about a mile up the road. I fancy a few drinks so we'll walk — it's stopped raining now."

"Lead on."

We leave the house and stroll through the dark streets towards the pub, Clement whistling the closing track to Toy Story: *You've Got a Friend in Me*.

"Alright, enough with the whistling please."

He continues for a few seconds before deciding to keep his lips busy with a cigarette instead.

"So, doll, you worked out how you're gonna spend the cash once Powell coughs up?"

"I've got some ideas. The house needs some work, and I really a holiday."

"A holiday?"

"Yep. Somewhere relaxing."

He takes a long drag of his cigarette and exhales slowly, seemingly deep in thought.

"I've never had a holiday."

Was that a hint he'd like to join me? No, surely not. He's not that subtle.

"Seriously? You've never had a holiday?"

"Nope. Although I did go to Llandudno in North Wales, for a while. Suppose that was a bit like a holiday."

"Why did you go to Llandudno?"

"Didn't have much choice in the matter. Most kids were evacuated from London when the Blitz started."

Despite the dynamics of our relationship changing for the better over the last few days, I'm still struggling to comprehend

Clement's delusional tales. If I'm honest, I'd rather he just didn't talk about his supposed past life, and that way, I can pretend everything is perfectly normal. It almost feels like having an affair with a married man — tip-toeing around the parts of his life you'd rather not think about. In Clement's case, there is no two-timed wife I'd prefer to ignore, just his delusions.

"It was nice there though," he continues. "Stayed with an old Welsh couple, Ivor and Megan Davies. Good people."

It takes some effort not to encourage Clement with any questions. Unfortunately, it doesn't curtail his wistful reminiscence.

"I think I was six or seven, and I'd never seen the sea before, never seen a beach. It felt like the world was ten times the size up there."

I can't help myself. "What do you mean?"

"Can you imagine what it's like when all you've ever known is a view of brick walls, to stand on a beach and look out to sea? The sky was so big, like it had no beginning and no end."

"How long were you there for?"

"Can't remember, but I do remember leaving, and that final day at the train station. All the other kids were so excited about going home, to see their parents. Don't think I was quite so keen to leave."

He flicks his cigarette butt into the gutter.

"That's what a holiday is like though, ain't it? You don't want it to end?"

"No, I guess not."

We turn a corner and, to some relief, the Slug & Lettuce is just across the road.

"You hungry?" I ask, firmly putting a lid on the previous conversation.

"Starving."

We cross the road and enter through a set of double doors, into the small saloon bar.

I used to visit the Slug fairly frequently, when I first started dating Karl. Over time, and I guess like most couples, we lost the motivation to go out, preferring takeaways and cheap alcohol from the fridge.

It's surprisingly busy for a Monday evening and the dozen tables in the saloon bar are all occupied. I peer through an archway towards the dining area, and I'm relieved to see there are plenty of empty tables.

"We'll grab a drink and then go through."

Clement nods and we saunter up to the bar.

"Lager?" I ask.

"Yeah, ta."

We wait until a young barmaid, sporting too much blusher and too much cleavage, comes to serve us.

"What can I get you?" she asks.

"A pint of Fosters and a glass of dry white wine. Large please."

I look across at Clement. "Fosters okay with you?"

He doesn't look back, his gaze fixed on the barmaid's chest as she pulls his pint.

I stand on tip-toes and whisper in his ear. "A woman's cleavage is like the Sun, you know?"

He pulls his attention away long enough to throw me a quizzical look.

"It's okay to take a quick glance, Clement, but don't stare at it."

He shuffles awkwardly and grabs his pint from the bar. "Dunno what you're talking about."

"Course you don't."

The barmaid delivers my glass of wine and I open a tab with my credit card. Furnished with much-needed alcohol, we wander into the dining area and take a table near the window.

We spend ten minutes surveying the menu and decide not to bother with starters, in lieu of oversized mains. Clement opts for their largest mixed grill, aptly named 'the meat wagon'. I play safe and go for something less likely to induce a coronary — Cumberland sausages with mustard mash.

I skip back to the bar and place our order. Having already downed half a glass of wine, I decide we also need more drinks.

By the time I return to the table, Clement's glass is nearly empty.

"Thirsty were we?" I ask.

"You can talk," he scoffs, nodding at my glass.

"Yes, well, we're supposed to be celebrating, and it's been a long time since I let my hair down."

"I'm all for letting hair down, doll. "

He raises his glass towards mine and we clink them together.

"But before we get too pissed, did you think about what I mentioned on the phone earlier?" I ask.

"The money laundering?"

"Shh," I hiss.

Clement turns his head and surveys the near-empty room.

"Yeah, I did."

"So, what can I do to...erm...clean the money?"

"You use the shop."

"Eh? How?"

"All your stock is second hand, right?"

"Correct."

"So there's no invoices for the stock coming in?"

"I produce receipts for each box, but not for individual items, no."

"There you go then — the perfect cleaning set-up. If nobody knows how much stock you've got coming in, and there's no paper trail, you slowly filter the dirty cash through the till as sales and it comes out clean."

"Won't it look odd if my turnover dramatically increases?"

"Not if you do it gradually. There's no quick way of laundering large amounts of cash, unless you're willing to physically take it to an overseas bank where they're less concerned about where it came from."

It's not quite the ideal solution I'd hoped for. It could take a couple of years to filter ninety grand through the shop, and I'll have to pay tax on it, but I suppose it's my only option.

"And you can still make a few lump sum payments into your bank account," he adds. "As long as you're sensible about it. People sell shit all the time and pay money into the bank. You could say you've sold your car, or your TV, or anything of high value."

"Thanks, Clement. That's good advice."

Just as I'm about to start drawing up a list of fictional assets to sell, a slim, dark-haired waitress arrives with our meals.

She places my bowl of sausage and mash down, and then Clement's veritable farmyard of meat.

"Enjoy your meals," she chirps.

"Don't worry, love, I will," Clement replies, a pork sausage already skewered onto his fork.

As she sashays away, I look across at Clement, half-expecting him to be ogling her polyester-clad backside. It seems, however, food takes priority, and he's too busy gnawing away at his sausage to notice.

We try a half-hearted attempt at small talk as we devour our food and empty our glasses. It's not exactly scintillating conversation and quickly peters out.

Only when Clement's plate is empty does he offer anything more than a few syllables.

"That was top notch, doll. No room for pudding though, I'm stuffed."

Swallowing my final mouthful of mash, I have to concur.

"I think dessert should be of the alcoholic liquid variety, don't you?"

"Yeah, shall I get them in?"

I give him a thumbs up while trying to stifle a burp. He gets up and strides off to the bar, no doubt hoping Little Miss Cleavage is still serving.

He returns with our drinks five minutes later.

"You didn't tell me they've got cabaret on tonight, doll."

"Cabaret?"

"Yeah. I heard a woman singing."

"It was probably the juke box in the public bar."

"Nah. It was definitely live."

"Ohh, right, of course. That's not cabaret — it's karaoke."

"It's what?"

"It might be easier for me to show you."

We grab our drinks and wander back into the saloon bar.

"It's through there."

Clement follows me through a door in the corner, leading into a narrow corridor. We pass the ladies and gents toilets, and through another door into the much larger, public bar.

We're greeted by the dulcet tones of a chunky, middle-aged woman in jeans and vest top, standing on a small stage in the corner. There are a few dozen tables, most of which are occupied by enthusiastic patrons. Clearly Monday-evening karaoke is popular.

I nudge Clement and point to an empty table in the corner. We work our way across the room and claim our seats.

"Whatever they're paying her, doll, it's too bleedin' much."

"They're not paying her. Anyone can get up and sing."

"Anyone?"

"Yep."

"Don't matter if they can't sing?"

"Nope."

"Christ."

"Don't worry, Clement. The more we drink, the better they'll sound."

For the next few hours, we thoroughly test that theory. The drinks flow freely and we spend our time harshly critiquing every poor sod who takes to the small stage, like we're the judges in a sweary version of X-Factor.

The only mild annoyance is Clement's insistence he's never heard many of the songs being murdered. Even when some deluded chap starts wailing his way through Pink Floyd's *Another Brick in the Wall*, Clement insists he's never heard it before.

I'm probably being churlish though, and I have to admit to enjoying myself more than I have in a long while. Maybe it's the alcohol, or maybe it's the thought of the cash coming my way tomorrow, but I feel relaxed, happy even.

Clement offers to get the next round and heads off to the bar, returning a few minutes later.

"I have to admit, Clement," I slur, as he places my glass on the table. "I'm feeling just a tiny bit pissed."

"Lightweight. I'm only just warming up."

"Yeah, well, you've got about ten stone on me."

"Granted."

"And I need to pee."

"What is it you say, doll? Too much information?"

"Ha! You do listen to me sometimes."

"Sometimes."

I pat him on the shoulder as I stagger off to the toilets.

Once I'm sitting in the cubicle, I close my eyes for moment, hoping the walls don't spin. The warbling from the bar ends with a cheer, and I'm able to enjoy a much-needed pee in relative peace. I feel so relaxed I have to make a conscious effort not to nod off.

I finish up, flush, and clack across the tiled floor to the sinks.

"Evening, Miss Baxter," I giggle to myself, my reflection grinning back at me from the mirror.

The woman in the mirror looks very different from the sad cow who has stalked me for the last week. This woman looks like she knows where her future is heading. She appears content, confident, and happy in her own skin.

"Thank you, Clement," I whisper.

She smiles in agreement.

I wash my hands and wait for the underpowered hand dryer to do its job. With a final check of my make up, I leave the toilets and head back to the public bar.

I swing the door open and look across to the corner, expecting to see Clement sitting there, supping his pint.

He's not there. I assume he's gone to the gents.

The sound of a piano tinkles from the speakers by the stage. It seems the next karaoke victim is about to start so I make my way over to our table and collapse onto my chair. A large gulp of wine and I look back to the door, expecting to see Clement walk through at any moment.

The piano notes continue, until they form the intro to a song I recognise. It happens to be a song from a film; one which came up in conversation just this afternoon.

My head snaps towards the stage.

"Ohh, shit."

Clement is not in the gents. Clement is standing on the stage with a microphone in his hand, staring at a monitor displaying the lyrics to a song I hope he's not about to sing.

I put my fingers in my ears and stare at the floor, wishing to God I was anywhere but here. Clement is yet to sing a note, but the embarrassment is already crippling. What the hell is he thinking? And of all the bloody songs he could have chosen, he decides to sing *Let it Go* from *Frozen*.

So, so inappropriate.

Yet, it begins.

I await the chorus of laughter and jeers from the now-intoxicated crowd, and pray it will drown out his singing.

I press my fingers deep into my ears and squeeze my eyes closed.

Please, stop. Please, stop.

I will never be able to set foot in the Slug ever again. I'll probably have to move home.

However, I don't hear any jeers or booing. I hear what sounds a lot like cheering and clapping.

I slowly open my eyes to see half the crowd on their feet. Incredibly, they appear to be lapping up Clement's performance.

They must be beyond drunk.

I remove my fingers from my ears, cringing in anticipation.

"Oh. My. God."

I'm not sure what I expected to hear, but it certainly wasn't this. Clement's voice is...incredible, his rendition note perfect. Even though the song was written for a female voice, Clement is blasting through it as if it was written for him; the tone of his voice somewhere between Bruce Springsteen and Rod Stewart.

I sit up and look across the room. Nobody is laughing and nobody is jeering. In fact, they're either standing in admiration, or sitting transfixed at the giant man on the stage.

He hits the final chorus and delivers it with such power, the hairs on the back of my neck stand up, along with everyone in the room. The end note brings rapturous applause and an embarrassed smile from Clement as he steps down from the stage.

As he makes his way back to our table, hands slap his back or clap in appreciation. I've probably been to a dozen karaoke nights here and I've never seen anything like it.

He eventually reaches our table and grabs his pint, necking almost half of it in one gulp. As the crowd quietens down for the poor woman who has to follow Clement's act, he leans over the table.

"Fancy a smoke?"

I nod, still speechless, and point to the door to the beer garden.

I follow Clement as we edge our way across the room. People look up from their tables as we pass, throwing glances in Clement's direction. Some of the men nod in begrudging admiration, and a few of the women flutter their eyelids. It's funny to think that just a few days ago, when I first stepped out in public with Clement, I was embarrassed to be seen with him. Now, the opposite is true.

We exit the bar to the quiet sanctuary of the beer garden.

Clement plucks his Marlboro packet from his pocket. He flips it open and extracts two cigarettes, handing one to me.

"I shouldn't," I half-heartedly object as I take it. "But go on then."

The Zippo is then ignited and Clement holds it towards the end of my cigarette as I draw deeply. I puff a plume of smoke into the air as Clement lights up.

"So, Mr Clement," I playfully venture. "Shall we talk about what just happened in there?"

"Nah."

"Oh, come on. How can we not? That was amazing."

"I was just clearing the rust from my pipes. No big deal."

"Don't be so modest. Where did you learn to sing like that?"

He shrugs his shoulders and stares up at the dark sky.

Despite consuming numerous pints of lager, there is little in Clement's demeanour to suggest the alcohol has had any effect on him. Much to my annoyance, there is no loosening of his tongue when the conversation veers in a direction he doesn't want to go. I really thought he'd let his guard down after half-a-dozen pints, and maybe let something slip to undermine his delusional claims.

I have clearly underestimated his tolerance for alcohol.

However, my own alcohol levels provide the confidence to persist.

"Have you always been able to sing like that?"

"Sort of," he mumbles.

Progress, I suppose.

"Have you had lessons?"

"You're a nosey mare, ain't you?"

"I'm not nosey, just interested, Clement. I thought we were friends, and friends share things, don't they?"

"Suppose so."

Just when I think he's about to shut me out again, he nods towards a picnic bench on a patchy area of grass bordering the patio on which we're standing.

"Let's sit down."

We take a seat on the bench, facing one another.

He takes a long drag of his cigarette, and then clears his throat.

"Annie taught me to sing."

"That's the third time her name has come up. I'm guessing you were more than friends?"

"You could say that."

"How did you meet?"

"I told you I used to do a bit of minding, for bands?"

"Yep, I recall."

"Annie was a backing singer for some shitty band I worked with for a while. I used to help her with the sound checks, and we got friendly. The band were bleedin' awful and the lead singer was tone deaf, but Annie could properly sing, and she carried them."

"And she gave you lessons?"

"Yeah. I made up some bullshit about wanting to start a band and asked her to teach me. It was just a ruse to see her more."

"Forgive me for saying so, but you don't strike me as the sort of man who resorts to subterfuge to chat up women."

"I don't usually, but Annie was different. She was a Yank, from Pennsylvania and, I dunno, there was just something about her."

"What happened?"

"We started dating, and after about six months things got serious. We rented a little flat together, in Soho, and everything was just about perfect for a while. We talked about getting married and maybe moving to America to start afresh."

"That would have been tricky, without a passport."

"In my line of work, getting a fake passport wouldn't have been a problem."

"Sounds like you had it all planned out?"

He pulls a final drag on his cigarette and flicks the butt away. "Plans don't always work out the way you want."

"How so?"

"In February, she found a lump in her breast. She didn't see Christmas."

His brutally frank revelation pierces my drunken bubble, sobriety returning in an instant.

"I...don't know what to say. I'm so sorry."

He doesn't answer, but lights another cigarette. He holds the Zippo for a second, turning it around in his big fingers. A chink of light from the bar catches the engraving.

I make the connection and murmur the words again. "*For the dark times.*"

Clement nods.

"Annie gave you the lighter?"

"Once she knew...the end was close, she had it engraved and insisted I took it. Her old man gave it to her as an eighteenth birthday present; it was the only thing of value she owned."

I lean across the table and grab his hand, squeezing it tightly.

"I wish there was something I could say."

"Nothing to say, doll," he sighs. "Which is why I don't see the point in talking about it. You asked though."

I know, from my own experience, there is nothing to be gained by pursuing this subject. I give his hand another squeeze and say the only thing I'd want to hear if the boot was on the other foot.

"I know how hard it is to talk about losing a loved one, so I'll consider the subject closed."

He replies with a slight nod of the head.

"Fancy another drink?"

"Nah. I've had enough, doll. And I think you probably have too."

"Shall we go home then?"

"Yeah."

We leave through a gate in the beer garden and make our way home. I lock my arm into Clement's so I don't fall over, but mainly because I think we both need a little comfort in the darkness.

36

"Are you gonna eat that?" Clement asks, pointing to a slice of fried bread on the edge of my plate.

"You've got to be joking," I groan.

It was Clement's idea to visit a greasy spoon cafe for a full English breakfast. He assured me it would ease my hangover.

It hasn't. Quite the opposite in fact.

Sitting beside a condensation-misted window, I can almost feel the grease in the air, and the lingering stench of sweaty men in damp overalls. What I wouldn't give to be in the contemporary confines of a coffee shop, supping on a tall latte, my thumping headache eased by some soothing classical music.

But, no. I have to endure a plate of greasy offal, and tea so strong I could paint my lounge walls with it. And as for music, a slightly out of tune radio is currently blasting some noise credited to The Sex Pistols, I think.

"I don't feel well. Can we go?"

"What about your bacon?"

I can barely look at my plate, let alone contemplate eating anything else on it. I shake my head and get up from the table.

Clement pincers the rasher between his thumb and forefinger, tips his head back, and lowers it into his mouth.

I slap my hand across my mouth while trying to control my gag reflex.

"Waste not, want not," he says, while noisily chomping away.

It's just gone nine thirty in the morning and I'm suffering the fallout from last night's excessive wine consumption. Clement, on the other hand, is annoyingly chipper. I suppose I should be grateful one of us is fit enough to drive, although I felt anything but grateful on the short journey to the cafe.

While Clement finishes my leftovers, I traipse over to the counter and ask a man in a stained apron if I can settle our bill.

"Was there anything else, love?"

"Do you sell bottled water?"

"Still or sparkling?"

I'm mildly surprised they stock either. "Still, please."

He turns around and plucks a bottle from the chiller, placing it on the counter.

"£1.50 for the water, which makes..." He jabs the till with a fat finger. "£12.80 in total."

"Do you take credit cards?"

He looks at me as if I'd asked for the vegan-friendly breakfast menu.

"No. Cash only."

I scrabble around in my purse and just about scrape thirteen pounds together, mostly in coins.

"Keep the change," I mindlessly mumble as I hand over the cash.

"Very kind of you," he replies dryly. "I'll let the kids know we can book a holiday now."

I return an embarrassed smile, grab the bottle of water and scurry towards the door where Clement is waiting.

"Let's get out of here."

We exit the cafe into drizzly rain and dash along the hundred yards of shiny pavement to where we parked the car. Once Clement has squeezed himself into the driver's seat, I setup the sat nav to direct him towards Powell & Partners.

As the route is calculated, I offer another warning about his aggressive driving style.

"Remember, we're not in London now so please take it easy, unless you want a lapful of warm sick."

"That's classy."

"I'm just warning you. My constitution couldn't cope with another one of your getaway chases."

He smiles as he turns the ignition key. "Trust me, doll."

My memories of last night, after we left the pub, are hazy. I remember walking home, just. And somehow, I managed to get undressed and put my pyjamas on. I have a horrible feeling I might have asked Clement to sing for me, but my memories are patchy and I daren't ask him.

It's not exactly a sedate drive but I manage to keep the content of my stomach in situ. We pull into the parking bay outside Powell & Partners with a few minutes to spare. Clement cuts the engine and looks across at me.

"You up for this, doll? You can wait in the car if you like."

"I'll be fine. After everything we've been through to get here, I'm not about to let a hangover ruin the moment."

"Fair enough."

We climb out of the car and I retreat to the pavement while Clement collects the rucksack from the boot.

The drizzle has eased but the low black clouds suggest heavier rainfall is imminent. Maybe it's my hangover, or maybe it's the sombre skies, but the street vista appears almost dystopian against the bleak, monotone backdrop. It's odd to think my financial dreams are about to be realised in such a joyless shit-hole.

"You look like total crap," Clement observes as he joins me on the pavement.

"Gee, thanks for the ego boost."

"Just saying."

"Tact isn't your strongest attribute is it?"

"You'd prefer it if I lie?"

"Well, no, but sometimes it's better not to pass comment at all."

"And sometimes it's better to be told the truth."

"Not when it comes to telling a woman she looks like crap."

"Ahh, so you want us blokes to be honest, but only when we're saying what you want to hear?"

"Um...no...that's not what I'm saying."

"What are you saying then, doll?"

I am in no fit state to defend my position, even if I had a position worth defending. Probably best to adopt the fifth amendment on this one.

"No? Nothing else to add?" he asks.

"Can we just get on with this, please?"

A smirk breaks on his face. "Sure. Come on then."

Clement strides towards Oswald Powell's shop, the rucksack strap gripped firmly in his left hand. I follow behind, every step pounding a dull thud through my head.

We step through the door almost on the dot of ten o'clock.

Unlike our last visit, Mr Powell is standing behind the counter, presumably awaiting our arrival.

"Very punctual," he observes as we approach.

"I'm a stickler for time, Mr Powell," Clement replies. "And we don't have much to spare this morning so let's get on with this shall we?"

I watch, sipping on my bottle of water, and slightly in awe of the way Clement cuts through the bullshit and gets straight down to business.

"Yes, of course. Do you have the merchandise?" Mr Powell enquires.

Clement holds up the rucksack.

"Do you mind if I see it? I need to take another shaving."

"Why? You already tested it."

"Considering the amount of money at stake here, you can't blame me for being cautious. With respect, the bar I assume is in your bag might not be the same bar you brought in yesterday."

Clement slips his hand into the rucksack and pulls the bar out. He steps towards the counter and carefully places it in the centre.

"It's the same bar, but do what you gotta do. Just make it quick."

Mr Powell nods, and ducks down below the counter.

"Bear with me a second," he calls out. "Just looking for the knife."

Clement slings the rucksack over his shoulder and leans against the counter.

Another minute passes and Clement's irritation at the delay appears to be simmering nicely.

"What you doing down there, old man?"

"Just a second."

He finally emerges, holding the same scalpel-like knife he used yesterday.

"Sorry about that. I'm a bit disorganised this morning."

Mr Powell then goes through the same routine of carefully scraping a tiny fragment of gold onto the knife blade. Once his sample is secured, he heads towards the door behind the counter.

"If you can give me five minutes, I'll put my mind at rest and we can conclude our business."

Clement answers with a scowl, ensuring Mr Powell is aware of his growing impatience. Judging by his nervous twitching, I assume Mr Powell received the message loud and clear, and he quickly scurries through the doorway into the back of the shop.

Clement returns the bar to the rucksack and places it on the floor between his feet.

"You want a sip of this?" I ask, offering him my bottle of water.

"What is it?"

"Water."

"Like water out of a tap?"

"No, it's spring water."

"What's the difference?"

"It's...err...pure."

He grabs the bottle and takes a sip. "Tastes like water."

"Well, that's because it is water."

"How much did you pay for that?"

"£1.50."

"You paid £1.50 for something you can get out of a tap, for free?"

"It's not the same."

"Somebody is having a laugh at your expense, doll. Charging £1.50 for bleedin' water."

He hands the bottle back, almost in disgust, and returns to his position, leaning against the counter.

As the clock on the wall ticks the seconds away, I begin to share Clement's impatience.

"What's taking him so long?"

"Dunno, but he's got one more minute before we sod off."

Clement's answer is purposely delivered with enough volume for Mr Powell to hear.

"Just coming," a thin voice replies from the back room.

Precisely at the moment Mr Powell returns, the front door swings opens, the bell chiming the arrival of another customer.

It's not one customer that enters, but two, dressed in jeans and black hoodies.

The two men stand side-by-side just in front of the door. Their hoods are up, and the lower part of both their faces are covered with red bandannas.

Two pairs of beady eyes scan the shop.

Their attire suggests they're either ridiculously early trick or treaters, or there's a more sinister purpose to their visit. When the man on the left slowly raises a pistol, it becomes clear they're not here for confectionery or loose change.

37

Every gun I've ever seen has been confined to the screen on TV or in films. To me, a gun is nothing more than a lump of forged metal, utilised by the hero to deal with the bad guys. I've never had reason to think of a gun in any other way — until now.

This gun is very real and currently being pointed at me by a real bad guy.

A slight contraction of a forefinger is all it would take to end my life. That fact is not lost on me as a cold sweat creeps across my skin.

"Move, move. Up against the counter. Now." the man with the gun orders.

I expected a voice to match the physical menace, but it's high-pitched, and quite nasal. His companion remains silent, his purpose unclear.

I shuffle backwards, my hands instinctively raised in surrender. My back comes into contact with the edge of the counter and I turn to Clement, about ten feet away. He looks across at me, the corners of his mouth turned upwards by just a fraction, possibly to offer reassurance.

I do not feel reassured.

The silent companion approaches the counter and pulls a carrier bag from the back pocket of his jeans.

"Fill this up," he yells at Mr Powell, as the bag is thrown onto the counter. "Cash and jewellery."

The companion's voice is also distinctive, inasmuch it sounds like he's got bronchitis. There's a distinct rattle in his chest, his words raspy.

Mr Powell, standing with his hands above his head, is probably wishing he'd stayed in the back room, behind that sturdy door. He slowly lowers his hands and grasps the carrier bag.

"All the cash and stock is out back," he whimpers.

"Get it, now," bronchial man shouts.

Mr Powell edges backwards, slipping out of sight beyond the doorway.

"Anyone moves, and they're dead. Geddit?" The squeaky gunman squeals as he traces the gun left and right, between us. Clement remains still, nonchalantly leaning against the counter, and the only part of me currently moving is my twitching sphincter.

The clock ticks away as we wait for Mr Powell to return with the carrier bag. Based upon our prior experience, I suspect our guests might be in for a bit of a wait.

As terrified as I am, there is some comfort in knowing this will be over pretty quickly. As soon as Mr Powell hands over the bag, these two will be gone. Whether he drops our ninety thousand pounds into the bag remains to be seen, but if he is stupid enough to do so, it's his loss. There will be other pawnbrokers.

The ticking of the clock appears to get louder with every passing second, or it could be my heart thumping away. The wait is excruciating.

"What's in the rucksack?" The gunman suddenly asks, turning his attention, and the gun, to Clement.

Shit. No, no, no.

"Nothing to interest you, mate," Clement replies.

The gunman moves within four feet of Clement, keeping the gun aimed low.

"Fuck you freak," he squeaks. "I said, what's in the rucksack?"

Bronchial man sidles up to his companion, and for one moment, I fear he's going to snatch the rucksack. However, the two men clearly realise Clement is a threat, but as long as they keep their distance, he can't do anything with a gun pointing at his crotch.

Clement looks down at the rucksack, and then slowly raises his head to meet the gunman's stare.

"This rucksack?"

"Yeah, you prick. That rucksack."

"It's just my lunch," Clement replies.

"Bullshit. Let me see."

"Help yourself."

"Fuck you," he scowls. "Pick it up, slowly, and hand it to my mate."

This is game over, surely? Once they look in the rucksack, they'll realise all their Christmases have come at once. We might come out of this unscathed, but there will be no gold, and no cash windfall.

If I didn't feel sick earlier, I sure as hell do now.

Clement bends his knees and reaches down for the rucksack, all the time maintaining eye contact with the gunman. It's painful to watch, and Clement is dragging it out with his ponderous movements.

Once his right hand is clasped around the strap, he slowly straightens his back, gingerly raising the rucksack as if it contained volatile explosives.

Inch by inch, he raises his arm until it's parallel with the floor and the rucksack is held at arm's length.

"Grab it," The gunman squeaks to his companion.

Bronchial man takes a step forward while raising his hand to take the rucksack. That hand gets within inches of the target when Clement suddenly releases his grip on the strap.

Three heads, including mine, drop and follow the trajectory of the rucksack as it falls to the floor.

It's a distraction which lasts a split second, but time enough for Clement to enact whatever plan he's been plotting.

Neither man saw it coming, and neither has time to react.

Clement's right arm, still held out horizontally, snaps downward, towards the gunman's wrist. He grabs it, and twists, so the gun is pointed towards the floor. Almost in the same movement, Clement takes a stride forward and thrusts his lowered forehead towards bronchial man's face.

I don't know if it's possible for a nose to actually burst, but the second Clement's forehead meets bronchial man's face, that is what appears to happen. It's greeted by a sound I'll be hearing in my nightmares for weeks — a rasping squeal-come-scream as bronchial man falls backwards, his hands covering the remnants of his splattered nose and the bandanna tangled around his neck.

I can scarcely contain my horror as he thrashes around on the floor like a grounded fish on a river bank.

We are still in a shop with an armed man though, and my attention quickly turns to the greater threat.

With his gun hand contorted in what appears to be an extremely uncomfortable position, the squeaky assailant is currently rendered powerless. He's a sitting duck for Clement's gnarly fist as it hones in on its target. The gunman's beady eyes widen once they realise what's heading their way.

Clement's fist makes contact and another nose bursts. Another face is showered in blood and splintered cartilage.

It's sight enough to propel the contents of my stomach back towards my throat. I bend double, bile burning. Only a desperate gulp stops vomit exploding from my mouth.

By the time I lift my head, both men are on the floor, incapacitated, and both wailing through hands clamped to their faces.

Clement steps over the prone body of the gunman, moving towards me.

"You alright there, doll?"

I stare at him, then down at the gunman. Blind panic suddenly grips me.

"The...the...gun," I pant. "It's on the floor."

"Won't help him. It's a starting pistol."

"It's what?"

"A starting pistol. Only shoots blanks."

"Jesus bloody Christ, now you tell me."

"I'll send a telegram next time."

I take a few deep breaths and try to find some composure. "That was horrific. Is Mr Powell okay?"

"Probably. But not for long."

I don't get a chance to question his reply before he leaps over the counter. I hear muffled voices from the back room — one growling, one pleading.

The voices continue for twenty, maybe thirty seconds, and I'm becoming increasingly concerned for the wellbeing of the two men on the floor. I think bronchial man has passed out as he's no longer whining, or moving.

Mr Powell emerges from the doorway, Clement behind him. It's only when Mr Powell's upper body is thrust towards the counter do I realise Clement has a handful of his shirt collar.

"Bloody hell!" I shriek. "Leave the poor man alone. Don't you think he's been through enough?"

"He set us up."

"What?"

"This was no robbery. They only wanted the gold."

"Don't be ridiculous," I chide. "They told Mr Powell to fill a bag with cash, and jewellery."

"Yeah, and then they sent him out the back, where he could have called the old bill, or done a runner, or at least shut the bleedin' door. They're a pair of fucking idiots, but I don't think they're that stupid."

If I'd experienced our ordeal as a scene in a novel, Clement's revelation might have occurred to me earlier. But living through it first hand, blinded by fear and panic, it's an unexpected twist I never saw coming.

"What are you going to do with him?" I murmur.

"I'd quite like to ring his scrawny neck, but I'll let you decide."

I step towards the counter and bend down so my face is at the same level as Powell's. He doesn't look comfortable, and as much as I hate to admit it, I'm glad.

"You nasty old man," I spit.

"Yeah, don't hold back, doll," Clement interjects, somewhat sarcastically. "I'm sure that really stung."

"What am I supposed to do, Clem…Cliff? Jab him in the face a few times?"

"That'd be a start."

Tempting as it is, I shake my head and stand upright.

"Let's just get out of here," I huff. "We've got more important things to do than beat up old men."

"You're the boss."

Clement drags Powell to his feet and spins him around. Instinctively, Powell backs up until he meets the wall behind. Clement takes a few steps forward and places his hand around Powell's throat. For a second, I worry he is going to wring the old man's neck, but I'm hoping I know Clement well enough now to spot a bluff.

"You listen to me, you scrawny bag of shit. If you call the police, I'll come back and rip you a new arsehole. If either of those two idiots tells the police what happened, I'll come back and rip all three of you a new arsehole. Got it?"

Powell tries to nod; not easy with an enormous hand around your throat.

"Got it," he gasps.

Clement releases his grip, smiles, and playfully slaps the old man across the cheek. Not hard enough to cause any damage, but hard enough to make his point.

"Good man."

Clement leaps back over the counter and picks up the gun, tucking it into the waistband of his jeans.

"What do you want with that?" I ask.

"I'm gonna get rid of it. I'm sure as hell not gonna leave it with these two so they can terrorise some other poor bastard."

"Fair point, although I suspect they might re-think their life choices after this morning's events."

I think their revised life choices might begin with a decision about cosmetic surgery. How they're going to explain their injuries to a doctor is beyond me, but I don't think they'll be keen for Clement to pay another visit.

"Shall we get going?"

With a final glance at the grisly scene on the floor, I make a hasty exit with Clement bringing up the rear.

We step into dusk-like gloom and the promised rain. Deep puddles are already forming on the pavement, and only a frantic dash to the car prevents a proper soaking.

Once we're in our seats, Clement hands me the rucksack. "Feel free to put it in the boot."

With rain now hammering on the car roof, I'm not keen. "I'm sure it'll be fine in here."

I tuck it into the footwell as Clement starts the car.

With nothing more than a cursory glance, he reverses out of the parking bay and slams the gear lever into first. The tyres spin until they find traction on the slick road surface, and we lurch forward.

"Where are the wipers, doll?"

We've already covered a hundred yards before he chooses to address the fact we're driving blind.

"Twist the right stalk."

The wipers clear the screen and Clement works through the gears, putting a reassuring distance between our location, and what is now a crime scene.

"So, that went well," I sigh.

"Could have been worse. Could have been a real shooter."

"Would you have done anything differently, if it had been real?"

"Yeah. I'd have shot the little fuckers before we left."

"Very funny."

The fact he doesn't respond suggests he probably isn't joking.

"How could you tell it wasn't a real gun?"

"Experience."

"Specifically?"

"If you're gonna threaten somebody with a shooter, you hold it level so they can see straight down the barrel. Ninety-nine times out of a hundred, that's enough to get your point across. The dickhead back there kept the shooter low the whole time. Starter pistols have a bung in the barrel and I'd have seen it if he'd raised it to my line of sight."

"Seems a pretty flimsy theory to me."

"That, and the maker's mark on the barrel sorta gave it away."

"Oh."

We continue onwards through rain-soaked streets with no direction in mind. I'm happy to let Clement drive aimlessly while I try to process what just happened.

"Can I ask you something?"

"You're not gonna ask me to sing again, are you?"

"Um...no."

Bugger. He remembered.

"Go on then."

"Do you ever get scared?"

"Scared? Of what?"

"Well, those two men in the shop for starters."

"Those two streaks of piss? Nah."

"But they had a gun, and even if you thought it wasn't real, they could have had knives."

"So? What's the worst that could have happened?"

"You could have been shot, or stabbed. Christ, Clement, they could have killed you."

He looks across at me, eyebrows raised. "You know that's not really a concern."

What is a concern, certainly for me, is that Clement's delusions are now moving into dangerous territory, validating his reckless decisions. That worries me, but if I've learnt anything about him, it's that nagging doesn't work. I need to take another tack.

"I was scared. Petrified, if I'm honest."

My declaration is met with silence; a slight crease across his forehead the only indication he heard me.

"Clement?"

"I heard you, doll. There's no reason for you to be scared."

"Why?"

"As long as I'm around, you've nothing to be scared of."

"And when you're gone, and I'm on my own again?"

The crease returns to his forehead, deeper this time. Seconds pass and he remains silent.

"Anyone ever told you, Clement, you're hard work sometimes?"

"Possibly."

"Well? Are you going to answer my question?"

We come to a stop at a red traffic light. Finally, he looks across at me.

"You're not on your own, doll. Never have been, and never will be."

"Eh? What do you mean?"

The lights change and Clement pulls away, leaving my question unanswered at the lights.

38

Of the five men I've dated over the years, all of them have accused me, at one point or another, of being obstinate, testy, and standoffish — usually during an argument which I probably started.

I've never considered those accusations to be fair, perhaps because it's hard to recognise your own flaws. I can see them in Clement, though.

Since he dropped his cryptic statement, any attempt on my part to press him has been met with either silence, a dismissive grunt, or a shrug of the shoulders.

Ten minutes pass before I give up.

"Can we at least discuss what we're going to do next?"

"Back to the first plan."

"We try another pawnbroker?"

"Yeah. Let me know when you've worked out where we're heading."

I refer to my phone and locate the nearest target from my original list of possibilities. It's only three miles away.

"Keep going along this road for another mile. I'll direct you from there."

He nods and we continue in silence.

As we navigate closer to Barlow Brown Pawnbrokers, I'm relieved to see the general area is several notches up the social scale from that of Powell & Partners. We pass a couple of antique shops, a coffee house, and a car dealer with a forecourt full of premium German motors.

"This feels a bit more affluent."

"Definitely some money here, doll. Dunno if that's such a good thing though."

"Why?"

"Respectable businesses are less likely to break the rules."

"And less likely to attempt an armed robbery."

"I'll give you that one."

We turn into Churchill Road and I point to the premises of Barlow Brown, sited on the corner. Clement drops into second gear and we cruise slowly along the narrow street, looking for somewhere to park. We find a space sixty yards along, and Clement pulls in.

"Second time lucky," I chirp as I grab the rucksack from the footwell.

As we step out of the car, Clement looks up and down the road. He then removes the starting pistol from his waistband and drops it into a drain. Even though it's not a real gun, I'm glad to see the back of it.

After a quick dash through the light drizzle, we reach Barlow Brown Pawnbrokers and stand outside. The external facade certainly looks more upmarket than Powell & Partners. The brickwork has been painted a deep shade of blue, and the business name above the window is formed in foot-high gold letters in a Roman-style font.

The other difference is the locked door. A sign in the window tells us we have to press a button to gain access.

I press the silver button and a buzzer sounds on the other side of the glass. A few seconds pass before the latch clicks, and Clement pushes the door open.

The inside of Barlow Brown is more like a jewellers than a pawnbrokers. There are waist-high glass display cases positioned against the walls to our left and right, stocked with watches, bracelets, rings, and necklaces, all beautifully arranged. Another display case, running parallel to the rear wall, serves as a counter, with a till on top and a narrow archway behind.

A man appears from the archway and sidles up to the counter.

"Good morning, folks. Rotten day out there," he says with a warm smile, his middle-class voice as smooth as butter.

As we approach the counter, I'm struck by how handsome he is. He must be in his mid-forties, judging by the flecks of grey peppering his collar-length brown hair, and the fine lines around his chocolate-brown eyes. His broad shoulders and tapered torso are cloaked in a white cotton shirt; the sleeves rolled-up to the elbows to reveal tanned forearms. I notice the absence of a wedding ring.

"Are you the boss?" Clement asks.

The man's smile broadens, revealing a set of platinum white teeth.

"Well, I pay the bills, so I guess I am. Richard Barlow, nice to meet you."

Handshakes are exchanged and my cheeks adopt a rosy hue as Clement introduces me as Louise. Just my luck I look like a sack of shit this morning.

"So, how can I help?" Richard asks.

Please, Clement. Don't call him Dick.

"It's a bit of an odd one, Dickie."

Is that better or worse than Dick?

"An item has come into our possession and we're not really sure what to do with it."

"Sounds intriguing."

"Louise will explain."

Richard's gaze turns in my direction, his seductive eyes prompting a flutter in places that really shouldn't be fluttering.

I do my best to relay the story of how we found the gold under my floorboards, but it feels rushed, flustered.

"So, Richard, we were wondering if you might be interested." I coo.

To my relief, his smile is still in situ and his body language remains open, cordial.

"I'd be lying if I said I wasn't tempted," he replies. "But I'm afraid I can't take it."

"Why not?" Clement interjects.

"All pawnbrokers have to be licenced, and to secure a licence you have to agree to certain rules, many of which relate to the way we purchase goods. Buying or pawning an item without completing a raft of paperwork and obtaining official ID is a big no-no, and we certainly can't take an item we suspect might be stolen."

"You can't bend those rules, Dickie?"

"Afraid not. If you get caught, you lose your licence. You can't trade without one, so no matter how lucrative the potential reward, the risk is just too great. I'm sorry."

"So you reckon no pawnbroker will touch it?"

"Maybe one in hundred, if you're lucky, but not in this part of the world. I know nearly all my local competitors and I can say for certain none of them would touch it."

"What about Oswald Powell?"

Richard's face puckers as if he's just caught wind of a particularly bad smell.

"Oswald Powell was the one in a hundred and lost his licence six months ago. He shouldn't be trading, and certainly not as a pawnbroker."

I exhale a resigned sigh and offer my hand to Richard.

"Thank you anyway, Richard. Lovely to meet you."

He shakes both our hands and we turn to leave. We take barely three steps when a thought appears to strike Richard.

"Actually, guys, there might be another option."

We spin around and stare at him, expectant.

"But you never heard this from me, right?"

I nod, and Clement gives him a thumbs up.

"Jewellers aren't licenced so they can buy whatever they like, and some of them do accept scrap gold. If you're prepared to provide a name and address, I think I might know a jeweller worth talking to — Gerrard Clarke."

"We have to provide a name and address?" I parrot.

"Yes, but I didn't say whose name and address," he replies with a wry smile. "Gerrard Clarke is more inclined to bend the rules than most."

He tears a slip of paper from a notepad and scribbles something down.

"Here's Gerrard's address."

I reach out and grasp the slip of paper, taking the opportunity to stare into Richard's deep brown eyes one final time.

"Oh, and here's my card," he adds. "If you need any advice on, shall we say, more legitimate items, please give me a call."

I take the card and reciprocate his flirtatious smile, although I fear my attempt is more of a gurn.

We leave Richard in peace and scuttle back to the car.

"He was helpful," I comment as we buckle up our seatbelts.

"Yeah, considering how you virtually threw yourself at him."

"I don't know what you're talking about."

"You were about as subtle as a sledgehammer. Honestly, doll. That made my toes curl."

I feel my cheeks flush again, and try to turn the tables.

"Yes, well, we could have avoided all of this if you'd known pawnbrokers had to be licenced. It was your suggestion."

"I did know, but licencing only came in during the mid-sixties, and plenty of them didn't play by the rules back then. How was I to know they're all bleedin' saints these days?"

We reach an uncomfortable stalemate.

"Anyway, let me check the address of this Gerrard character."

Clement does a three point turn and by the time he swings back onto the main road, I've entered the address in to the sat nav.

"It's about nine miles away."

"Triffic."

For the first few miles we don't talk. When Clement does decide to get chatty, I wish he'd remained silent.

"You fancy him then?"

"Who?"

"You know who I'm talking about. Dashing Dickie."

"No. I don't fancy him," I lie.

"Word to the wise, doll — you can't bullshit a bullshitter."

"Okay. I admit he was quite pleasant."

"You gonna call him?"

"I don't know. Probably not."

"Why?"

"What is this, Clement?" I snap. "Why are you suddenly interested in my abysmal love life?"

"You should call him," he replies, ignoring my question.

"Just for a moment, let's overlook the fact I'm not in the market for a new man, and not likely to be for some time — why is it any of your business?"

"Just looking out for you, doll. He seemed like a nice bloke, that's all."

It's not the answer I was expecting, and it catches me off guard.

"Yes, well, it doesn't help that he thinks my name is Louise. Lying about your own name is not a great way to start a relationship."

"Look at it another way. Beth had all that shitty luck with men. Now you can be Louise, and make a new start. Reinvent yourself."

My gut instinct is to dismiss the fanciful suggestion, but the more I think about it, the more I warm to his thinking. Maybe it is time for a complete overhaul of my life.

"Doesn't matter anyway. You're also overlooking the fact he probably didn't fancy me."

"He fancied you. Trust me."

"Really? You think?"

I inwardly cringe. That did not sound as indifferent as I hoped.

He turns to me with a broad grin. "Yeah, I think."

I try to hide my smile for the remaining fifteen minutes of the journey. It only fades once we turn into Bullers Road; our destination, and hopefully, the final hurdle before I can start planning this new life.

We slowly cruise along the entire length of Bullers Road, beyond the spot where the sat nav claimed we'd reached our destination. There is no jewellers. We turn around and try again, checking we haven't missed the obvious.

"Where the hell is it?" I groan.

A horn blasts from a BMW behind us. Clement ignores it and continues at a pedestrian pace. The horn sounds again and Clement glances at the rear view mirror.

"No bleedin' patience, some people."

"Shall we just park up and check on foot?"

"Seems a waste of time to me, but if you want."

We pull alongside a space between two parked cars and Clement slides the gear lever into reverse. He then twists around in his seat as he prepares to parallel park into the tight space.

"I don't believe it. He can see I'm trying to bleedin' reverse but he's right up my arse."

The horn blasts again. It's one blast too many, and Clement has apparently had enough.

Before I can tell him to calm down, his seat belt is off and he's out of the car. I twist around in my seat to see what's happening, although experience tells me I probably don't want to know.

I watch as Clement strides purposefully towards the BMW. He raises his hand, beckoning the driver to get out of his expensively-engineered cocoon.

I can't see the driver's face but I suspect it's full of panic, and regret.

Clearly not keen to accept Clement's invite, the tyres suddenly spin and the BMW reverses at speed. He doesn't stop until there's at least a hundred yards of tarmac between us.

Clement turns around and strides back to the car. He clambers in, and without a word, reverses into the parking space.

I should probably warn him against the dangers of road rage, but I'm secretly pleased he scored a small victory against impatient idiots in expensive cars.

We get out of the Fiat and check the number of Gerrard Clarke's premises — number forty two.

"Even numbers are this side of the road," I comment.

We pass half-a-dozen shops, none of which are a jewellers. Most of the shops don't display a number so we have to work backwards from number sixty; a sandwich shop.

We pass a dry cleaners and Clement suddenly stops. He turns towards a door set in an alcove.

"That address ain't a shop," he says, pointing to the door, painted gloss red. "It's an office above a shop."

We move towards the door and a small silver plaque fixed to the wall. Printed in embossed letters, barely readable, is the number forty two, and the name, 'Clarke Jewellers'.

"No wonder we couldn't bloody see it from the car," he grumbles.

Below the plaque is a doorbell, with a crudely printed sign next to it — 'Visitors by appointment only'.

"Do you think we should make an appointment?" I ask.

Clement shrugs and presses the doorbell, answering my question.

"Let me do the talking, doll."

I'm not going to argue. The breaking of any rule, no matter how trivial, puts me in a fluster.

We wait, and just as Clement raises his hand to press the doorbell again, the door opens.

A chubby man with a shock of curly black hair stares at us.

"Yes?" he snaps.

"We're looking for Gerrard Clarke," Clement replies.

"Who are you?"

"We're looking to sell some gold. We were told he was the man to speak to."

"If you're looking to flog a bit of nine-karat tat, I'm not interested."

"It's not. Are you Gerrard Clarke?"

"Maybe."

"Don't piss me around fella," Clement growls. "I was told this Gerrard bloke was a serious player, but if you wanna stand here playing guessing games, we'll take our business elsewhere."

The male ego is a fragile thing, and the man takes the bait.

"Yes, I'm Gerrard Clarke."

"Good. Now, are you interested in buying some gold?"

"Depends on quantity and quality."

"Hundred and fifty ounces. Pure."

A smile forms on Gerrard's moon-like face. "In that case, come on in."

He turns and lumbers up a flight of stairs. Clement leads and I follow the two men up to a landing with four doors leading off it.

"Come through here," Gerrard says as he opens one of the doors into a large room that appears to function partly as an office, and partly as a workshop of sorts. There are no windows, but two square skylights, set in the ceiling, offer some natural light from the ashen grey sky.

Gerrard switches the lights on and flops down in a battered office chair.

"What sort of jeweller are you?" Clement asks as he casts his eye around the room.

"The sort who knows the High Street jewellery trade is dying on its arse. There's no money in shops these days, so I focus on trading gold, gems, and I've also developed a decent manufacturing set up. We do quite well selling mid-range gear online through Amazon and eBay."

"Amazon and eBay?" Clement repeats.

"You know? The websites?"

I jump in before Clement has a chance to make a fool of himself. "Sorry Gerrard. He's a bit of a technophobe. The Internet passed him by somehow."

"Bit like my old mum," he chuckles. "She doesn't get it either."

With the small talk out of the way, Gerrard belatedly invites us to take a seat in front of his desk. I assume it's a desk, but it's so crowded with paperwork, tools, plastic tubs, and Red Bull cans, I can't be sure.

"So, you mentioned a hundred and fifty ounces of pure gold. Have you got it with you?"

Clement opens the rucksack and removes the bar. He places it on the desk and sits back in his chair.

"There you go. And just so you know, we want cash. No paperwork and no questions."

Gerrard sits forward and runs a hand through his curly mane.

"Good Lord. I didn't realise you meant a whole bar."

"Is that a problem?"

"No. It's just we don't see them very often, least not this size."

"And the cash?"

"I can do that, as long as you're realistic with your price. At best, this is scrap gold so don't be expecting market value. And I'll have to take a trip to the bank."

"Fair enough."

"You mind if I take a closer look?"

"Help yourself."

Gerrard reaches across and picks the bar up. Holding it in both hands, he slowly turns it around and studies the hallmarks. Seemingly satisfied, he places it back down on the desk.

"Okay. I'm definitely interested, but I need to run some tests on it first."

"Do what you like, mate, but we had it tested this morning and it's the real deal."

"How was it tested?"

"The bloke shaved a bit off and did something with it."

"Probably an acid test. My testing is a bit more thorough than that."

He picks the bar up and waddles across the room to a workbench, positioned against the wall.

"Come over here," he calls across to us.

We do as instructed and join him at the workbench.

Besides an array of hand-tools, boxes of brightly coloured gems, and more Red Bull cans, the workbench also houses a boxy silver-coloured gadget; a similar shape and size to a microwave oven.

It's that gadget Gerrard wants to demonstrate.

"This little beauty can tell me the composition of any metallic object. It cost a fortune but, if you pardon the pun, it's worth its weight in gold."

My eyes meet Clement's and we share a puzzled look.

"Almost a quarter of the jewellery I'm offered is not what it seems," Gerrard adds, noting our perplexed expressions. "For example, only yesterday I was offered an eighteen-karat gold bangle. When I put it through this device, turned out it was only gold plate over a tungsten core — basically it was a fake, cleverly designed to look like solid gold. This device saved me from paying a grand for something worth barely a hundred."

"And what will it tell you about our bar?" I ask.

"It will tell me the exact purity, and I can't emphasise enough how important the purity is. If it is pure, or at least very close, you've got something of significant value on your hands, darling."

I want to tell him not to call me darling, but considering he's about to pay me many thousands of pounds, I'll let it slip.

We watch as Gerrard prepares the machine. He flicks a catch and a digital display flips up. The screen receives a few prods and a low whirring noise begins. A few more prods of the screen and then he pulls open a door on the front. He carefully places the gold bar inside and closes the door. A switch is flicked, and with a final prod of the screen, he turns to us.

"This'll just take a minute."

"You wanna talk about money while we wait?" Clement asks.

"Let's see what we're dealing with first," he replies. "A difference of even a few percentile points in purity can have a significant impact on the value."

The three of us then stand and stare at the machine for a minute — an extremely long minute.

Finally, it emits three loud beeps and the whirring noise ceases.

"Grubs up," Gerrard jokes. We don't laugh.

He leans over the device and runs his finger down the screen, studying the data.

"Well?" Clement prompts, his patience wearing thin.

Gerrard turns and faces us. I can't tell from his expression what he's about to reveal.

"Do you want the good news, or the bad?"

"The bad." Clement replies.

"I'm afraid your bar is not pure gold."

"And the good news."

"I don't need to visit the bank."

39

For a brief moment, I worry Clement might throttle Gerrard.

"If you're trying to pull a fast one, I'll knock you into the middle of next week."

"I promise you, I'm not," Gerrard pleads. "The analysis shows it's only fourteen percent gold."

"What's the rest of it then?" Clement booms. "Scotch mist?"

"It's mainly lead, I'm afraid, plus a few other elements I suspect were introduced during the moulding process."

"That can't be right," I intervene. "It was tested this morning, and the guy made us an offer of ninety grand. Why would he offer us that amount of money for something that isn't pure gold?"

"You said he tested it by taking a sample?"

"Yes. Twice in fact."

"Okay. He would have then conducted an acid test on that sample, and I think I know why that test might have shown the bar to be pure gold."

"Go on."

"Well, I think what you have is what's known as a salted bar."

"A what?" Clement barks.

"There are basically two types of fake gold bar. The first type is plated, where a bar of base metal, usually tungsten, is coated with a few microns of gold. Those are easy to spot as you can literally scrape the gold away."

"But our bar isn't plated?"

"No, it's definitely a salted bar, and quite an old one. Basically, it's a lump of lead with a comparatively thick coating of gold. When you scrape a sample, you're cutting into pure gold and that's how it passes an acid test."

"I still don't get it," I grumble. "Why would anyone bother making a bar like that if any backstreet jeweller can tell it isn't pure gold?"

"Throughout the sixties and seventies, salted bars were used as currency amongst the criminal fraternity. Obviously they never had the technology to determine the true composition, and because they passed an acid test, they were incredibly difficult to spot as fakes. If you were offering a bar like this in exchange for guns or drugs, the last thing you wanted was the seller realising it was fake. It's quite ingenious when you think about it."

I don't share Gerrard's admiration for the forger's ingenuity. His revelation has just destroyed my hopes in one crushing instant.

"So, it's bloody worthless?" Clement asks.

"Well, not quite. You've still got over twenty ounces of gold in there."

"Worth?"

Gerrard waddles over to his desk and unearths a calculator. He jabs the keys with a fat finger.

"I could offer you nine grand."

"Nine grand?" Clement spits. "Is that it?"

"But, Gerrard," I add. "I thought gold was worth a thousand pounds an ounce."

"It does trade about that level, you're right, But we're talking about scrap gold here. It needs to be smelted to remove the lead and that process takes time and money. Nine grand is a fair price."

Clement chips in. "Make it ten and you've got a deal."

Gerrard chews his lip for a few seconds, perhaps considering the pitfalls of haggling with a giant man on a short fuse.

He finally relents. "Okay, ten grand, but that's it."

I'm not sure it really matters if we walk away with nine or ten thousand — it's still not enough to pay Sterling, let alone fund all the things I had planned. No repairs to the house, no remodelled lounge, no holiday, and my hundred thousand pound mortgage remains fully intact.

But as much as I'd like to wallow in self-pity for the loss of soft furnishings and spa breaks, I have more pressing concerns. Where the hell am I going to get ten grand in two days?

I return to Gerrard's desk and slump down on a chair. Right on cue, heavy drops of rain begin to thump against the skylight above my head. I look up at the stormy grey clouds as they gather together. No view could be more fitting.

Ten thousand pounds.

Two days.

Fuck my life.

I press my fingers into my temples, trying to quell the headache which is now approaching migraine status. A glimmer of light is reflected from the diamond in my engagement ring.

A thought occurs and I spin round in my chair.

"Gerrard. You said you trade in jewellery?"

"Yes, I do, amongst other things. Why?"

I tug at the ring until it reluctantly pops from my finger. "How much would you offer for this?"

He walks over to the desk and takes the ring. After a cursory glance, he returns to the workbench and examines it under a magnifying glass.

Inspection complete, he makes his offer. "I'll give you a grand for it."

"Is that all?"

"Sorry, darling, but that's my best offer. Rings like this, as nice as it is, are ten a penny."

"Fine," I sigh. "I'll take a thousand."

"Okay, let me sort out some cash. Give me a few minutes."

Gerrard disappears and we're left to dwell on what might have been.

"You alright, doll," Clement murmurs.

I look up at him from the chair. Maybe it's the muted light from the skylight, but his face is a stony shade of grey.

"Not really."

It's not just the money, as devastating as that is; it's the sense of failure. We took on the most improbable of challenges, and against all the odds, we prevailed, only for our victory to be snatched away at the very last second.

"It's like that bleedin' cup final all over again," Clement mutters to himself, as if he'd read my thoughts.

"At least we made it to the final, if it's any consolation."

It's a weak attempt to lift the sombre atmosphere, as much as it is a crass analogy.

Ignoring my effort, Clement disappears inside his own thoughts as he strokes his moustache. The rain begins to fall harder as the clouds darken above us.

Seconds pass and rain falls. Clement eventually turn and calls across to me.

"We're not done yet, doll."

I'm about to ask what he means when Gerrard returns, clutching a large brown envelope.

"I hope it's okay with you," he chirps. "But I do need to complete some paperwork on the ring. I can't resell it without proof of ownership."

"Fine."

As Gerrard flops back behind the desk and searches for a pen, Clement steps across from the workbench and joins us.

He sits down and opens the breast pocket of his waistcoat.

I tap him on the arm. "You can't smoke in here."

"I'm not."

He pulls out his Zippo and places it, carefully, deliberately, on the desk.

"You interested in buying that?" he asks Gerrard.

My heart melts at the kindness of his gesture. He has literally nothing to his name, and yet he's prepared to sell something of immeasurable sentimental valuable, just to help me. I don't have the heart to point out the obvious — the value of a lighter is barely a drop in the ocean compared to the sum we need.

I put my hand on his shoulder. "Bless you, Clement, but you keep it."

As I turn back to Gerrard, intent on telling him to ignore Clement's proposition, he already has the Zippo in his hands, inspecting it with more intensity than he afforded my engagement ring.

"You know what it is, right?" Clement says.

"Indeed I do," Gerrard replies with obvious enthusiasm. "Although I've never seen one in the flesh, so to speak."

For a moment, I wonder if I've stepped into some parallel universe where battered cigarette lighters are the most interesting thing in the world.

"Am I missing something here?"

Gerrard finally shifts his gaze from the Zippo and looks across at me, wide-eyed.

"This, darling, is a 1933 Zippo," he says, his voice low, reverent.

"And that is interesting, why?"

He turns to Clement. "You want to educate her, or shall I?"

Clement shrugs. "Stage is yours, mate."

Gerrard delicately places the Zippo back on the desk and locks his hands together. He then clears his throat as if he's about to deliver a sermon.

Christ, man. Just get on with it.

I roll my eyes, which is enough to prod Gerrard into action.

"The Zippo Manufacturing Company was founded in 1932, in Pennsylvania. They only made 25,000 lighters in their first year of operation — 1933 — so any lighter from that year is an extremely rare object. What your friend has here is an original 1933 model."

"Okay, it's rare, but it's just a lighter."

"Not to collectors it's not. This is the holy grail of Zippo lighters, and they can change hands for significant sums of money."

My interest is suddenly piqued. "How much money?"

"Well, in auction, and despite the fact it's not exactly in pristine condition, I can see it going for as much as twenty thousand."

"Holy shit! Really?"

"Oh, yes. Without question."

Clement, apparently bored with the lesson, breaks our conversation.

"I'm more interested in what you'll pay for it here and now, mate."

Gerrard sits back in his chair and puffs his already bulbous cheeks.

"I honestly think you'd be better served putting it into auction. As much as I'd love to buy it from you, I doubt you'd be very happy with my offer. And, if you don't mind me saying, I wouldn't want to see you when you're unhappy."

"Yeah, I know we'd get more money at auction, but we don't have time. What's your best price?"

Gerrard fidgets nervously. "Eight thousand is my absolute best offer," he ventures, his voice barely a squeak.

Clement turns to me. "Your call, doll. It puts us just a grand short when you add it to the gold and the ring."

I could raise a thousand pounds if I sold my car, but that's academic as far as I'm concerned.

"Clement, you don't have to do this."

"Don't I?"

"No, you don't. I know it has a lot of sentimental value but I didn't realise it was worth so much money. I can't ask you to sell it. I just can't."

It appears my protest was in vain as he reaches across the desk, his hand extended.

"Alright, mate. Eight grand. Deal."

"Clement. No," I plead.

"It's not up for debate, doll. We need the cash more than I need a lighter."

"But..."

"Drop it. You sold your ring so it's only fair I sell something of mine."

I can't bring myself to tell him the ring means nothing to me, least not sentimentally.

Gerrard leans across the desk and shakes Clement's hand. The deal is done, irrespective of my objection.

Of the three people sitting in the room, one is delighted, one is swamped with a mixture of guilt and gratitude, and one is typically Clement.

With our deals concluded, I just want to go home and curl up on the sofa. The reality is that I've got paperwork to go through with Gerrard, and then I need to get back to the shop. With my fortune gone before it even arrived, I have to earn a living the hard way.

Gerrard counts out ten thousand pounds, payment for the gold, and stacks the pile of notes on the desk. I give him my bank details and he makes a payment of nine thousand pounds, for the ring and the Zippo, straight into my account. Neither were acquired through dubious means so it makes no odds if he has my name and address.

With a final shake of hands, we leave Gerrard to savour his good fortune. He must be delighted we turned up today, even without an appointment.

We trudge back to the car and I set the sat nav to direct us home.

"Drive back to my place, but then I must get back to the shop. I need every penny I can lay my hands on now."

Clement nods and we pull away. As we crawl through heavy traffic my mind buzzes with what-ifs and unanswered questions.

"Don't take this the wrong way, Clement, because I'm more grateful than you'll ever know, but if you knew your lighter was so valuable, then why didn't you just offer to sell it the night you walked into the shop? We might have got a much better price if we had had time to find the right buyer."

"I didn't know it was worth as much as twenty grand."

"Shame. We missed an opportunity there, don't you think?"

"Opportunities are like buses, doll — they come and they go. No point dwelling on the one you missed."

"Maybe, but doesn't it bother you we could have avoided all that hassle of schlepping around London?"

"No. Why would it?"

"Because it was a waste of time, all of it."

He turns to me, a deep scowl plastered across his face. "Do you really think everything we've been through has been a waste of time?"

"Well, it was, wasn't it?" I snipe back, perhaps too defensively. "Harry's gold turned out to be almost worthless, and Sterling's money could have been raised with something you had in your pocket the moment we first met. Of course it was a waste of time."

He shakes his head and turns back to the road. "Jesus wept, doll. Have a word with yourself."

40

I leave Clement sitting in front of the TV with a cup of tea.

It would be fair to say our conversation was muted after our testy exchange. That's not to say Clement's words didn't strike a nerve, and I spent the remainder of our journey home in a state of quiet introspection.

And even now, driving towards the shop, that introspection continues.

Four days since Clement appeared in the shop, and what we've been through in that time beggars belief.

Plenty of miles driven, plenty walked. I met good people, and some particularly bad people. There was the thrill of adventure, and the bruising disappointments. I laughed hard, I cringed, and I cried. Tantrums were thrown, and fortitude found. My shame became pride. I looked beyond delusions, and discovered wisdom in the least likely of places.

Two strangers. One unlikely team.

Was it really all a waste of time?

Absolutely not.

It's taken almost an hour, but I now understand the point Clement was trying to make. We've as good as secured Sterling's cash, but, more importantly, I have regained something beyond monetary value – belief.

It's funny, but as I open the shop, I'm not bothered I've missed half the lunchtime trade. I'm no longer bothered about the small fortune that slipped through my fingers. I don't think I'm even bothered about Karl, or David Sterling.

But amid all my positivity, there is one thing still bothering me.

Clement has done more for me in the last four days than any of my partners ever did – period. He protected me, guided me, and encouraged me. He forced me to address my shortcomings, and tested my resolve. Above all, though, he was there for me when I really needed him, and that is something I can't say has ever been true of any other man in my adult life.

The thought that he might disappear just as abruptly as he arrived pains me more than I care to admit.

And I think I know why.

In lieu of a father, or any male siblings, I've tried to fill a hole with the wrong kind of love, and the wrong kind of man. My staunchly independent principles would never have allowed me to accept it, but I guess all I ever wanted was somebody to look after me.

Is that so wrong? Doesn't everyone want to feel protected, feel safe?

Clement has made me realise what's missing in my life. I owe him, and now it's my turn to fight on his behalf.

Once I've got settled behind the counter with a strong cup of coffee, I scroll through the contacts in my phone. I find the name I'm looking for and tap the dial icon.

It rings five times before Juliet answers.

"Hi, Juliet. It's Beth. Beth Baxter."

"Hiya, Beth. How's the wonderful world of books?"

Juliet has been one of my best customers for years. She pops in two or three times a month and always leaves with a handful of books. Over the years, we've got to know each other well, and chatted over countless cups of tea while we critique books and put the world to rights.

But it's not her opinion of the latest Jodi Picoult novel I'm interested in today. It's her professional advice as a mental wellbeing counsellor that I need.

We spend a few minutes chatting idly before I steer the conversation towards the reason for my call.

While Juliet patiently listens, I try my best to explain Clement's delusions. There are certain parts of his psyche I skirt past, mainly because I don't know how to properly explain Clement's complex personality. Within a few minutes of unloading to Juliet, it becomes apparent how much I needed to share my concerns with somebody — something I've been unable to do until now.

"So, what do you reckon, Juliet?"

"Honestly? From what you've told me, I think you're right to intervene. This is not my area of expertise but if I was to offer a prognosis based purely on what you've told me, I'd say it's likely your friend is suffering from a deep-rooted delusional disorder. In acute cases, which this might be, the patient's delusions become their reality — they are just as real as your memories of what you had for dinner last night. In your friend's case, it's highly likely he genuinely believes he died in 1975."

"I'm so relieved to hear you say that. I was starting to question my own sanity. The way he acts, the things he says — it's so credible it almost unnerving."

"If it's any consolation, your feelings are not uncommon, and many a medical professional has felt exactly the same. Unless the patient is claiming they were abducted by aliens, or in your case, claiming they returned from beyond the grave, some delusions can be extremely difficult to diagnose and treat."

"So, what can I do?"

"No doubt about it. He needs to see a doctor for a preliminary assessment, and urgently."

"Ahh, that's my problem. I might have suggested to him that perhaps he should see a doctor."

"He didn't respond well?"

"No, he did not. He flatly refused because as far as he's concerned, there's nothing wrong with him."

"That's not uncommon."

"So, and I'd understand if you said no, would you be willing to meet him? I think I can persuade him to speak to you as long as it's at my place, and he doesn't feel like he's being press-ganged. He's not the sort of man who can be forced to do anything he doesn't want to do."

"I'm not sure, Beth. It goes against our protocols."

"Please, Juliet. I'm worried he's just going to wander off and I'll never see him again. He won't seek help on his own so I need to subtly bring the help to him."

The line goes quiet. I can imagine Juliet at the other end, working through number of ways this could come back to bite her.

"Listen, Beth. Your problem raises several ethical issues for me, but I do understand your dilemma. I need to stress that your friend urgently needs to seek help, but if he's reluctant, maybe you could invite me over for coffee on Friday at one o'clock. If, by pure chance your friend was there, I could have an informal chat with him."

"Oh, Juliet, thank you. You have no idea what a relief that is."

"It's okay, but in the interim, I want you to promise you'll keep trying to persuade him to see his doctor. I'm not qualified to be anything other than a second opinion, and maybe help him to make contact with a professional. He really needs to see a doctor, Beth. Understood?"

"Totally."

"Okay then. I'll be at the shop at one on Friday."

She rings off and I breathe a sigh of relief. It's a small step, but one in the right direction.

Now all I need to do is decide when to tell my delusional friend. Perhaps it would be better to leave it until Friday morning, once I've got Sterling out of my life and I can focus fully on helping Clement.

With that problem in hand, if not solved, I can turn my attention to raising the final thousand pounds I need to hit my twenty thousand pound target. And that means selling my beloved Fiat.

I revert to Google and check the value — just over two thousand pounds. At least I'll be able to buy a cheap runaround with the excess cash.

I spend the next hour ringing round a dozen local car dealers until I find one who isn't either a patronising git, or a piss-taking chancer. He has a Nissan Micra he's prepared to swap for the Fiat, plus an additional thousand in cash. The only slight issue is the car won't be ready until Thursday afternoon, but I agree to pop over a few hours before Sterling is due. Nothing like cutting it fine.

With both Clement and the car sorted, I only have my ailing hangover to address. Alas, I don't think anything other than a good night's sleep will remedy that. I shouldn't be pleased about it, but the incessant rain has ensured a quiet afternoon in the shop.

By the time five thirty comes around, I've barely made thirty pounds. This can't go on. I refuse to accept the rest of my life will be spent standing at this counter, peddling second hand books and praying my life will miraculously change.

Clement isn't the only one suffering from delusions.

It's time to accept a few truths of my own.

41

Good morning Wednesday.

Ten minutes since my alarm sounded and I'm still lying in bed, staring up at the ceiling. In part, I'm revelling in the fact my hangover is no more — eleven hours of sleep saw to that. However, the main reason I've not ventured beyond my duvet is because my head is buzzing with ideas, with plans. So much to do, but I can honestly say I'm relishing the challenge.

I skip to the bathroom, take a quick shower and get dressed. There's no sign of life from the spare bedroom so I rap on the door.

"Wakey, wakey, Clement."

He replies with a guttural groan and a few profanities. I chuckle to myself and barrel down the stairs.

By the time Clement joins me in the kitchen, I'm already halfway through a bowl of granola.

"Morning."

"Yeah, it is."

"Sleep well?"

"Need a brew," he grumbles.

And they say I'm not a morning person.

Clement makes himself a cup of tea and declines everything on my breakfast menu.

"Have you got any plans for the day?" I ask.

"Nah. What are you doing?"

"I'm heading to the shop so I'll be there all day. I've got a lot to do."

"Guess I'm stuck here then."

"No, not necessarily. Is there anything in particular you wanted to do?"

He sits down at the table and takes a sip of tea.

"Don't suppose there's a zoo nearby?"

"A zoo? Um, yes, I think there's one about half-hour away. Why?"

"Never been to a zoo before."

"Seriously?"

"Planned to, once, with Annie. Never happened."

My initial inclination is to suggest it's a bad idea. I'd rather know precisely where he is, at least until we've dealt with Sterling and he's spoken to Juliet. But the mention of Annie, and a new found resolve to kerb my controlling ways, softens my stance.

"Right, well, if that's what you want to do, I can drop you at the train station."

"You gonna give me some cash?"

"Of course. Do you want me to print off the journey details, and a map?"

"I'm not twelve, doll," he scoffs. "I think I can find my own way. Just tell me where it is and drop me at the station."

"Right, yes. Sorry."

With our respective plans in place, we leave the house and head for the train station. Despite my best efforts, the conversation is strained, and Clement appears reluctant to talk; more so than usual.

Once we pull into the station forecourt, I hand him fifty pounds and my mobile number. "Give me a call when you get back and I'll pick you up."

He nods, mumbles a goodbye and gets out of the car.

I sit and watch him as he strides towards the station entrance. He reaches the ticket machines and pulls out the pack of Marlboros. He then taps both his breast pockets before his head drops. No Zippo.

I wish I'd just driven away the moment he got out of the car.

419

A man in a suit walks past Clement, smoking a cigarette. I can't hear what's being said but the man suddenly stops and digs a hand into his jacket pocket. He offers Clement a lighter. Once his cigarette is lit, Clement hands the lighter back and nods at the man in the suit.

I pull away from the kerb and head to the shop with a weighty sack of guilt sitting next to me.

Fifteen minutes later, I'm standing behind the counter in an empty shop, cup of tea in hand. My plans have taken a temporary backseat as I ponder Clement's behaviour this morning. Assuming she was a real person and not another figment of his imagination, this Annie obviously meant a lot to him.

That begs an interesting question. Actually, it begs many questions.

If Clement is so convinced he really did die, and he's been sent here to make amends for his past life, surely that would mean he's also convinced there is an afterlife. And if there is an afterlife, wouldn't that be where Annie now resides? If that's the case, he'll get to see her when he's done here, won't he?

That doesn't tally with his mood this morning. I would have thought he'd be positively chipper considering he's on the cusp of a celestial reunion with his partner.

Maybe I've just unearthed a chink in Clement's claims.

The next question is: do I confront him with it?

It takes about half a cup of tea for me to decide it's not a good idea.

As well as the fact it could mess with his already fragile mind, there are too many ways he could rationalise my concerns. I mean, he could say anything, and I couldn't disprove any of it. As far as I'm aware, there is no set agenda for what happens to us once we shuffle off this mortal coil. Do we end up in either heaven, or hell? Do we get reincarnated as plankton? Or do we simply cease to exist — an eternity of nothingness?

That final possibility sends a cold shiver down my spine.

Whichever way you cut it, I can't argue what I can't substantiate, so any conversation on the subject is probably ill-advised. I'd also prefer not to dwell on such dark subject matter any longer.

Hopefully my questions will become moot after he's had a chat with Juliet.

Happy to move on from Clement's delusions, I start thinking about my plans for the future, here on planet sanity.

I grab a pad and start compiling a list of tasks.

The first task prompts me into immediate action, and I call the bank to arrange a nine thousand pound cash withdrawal. I'm told it will be ready tomorrow morning. First task completed.

The next task couldn't be less routine than the first.

I google commercial estate agents and find three candidates within five miles. I call the first one listed in the search results.

"Good morning. I'd like to speak to somebody about selling my business."

I spend twenty minutes on the phone to Howard; an extremely knowledgeable and helpful chap. He happens to know my landlord, and actually handled the lease for the previous tenants of my shop. We talk through my income, which puts a slight dampener on his enthusiasm, and probably his valuation of the business. However, Howard does seem more enthusiastic when I tell him the very attractive terms of my lease, and the stock which the buyer will inherit. I don't mention the small mountain of mummy smut.

Once he has all the relevant numbers, he promises to call me back later with a ballpark valuation.

I'm tempted to call the next agent listed in the search results, but I have a good feeling about Howard so I'll see what he comes up with first. Besides, I want to take a moment to reflect.

As decisions go, this one falls into the monumental category.

My shop, founded to create a legacy from my father's inheritance money, has sadly become a millstone. Thirteen years of my life and what do I have to show for it? It's the longest relationship I've ever had, and like most relationships there have been some truly great times, and some particularly hard times — too many of late. It's now time for a clean break and an amicable parting of the ways.

I guess, in part, I have Clement to thank for helping me reach this decision. Despite the fact it didn't quite pan out the way I hoped, our journey over the last five days has taught me the value of being decisive, of taking a chance, of daring to dream.

Lesson learnt.

Armed with a fresh perspective, I return to my pad and while away an entire hour in a frenetic brain dump. The fact I don't see a single customer in that hour, or the next, only validates my decision.

It's late morning before the door finally opens. That customer browses the shelves for twenty minutes and leaves empty handed.

Lunchtime comes and goes. The till is opened seven times. Any lingering doubts about my decision to sell the shop are quashed when a dumpy, sour faced woman enters, and demands a refund for a paperback novel she purchased last week.

I point to a sign on the wall behind me.

"Sorry, madam, but as the sign clearly states, we don't offer refunds."

"I want to speak to the manager."

"You are."

"This is preposterous," she whines. "This book is not fit for purpose."

"It's a novel. What purpose were you hoping it would serve?"

"It's supposed to entertain. I hated it."

"Well, I'm sorry about that, but no book shop offers refunds just because the book wasn't to the customer's liking. It's subjective."

"You obviously don't care about your customers then."

Thirteen years of smiling politely while sucking up all the whinging and whining. Something inside me snaps.

"Madam. May I make a suggestion?"

"What?" she snaps.

"Take your book and get the fuck out of my shop."

Clearly shocked, her face reddens but she appears unable to find a reply. The book is snatched from the counter and she storms out of the shop, presumably never to return.

I know it was wrong, but boy, it felt good. Clement would have been proud of me.

With no further customers to serve, or offend, I return to my note pad. In between my note taking, I make calls to the various leaders of the book clubs who use the shop for their gatherings. I tell them I won't be able to host their meetings for a few weeks because I'm going through some personal issues. There are a few grumbles but on the whole they're fairly understanding.

At three o'clock I decide to treat myself to tea and biscuits. Just as I put the kettle on, my mobile rings. It's Howard, the commercial estate agent.

For ten long minutes he explains the process of putting the business on the market, in intricate detail. Several times I'm tempted to scream down the phone that I just want to know the bloody valuation figure, but I manage to find some self-control this time.

He eventually gets down to business.

"The retail sector isn't particularly buoyant at the moment and there are plenty of empty units in the town centre."

"Right."

"But the fact you're selling a going concern does set you apart, and coupled with your favourable lease, I do believe you have a good chance of finding a buyer."

"Great. And what price do you think I might achieve?"

"Always tricky to say for sure, but I'd estimate you could achieve a figure somewhere between thirty and forty thousand."

Not much to show for thirteen years of hard slog, but it's enough to enable my grand plan.

"That's fine, Howard. How long do you think it will take to find a buyer?"

"Oh, shouldn't be too long. Maybe four to six months."

My jaw drops. "That long? Really?"

"I wish I could be more precise. The right buyer could walk through my door tomorrow, but we do need to be realistic. It's a small market we're working with."

Now I've made the decision, I just want to get on with my life. Waiting in limbo for months on end wasn't part of my plan.

"Okay, if that's the case, I'd like to get things moving as soon as possible."

We arrange for him to pop by tomorrow morning to measure up and go through his contract. I was hoping I wouldn't have to see another Christmas in the shop, but that now sounds like it might be optimistic.

Not much I can do about it, I guess.

I continue making my tea and sit down in the staff room to drink it, accompanied by a packet of chocolate digestives. Not a wise move.

Five biscuits later, I have an acute bout of binge remorse, and a growing reluctance to move from the chair. Sods law – the front door opens.

I clamber to my feet and wander back into the shop.

"Alright, doll."

"Oh, it's you. I thought you were going to call me for a lift?"

"Fancied a stroll."

"How was the zoo?"

"Okay."

"Gosh, you're chatty. What's the matter?"

"Nothing."

"Do you fancy a cup of tea?"

"Yeah. Ta."

He follows me back out to the staffroom and sits on the edge of the table. I put the kettle on and grab a cup from the cupboard.

"Here we are again," I say over my shoulder. "Just like Friday evening."

"What?"

"You know? When you, um...appeared in the shop. I made you a cup of tea, didn't I?"

He doesn't answer.

I finish his tea and hand it to him. No thanks are offered.

"What is it, Clement? You've been in a strange mood all day."

"Nothing."

I gently place my hand on his arm. "You can talk to me, you know?"

"I'm not big on chatting, doll."

"I gathered, but if there is something bothering you, maybe I can help."

"I doubt it."

"Try me."

He takes a sip of his tea and places the cup on the table.

"Tomorrow," he murmurs.

"What about it?"

"It'll be all over."

"Right, but that's good, isn't it?"

"For you, yeah."

"But I thought the whole point of you being here was to help me? You've done that, so what's the problem?"

"The problem is…"

His voice trails off without an answer.

"Clement?"

"What happens to me, doll?"

"I'm not with you."

"I don't know how I got here, who sent me, or what happens next. That's the bleedin' problem."

His frank confession does nothing to ease my concern for his mental state. With nothing to keep his mind occupied all day, I fear his delusions have been allowed to fester unchecked. I should have insisted he stayed with me today. I could have kept him busy, kept his mind elsewhere.

"It'll be okay, Clement. I promise."

"You reckon?"

Should I tell him about Juliet? It might provide some assurance, but it could just as easily scare him away.

I am so out of my depth here.

"Let's just take things one day at a time. We'll deal with Sterling and then, on Friday, we can focus on you."

He looks me straight in the eye, and perhaps for the first time since we met, I see something approaching vulnerability.

"If I'm still here on Friday, doll."

42

I can't face breakfast.

Despite yesterday's confession, Clement appears back to his usual self this morning, chewing on a piece of toast at the kitchen table. I'm far from my usual self though. I'm a total bag of nerves.

I take a few deep breaths and focus on how I'll feel at six o'clock tonight. By then, everything will be sorted. The shop will be up for sale, the car will be sold, and most importantly, Sterling will have his cash and I can finally be rid of him.

Nearly there, Beth. Nearly there.

I gulp down my tea and prepare to face what could be the longest ten hours of my life.

We agreed that Clement should spend the whole day with me today. I say agreed, but it was never really up for debate.

After we got back to my place yesterday evening, I did everything I could to keep his mind distracted. I conscripted him to help prepare dinner, and after we ate, we washed up and put everything away. By eight o'clock we were sitting in the lounge watching, or in my case enduring, two films back-to-back — over three hours of *Shrek*. Not my idea of a fun night in, but Clement seemed to enjoy both films and I suspect he found a kindred spirit in the grumpy green ogre.

We arrive at the shop and my first task is to squirrel away the ten thousand pounds of used notes in the stockroom. Then, once the opening routine is completed, I set Clement up in the staffroom with my laptop, and introduce him to YouTube.

"There are millions of videos on here covering every subject you can imagine. It should keep you occupied for a few hours."

"Every subject?"

"Pretty much. Let me show you."

I quickly think of something which might hold his interest, and search for 'Arsenal in the 1950s'. A whole raft of British Pathé videos pop up. I click the first one, something to do with a cup final, and the grainy black and white video begins.

Clement sits bolt upright and stares intently at the screen. "Bloody hell," he murmurs.

"Do you want to try searching for something?"

"Yeah."

It is at this point my tuition hits a brick wall. Clement claims he has never used a computer before, so even words like 'cursor' and 'link' are totally alien to him.

Then there's Clement's painstakingly slow keyboard strokes, administered with one finger — a whole different league of frustration.

"Have you never typed before?"

"Annie had a typewriter. Used that once."

It soon becomes clear why I could never have been a teacher. After half-an-hour, my paper-thin patience is spent and I decide to leave him to it.

"Just give me a shout if you get stuck."

"Will do."

I return to the shop and he shouts for help five times within an hour. Why didn't I just give him a book?

It's a blessed relief when a grey-haired man in a suit walks in.

"Miss Baxter? I'm Howard Grant."

"Nice to meet you, Howard, but please, call me Beth."

I give Howard a guided tour of the shop, pointing out the various fixtures and fittings that will be included in the sale. The denim-clad giant in the staffroom takes a little more explaining.

"Excuse my friend, Howard. I'm just helping him to polish his IT skills."

Clement nods at Howard. "Alright, mate."

"Very well, thank you."

I quickly escort Howard back into the shop and we go through the contract. He hands me a pen and points to where my signature is required.

I pause briefly, the significance of the moment not lost on me.

Just sign it, stupid.

The contract is signed and Howard snaps a few photos of the shop, both inside and out.

"I'll have the sales particulars drawn up by Monday. I'll email them over as soon as they're ready."

Howard departs with a reassuring smile and a handshake.

As soon as the door closes, I take a minute to reassure myself I'm doing the right thing.

"Who was that bloke?"

I spin around to find Clement standing in the doorway.

"Oh, him? He's a commercial estate agent. I've put the shop up for sale."

"What are you gonna do, for a job?"

"I'm...erm, going to concentrate on trying to write a book," I reply hesitantly.

As soon as the words leave my mouth, I regret sharing them with Clement.

"Good for you, doll."

It wasn't the reaction I was expecting.

"No punchline?"

"Nah. You gotta do what makes you happy."

"I appreciate that, Clement. It means a lot."

"No worries. Can we have lunch now?"

With my stomach in knots, food is the last thing on my mind. I give Clement some money and point him in the direction of a sandwich shop.

By the time he returns, a handful of customers are browsing the aisles. He wanders straight through to the staffroom, lunch in hand.

If ever there was a time I needed the shop to be busy, today would be it. As the meeting with Sterling looms closer, I feel increasingly nervous, and I'm not sure why. I have his bloody money, and I'll have Clement on hand if he threatens me again. The transaction should take no more than five minutes — his bogus contract will be torn up and I can get on with the rest of my life.

But I don't trust him one iota. He's already proven to be devious and dangerous so I'm taking nothing for granted.

As it happens, the gods are smiling on me today, and I'm kept occupied dealing with a steady stream of customers.

At three o'clock, I receive a call from the car dealer to say the Micra is ready, as is my cash. I put a sign in the window, stating we'll be closed for the rest of the afternoon, and lock up.

Clement is still sitting in the staffroom, watching a black and white newsreel.

"I've got to go to the bank and pick up my new car. Are you coming?"

"Yeah. I'm going stir crazy in here."

We head through the town to the bank and return to the shop with nine thousand pounds in cash. I stash it in the stockroom with the rest of the cash, hidden behind a pile of books even the most thorough of burglars would probably ignore.

The car dealer is only a few miles away and we arrive just before four o'clock. The man I spoke to on the phone, Bernard, introduces himself and leads us behind a portacabin where my new car is parked. He takes the keys for the Fiat and invites me to check the little red Micra over, and take it for a quick test drive.

Once Bernard disappears, I take the opportunity to walk around the Micra. I kick the tyres a few times, and turn the engine over.

"Do you know much about cars?" I ask Clement.

"A bit. Want me to check under the bonnet?"

"Please."

It takes five minutes to find the bonnet catch, and thirty seconds for Clement to declare he doesn't know what he's looking at.

"Sorry, doll. It looks nothing like the engines I used to tinker with."

"Never mind. Let's take it out for a spin."

Despite the fact it smells of cheap aftershave, and the upholstery has a few dubious stains, it's not a bad little car. It lacks the character of the Fiat, and it's travelled plenty more miles, but it should serve my needs for a year or two.

By the time we return to the car lot, Bernard is ready with a mountain of paperwork for me to complete.

Half an hour later, I am the proud owner of a Nissan Micra, and a bundle of fifty pound notes.

We arrive back at the shop half an hour before Sterling is due, and the moment I walk through the door, my nerves begin to jangle.

I thought I was doing a reasonable job of hiding my apprehension, but Clement can tell something isn't right.

"Don't worry, doll. It'll be over soon."

"I know, but I just can't stand the man — he puts me on edge. The thought of being in the same room as him, even for just a few minutes, makes my skin crawl."

"Don't see him then. Let me handle it."

It's a tempting offer, but this is more about closure than control. I need to be completely sure Sterling is out of my life once and for all.

And if I'm honest, Clement's propensity to handle confrontation with extreme violence does concern me. This could easily escalate if not handled properly, and I don't want to risk anything going wrong at the last minute if Sterling goads him. After everything I've been through, I just want to draw a line under it.

"I appreciate the offer, Clement, but I have to see this through myself. I need to be totally sure it's over."

"Your call, doll. Shall I hang around out back, just in case?"

"I'd really appreciate that, thanks. Promise me you won't come steaming in though, unless I call you for any reason."

"I can't even give him a quick slap?"

"God, I'd love you to, but no. Please, just stay in the staffroom."

"Don't worry. I'll keep out of the way."

I collect the cash from the stockroom, add the thousand Bernard gave me, and drop it into a carrier bag. It's been a long, long time since there was so much cash in the shop. I stare into the bag at the pile of bundled notes, trying to stifle my anger. It riles me I have to give it all away for a debt that was never mine. I suppose I never paid for the ring or the car, but the ten thousand pounds for the gold really stings.

Easy come, easy go, I suppose.

Perhaps not so for Clement's Zippo though.

With another fifteen minutes to kill, I put the kettle on and make myself a cup of camomile tea. Clement isn't keen to give it a try so I make him a cup of builders tea. He then settles down to watch the 1971 cup final on the laptop.

"Sterling will be here in a minute so I'm going to go through to the shop."

"Alright, doll."

"And you promise to stay in here, and not interfere?"

"You know I don't do promises, but don't worry. I'll stay put."

I pat him on the shoulder and turn to walk into the shop.

I make it to the doorway when he calls after me.

"Doll."

I turn around. "Yes."

"Any trouble, you shout for me. Okay?"

"Okay."

I close the door behind me and with the carrier bag in hand, trudge across to the front door and unlock it. I remove the sign and take refuge behind the counter.

I close my eyes and take a few deep breaths.

Ten minutes and this will all be over.

As I open my eyes, I catch a flash of red beyond the window. A huge car, a Bentley I think, pulls up to the kerb opposite the shop. A portly man in a grey suit gets out from behind the wheel and scuttles around to the other side of the car. He opens the rear door and virtually stands to attention.

An elderly man climbs out, adjusts his navy blazer, and nods at the portly man.

He turns, taps the roof of the car, and strides towards the shop.

I'll give David Sterling one thing — he's punctual.

43

"Evening, Miss Baxter. I trust you are well?"

Sterling closes the door behind him and looks around the shop. In his navy blazer, crisp white shirt, and yellow cravat, he looks no more threatening than the chairman of a bowls club committee. The look in this case, is absolutely deceiving.

He casually saunters up to the counter.

"How's your mother?"

"None of your business," I hiss.

"I had to visit the hospital again on Monday. You can probably guess who I was visiting."

I glare back at him. "No."

"My associates, Miss Baxter. Mr Black has been discharged, but I'm afraid Mr Blue will be in hospital for some time, and I suspect he'll be walking with a stick for the rest of his life."

"What a shame."

"It is, and quite an inconvenience for me. Still, I've got other good men I can rely upon."

He then turns his head and nods towards the window.

"See the two men in my car? Donald and Terence — both highly-respected, retired police officers with distinguished careers behind them. Donald is my driver, and Terence handles security for all my property investments."

I look across at the Bentley. One of the two men is the portly driver but I can't quite see the other, not that I really care.

"So what?"

"I don't like taking chances, Miss Baxter. Would I be right in assuming the man who put my associates in hospital is nearby?"

I don't answer, but I don't have a particularly good poker face it seems.

"I thought as much. Well, assuming he is, you should know that Donald and Terence are watching, and they'd make excellent witnesses. If there is even the hint of violence, the police will be here in seconds and I'll ensure the perpetrator is punished to the full extent of the law."

"Whatever. Let's just get this done."

"That would suit me," he says flatly.

I reach down, pick up the bag of cash from the floor, and place it on the counter.

"It's all there, but I want that contract first."

He slides his hand into the inside pocket of his blazer and extracts a folded piece of paper.

"You mean this?"

"Yes."

"I'm more than happy to hand it over..."

He pauses and holds the contract in the air, tantalisingly close enough for me to grab.

"...to Mr Patterson."

"Eh?"

"I said, Miss Baxter, I'm happy to hand it over to Mr Patterson."

"Tough luck," I snap. "He's not here."

"Where is he then?"

"How the hell should I know? That man is dead to me."

"Oh dear. That is a shame."

He slowly and deliberately tucks the contract back in his blazer pocket.

"It doesn't look like we're going to conclude our business then. I'll get the memorandum of sale drawn up for the purchase of your property."

"What? No. I've got the money, like you asked."

"Clearly you weren't paying attention, Miss Baxter. I wanted Mr Patterson to repay the debt — in person."

"You never said that."

"I'm sure I did. Perhaps you weren't listening."

My mind flashes back to the two previous encounters with Sterling. Did he mention Karl handing over the money? Surely if he had, I'd have picked up on it.

Whether he did or he didn't, it's now academic. The only thing that matters now is that he wants something I can't give him — Karl.

The goalposts, which I thought were within shooting distance, are now several miles down the road.

"What difference does it make? I've got your money so give me the contract."

He sidles up to the counter until there's barely four feet between us.

"You stupid girl," he says, his voice low. "Do you really think I give a damn about twenty poxy grand? Your fiancé was of much greater value to me when he was employed in the planning office. I want him back here, and behind that desk where he can influence my future developments."

"But...I don't know where he is. His phone has been disconnected."

"Then you are in default. If Mr Patterson is not here to signoff the contract, it remains in force, irrespective of your efforts. And you know what that means?"

"I don't care what it means. You can't do this."

"Oh, I think you'll find I can. And I will."

Desperation arrives and I seriously consider calling Clement in. I'm banging my head against a brick wall here, and I'm minded to damn the consequences and let Clement literally bang Sterling's head against a brick wall.

The only thing stopping me is my own stubbornness. Maybe time for another tack?

"Please," I beg. "Just take the money and leave me alone."

He drums his fingers on the counter. Maybe my revised tack has worked.

"Tell you what I'm willing to do, as a gesture of goodwill. I'll give you three days to find Mr Patterson and bring him to me. Do that and we can put this unpleasantness to bed."

"I told you, I don't know where he is. If he's so important to you, why don't you find him yourself?"

"You really are unbelievably thick," he snipes. "Do you want me to spell it out for you?"

My blank expression suggests I do.

"You're the only person he's likely to come back for. You are my leverage, Miss Baxter."

As much as it pains me to admit it, Karl was right. Well, partly. Sterling no doubt assumed I'd never get the money together, and I'd therefore concentrate my efforts on finding Karl. If he'd made that clear in the first place, I might have spent the last seven days trying to find my errant ex-fiancé, rather than the cash.

But knowing the true reason, and being able to do anything about it, are very different things.

"Three days is bloody ridiculous," I protest. "I wouldn't even know where to begin."

"It's the only concession I'm prepared to make, Miss Baxter. Three days to find him or I buy your home for the price of my choosing."

Clearly pleading didn't work and my subservience is clouded out as a red mist descends.

"No. Fucking. Way."

"I beg your pardon."

"There is no way on God's earth I am letting you take my home."

He leans across the counter, the spotlights deepening the shadow along his scar.

"You listen to me young lady," he snarls. "If I'm going to lose Patterson's influence, I want sufficient compensation. You will sell your house and you will accept whatever price I damn well see fit. And because of your insolence, that price is now half the market value."

"I'm not selling my home."

"Then you leave me no other choice."

He withdraws from the counter and pulls a mobile phone from his pocket. With needle-like fingers, he prods the screen a few times.

"You had your chance, Miss Baxter. I'm afraid your mother will now bear the consequences of your bloody-mindedness."

"For God's sake. Leave her out of this."

He turns to me, his finger poised over the phone screen.

"I send this text message and your mother is as good as dead. Last chance — are you going to find Patterson or sell your home to me?"

I'm out of options.

"Clement!"

The door from the staffroom crashes open.

"You wanna repeat that?" Clement booms.

If Sterling is alarmed at Clement's sudden appearance, he doesn't show it. He casually slips his phone back in his pocket and turns to face him.

"Ahh, so you're the man who put my associates in hospital?"

Clement doesn't answer as he strides towards us, his fists balled tightly. He stops dead, about six feet short of Sterling. I breathe a sigh of relief his opening salvo isn't administered with his fists.

"I assume you were eavesdropping?" Sterling says, matter-of-factly. "So, you'll know I have witnesses, two former police officers, just twenty yards away. Touch me, and you'll find yourself in the back of a police van pretty sharpish."

Clement takes a step to his left, tilting his head slightly, as if weighing up his opponent.

"What's your problem, old man?" Clement growls. "You get some sort of kick out of threatening women?"

Sterling chortles to himself. He's either incredibly brave or incredibly stupid.

"How chivalrous, but this is none of your business, unless you're interested in a job? I could do with a little extra muscle now I'm two men down."

"Yeah, as if I'd ever work for an arsehole like you."

"Your loss. Anyway," Sterling says, turning to me. "Where were we?"

"You were going to take the money and leave me in peace."

"Nice try, Miss Baxter. But I'm sure I was about to send a text message, wasn't I?"

I glance across at Clement, hoping he'll intervene. He remains worryingly impassive.

"Look, I've got your money. Just go will you?"

Sterling looks to the ceiling and shakes his head. "I'm not a patient man, Miss Baxter, but for the sake of clarity, I'll confirm your options. You either bring Patterson to me by Monday, or you agree to sell your home. I assume you'd rather not explore the third option."

"I don't know how many times I have to tell you — I don't know where Karl is."

"In which case, you only have one option...unless you'd like me to send that text message instead?"

He slowly moves his hand towards his blazer pocket, smirking all the way.

It appears Clement has nothing to offer as he continues to stand motionless, gawking at Sterling almost as if he's star struck. What the hell is wrong with him?

"Okay. I'll sell the house," I murmur through gritted teeth.

"Good. I'll have the necessary paperwork delivered to you tomorrow. And if you mess me around, or attempt to delay the process, that text message will be sent."

He offers his hand to me, knowing full well I'd rather stick my hand up a cow's arse than reciprocate.

"No? Oh well, there's no accounting for manners with some people."

With a final leer, he turns to leave. He makes two steps before Clement throws him a question.

"I'm told you used to be some sort of big shot in London during the sixties. That true?"

It seems Sterling can't resist an opportunity to brag.

"I was, which is why I'm not a man to be crossed."

Clement approaches Sterling and stoops down to inspect the side of his face. The old man edges backwards, clearly affronted at the invasion of his personal space.

"How did you get that scar?" Clement asks.

"None of your damn business."

"He said he got it in a motorbike accident," I call across.

"Really? That's interesting."

Without clarifying what he found so interesting, Clement marches across the shop, locks the front door and drops the key in his pocket. He then folds his arms and takes up a position like a nightclub bouncer.

"What the hell are you doing, man?" Sterling yells.

"Thought we'd have a quick chat. Get to know one another."

"Unlock the door. Now."

"Don't piss your pants, Sterling. It's in your best interests to hear me out."

"I'll count to five and if you don't unlock the door, Miss Baxter's mother won't be the only one in grave danger."

"Nah. I don't think so. And you're the only one currently in danger."

Sterling's face reddens as his control of the situation slowly ebbs away.

"Your scar? Motorbike accident, eh?" Clement asks as he edges closer to Sterling.

"What? Yes."

"Funny that, because it looks a lot like a Glasgow smile."

Sterling shuffles backwards in an attempt to maintain his distance from Clement.

"What's a Glasgow smile?" I ask.

"It's like a branding, doll. A semi-circular cut from the corner of the mouth to the ear, which is why folks call it a smile. It's a gangland thing, usually done to people who grass, and other scumbags. Ain't that right, Sterling?"

"I...I don't know what you're talking about."

"Are you sure?"

Sterling turns to face me. "I'm warning you. Tell him to unlock the door or, so help me God, I will send that text message."

The confidence in his voice is gone, replaced with a distinct sense of urgency. As intimidating as Clement is, I don't understand why Sterling has withered to a shell of his arrogant self.

"He's bluffing, doll. He ain't gonna do a thing."

Sterling dips his hand into his pocket and extracts mobile phone again. With a shaky hand, he tries to unlock the screen.

"I've had enough of this. I'm calling my men in."

Clement peers out of the window towards the Bentley.

"Those two?" he sniggers. "What are they gonna do? Challenge me to a game of dominoes?"

"They'll call the police. You're holding me here against my will."

"Go on then. Get them to call the police — let's see how that pans out for you."

Sterling switches his focus from the phone to Clement.

"I'm not bluffing. This is your last chance — open the damn door."

"In a minute. But first I want to put a proposition to you. You run a property business don't you?"

"What of it?"

"I've got an investment opportunity for you. This place is up for sale, ain't it doll?"

I nod.

"And what's the asking price?"

"Forty thousand," I reply.

"Maybe you'd like to buy it, Sterling?"

"Why the hell would I buy a book shop?"

It's a question I'd like answered too.

Clement fixes a fierce stare on the old man. "Why? Cos' I said you're going to buy it. Let's say...double the asking price?"

Sterling appears to find some resolve. "Are you insane, man?" he scoffs. "Not a chance."

Clement strokes his moustache and poses a question in my direction. "What do you think, doll? Am I insane?"

Sterling turns to me, his sneering face now a picture of bewilderment. I still don't have the first clue what Clement is up to, but I'm happy to play along as it appears to be making Sterling uncomfortable.

"Between you and me," I say in a hushed voice. "He might well be insane."

"We gotta deal then?"

Sterling's head snaps back in Clement's direction. "No, and I've had enough of this. Unlock the door."

"No can do."

The two men appear to have reached an impasse. Clement moves across the floor and leans up against the counter. He looks totally relaxed while Sterling appears paralysed by indecision. I don't understand why, despite his threats, he still hasn't called the police.

"Just forget Patterson," Sterling suddenly blurts. "I'll take the money and you can have the contract."

Clement reaches across and grabs the carrier bag of cash from the counter.

"Here you go then. Gimme the contract first."

Sterling steps forward and pulls the contract from his pocket. He tentatively holds it out and it's snatched from his fingers. Clement then passes the contract to me and holds the bag of cash out at arm's length.

Sterling reaches for the bag but Clement pulls it away and drops it back on the counter.

"Bad luck, Norris. We're keeping it."

What? Who is Norris?

Sterling's mouth drops open, his face plastered with much the same fear as a man being told he has only weeks to live.

"What's the matter, Norris? You look a bit peaky."

Sterling's face is now so white I can barely see the scar. His lips twitch as if he's trying to reply but he appears unable to find any words.

"Sorry, Clement," I interject. "Why are you calling him Norris?"

"Cos' that's his real name, and he certainly was a big shot in London...amongst the nonces."

I stare at Sterling, and then at Clement. "I'm not with you."

The big man is more than happy to explain. "The moment I saw him, I knew I'd seen his face before. Couldn't quite place it though. His real name is Norris Durbridge, and he got his Glasgow smile during a four year stretch in Wormwood Scrubs."

"Prison?"

"Yeah. Norris here had a thing for young boys, didn't you Norris? Thing is, most prison inmates aren't keen on nonces and like to dish out a bit of extra punishment. And a Glasgow smile is reserved for the lowest of the low."

Sterling suddenly finds his voice. "No...you're mistaken," he splutters.

"Shut up, Norris. With a beak like that, you're not easy to forget. Your ugly mug was all over the papers — what was it they called you? Norris the Nonce, wasn't it?"

"Absolutely not."

"Don't bother denying it. We can easily check with Beth's goggly thing."

"Google," I suggest.

"Yeah, that."

Backed into a corner, Sterling, or Norris, or whatever his name is, decides attack is his best form of defence.

"This is preposterous," he huffs. "Your claims are slanderous and I have a very good lawyer. I'll sue you both for every penny you have."

"It ain't slander if there's proof you're Norris Durbridge."

"And what proof could you possibly have?" Sterling taunts. "Anything and everything tying me to that man is long gone."

"I'm sure you've done a good job burying your past. But there's one thing you've overlooked — fingerprints."

"What?"

"Your fingerprints on the contract you just handed me. I'd bet my last quid they're an exact match for Norris Durbridge's."

The look on Sterling's face is almost worth twenty thousand pounds.

"So, Norris, if you wanna try taking us to court for slander, go ahead. I'd love to see your fancy lawyer explain that."

Checkmate.

With his short-lived defence already in tatters, Sterling visibly shrinks.

"You know nothing," he whimpers. "It was a fit up. I'm innocent."

"Bullshit. All seven boys testified against you. All liars were they?"

"The police were corrupt and they coached those boys. You weren't there — you don't understand what it was like back then."

"Don't I?"

No, Clement. Please don't.

He stares intently at Sterling for a second, and poses another question.

"You ever watch the programme *Mastermind*, Norris?"

Sterling nods.

"Well, if I ever got to sit in that big chair, my specialist subject would be London in the sixties and seventies. I know exactly who you are and I know what you did, so you're wasting your breath trying to tell me otherwise."

Nicely done.

Clement moves from the counter and stands a few feet in front of Sterling, looming over him, both physically and, I suspect, psychologically. The man who walked through the door with a confident swagger only ten minutes ago is no more. The arrogant, despicable old man, broken without a single punch being thrown.

"Let's not piss around here," Clement scowls. "You're not gonna walk away with any cash, but you are gonna buy this place for double the asking price."

I can almost hear the cogs turning in Sterling's head. He has nowhere to run.

He avoids eye contact with Clement and mumbles a response. "And if I don't?"

"Your dirty little secret will become public knowledge. We'll see how popular you are with your mates in the police once they know who you really are."

Silence.

From my position behind the counter, I've stood and watched this drama unfold, almost in disbelief. One moment my mother's life is being threatened. The next, I'm about to be offered another winning lottery ticket, courtesy of the carrier bag of cash and Sterling's imposed purchase of the shop. And much like my entire journey with Clement, I've felt a little bit like a passenger on a runaway train — staring out of the window as good fortune and bad fortune zip past.

Now it's time to get off and take control.

I move from behind the counter and approach Sterling. He now looks every one of his seventy-plus years.

"Do we have a deal then, Sterling?" I ask. "Or do you prefer Mr Durbridge?"

"It appears I don't have much choice," he mumbles, his voice barely audible.

"Sorry. I didn't catch that."

He won't even look at me. Coward.

"Yes. I'll buy your damn shop."

"Good. And in return, I'll resist the temptation to post details of your indiscretions on Facebook."

"I want a non-disclosure agreement signed," he mutters as a final act of defiance.

"Fine. Oh, and Sterling, I want this done and dusted within two weeks. Understood?"

He moves his head a fraction, barely discernible as a nod.

"My estate agent is Howard Grant. I'll expect you to make your formal offer by lunchtime tomorrow."

As I savour the moment, Clement moves up behind me and delivers a coup de grâce in his gravelly voice. "One thing before you crawl back to your hole, Norris. I'll be watching you, just in case you have any ideas about retaliation, or doing a runner."

Sterling remains mute, head bowed.

Clement continues with his hands placed protectively on my shoulders. "And if anything happens to Beth or her mother, or you don't come good and buy this place, I'll blow your secret myself. Then, once you've suffered the humiliation, I'll hunt you down and I will kill you. Clear?"

David Sterling nods, and Norris Durbridge asks if he can leave.

Pathetic.

Clement retrieves the key from his pocket and strides over to the door. He unlocks it and holds it open.

"Seeya then, Norris."

Sterling doesn't need a second invitation and scurries out of the shop, back to the confines of his Bentley. I doubt he'll find safety there, or anywhere else now.

Clement shuts the door and locks it.

"Did that just happen?" I ask, still trying to process events.

"Yeah, it did."

"Incredible. I'm honestly lost for words."

"That'd be a first."

I skip over to Clement and, standing on the very tips of my toes, plant a kiss on his cheek.

"You never cease to amaze me, you know?"

"It was nothing."

I gaze up at him. "I still don't think I can quite believe it. What were the chances of Sterling having such a dark secret, let alone you recognising him?"

"Yeah, fancy that," he replies, his eyebrows arched. "Was it enough to change your mind?"

"About what?"

"You don't remember?"

"Remind me."

"When I first pitched up here — I asked if you believed in miracles."

"Oh, yes. Right."

"And you said you didn't."

"Did I?"

"Yeah, you did. And now?"

"I...err, don't know. I believe I've been extremely lucky."

"Yeah, right," he snorts, shaking his head. "Nobody is that lucky, doll."

44

It's over. Done.

The feeling isn't too dissimilar to the moment I received my university exam results in the post. A distinct line in the sand, separating two periods of my life. So much effort, culminating in one moment of elation.

No more looking back. Everything to look forward to.

But the one key difference between overcoming David Sterling, and passing my exams, is luck. At university, my destiny was in my own hands. If I studied hard, I knew what the outcome would be. This time, and despite Clement suggesting otherwise, I have been gifted some incredibly good fortune.

And that, as far as I am concerned, is all it is.

The rationale behind that assumption is also drawn from my time at university.

Danny, boyfriend number two, was a historical literature buff. Besides the occasions when he was busy fellating his tutor, he always had his head stuck in a book. He had a particular passion for the life and work of Byron, and amassed an encyclopaedic knowledge of the man. I'd even go as far as to say Danny was obsessed with Byron. Whenever he talked about him, which he did a lot, he spoke as if he actually knew him. And when he waxed lyrical about an event in Byron's life, he did so as if he'd actually been there.

It's now clear Danny and Clement share a similar trait. One painted a convincing picture of life in nineteenth century Europe, while the other paints an equally convincing picture of London in the sixties and seventies.

It is, I would venture, not too much of a stretch to assume Clement has studied his subject to the same obsessive level as Danny. With that in mind, it is also not too much of a stretch to assume Clement might have studied the crimes of Norris Durbridge.

Call it a freakish coincidence, a stroke of luck, or ridiculously fortuitous, but there *is* a rational explanation to Clement and Norris Durbridge occupying the same room. Hell, for all I know, Clement found Sterling and worked out he was Durbridge before he turned up at my shop that evening. It isn't inconceivable that Sterling inadvertently brought Clement to me, rather than the other way around.

Muddy waters perhaps, but what is clear is that Juliet's visit tomorrow can't come quickly enough.

For now though, I'm going to kick back, take stock, and get raucously drunk.

"I reckon we deserve a few drinks, Clement. Don't you?"

"Could be my last night here, so yeah, I do."

I choose to ignore his prophetic comment and grab the bag of cash from the counter.

"And we don't need to worry about the tab this time," I say, shaking the bag.

"Good. I'm overdue a proper hammering."

I dread to think how much alcohol might be required to fulfil that hammering. Erring on the side of caution, I extract two fifty pound notes from the bag and tuck them into my pocket.

"We'll go back to my place first. I want to grab a quick shower and change."

He nods, and follows me out to the car. I lock the back door and we clamber into the Micra.

As we travel the congested roads back home, my mind turns to the carrier bag of cash, stuffed below my seat. While it has provided a more than generous kitty for the pub later, it strikes me that I've been incredibly presumptuous regarding what should happen with the rest of it. Why do I have any more right to it than Clement? If anything, he has the greater claim.

"I was thinking, Clement, about the money."

"What about it?"

"Well, at least half of it is yours. How are you going to spend it?"

"It's no use to me, doll. You keep it."

"All of it?"

"Yeah."

"No, that's not fair. If it wasn't for you, there wouldn't be any cash."

"I don't want it, doll. Any of it."

"But, what about your Zippo? We could speak to Gerrard in the morning and buy it back."

"I doubt he'll sell it unless we offer him stupid money."

"I'm sure you could convince him to sell it back to us with a small profit."

"Forget it. It don't matter now."

There is no sense arguing with him. While I appreciate his generosity, I'm puzzled why he wouldn't at least want his Zippo back.

I decide to change the subject.

"Have you got any plans for tomorrow?"

"Yeah, right," he huffs. "As it is, I can't see much point in planning anything beyond the next ten minutes."

"What do you mean by that?"

"Nothing. Forget it."

"Come on, Clement. You worry me when you say things like that."

Three strokes of the moustache while I wait for an answer.

"Look, doll," he sighs. "Whether you believe how I ended up here, or not, you're sorted now. My job is done and I don't have the first bleedin' clue what happens next."

I don't believe him but that's not my immediate concern.

"Okay, but tomorrow?"

"What about it?"

"Will you promise me you won't disappear before tomorrow afternoon?"

"What's so special about tomorrow afternoon?"

"Just trust me. Please?"

"Alright."

"You promise?"

"I've told you, doll. I don't..."

"I know, I know. You don't do promises. But just this once can't you make an exception, for me?"

He draws a deep breath as his gaze falls to the footwell.

"I promise I'll be around tomorrow afternoon...if it's my decision to make."

"Thank you."

Unless some omnipotent deity comes calling for him, which I highly doubt, I think I can count on him meeting Juliet tomorrow. What happens from there is out of my hands, but I can at least say I tried to help him.

There is no further talk, small or otherwise, for the rest of our journey home. I eventually turn into Elmore Road and my good fortune continues as I secure a parking space right outside my house.

I grab the carrier bag of cash from beneath the seat and we exit the car. As soon as I'm standing on the pavement, I draw a lungful of semi-fresh air and make a mental note to purchase an air freshener for the car.

"I assume you're hungry, so shall we go back to the Slug?" I ask as I unlock the front door.

"The Slug?"

"The pub we ate at the other night."

"Yeah, okay."

"I'm afraid there's no karaoke tonight. Still, a few of your adoring fans might be in."

"Ha bloody ha."

Clement follows me into the hall and I hang my coat and handbag up. I take the carrier bag of cash and stash it in the small cupboard housing the electric meter. There's no reason to hide it other than my own paranoia that I'll inadvertently throw it out with Karl's junk, which is still piled up in the hall.

"I think there might still be a few cans of lager in the fridge if you fancy some pre-loading?"

"Pre-loading?"

"It's what the youngsters do these days. They fill up on booze at home before going out."

"Why?"

"You haven't been paying attention have you? Didn't you notice a pint of lager can cost as much as a fiver these days?"

"A fiver? For a pint? Shittin' hell."

"Not that it's an issue for us, but no harm in having a few cheeky drinks before we leave, is there?"

"None at all, doll."

We wander through to the kitchen and Clement sits down at the table. I open the fridge and extract a bottle of white wine and a can of lager.

"Here you go."

"Cheers."

I open the wine and pour myself an overly generous glass. Just as I turn to join Clement at the table, I catch a glimpse of movement from the corner of my eye. I turn towards the utility room door.

It takes a second for my brain to piece together what I'm looking at.

As the picture completes, my heart stops beating when I realise it's not a *what*. It's a *who*.

The glass slips from my hand and shatters on the floor.

"Clumsy bitch," a nasally voice rumbles.

I recognise the voice immediately. It's not one I'm ever likely to forget.

Mr Black moves from beyond the door.

My eyes dart between two prominent features. The first is the dressing, strapped across his nose. The second is the gun which he's holding level, pointing squarely at my face.

I look straight down the barrel and recall Clement's words. It doesn't take long to conclude it's not a starting pistol aimed at me on this occasion.

As Mr Black takes a step forward, I glance towards Clement, positioned in the worst possible place, at the table. Whether it was planning or good fortune, I now form a handy barrier between the two men. By the time Clement gets out of his chair, a bullet could already be sailing towards my head.

This is not good.

"What...what do you want?" I splutter.

"What do you reckon?" he growls back.

"Look, we've already come to an arrangement with Sterling. It's over."

"Like I care."

"Just call him. He'll tell you this isn't necessary."

He takes another two steps towards me, shrinking the distance to barely six feet. I don't suppose a few feet matter one way or another — a bullet shot at such close range isn't going to miss its target.

"I ain't here cos' of Sterling. I'm here cos' of what that fucker did to my brother."

He nods towards Clement, just in case we were in any doubt which fucker he was referring to.

"Sorry. Your brother?" I query.

"Mr Blue."

"Oh, I didn't..."

"Shut it, bitch."

I shut it.

As if this situation isn't bad enough, the reason for Mr Black's visit is now graver than I had initially imagined. A thug with obvious anger issues, brandishing a loaded gun, and bearing a significant grudge. In some way, I wish he was here to do Sterling's bidding.

But he's not here to enact another man's instructions. He's here seeking revenge.

This is not good at all.

I revert to my first question.

"What do you want?"

"Eye for an eye. I'm gonna blow your fucking kneecaps off — both of you."

In any other circumstance, I might have admired his candour.

I glance at Clement again, and I'm horrified to see he's casually sipping from his can of lager.

"Look, Mr...err, Black. Can we not sort this out without violence?"

"Like your man did?"

"Well, no, but surely there's a way we can come to an agreement?"

"You gonna fix my brother's leg?"

"Um, no, but..."

"No, course you ain't," he bellows. "You can stick your agreement up your arse, bitch. I ain't interested."

Negotiations over.

Mr Black takes another three or four steps towards me. I instinctively edge backwards until my shoulder blades meet the fridge door.

He lowers the gun until the barrel is pointing at my knees. He then turns to Clement.

"I'm gonna do her first, so you can hear her scream."

Finally, Clement has something to say.

"Get on with it then, shit-head. I'm knackered."

Clement then leans back in his chair and lets out a yawn. He slowly stretches his arms out wide, the lager can still in his left hand.

All I can do is stare at him, open mouthed.

You fucking arsehole, Clement.

His yawn peters out and he swings both arms upwards. Then, as his left arm approaches a vertical position, he suddenly releases the lager can from his grip.

The momentum of his swinging arm is enough to propel the can across the kitchen in a lazy arc. It travels through the air almost as slowly as a ball pitched by a parent to a toddler.

Quite what Clement hoped to achieve is anyone's guess. Its trajectory is so laboured, Mr Black has ample time to step out of its path, and probably read a paper while he waits for it to land.

As I watch the can loop towards Mr Black, spilling its frothy contents as it turns, Clement's true intentions become abruptly clear — distraction.

The first thing I hear is the scrape of a chair leg. Then, a dark shadow looms in my peripheral vision.

An arm suddenly encircles my waist, and I'm hauled backwards, while another arm flashes past my face towards the fridge door.

I blink once, and in that millisecond, Clement's hand is on the fridge door. He tugs at the handle with enough force to rip it clean away, and the door swings open towards Mr Black's face.

The door must have made contact with something because the frenetic action is followed by an immediate succession of sounds.

First, a muffled yowl, and then the dull thump of a large object falling against the larder door.

The third sound is unmistakable.

The gun is fired.

I knew it was the gun firing because the bullet is already embedded in the wall somewhere behind me, having passed through my leg on its journey.

The pain is grotesque, like a searing, white-hot poker thrust into my calf, just below the knee. It spreads through my leg, as if my veins are coursing with battery acid. A pain so fierce it takes my breath away, and with it, any chance of screaming.

Unsurprisingly, my right leg gives way and I slip from Clement's grasp.

I go down, nothing to stop me.

I hadn't given it much thought until now, but I'm suddenly struck by the way a brain can process so much information in an almost imperceptibly short period of time.

I know I'm falling, and I know I need to raise my arms to cushion my landing. However, that message took just a fraction too long to be sent and my arms won't arrive in time. My eyes are more nimble though, and they flick from the soles of Mr Black's shoes to Clement's boot sailing through the air. I suspect Mr Black is currently sitting on his arse with his back against the larder door. Whether he meant the gun to go off is an irrelevance now. Clement's boot will reach some part of his anatomy before my fall is complete.

As my eyes continue their journey from left to right, they have just enough time to capture another image — the thick edge of the kitchen table.

That image rapidly fills my vision until I can clearly see the grain in the wood.

Three inches.

Two.

One.
A brilliant light explodes behind my eyes.
Goodnight.

45

The computer in the shop is way past its sell-by date. It takes forever to boot up, and clunks through tasks with all the urgency of a sloth on holiday.

I am that computer.

One by one, my senses slowly come back online.

The first sense to drag me away from the darkness is my hearing. There's nothing distinct; just a low, intermittent rumbling sound.

My hearing is joined by taste. I tentatively probe my tongue around an arid mouth. It returns a vile, bitter tang.

Next up, smell comes into play. Disinfectant, I think. And lilies? Maybe orange blossom? There's a familiarity to the latter scent. Perfume?

My eyelids flicker as vision joins the party.

I'm suddenly aware of a warm hand squeezing mine.

I understand the human body is approximately sixty percent water. As I try to peel open dry lips and crusty eyelids, I can only conclude my body must be some way below that level. I have never felt so thirsty.

I blink hard, six or seven times, in an attempt to clear the opaque mist clouding my vision.

Blink by blink, the mist clears and an oval shape comes into focus.

A face. My mother.

She's smiling but her expression is anything but happy. A single tear rolls down her cheek.

"Oh, thank God," she whispers. "It's okay now, my darling. I'm here."

What's okay? Where is *here*?

I try to speak but my first syllable is nothing more than a wheeze.

"I'll get you some water."

She disappears for a moment, leaving behind a bare magnolia wall. As I move my eyes to the left, the mist returns. I squeeze a few more blinks and my precise location becomes apparent — a hospital bed. I'm not in a ward though, that much is clear. No other beds, but trolleys, laden with an assortment of unfamiliar devices; their function lost on me.

My first time in a hospital bed. My worst nightmare.

Sudden panic brings a flush of adrenalin, and with it, a dozen questions. I scour my mind for answers but the same mist which clouded my vision seems to have permeated my memory.

In lieu of answers, the two most pertinent questions taunt me: why I'm in a hospital bed, and what's wrong with me?

"Here you are, darling. Take a few sips."

A paper cup is held to my lips and I instinctively raise my hand to hold it. Something doesn't feel right. I bring my hand closer to my face and stare in horror at the sight of a transparent tube, disappearing beneath a plaster, into my wrist.

"It's alright, darling," Mum says softly. "It's just a drip."

Keep it together, Beth. Deep breaths.

I pull back from the edge and sip at the water. It's tepid, and overly chlorinated, but water has never tasted so sweet. I take the cup in my hand and the sips become thirsty gulps until the cup is empty.

I smack my lips a few times and finally manage a few words. "What happened, Mum?"

"You had a bang on the head, darling. You're going to be fine though, so there's no need to worry."

Isn't there?

"I should get a doctor to check you over. I'll just be a second."

461

Mum takes the empty cup from my hand and gently brushes her hand across my cheek. A reassuring smile and she slips from view.

I close my eyes and dredge my memories, searching for the moment I apparently banged my head. Nothing comes, other than a dull headache.

Minutes pass and my frustration mounts. Something is in there — I know it is, but I can't quite reach it.

A door creaks open, as do my still dry eyes.

An impossibly young doctor approaches the bed, my mother hovering at his shoulder.

"How are you feeling, Beth?" he asks.

Despite the fact he looks more like the lead singer of a boy band, his white coat, ID badge, and clipboard affirm his medical credentials.

"Confused," I wheeze.

"Don't worry, that's to be expected. I'm Dr Potter, by the way, but just call me Robbie."

Even his name sounds boy bandish.

I reply with a faint nod. He beams a bedside smile and consults his clipboard.

"Okay, let's bring you up to speed," he chirps. "You took quite a nasty bang to the head which resulted in some minor swelling to your brain."

"Uh?"

"We had to put you into an enforced coma while we waited for the swelling to subside."

Brain swelling? Coma? Truly alarming words delivered with casual abandon.

"Don't worry though. The latest scan results look good and the swelling is gone. I think it's safe to say you should make a full recovery."

He returns to his clipboard.

"Oh, and your leg injury is clearing up nicely. Thankfully, it was a remarkably clean intrusion."

I instinctively shuffle my legs and feel the dressing wrapped around my right calf.

"You were very lucky, considering how much blood you lost."

"Blood? Lucky?"

"Yes, really. I've only ever treated a handful of gunshot wounds, but they can be catastrophic. Beyond the threat to life, the damage can leave permanent disabilities."

A gunshot goes off in my head.

Then another, and another — each one accompanied by a vivid image. A salvo of memories burst through the mist.

"You okay, Beth?"

I can't answer him. Not because I don't know if I'm okay, but because I don't want anything to shift my concentration. With more and more memories landing, I try to organise them into a coherent timeline. Slowly, the picture builds: the shop, Sterling, the cash, my kitchen, Mr Black, the fridge.

"Beth, darling?"

"Clement," I whisper.

My mother and the doctor stare at me blankly.

"What's that, Beth?" the doctor asks.

"What...what happened to Clement?"

"One second, Beth," Dr Potter says. "Let me check your pupils quickly.

Without waiting for permission, my eyelid is held open while the doctor shines a piercing light in my right eye. He then checks the left and turns to my mother.

"Nothing to worry about, Mrs Goodyear."

My mother leans in. "Who is Clement, darling?"

Jesus. That's a question even I can't really answer.

"Um...sorry. I'm...not sure."

The doctor takes my mother by the elbow and guides her a few steps away from the bed.

"She's probably still suffering the effects of the medication. I'll pop back in half an hour, and hopefully she'll be a little more lucid by then."

Hello. I am here, you know.

Somebody should tell the doctor that being shot does not rob the victim of their hearing.

He disappears and my mother perches herself on the edge of the bed.

Beyond Clement's whereabouts, there are a number of other questions I need answers to. I ask her for another cup of water, which I quickly down, and then try to ask those questions while appearing as lucid as I'm apparently supposed to be.

"The shop..."

"Don't worry, darling. Everything is in hand."

"In hand?"

"Stanley has been opening up and keeping things ticking over for you. Oh, and he's been dealing with your agent chap."

"Howard?"

"That's him. When were you going to tell me you were selling up?"

"I only decided last night."

"I don't think it was last night, darling. You've been in here for over a week."

"Eh? What day is it?"

"Friday."

Eight days. Shit.

"Have I had any visitors?"

"A few. Your friend, Juliet, popped in, and a lady from one of your book clubs. Sorry, I can't recall her name."

"Are you sure nobody else has visited?"

"Well, I've been sitting here every day, with Stanley of course, and we haven't seen anyone else. I have to say, darling, he's been an absolute rock."

I may have seriously misjudged Stanley. And I may have also seriously misjudged Clement. Why hasn't he been to see if I'm okay?

"Is Stanley coming in today?"

"He'll be here this evening."

"Good. I need to thank him."

While I might still have unanswered questions, it seems my mother has some questions of her own she's keen to pose.

"Do you remember what happened, darling?"

I do, but that doesn't mean I wish to share it with anyone.

"Not really."

"I mean, how on earth did you manage to get yourself shot?"

"I...don't know."

"This is like something you only read about in the papers, but you never expect it to happen to your own daughter, in her own home of all places."

I don't know what to say to her. Truth is, there isn't anything I can say without having to explain the whole back story. And that would mean trying to explain the unexplainable.

"I'm sorry, Mum."

"It's okay, darling. You've nothing to be sorry for."

Her voice is strained and I'm suddenly struck by just how exhausted she looks. Whatever I've been through in the last eight days, my poor mother looks like she's been through an equally arduous ordeal.

"You okay, Mum? You look shattered."

"I'm fine, darling. Don't worry about me. You just concentrate on getting better."

"I'll try."

"And I'll tell the police they'll have to wait until tomorrow."

"The police?"

She bites her bottom lip — a tell-tale sign she's opened her mouth without thinking.

"Yes, darling, they're...err, quite keen to talk to you. They did ask me to call as soon as you woke up."

"Why?"

"Oh, um, no particular reason."

I know when my own mother is lying.

"Mum? What do they want?"

"Honestly, darling, I really wouldn't worry."

Her attempt to dismiss my concern is as half-hearted as it is futile. When somebody tells you not to worry, it's usually a sure sign there's something to worry about.

"Christ, Mum. Tell me, please."

I know she doesn't want to tell me, but she also knows I won't stop asking.

"A man, err..."

"Mum?"

"They found a man in your kitchen."

"What?"

"And he died, I'm afraid."

"Who? What man?"

"I don't know darling. They wouldn't tell me."

"They must have told you something."

"Not really. Just that it was a middle-aged man."

"What did he look like? What happened to him?"

"I honestly don't know. I promise you."

A middle-aged man, dead. No sign of Clement in eight days.

The machine next to my bed screams an alarm. I gasp short, shallow breaths as my panic-stricken mother looks on. My heart feels like it's about to burst from my chest and that only serves to increase my own level of panic.

We stare at one another, eyes wide. Different fears but the same obvious distress.

The door bursts open and a nurse shoos my mother from my side. She silences the screaming machine and takes my wrist.

"Beth. Look at me," she orders. "Take slow, deep breaths."

So easy to say.

"Come on, Beth, look at me. Breathe in. Breathe out. Nice and slowly."

I focus on her hazel eyes, her smooth ebony skin. There's a slight Caribbean lilt to her voice and the tenor is almost melodic.

"That's it, my girl. Breathe. Breathe."

Gasps become gulps as my lungs finally draw in air. My racing heart eases and I find some rhythm to my breathing. It's still laboured, but I no longer feel like I'm about to suffocate.

"What's wrong with her," my mother cries.

"Nothing to be alarmed at, my love. I think she's had a little panic attack."

The nurse glances across at the machine and pats my hand.

"You did good, my girl. You feeling okay now?"

The symptoms might be under control but the root cause is far from cured. I nod as I continue to consciously control my breathing.

Words are exchanged between the nurse and my mother but they drift over my head, unheard. My mind is already elsewhere.

Scene by scene, patchy memories are sifted as I try to reach any conclusion other than the one that just triggered a panic attack.

I can see Clement's hand on the fridge door. He yanked it open and it struck Mr Black. The gun went off and...God, that pain. Then what? I fell forward and it couldn't have been more than a second before my head hit...the table.

467

I wince at that memory.

But what did I see? There was Clement's boot, heading in the direction of Mr Black, I think.

Did it ever reach him? Was there another gunshot?

I ignore the pounding in my head and try to eke out whatever remains. There has to be something, anything.

There is neither something or anything. There is nothing. I was no longer conscious when whatever happened to Clement, happened. I can search those memories for the rest of my days but it's a futile exercise.

No matter how big he is, how tough he is, gun trumps man every time. And coupled with Clement's failure to visit, there is only one conclusion I can draw.

"Beth? What's the matter, darling?"

My mother's voice breaks through.

"Why the tears?"

As much as I want to unburden myself, this is a cross I'll have to bear alone.

My friend. My grief.

46

Tiredness arrives without warning, and I'm instructed to rest. I don't want to sleep but I have no energy to resist.

It scares me that I might wake up and not remember the last hour. I'll return to this unfamiliar room and I'll repeat the same cycle of confusion, dread, and damning realisation.

So tired though.

I slip away.

There is no natural light in the room so time becomes blurred. Sleep comes when it comes. I awake when I awake.

In between, I encounter a series of groggy vignettes in which various characters come and go: my mother, Dr Potter, nurses, and Stanley. The one person I want to see only visits when I slip back into another fitful sleep.

And the cycle continues for three more days. Apparently.

By Monday morning, I feel stronger. I eat a little, I drink weak tea, and I'm deemed fit enough to be moved to a room with a window. When you've been deprived of natural light and non-conditioned air for days on end, even a cold draught and a view of a dreary sky is welcome.

As a nurse bustles around the room, my mood is not as cheery as it should be for somebody who has seen off a brain injury and a gunshot wound.

It's been eleven days since Clement's death. There is a constant dull ache in my chest, and when nobody is around, I allow myself to shed a few tears. Grief is hideous, and no more so than when you're forced to bottle it and drink alone.

To make matters worse, the police will be here shortly. They'll have questions; plenty I'm sure. They'll get no answers from me though.

I'm hoping Dr Potter will deem me fit enough to go home by the end of the week. With the prospect of fourteen sleepless hours ahead, I'm sure boredom will arrive soon, and quickly outstay its welcome. I have a TV, magazines, and Mum brought me a notepad and pen, but it's not enough. I have a Clement-sized hole to fill and I don't think I can properly grieve, or move on, while I'm trapped in this magnolia limbo.

There is also the small question of the shop sale to deal with. Stanley, bless his heart, has been liaising with Howard, and while he awaits my confirmation to proceed, the legal groundwork is already well underway. I'm maybe ten days and a few pen strokes from eighty thousand pounds and a new career.

The fact Sterling actually kept his word does surprise me. I don't know if he's aware of what happened, but if he is, I'd bet he prayed I wouldn't pull through. With Clement gone, I am the last person alive who knows his dirty secret. It's a stick I intend to wave until that money is in my bank account.

My only enemy now, is time.

Long hours, watching TV and reading magazines while I try to distract myself from thoughts of Clement.

I reach for the remote control and switch the TV on. The Jeremy Kyle Show — God help me.

Twenty minutes into it, and just as I'm about to discover if Daz really is the father of Tanisha's baby, the door from the main corridor opens.

"Miss Baxter?"

"Yes."

I switch the TV off.

"Detective Inspector Brampton and Detective Constable Marsh."

The man offering the introductions, DI Brampton, is every bit a caricature of a TV detective. He looks like he slept in his suit, and I'm guessing he probably isn't as old as his craggy features suggest.

The two detectives march across the room and stand side-by-side at the edge of my bed. Warrant cards are shown, and sympathetic smiles are offered before they each pull up a chair.

As they sit, I size up DC Marsh. She's the polar opposite of Brampton. Fresh-faced and younger than me by a few years, I'd guess. Her ill-fitting, navy blue trouser suit does nothing for her. Together, they look an unlikely partnership. But if I've learnt anything of late, it's that not all partnerships are what they first appear.

"How are you feeling?" DI Brampton asks.

If I never hear that question again, it will be too soon.

"I'm okay."

"And you're up to answering a few questions?"

"Yes, although I'm not really sure what I can tell you."

"Don't worry. Anything at all would be a help."

DC Marsh pulls a notepad from inside her jacket, and flips it open. I'm not sure if it's a rank thing or a sexist assumption that she should be on secretarial duties.

"Let's start at the beginning shall we?" DI Brampton begins. "Tell me what you remember about that Thursday."

I had already guessed this would be their opening question. Clearly I can't tell him I was in the shop, busying myself with a former gangland fixer; the two of us blackmailing a local businessman who just happened to be a notorious sex offender.

"Just a normal day. I closed the shop and went home."

"Right. Then what happened."

"I remember walking through the door, hanging my coat and handbag up, and then I went into the kitchen."

"And then?"

"Sorry. Nothing."

"Nothing?"

"No."

DC Marsh stops scribbling and DI Brampton frowns.

"So let me get this right. You had a perfectly normal day at work, and then you went home?"

"Yes."

"And you hung up your coat and handbag, and then went into the kitchen?"

"Yes."

"And from that point, you have no memory?"

"I don't know what to say, Inspector. That's all there is."

"Okay. Let's leave that for the moment and concentrate on what we do know."

He loosens the knot in his tie and crosses his legs.

"We found a man in your kitchen, close to death. Unfortunately, he died on the way to the hospital."

His blunt statement hits me like a sledgehammer. Perhaps that was his intention.

"You weren't aware of a man in your kitchen when you entered?"

"No."

I can feel the panic returning. I consider switching to a 'no comment' strategy, but I fear that will only fuel their theory I'm not telling the truth.

"Does the name Kenny Bingham mean anything to you?"

"No. Should it?"

"Considering he was the man in your kitchen, maybe."

"I...I've never heard of him."

Clement is, or was, Kenny Bingham? Why did he use a false name, unless he had good reason to?

"Well, the late Mr Bingham was certainly known to us, Miss Baxter. He has a long list of convictions going back almost twenty years."

Nausea starts to build. I reach across to a table by the bed and grab a glass of water. As I lift it to my mouth, I have to consciously stop my hand from shaking.

I take a few sips while the detectives watch on. They can smell my trepidation — I'm sure of it.

Nauseous and fearful I might be, but the need for answers is overwhelming.

"What convictions, Inspector?" I ask in a feeble voice.

"Where to start? Lots of petty stuff when he was young, but more recently he's been on our radar for a whole host of offences: demanding money with menaces, grievous bodily harm, and extortion, to name but a few. Unfortunately, witnesses willing to testify against Mr Bingham have been in short supply."

DI Brampton then turns to DC Grace. "So whoever killed him probably did us a favour, eh?"

DC Grace concurs with her boss by nodding slowly.

"But, we still need to establish what happened to him," he continues. "We can't be having gun crime on our patch, Miss Baxter."

"No," I mumble.

Their rap sheet doesn't tally with the man I knew. Maybe that's the problem — I never really knew Clement.

"So you're absolutely sure you've never heard of Kenny Bingham?"

"No."

"Okay, maybe you don't know the name, but perhaps the face might be familiar. Can we show you his photo?"

I fear I won't be able to look at Clement's photo without breaking down, but what possible excuse could I use not to?

No way around it. I nod.

DC Marsh delves into her pocket again, this time withdrawing a piece of paper. She unfolds it and hands it to me.

I tentatively take the sheet of paper.

"That's Kenny Bingham," she says.

I steel myself and snatch a quick glance at the picture.

No. That's Mr Black.

I cannot imagine a picture of Kenny Bingham, or his alterego, Mr Black, has ever provoked such joy, such relief. It takes a monumental effort not to let those emotions show on my face.

"Sorry. I've never seen him before."

"Are you totally sure?" DI Brampton asks.

"Positive."

As another lie slips a little too easily from my mouth, it triggers two questions of my own. What happened after I hit my head on the table, and where the hell is Clement now?

I hand the picture back to DC Marsh. The two detectives swap glances and DI Brampton exhales a deep breath.

"Well, Miss Baxter. We have quite the mystery on our hands and very little to go on. I was kind of hoping you might be able to fill in a few blanks for us, but your memory loss is...how can I put it...disappointing."

"I'm not sure what you want me to say."

"Are you absolutely sure you entered your house alone?"

"Yes, of course I'm sure."

"And that is our problem. S*omebody* killed Kenny Bingham, Miss Baxter, and yet you say you entered your home alone."

There is more than a hint of an accusatory tone in his voice.

"I hope you're not suggesting I killed him."

"No, I'm not. That much we can be pretty certain of."

I need answers just as much as DI Brampton does, although to different questions. Despite my best efforts to portray a calm, indifferent exterior, I'm sure he's experienced enough to read my body language, which says something different.

"You're curious, Miss Baxter?"

"Sorry?"

"I detect you're curious how we can be certain you didn't kill Bingham."

"Erm..."

"We know you didn't kill him because of the way he died."

The detective leans forward in his chair and looks me straight in the eye.

"Somebody punched him in the head with such force, his brain bled out before the ambulance reached the hospital."

I reach for the cup of water again. Anything to mask my internal horror.

"And I hope you don't take this the wrong way, Miss Baxter, but that *somebody* had to be significantly bigger and stronger than you."

He sits back in his chair and a tense silence fills the room. I continue to sip at my water while I process DI Brampton's revelation.

"Now, we know it was Bingham who shot you, because of the residue on his hand," he continues. "But we're no closer to establishing who killed Bingham."

"Or, who rang for an ambulance," adds DC Marsh.

"That's right. And whoever did call used your home phone. A man with a distinctive London accent if that helps?"

I decide to adopt a new strategy — act dumb and say as little as possible.

"Can't help you."

"Come on, Miss Baxter," he huffs. "We know somebody else was in your home. We've dusted your entire kitchen for fingerprints and there is one set we can't account for. And those same fingerprints were on the phone used to call the ambulance, so who do they belong to?"

"I don't know."

"Right. Well, maybe this will help jog that memory."

He nods to DC Marsh. She pulls out her phone and taps the screen a few times. She holds the phone towards me, close enough I can see the grainy still photo; almost certainly pulled from a CCTV camera.

"Who is he?" she asks, pointing to Clement's pixelated face. "The image was captured in the town centre. This man, and you, together."

Shit. Shit. Shit. What do I say?

I press my fingertips into my temples and close my eyes. I don't know how the detectives will interpret this action, but I need to buy some time.

Seconds turn into a minute and their patience wears thin.

"Who is he, Miss Baxter?" DC Marsh repeats.

Something of Clement's prior advice strikes me — If I'm going to lie, keep it close to some version of the truth.

"He was...he was...an odd job man," I splutter.

"And does he have a name, this odd job man?" DI Brampton asks.

"Cliff."

"Cliff?"

"Yes."

"Cliff what?"

"I don't know his surname. Honestly."

"Where does he live?"

"Not sure. I think he said he was originally from North London."

"And does he still live in North London?"

"No. He said he moved around a lot."

"Okay. So how did you meet him?"

"He just turned up at the shop one day."

Clement's technique is surprisingly effective, and with every question I answer, the detectives become increasingly frustrated.

I confidently offer a version of the truth that sounds believable but provides no real answers.

They eventually give up.

"If you hear from this Cliff character, Miss Baxter, it is imperative you tell us. We understand he might well have been acting in self-defence, but we need to hear his side of the story."

The detectives stand and offer me their token wishes for a speedy recovery. DC Marsh then slides her business card onto the table by my bed and they leave.

The moment the door swings shut, I drop the card in the bin.

I have no idea how I managed to busk my way through their interrogation, but their departure brings some sense of closure, at least on any further probing by the police.

It doesn't however, bring any closure on Clement. The fact the police are looking for him might explain why he's gone to ground, but for somebody as resourceful as Clement, I don't understand why he hasn't made any effort to let me know he's okay.

Eleven days and not a peep.

As I lie back on the bed, a swarm of emotions buzz around my mind. Of all those emotions, one cuts deeper than the rest — sadness.

As much as I don't want to face the only conclusion I can possibly draw, I have to.

Clement is gone and he's not coming back.

47

Saturday brings an end to my sixteen day stay in hospital.

It also brings down a curtain on any lingering hopes I'll ever see Clement again.

I've spent an unhealthy amount of time just staring at the door, and every time it opened, I prayed a big man in double denim would wander in.

It was never Clement.

As much as I'd rather be anywhere else, I have tried to make the most of my stay. I managed to plot a semi-decent outline for my new novel, and in turn, I had the opportunity to reflect on everything I've been through.

An incredible, ridiculous, unbelievable journey, alongside an incredible, ridiculous, unbelievable man.

But now that journey is over and I must move on. Alone again.

On Monday, I called Howard and confirmed my instructions to proceed as quickly as possible with the sale of the shop. All being well, that sale should conclude next week. I have no idea what Sterling is going to do with a book shop, but I suspect Baxter's Books has probably sold its last copy of *Fifty Shades of Grey*. Saying that, I suspect Baxter's Books has sold its last copy of anything, as I won't be returning. I've only been discharged on the strict understanding I convalesce at home for the next three weeks.

Mum and Stanley have insisted they move into my spare bedroom for the time being. They've both been so good to me, and Stanley in particular has been an absolute hero through all of this. Considering my appallingly brattish behaviour towards him, he had every reason to turn his back on me, and my mother. I doubt he'll ever win an award for businessman of the year, but his heart is very much in the right place.

Now, the moment has arrived I can leave this damn place. I sit on the edge of the bed, waiting for my lift.

Dr Potter enters the room.

"How's my favourite patient this morning? All set?"

I confirm I am with a half-hearted smile and a nod.

"Good, good."

He spends ten minutes listing all the things I can and cannot do, with greater emphasis on the latter.

With his job done, we shake hands and I offer my thanks for all his care. His is not a job I envy one bit.

As the doctor leaves, Stanley arrives — a vision in corduroy and tweed.

"Morning, Bethany."

"Morning, Stanley."

He approaches the bed, still noticeably uncomfortable in my company.

"It's just me I'm afraid. Your mum was going to come with me but she's still busy back at your place."

"It's fine, Stanley. What's she doing?"

"The police left the kitchen in a bit of a mess. She wanted everything looking nice for you."

"Ahh, right. Bless her."

He picks up the bag containing my nightclothes and toiletries. "Shall we?"

"Yes, but I wanted to say something first, Stanley."

"Oh. What have I done now?"

I gingerly stand up and shuffle over to him.

"I wanted to say thank you, and I'm sorry for the way I've behaved. Mum is very lucky to have you in her life. We both are."

His ruddy face blossoms into a deep shade of scarlet. "There's really no need," he says quietly.

"There is, and I think I owe you a hug, don't you?"

I put my arms around him before he has a chance to answer.

I complete the hug with a peck on the cheek. As I step back, Stanley looks like he's about to cry. Soppy old sod.

"Come on then, Stanley. Let's go home."

He offers me a ride in a wheelchair, which I decline. The hospital has provided me with a set of crutches and I need the practice. My leg doesn't hurt that much and the gunshot wound is healing nicely, but I can definitely feel it if I put too much pressure on my right leg for any amount of time.

We take a slow walk to the exit.

"You wait here and I'll go fetch the car."

"Sure."

Stanley heads off to the car park and I take a seat on a bench just outside the main doors. It's been raining, and a frigid wind is gusting, but the relief of being outside the hospital walls tempers the miserable weather.

I watch people come and go, perhaps hoping I might spot a big man amongst them. I spot a few, but they're not the big man I'm looking for. I wonder just how long I'll keep looking. A few days? A few weeks? Will I ever accept Clement walking out of my life as abruptly as he entered it?

I guess I have to.

A silver Honda pulls up to the kerb and Stanley hops out.

"Your chariot awaits, my lady."

He opens the passenger door and takes my arm as I delicately lower myself in. My crutches are deposited in the boot before Stanley takes up position in the driver's seat.

"Let's get you home."

I take a final glance at the hospital and offer a silent prayer I never have reason to return.

Stanley pulls away and I let myself relax a little.

Within a few minutes it's clear Stanley can't handle sitting in silence, and he makes an attempt at small talk.

"I quite enjoyed working in the shop. Will you be sad to see it go?"

"A little, but unfortunately it's had its day. Time to move on."

"Won't you miss the customers?"

"Not really," I chuckle. "Although they weren't all bad."

"I thought they were all fairly pleasant, despite the fact I didn't have the first clue what I was doing."

"You're right, they are, and I'm probably being unfair. I guess when you've stood at that counter as long as I have, you get a little tired of...I don't know, people I suppose."

As we pull up to a roundabout, he turns to me and smiles. "I know what you mean."

He pulls away and we continue on our way.

Stanley's driving style could best be described as cautious, and the journey is taking significantly longer than it would if I were at the wheel. Maybe this would have irritated me once, but I'm now happy to sit and watch the world drift past. Ever so slowly.

"Oh, by the way. Some chap called in with a box of books."

"Eric?"

"Yes, that's the chap. I wasn't sure what to tell him, so I said you'd give him a call when you were up to it."

"Right. Thanks, Stanley."

"And another chap left a parcel for you."

"Okay."

"I suspect he found himself in trouble when he got back to the depot."

"Why?"

"He forgot to ask for a signature."

"Those guys are on such tight schedules. It wouldn't be the first time."

"Probably."

"What did you do with it?"

"Oh, I took it back to your place."

The last thing I want is shop stock cluttering up my home, but it would be churlish to say anything.

"Okay. It's probably a customer order. I'll deal with it once I'm back on my feet."

"I don't think it's for a customer."

"No? Why's that?" I reply wearily.

"He said...let me think. Oh, yes, that's right. He said I should make sure you get it because it was really important. That's why I dropped it at your place."

"Knowing my luck, it's probably a court summons for an unpaid bill."

"I'm afraid I've had too many of them myself," he replies. "And speaking from bitter experience, I hope for your sake it's not."

"It's okay. I'll have the money to settle all my bills as soon as the shop sale goes through."

We get within a mile of Elmore Road and Stanley stops at an amber traffic light.

"Was there anything else I need to be aware of, Stanley? Any problems?"

"No, I don't think so. Your friend, Juliet, popped in on the Friday, and I told her you were in hospital. I hope that was okay?"

She never did get to see Clement. I owe her an apology and an explanation.

"And that was it really," Stanley adds. "I left the parcel on your kitchen table, like the courier asked."

"Okay, thanks, I'll deal...hold on. He asked you to put it on my kitchen table?"

"Yes. He was quite insistent on it."

"Did he say anything else?"

"Um, let me think."

He thinks, and the lights change to green. He slips the car into first gear and moves away.

"Stanley? Did he say anything else?"

"No. That was it."

"So let me get this clear. He delivered a package and told you it was important, and to put it on my kitchen table?"

"More or less."

I've got a horrible feeling that parcel might contain something far worse than a court summons. The one thing about sitting around in a hospital room. With nothing to occupy your mind, your imagination is allowed to run wild. After learning of Mr Black's unfortunate passing, it dawned on me that his brother might want to seek revenge of his own.

Clearly the courier was not from a reputable parcel company. God only knows what horrors await me in that parcel.

"This man, Stanley. Did he use a walking stick, or walk with a limp?"

"No, not that I recall."

"Can you remember what he looked like? And please think carefully because it might be connected to the man who shot me."

"Oh, good grief," he splutters. "Do you think so?"

"Maybe."

"Now you come to mention it, he did look like trouble."

"In what way?"

"Well, he was bloody enormous for one thing. Hands like shovels."

"Anything else?"

"Um...yes, there was one other thing. He had a huge droopy moustache. I've never trusted a man with a moustache, they're..."

Oh, my God!

"Was he wearing a denim waistcoat?" I screech at poor Stanley.

"Yes. Yes he was, and a sweater that looked like it had shrunk in the wash."

"Stanley — put your foot down. I need to get home."

Stanley's idea of putting his foot down is travelling a fraction over the speed limit. If it weren't for the fact we're less than a mile away from my house, I swear I'd have throttled him.

He eventually pulls into Elmore Road and painstakingly reverses into a parking space.

"Can you grab my crutches, please?"

"Of course. Shall I go and fetch your mother first?"

"No, Stanley," I bark. "Please. The crutches."

He doesn't need telling twice and within seconds he's at my door, crutches in hand.

"Thanks, Stanley, and sorry for snapping. I just want to get inside."

"It's forgotten already."

By the time I reach my front door, the crutches have become more an accessory than a practical walking aid.

My key is in my bag, inside the house, so I'm forced to rap the knocker and wait for my mother to answer. Stanley brings up the rear, carrying my bag.

"She's probably up to her elbows in flour," he says.

"What? Sorry?"

"I think she wanted to cook you something nice for dinner, you know, after all that hospital food."

I turn and reach for the knocker, and the door swings open.

"Darling," my mother squeals. "Welcome home."

She takes my bag from Stanley and immediately sends him off on a mercy mission for the eggs she forgot. I throw him a smile before I hop through the door.

Stanley dealt with; she closes the door and starts clucking. "How are you feeling, darling? Is your leg okay?"

Aghhhh!

"It's all good, thanks, Mum. I need to get something from the kitchen, though."

Before she can pose any further questions about my wellbeing, I begin limping down the hall towards the kitchen.

"Shall I take your bag upstairs, darling?"

"Yes, please," I call back to her, not really giving a stuff what she does with it. I have much more important matters to attend to.

The second I step through the kitchen door, my sense of urgency is arrested. Although everything looks more or less the same, thanks to my mother, the spectre of what happened on that evening looms large. I take a moment to regain my composure, and cast aside the mental image of Mr Black, taking his last breaths here in my kitchen. It sounds horrible, but I'm just glad he hung on long enough to die elsewhere.

As a cold shiver subsides, I hop over to the table which is laden with an assortment of packets — ingredients for whatever my mother is cooking. I collapse onto a chair and frantically scan the table. My eyes lock onto a plain brown package, about ten inches long by eight inches wide, and less than an inch thick. My name has been scrawled on the front in pen.

With complete reverence, I gently lift the package from the table. I'm almost too scared to open it.

I turn it over and gently pick the packing tape from one end. As it curls away, I hear the wardrobe door creak open from my bedroom. I guess my mother has decided to unpack and put away the contents of my hospital bag. That buys me a few minutes of peace to deal with whatever is beyond the brown cardboard.

With the packing tape removed, I slide my fingernails under a flap and prise the package open.

What the hell?

A book?

I have no idea why Clement would send me a book, unless of course, it's hiding something else.

If he's paranoid about the police finding him, what better way to get a message to me? They wouldn't think anything of a book shop manager receiving a book. Very clever, Clement.

I flick it open and my eyes scan the inside of the cover. Nothing. Nor is there anything on the next.

I turn another page to find a few lines of scribbled text.

Alright Doll

Sorry I couldn't hang around but things didn't turn out the way they were supposed to. Seems there's no place in heaven for a bad man, even when that bad man had good intentions. I never meant to kill that arsehole, but shit happens and he probably deserved it. I won't be shedding any tears. Anyway, hope you enjoy the book. Don't ask me why, or how, but that voice in my head said you were supposed to have it.

Stay lucky.

Clem

PS: I did pop into the hospital to check you were okay, and some black nurse chick told me you were on the mend. Shame I was in a hurry — she had a cracking pair of knockers.

I drop the book on the table.

That's it. He's gone. Definitively.

That in itself is hard to take, but of greater concern is that his delusions have clearly worsened. All that crap about heaven and voices. He desperately needs help and I'm powerless to do anything. And why the hell does he think I want a bloody book? Christ, I've got a whole shop full of the damn things.

Far from alleviating my worries, Clement's parcel has achieved the opposite. I feel utterly helpless, and more than a little guilty for not insisting Clement sought help sooner.

"Shall I put the kettle on, darling?"

My mother's voice snaps me from my malaise.

"Please."

"I've put all your clothes away, and your toiletries back in the bathroom."

"Okay, thanks."

She busies herself making the tea as I slump back in my chair.

"I'm making your favourite for dinner, darling — sausage and onion pie."

I've never had the heart to tell her that sausage and onion pie ceased to be my favourite meal about twenty years ago.

"Great."

"And I thought we could curl up on the sofa this afternoon and watch a film."

"Sounds lovely."

She suddenly spins around, a look of concern on her face.

"What's the matter, darling? You don't seem yourself."

"It's nothing, Mum. I think things have just caught up with me."

Liar.

"Are you sure?"

"Honestly, I'll be fine. I promise."

She shuffles over and runs her hand through my hair. "I know you will, darling. You're just like your father — tough as old boots."

Just as she's about to return to tea-making duties, she spots Clement's book on the table. For some reason, she stands motionless and stares down at it, temporarily transfixed.

"You alright, Mum?"

"Eh? Oh yes, sorry." she splutters, her trance broken as abruptly as it arrived. "I'll get your tea."

"Seems I'm not the only one out of sorts," I chuckle.

She smiles down at me. "Ignore me. Just one of those silly moments."

"Something you want to share?"

"It's not important."

"If something is worrying you, then it is important."

"No, darling, you misunderstand. Nothing is worrying me, it's just..."

Her mouth drops a fraction and she lets a little sigh escape.

"It's just...that book."

"What about it?"

"*James and The Giant Peach* — your father bought a copy for you. To be honest, I'd completely forgotten about it until I saw it there on the table."

"Did he? I don't remember reading it."

She pulls up a chair and sits a few feet from me.

"No, you wouldn't. Your dad called me the day he bought it, and sounded so pleased with himself. He knew you'd love it."

"Right. So why didn't he give it to me?"

She swallows hard and takes my hands in hers. "Because, darling, it was the same day as his...accident. The book was in the car with him."

I hear my mother's words but making sense of them proves impossible.

And then, something connects. Clement's scribbled message...

Anyway, hope you enjoy the book. Don't ask me why, or how, but that voice in my head said you were supposed to have it.

How the hell could he have possibly known my dad bought the very same book for me, on the very day he died?

Unless...

ONE YEAR LATER...

THAMESVIEW TV STUDIO

LONDON

As the presenter of *Big Entertainment Live,* one of the network's most-watched weekly programmes, Libby Green is a well-known face on TV. She is now considered a 'Goldilocks presenter'; a label once used by chauvinistic producers to describe female presenters old enough to carry some authority with famous guests, but young enough to look good on camera.

Nobody dare use that label within earshot of Libby.

She has hosted *Big Entertainment Live* for over four years and reached the top of her game. That achievement also brings the power to make or break careers.

With only minutes remaining before the show is due to go live; the set is a hive of activity. Amongst it all, Libby sits serenely in a leather-bound chair while a make-up artist applies a few finishing touches to Libby's already flawless skin. As the makeup artist dabs away, a hairstylist fusses over Libby's blonde locks to ensure not a single hair is out of place.

"Thirty seconds, people," a voice booms.

The two stylists scamper away and Libby begins a series of vocal exercises.

"Ten seconds," the voice booms, with a little more urgency.

Libby takes a sip of water and calmly places her glass down on a coffee table, positioned between host and guest.

"Going live in five, four..."

On cue, Libby's face explodes into a welcoming smile as the camera zooms in for a head shot.

The studio audience of three hundred had prior instructions to clap and cheer as if their lives depended on it. They don't hold back.

Friday night, nine o'clock, and the show is live.

For the first ten minutes, Libby goes through a heavily-scripted introduction, covering highlights of the week's entertainment news. Carefully crafted jokes are dropped, and the audience laughs and whoops when prompted. To anyone watching at home, it all appears seamlessly spontaneous.

With the crowd warmed up, Libby moves on to introduce her first guest of the night.

"This lady has taken the literary world by storm and I'm delighted to welcome her to *Big Entertainment Live*. Ladies and gentlemen, please give it up for Beth Baxter."

Libby stands and joins the audience in applause as her guest enters through an archway at the rear of the set.

Dressed in a black, off-the-shoulder Dolce & Gabbana dress, Beth Baxter moves confidently across the studio floor. She reaches her host and they shake hands before taking their seats.

The audience quietens and Libby goes to work.

"Firstly, I must say what an honour it is to have you on the show, Beth. You're a lady in huge demand at the moment, aren't you?"

"The honour is all mine, Libby. And yes, it's been a crazy time for me."

Libby then turns to the audience, both in the studio and watching at home.

"For those of you who've been living in a cave for the last few months, Beth Baxter is the author of the best-selling novel, *The Angel of Camden*."

Returning her focus to her guest, Libby continues. "And I don't think it would be an exaggeration to say it's been a colossal hit, both here in the UK and in the US. How do you feel about that success, Beth, considering it's your debut novel?"

"If I'm honest, Libby, it's all been a bit of a whirlwind. In the nine weeks since it was released, my feet have barely touched the ground. I could never have dreamt it would take off in the way it has, and I'm incredibly humbled."

"And for the handful of people watching who haven't read *The Angel of Camden*, could you give us a quick overview of the plot?"

"Sure. The main protagonist, Louise, is the manager of a book store. And through no fault of her own, she finds herself in debt to a corrupt property developer."

"That's down to her fiancé, Kevin?" Libby interjects.

"That's right, Libby. And after Kevin disappears, poor old Louise faces the prospect of losing her home."

"And this is where things start to get a little crazy, right?"

"They do indeed, Libby. One evening, while Louise is doing a stock take in the shop, a man appears, seemingly from nowhere."

"Not just any man, though? Tell us about the hero of the story — Cliff."

"He's an absolute giant of a man and claims he was once a fixer in gangland London. He then drops the bombshell that he's Louise's guardian angel and has been sent to help."

"But Louise thinks he's a crackpot, doesn't she?"

"She does."

Libby then turns back to the audience.

"I have a confession to make at this point. Crackpot or not, I've developed a bit of a guilty crush on Cliff."

Exaggerated laughter peels across the studio.

"Well, you're not alone there, Libby. I found out the other day that Cliff now has his own fan page on Facebook, with over fifty thousand members."

"Really? That's incredible. I'll be straight on to Facebook after the show."

More laughter from the audience.

"So, Beth. Tell us what happens after Cliff barges into Louise's life."

"Okay, without giving any spoilers, Cliff comes up with a plan to find the money for Kevin's debt, and that plan turns into a bit of an adventure."

"They end up going on a sort of treasure hunt across London, don't they?"

"They do, and besides their search, the story focuses on the way their relationship develops."

Libby smiles at her guest and turns to face the camera. "We'll come back to that relationship in a moment. Join us after the break where we'll be chatting a little more with author, Beth Baxter."

As the audience claps, the camera moves from Libby and her guest, and sweeps across the sea of cheery faces.

The adverts roll.

A few miles across London, Jimmi Kumar is standing outside a terraced house in Stepney. He doesn't live in the house but he does own it, and Jimmi has just collected the weekly rent from his six tenants. Paid in cash, of course.

There are six bedsit rooms in the three-storey house. Numbered one to six, there are two located on the ground floor, three on the first, and room number six in the converted loft.

In that top room, the tenant is perched on the edge of a single bed, watching *Big Entertainment Live* on a portable TV. As the adverts begin, he kicks off his boots and lights a cigarette with a disposable lighter. He isn't supposed to smoke in the room, but considering the walls and ceiling were already stained with nicotine when he moved in, he doubts the landlord is that bothered.

In truth, Jimmi isn't bothered. He has no desire to get on the wrong side of the tenant in room six. Besides, he pays his rent on time and keeps himself to himself. If he wants to smoke, Jimmi isn't going to stop him.

Back at Thamesview Studio, a countdown begins on set — ten seconds until the adverts end. Presenter and guest sip water, and ready themselves.

The audience applaud, signalling the viewers at home are back, and the show is live once more.

The camera zooms in on Libby. "Welcome back to *Big Entertainment Live,* where I'm joined by the author, Beth Baxter.*"*

The camera switches to a smiling Beth.

"So, Beth. We were talking about the relationship between Cliff and Louise. I was fascinated by that dynamic because they were such different people."

"They are very different but in some way, they both needed one another. Cliff was out of his depth in a world he no longer recognised, and Louise was pretty blind to her own shortcomings, particularly her trust issues. For me, that part of the story was the most enjoyable to write."

"Fascinating. Now, let's talk about your journey. How did a book shop owner suddenly find herself a best-selling author?"

"Well, it started when I sold my book shop last year. That gave me both the time and money to concentrate on writing. I had a spell in hospital and used that time to formulate the plot of *The Angel of Camden.* When I was discharged, I was able to pen the entire book within three months."

"Good to hear something positive came from your stay in hospital. Is your book shop still open?"

"Unfortunately not. A few months after I sold up, I heard the buyer sadly passed away. Heart attack, I think."

"Oh, how tragic."

"It was, but he was an old man. He enjoyed a good innings."

Libby does her best to look sympathetic before quickly moving the interview along.

"It's been rumoured that besides the fact you and Louise both ran a book shop, there are other parts of the story that mirror your life. Can you tell us about that?"

"Well, I've never broken into a disused tube station, or lied my way into a church," Beth laughs nervously. "But yes, some of the story reflects my real life. I lost my father when I was young, and like Louise, I wasn't particularly lucky in love."

"And is that still the case?"

"I'm glad to say it isn't, Libby. I started dating a lovely chap called Richard about ten months ago, and we've just decided to move in together."

"Ohh, how lovely. Congratulations."

"Thank you."

"Is he anything like Cliff?"

"Quite the opposite," Beth chuckles.

"I know thousands of your fans will be dying to know the answer to my next question. Was Cliff based upon a real person?"

Beth's smile fades away.

"Yes. He was."

"Somebody famous?"

"No. A dear friend."

"And what does your friend think of the fact he's been immortalised in print?"

"I don't know. He's not in my life anymore."

Libby senses vulnerability in Beth. Never one to miss an opportunity of a scoop, she decides to dig a little deeper.

"Did you have a falling out?"

"Not in the traditional sense."

"We're intrigued now, Beth. Can you tell us what happened?"

"He told me something and I didn't believe him. Turned out that he was telling the truth all along."

"A bit like Cliff and Louise?"

"Yes, I suppose."

"And you never got the chance to apologise?"

"Sadly, I left it too late and he'd already moved on. He did leave me a gift, though — the greatest gift anyone could have wished for."

Libby moves the conversation back to more salient matters.

"Do you know where your friend is now?"

Beth pauses for a moment and then stares straight into the camera. "Unfortunately not, but wherever he is, I hope he found his own version of heaven."

In Stepney, the tenant in room six smiles to himself as he stares at Beth Baxter's face on the TV screen.

"Nothing like heaven," he mumbles. "But as far as purgatory goes, it ain't so bad, doll."

497

THE END

Before You Go...

Well, that was 'Who Sent Clement?' — I genuinely hope you enjoyed it. If you did, and have a few minutes spare, I would be eternally grateful if you could leave a review on Amazon. If you're feeling particularly generous, a mention on Facebook or a Tweet would be equally appreciated. I know it's a pain, but it's the only way us indie authors can compete with the big publishing houses.

As for Clement, his next adventure is entitled *Wrong'un,* and you can pick up your copy, in ebook or paperback format, from Amazon.

Stay in Touch...

For more information about me and to receive updates on new releases (everyone on my reader list receives a pre-launch discount), visit my website...

www.keithapearson.co.uk

If you have any questions or general feedback, you can also reach me, or follow me, on social media...

Facebook: www.facebook.com/pearson.author
Twitter: www.twitter.com/keithapearson

Acknowledgements...

There have been several people whose help has been invaluable in writing this book. I would therefore like to offer my sincere thanks to...

Ailsa Campbell — the lady who kicks my writing in the right direction. My books would be significantly less readable without Ailsa's hard work, advice, and honest feedback. I'm so grateful our paths crossed.

Tom Salter — not just a gentleman, but an absolute mine of information. Tom really helped me to capture the essence of London in the sixties and seventies. This book would not have been as authentic without Tom's input, and Clement wouldn't have been quite the same character.

Deborah Howard (Prestige Pawnbrokers) — very generous with her time and as a result, Deborah helped me to understand the realities of selling gold bars and the world of pawnbroking.

Andrew Acquier FRICS — the go-to guy for rock & roll memorabilia. Some fairly fundamental plot points rested on Clement's Zippo lighter. Without Andrew's expert advice, I suspect those plot points would have been flaky, at best.

Jane Lacey (St Michaels, Aldershot) — with so little knowledge of church-related matters, particularly bell towers, Jane was incredibly helpful in ensuring I got my facts correct.

Printed in Great Britain
by Amazon

75236301R00298